the Beat of my Heart

the BEAT of my HEART

LAURA WIGGIN

ORPHANED AT HOME

TATE PUBLISHING
AND ENTERPRISES, LLC

The Beat of My Heart
Copyright © 2012 by Laura Wiggin. All rights reserved.

No part of this publication may be reproduced, stored in a retrieval system or transmitted in any way by any means, electronic, mechanical, photocopy, recording or otherwise without the prior permission of the author except as provided by USA copyright law.

This novel is a work of fiction. Names, descriptions, entities, and incidents included in the story are products of the author's imagination. Any resemblance to actual persons, events, and entities is entirely coincidental.

The opinions expressed by the author are not necessarily those of Tate Publishing, LLC.

Published by Tate Publishing & Enterprises, LLC

127 E. Trade Center Terrace | Mustang, Oklahoma 73064 USA

1.888.361.9473 | www.tatepublishing.com

Tate Publishing is committed to excellence in the publishing industry. The company reflects the philosophy established by the founders, based on Psalm 68:11,

"The Lord gave the word and great was the company of those who published it."

Book design copyright © 2012 by Tate Publishing, LLC. All rights reserved.
Cover design by Shawn Collins
Interior design by Rtor Maghuyop

Published in the United States of America

ISBN: 978-1-62024-758-7
1. Fiction / Christian / Romance
2. Fiction / Family Life
12.06.28

To every child who has tried to be their parent's unfulfilled dreams,

to every child whose future is stolen by selfish-driven parents,

to every child who spends a lifetime faking it,

to every child who is forced to be something they're not,

to every child who spends their childhood
climbing someone else's ladder,

to every child whose ideas are abandoned,

to every child who will never measure up
to their parents' expectations,

to every child who feels like a constant failure,

*and to every adult who comes alongside
these kids and believes in them.*

to my friend
Cody

ACKNOWLEDGMENTS

Of course, there would be no book without God. So first off, I'd like to say that He has been there every step of the way. Every page has His handprints. The scars on His hands are the reason I write. I'm reminded of the people He came to this earth and died for on the cross. Without Him, this manuscript would've never been started, much less finished. But He has a message for someone out there. So my biggest thanks goes to my Jesus! It's an honor to be used this way, Lord.

Special thanks goes to the US military for sending us to a duty station on the coast of California. For over eight years, we vacationed almost every weekend. Most often, it included some form of beach. Whether camping on the sands and watching spectacular sunsets or building sandcastles in the morning fog, we loved it. Countless times, we simply sat and watched the dolphins play tag in the shimmering water. Or perhaps we would go to the aquarium and eat lunch over the bay, watching the seals clap their hands (fins) for food. Bonfires and singing at night to the crashing of the waves was a favorite. Walking the boardwalks, feeding the squirrels and riding bikes were everyday joys. Did I mention boogie boarding, skim boarding, and surfing of all kinds? Driving Highway 1 up the entire coastline, with the mountains on the right and the bluff on the left, hovering over the emerald sea, now that is a picture worth seeing. Seals on wheels and whales with tales will forever be in our memories. I have tried to bring those precious years alive in these pages. I've attempted to sketch the beauty of our time there for you.

I want to thank our friends we camped, surfed and roasted hotdogs around the bonfire with so many times. Our times at Knott's Berry Farm, Lego Land, and SeaWorld with our friends made special lasting memories. The times our children played on the beach while we prayed together meant more to me than you'll ever know. Our church times on the beach will never be forgotten. Each one of you is engraved on our hearts.

I must thank each of my boys who gave me enough *real live stuff* to fill a hundred books while living in California. We had so much fun. Don't worry. I didn't tell all our secrets. We learned the true meaning of *sand*wich. Many years later, we are still finding sand in places you wouldn't believe. I'm so thankful my boys got to spend much of their tender years out skateboarding, flying kites, riding bikes, and learning about God through His *waves* of grace.

Thank you to my husband, who worked so we could enjoy our time out in California. Thank you, Sherman, for every trip you pulled the travel trailer for camping in the Sequoias, Yosemite, and the Kern River and the many times you hitched it up to camp alongside the beach and every other adventure we had. Sorry about the hair that turned gray when you drove it without brakes. Yes, you're the best. You made all our memories possible. Thank you.

TABLE OF CONTENTS

Introduction 13

Chapter 1 15

Chapter 2 21

Chapter 3 29

Chapter 4 41

Chapter 5 51

Chapter 6 63

Chapter 7 71

Chapter 8 91

Chapter 9 103

Chapter 10 113

Chapter 11 117

Chapter 12 137

Chapter 13 151

Chapter 14 165

Chapter 15 193

Chapter 16 217

Chapter 17 237

Chapter 18 251

Chapter 19 271

Chapter 20 285

Chapter 21 299

Chapter 22 305

Chapter 23 311

Chapter 24 321

Epilogue 343

INTRODUCTION

You are about to take another kind of bus ride. It's completely different from Lilly's journey in the first book of this series, called *The Bus Ride*. In these pages, you will hop on the tour bus with Willy. His high spirit and evangelistic heart will keep you rollin' along.

All the places on the coast that the bus pulls into on the journey are real places that my family and I frequented during the time we lived on the coast of California. I've paved the way of this story with favorite places and personal memories. Many of the funny stories and scenes really happened, perhaps with some variations.

Orphaned at Home has a unique twist inside this book. Being orphaned at home has no respecter of persons. In these pages, you will find that it has affected the rich and famous in a way perhaps you've never thought of. Though I never knew Noel—her storyline is completely made up—I saw her every day. Every time we went to Los Angeles, I saw her. If I walked along the beach, she was there. I sat next to her on roller coasters. I toured vineyards beside her. She is every young person who has been rejected, cut from the first auditions, so to speak, her dreams dashed in exchange for her parents' *script* for her life. Every Noel that has been orphaned at home, abandoned to pursue their own dreams, walks around playing a role they were never meant to play.

Join Lilly in her ministry as she reaches out even to Hollywood to love an unwanted orphan who no longer wants to play the part in this make-believe land but wants to find the script to a real family.

So jump on the bus and tour the coast with our memories, Willy, the Mercy Seat Rockers, a mystery woman, and of course, Peter and Lilly.

CHAPTER 1

Willy plopped down on his bunk. It was a tight squeeze and not nearly as comfortable as his bed at home, piled high with quilts his mother had made, or the couch bed he used at Peter's apartment. But he wasn't going to complain. Touring with a Christian pop rock music group had been his dream for as long as he could remember. Willy smiled in the curtained-off section called his room, which only held his bunk and the area below it. He had a small light above his bunk, which, on nights like tonight, kept him company when homesickness tried to creep in.

He smiled as he thought about how he got his bunk on this very bus just a few weeks prior. He was a disc jockey for WAZE of the Master, a Christian radio music station. He chuckled to himself. *How many times have I said, "This here is YoYo Willy bringing you up when you down, comin' at ya with all the best hits from WAZE. The Ways of the Master are always the best," and then popping on the records?* He did miss that, but not for a million bucks would he trade what he was doing right now.

It happened one night when the Mercy Seat Rockers were in the studio for a live interview. After the interview, Willy asked where they were staying and told them some of the best places to eat. Then the lead singer popped off and snidely asked, "Well, since you seem to know where to find everything in this here small town, you think you can point me in the direction of a drummer replacement?"

The guy didn't expect an answer, but Willy was a great listener and burden carrier; thus, it was easy for Sky Blue to spill out on him.

Willy had the biggest smile cross his face. "You're not going to believe this, but I do know of an excellent drummer who might be just what you're looking for."

"Oh really?" The guy grunted. Not really thinking that this was possible, he started to turn away.

Willy called after him, "Yes, Sky Blue." He waited for him to turn around. "I'll make you a deal. If it doesn't work out, breakfast is on me."

Sky Blue perked his ears.

"Meet me at Waffle King at nine a.m. on West Street at the other end of town, and I'll bring you the guy who just might be the answer to your prayer."

Sky Blue was doubtful, but what did he have to lose? He'd already lost his drummer, and this kind of setback could easily wreck his tour. The last thing a band wants is to have to quit mid tour. He thought he could trust this guy. He heard himself agree to meet him and got directions one more time before shaking his head and leaving the studio.

After hearing that the Mercy Seat Rockers needed a new drummer, Willy wormed his way into a meeting with the lead singer, Sky Blue, as a prospective new drummer replacement. He grudgingly agreed to let Willy play for him. He *was* in desperate need of a drummer, after all. When Willy finished playing, Sky Blue's question of "When can you start?" was music to his ears. Soon after, he turned in his resignation at the radio station and joined the tour immediately. He was introduced to all the band members soon to become one of their own.

After he'd made arrangements, he packed up his clothing and all that he thought he'd need, and left a note on the table for Peter. He explained everything and requested that he bring Lilly over to the Barnabus House B&B that evening to meet the group. He then shut the door for the last time yet opened a new door he hoped would last forever.

When Willy and the crew arrived, both Peter and Lilly were already there. Wilma had a feast prepared, hot and waiting. Doug welcomed everyone. This was the heart of Wilma and Doug's place, the Barnabus House B&B. They hosted many people at their place and poured as much love and encouragement into their guest as possible.

After grace, Willy said, "Thank you, Mom and Dad, for having my new roommates here for a great feast and a real bed for the night. I'm going to have Sky Blue introduce everyone, as he knows them much better than me." He looked at Sky Blue for his cue.

Sky Blue put down his fork and began the introductions after he too thanked both Doug and Wilma for their generous hospitality. "This here to my right is Oscar Williams. We call him Cookie because his sweet wife is always sending him cookies, yet he never shares. He has two little boys of his own. He has been with us since day one of the band. He's the pillar and heart of the group. He has a passion for those contemplating suicide, as he has been on the edge himself before Jesus claimed his life. He plays bass guitar for us.

"Next to Cookie is Chester Strayer. We call him Chet. He's a bit green for the band. He started with us just over a year ago. He's our rhythm guitarist. He's very good, but I think he's a bigger camera ham. His particular calling is revamping secular music into Christian music, which really reaches a whole new group of kids for Christ." He looked at both of Willy's teen sisters. "Ladies, he's not available. I intend on getting plenty of stringing out of him yet." He was teasing but really meant it.

He pointed across the table. "That there is Jordan Croft. We call him Jordie for short. He's our lead guitarist, and he's a laugh a minute." Sky Blue stopped at the giggling around the table.

Everyone knew that Willy would give this guy a run for his money in the area of humor and smiles. There just wasn't another Willy. Sky Blue looked around the table. Obviously, there was some kind of family joke going on. He could tell. He ignored it and continued.

"Jordie is the funniest guy I know, as well as the best lead guitarist. He's an extremely accomplished and creative player. He has a passion for the hurting." Then he looked at the girls. "Neither is he available! I don't intend to let my string men get strung up with anyone anytime soon."

He continued with the introductions. "The lovely lady next to Willy is Kenzie Strayer. She's our pianist/keyboard player. She also has a lovely voice for our background vocals. She's fabulous on the ivory and is Chet's sister. She keeps him in line, and he gives her someone to be mad at besides me." He laughed at Kenzie and winked.

She gave him her best ever eye roll.

He pointed to the guy at the end of the table. "That there is Rusty. He's the special guy that makes all of us sound so good." He smiled at Rusty. "He's our sound guy, and sometimes he has to do flips to keep up with us or, rather, Jordie's tricks, but he always makes us the stars of his electronics. He's married and has a newborn. He also drives our equipment truck and keeps our equipment all in fine tune.

"Sitting beside Rusty is our terrific bus driver, Jonas Kelsey. He gives us all sweet dreams. He does the driving while we sleep and sometimes treats us to a dinner of his fabulous barbeque ribs. He has a heart for this mission and is always smiling and encouraging us in many ways. He's the oldest, and like it or not, I think we've all found ourselves at his knee, listening to some sound, older wisdom that has helped us in our walk with the LORD. We are thankful for you, Jonas," Sky Blue said with a tender smile.

Then he speared Willy. "And as far as our newest member, I was hoping you all would tell me about him." He paused at the uproar of laughter. "Why do I get the feeling this is going to be a year I'll never forget?"

Lilly spoke up. "Well, Willy, where shall we start, couch stuffin's, drumming on your hood, or beating the girls off with your drum sticks?"

"Let's see." Olivia, Willy's sister, joined in and told another whale tale on her brother, to everyone's delight, and then, before another word was spoken, Hannah piped up with an exaggerated fish story of her own. Between Peter, Lilly, and Willy's two teen sisters, Willy was about to crawl under the table. He certainly was being served what he usually dished out. Neither Wilma nor Doug needed to join in; everyone was doing a fine job describing their Willy through and through.

Finally, Willy put his hands in the air, "Okay, okay. That's enough. I'm going to wake up in the morning and find out these guys left without me," he said, laughing. Willy was shaking his head. "Return payment is rough."

Wilma spoke up in Willy's defense. "Willy will keep your heart challenged and, at the same time, young and encouraged." Wilma wiped a tear. "Even through all this teasing, we will miss him more than he knows. He's a precious son and brother."

Everyone in the family cheered. That this was indeed the truest of the stories told.

After dinner, all retired to the living room, where the group sang some songs using the piano in the corner. They had a great night fellowshipping in song. Then Doug led them all in a short Bible study. Afterward, they shared the heart of their ministry. And then Doug suggested a time of prayer. They all joined hands, and everyone took turns praying. The Spirit of God was upon them, and they worshiped through prayer in Spirit and in truth.

><

That night Willy laid his head on his pillow one last time and said to the Lord, *This night really rocked. You, the Rock of our Salvation, give us much to rejoice about. Thank You, Father. May I please You in all I do with this group in the days to come.* Then he drifted off to sleep listening to the beat of his heart.

><

All these treasured memories actually had him drifting off in his tiny bus bunk, listening to his skateboard roll back and forth. He rolled over with a smile. Indeed, he was blessed. Then he fell into a peaceful sleep.

CHAPTER 2

They were headed south after spending two weeks in the San Francisco area. Willy couldn't keep his eyes off the coastline. Jonas had purposely taken them down Highway 1, known as one of the most famous scenic highways in the US. The highway was twisty and narrow, sandwiched between the mountains on one side and the ocean crashing below on the other. The bus sat up high, overlooking the dangerous bluffs below. Willy had never seen anything like it. He was supposed to be practicing, but he kept messing up because he wanted to look out the window at the beautiful ocean.

Finally, Sky Blue told Jonas, "At Jade's Cove, pull in for a view chaser for new boy here."

That was Sky Blue's nickname for Willy. But thankfully Sky Blue had warmed up to Willy as a perfect fit to the team. He wasn't a man of many compliments, but several times, he'd slapped Willy on the back, telling him what a good job he was doing. And he'd been supportive about adding the skateboard ministry to the tour, which meant a lot to him.

About an hour later, they pulled into a gravel parking area. The ocean was sparkling like glitter. Willy didn't need an invitation. He hopped up without a word, skipped down the aisle, off the bus he went, jumping over the last two steps, and stood next to the railing. The wind was making a crazy arrangement of his hair, but Willy didn't care. He was so awestruck by God's beauty that he was frozen in place for a moment. Everyone in the bus had a chuckle at his expense. Then they saw him dash down the five flights of stairs, taking them two at a time, disappearing into the bluff below. In seconds, Willy's cargo shorts, t-shirt, and shoes had disappeared. Everyone else then got off the bus, except Kenzie.

They were about to go down, but Sky Blue held up his hands for them to wait. "Give the boy some time."

They nodded and then looked back down at the majestic ocean, surrounded by huge boulders and outcroppings of bluffs. Then they spotted Willy, his hands raised high in the air as the water lapped over his shoes. All knew what he was doing: praising his Savior.

Willy was so overcome by emotion. As he stood in awe of God's beautiful creation, *Lord, I'm undone at Your hand. I'm blown away by Your majesty. Your power is mightier than even these waves or mountains. Help me remember that Your grace is even bigger than these rocks and that this ocean, immense as it is, could not come close to holding the love You have for me and those up there on that bus and all the hurting and lonely people we see every day.* On he prayed and praised God while the sting of ocean spray splashed his face and the smell tantalized his senses. Then Willy took off running down the beach on the water's edge. He just had to run.

Cookie said to the crew as he went down the stairs, "Yeah. I remember the first time I saw the ocean up this way, it took my breath away that my God who made this here ocean loves me."

They all agreed and mentioned similar thoughts as they reached the bottom of the bluff stairs and dipped their feet into the sand.

By the time the group had dispersed, each to his own private time with God, Willy had come back, panting. He was leaned over, trying to catch his breath. It had been a good run, but the wind was a struggle.

Cookie laid his hand on Willy's back and said, "Makes ya feel kinda small, doesn't it?"

Willy stood up stretched his arms to get the kinks out.

"That's an understatement." Willy smiled as he looked around. "Yeah, I'd say I feel as small as a grain of sand." He swooped down, picked up a handful, and let it flow through his hands.

"Yeah, it's hard to fathom God as big as He is and how small we are, yet He desires a relationship with us." Cookie shook his head. "I hope I never lose my awe of that. Coming here is a clear reminder," he said getting choked up, "that the God who made all this wonder saved me." He paused, stemming his tears. "It's more than my heart can handle. That's what keeps me going on tour, so that others may know *this* God." He pointed to the vastness in front of him and then to his heart.

Willy was overcome by his words. "Yeah. Me too." Willy knelt down and reached up for Cookie's hand. "Let's pray for them."

Cookie smiled, took Willy's hand, and knelt in the sand with Willy. They both poured out their hearts to God on behalf of the unsaved, hurting, and lonely people. By the time they were well into passionate praying, the others had come up one at a time and joined in until all were huddled on the sand, pouring out their hearts to God. That was what really bonded this group together. Everyone eventually climbed the stairs back up to the bus.

Willy had wondered why Kenzie hadn't made it down to Sand Dollar Beach. He plopped down beside her on one of the few front seats of the bus located in the common area living room and asked, "So why didn't you come down to that gorgeous beach?"

Kenzie met Willy with a smile. "Yes, it's beautiful, and I did get to see God's glorious seaside painting."

Willy raised an eyebrow, challenging this news.

"I got out after you all left and enjoyed my view from the railing."

Willy wasn't sure why this bothered him. He knew she wasn't in danger, because Jonas was always on the bus. So he usually kept a close eye on the only lady of the bus. Willy had noticed that every time they left the bus, unless it was business, Kenzie wasn't in attendance. Whatever she needed to do, she did it on her own.

"How about a game of spades later?" he asked her with a smile then left her to go to his part of the bus.

Kenzie giggled to herself as she listened to Willy's shoes squish squash down the aisle, he had obviously forgotten to take them off before going into the water. Kenzie's section was up in the front, away from the others' sleeping quarters, for propriety's sake.

Sky Blue was standing leaning on the seat opposite Kenzie. He was looking down at her, his eyes trying to hide the feelings that had been creeping up in his heart about this certain piano player. "Didn't you feel up to going down to the beach?"

Kenzie looked into the eyes of what thousands of people looked at every weekend, the bluest eyes on earth. His dark, curly hair hanging just past his collar was the most gorgeous mass of hair she'd ever seen. He was very easy on the eyes, she thought. He was definitely tops in the looks department, from her view anyway. And his voice was what made the band possible. He had a voice smooth as silk, ever so lovely to the ears. Yes, she thought he would be easy to fall for. But she'd kept a close rein on her heart, as she didn't think she could take rejection from him. If it didn't work out, it would make things awkward. She just couldn't let Sky Blue know how she felt.

Changing the subject, Kenzie asked, "How was the water?"

Sky Blue ignored her question. "You know you don't have to be a hermit. I know I stressed the *rules*, but I do want you to get out some."

He was really in a pickle. He hated to see her so alone. This was intended to be an all-male tour group, but then she happened along, and because she was so great on the keys, he'd made it work. But she was left out of everything that had a personal level to it. But she knew this going into it, and thus far, God had strengthened her during the hardest of times.

Through their conversation, Sky Blue, suddenly realized what she was saying, or rather what she wasn't saying, he closed his eyes. *She's protecting me,* he thought. *She's protecting everyone on this bus.* He opened his eyes and sat down in the seat opposite her. He leaned over close to her face. "Look, Kenzie. I never realized the depth of the solitude I asked of you when joining the tour. If I'd known, I probably wouldn't have asked that of you. The faithfulness and loyalty you demonstrate to the group by hiding away is very touching. But I can't stand the thought of you suffering this way on our behalf." He looked caringly into her brown eyes.

"I'm thankful that we only tour two months at a time," she answered softly.

Sky Blue stood up. He needed a breather. Looking into her sweet face with her blonde hair framing it was getting to him. He became all business and said, "Do you have the books done and payroll coming along?"

"Yes. Anytime you want to go over them, I'm ready," she replied.

"Thanks. I'll let you know."

Then he walked to the back of the bus. He had a lot on his mind. He really wanted to tour—he loved doing it—but he had to admit that at times it had lost the luster it once had, and he hated that it took so much out of him. It wasn't that his heart for the lost had waned, but the bus life was hard. He was getting the urge more and more that he wanted to settle down and find a wife. Maybe that was why he seemed more irritated lately.

He'd no more thought the last thought than he tripped over Willy's skateboard that had rolled into the aisle, causing him to almost land face first on the floor. He growled and picked up the offensive piece of junk and threw it in Willy's bunk area.

"Can't you keep anything cleaned up around here?" he spouted like a volcano. "You can't just leave things in the walkway!" Then he stomped off to his curtained section. And not being able to slam a door, he jerked his curtain too hard and ripped it, which made him even more agitated.

Everyone just looked at one another and let out a low whistle. Everyone knew that when Sky Blue blew it, peace and quiet was in order. All went to their bunks for a rest.

They'd just set up for the Friday night's concert, and had about two hours left before rock time. So it was time to get down to some serious practice.

Sky Blue said, "Let's hit it for 'Casual Glances,' boys." He pointed to Jordie for the intro.

Chet had previously turned all of Jordie's drive and volume knobs up without him knowing it and conveniently forgot. Chet had a sore sense of humor, and he loved to watch Sky Blue blow his stack, so he was in for a real treat tonight.

Sky Blue covered his ears with his hands and whizzed around and clenched his teeth, about to make heads roll. He looked at Chet. Chet was sucking together his cheeks to keep from laughing, holding a straight face. He shrugged his shoulders like he didn't know how that happened. But he couldn't keep composure. He finally busted up laughing.

Sky Blue marched halfway over to him and said through clenched teeth, "Get it together, Chet, or you will find yourself strung up. Do you hear me? Man, you made his amplifier take a hike. Do it again, and you'll be the one taking the hike. Got it?" Then he turned around and walked back to his position.

Willy, loving this, did a victory drum roll. Everyone was quietly snickering. Chet thought it was worth it. They didn't play those pranks every time for fear they'd get fired. But they took turns adding a little life to the road, they called it. The only bad thing was that it was usually at Sky Blue's expense.

They went on through the rest of the practice. Thirty minutes before show time, they headed to their room to pray and be still before the LORD and quiet their hearts before the concert. Somehow, Willy knew it would be a special night.

"Three, two, one!" Willy hit the drums like a wild man in the intro to their last song. It was a lot of aerobic exercise playing the drums, but Willy loved it. He was an excellent drummer. After the song, he stuck the sticks in his back pocket and said, "That's a wrap!"

Then, as usual, Willy and Rusty immediately exited with the equipment while Sky Blue, Jordie, and Chet remained on stage to sign autographs and meet well-wishers. Kenzie and Cookie were in charge of the table with their albums, cassette tapes, and these new things called CDs, t-shirts, and other concert souvenirs. Willy and Rusty tore down everything and brought all the equipment out to Jonas, who gave them a hand in getting it all back in and situated. That was the usual routine, and it worked well for Willy since he was usually really pumped after a concert.

CHAPTER 3

On this night, though, he was about to have his routine rearranged like crashing cymbals. He had his arms loaded down with pieces of his drum set, to where he could barely see around them, and he was walking swiftly when he tripped over a large object in the alleyway while crossing to the bus and equipment truck. If Jonas hadn't been right there to catch the whole massive drums on legs (Willy always tended to carry more than he should in one trip, Jonas thought) it would have all landed splat on the ground, including Willy.

Willy caught himself just in time to look back at what on earth had jumped out and tripped him. Only he saw it was a *someone*, not a something. Jonas had already taken the things from him. Rusty had gone ahead and unburdened his arms and was standing over Willy as he went to the clump of breathing flesh. The body was on its side, curled up and face down, dressed in a black leather coat. It appeared to be a woman, as the red-highlighted brunette head of hair was midway down the back and curly.

Willy looked up at Rusty and then back at the clump. He gently turned the pile of flesh over, putting his hand behind the head and gently laying it on the ground. What he saw made him let out a low whistle. He looked back at Rusty and then back at the young lady and said, "I can't believe she didn't wake up! I tripped over her really hard!" Willy's heart was poured out for this girl.

There was an evident reek of alcohol, and she had a paper bag with a bottle in it clenched in her hands. Her face was pale, her makeup smeared as though she'd been crying, yet her lips sported untouched red lipstick. She still hadn't flinched a bit. It was Willy's assessment that she wasn't hurt but just skunk drunk.

Willy made an instant decision. "Hey, Jonas. Do you mind finishing up while I unhitch the jeep? I'm going to take this girl to a hotel. Can you help Rusty with the rest? Please."

Jonas had already made three trips. He didn't need to be asked. "Sure, man. Just don't leave alone." Then he patted him on the back and gave him a compassionate smile. Jonas shook his head. *I bet Willy brought home every stray puppy when he was a boy..*

Willy left the woman and went and unhitched the community jeep. It was shared by all the members on a first-come, first-serve basis. He loaded the gal into the backseat. She groaned but didn't wake up. He then waited for Rusty and Jonas to get back with the last load.

"Hey, Jonas. Thanks, man. I owe you one," Willy said.

"Anytime!" Jonas nodded with a wave of the hand as he began to load up the bus.

"Hey, Rusty, would you go with me?"

"Yeah, I'll go." He tossed the equipment truck keys to Jonas, "Hey, ask Jordie to drive for me, will ya?"

Jonas waved them both off.

Willy had no idea where to take her. He had no idea where she lived or what she was dong lying in the alley like that. So he prayed that he would find the right hotel. He sought out the Lord. Unbeknownst to Willy, Rusty was sitting beside him, doing the very same thing on behalf of his passionate friend Willy.

Not long after, Willy turned into a chain hotel that was well lit. He went into the office and got a room on the first floor. Then he drove right up to the door of the room.

Willy sighed. *Thank You, Lord, that this parking spot was empty.*

Willy opened the room door and pulled back the bed covers before returning for his mysterious passenger. Rusty helped get her out of the car, her body slinging every which way. She was so knocked out that it was easy for them to get her to the bed. Before they laid her down, they took off her coat and Willy slipped off her red high heels and tucked her feet under the covers and pulled them up over her red party dress. Rusty quietly stood back and watched all this.

Willy stood up and just looked at her. He thought that in all this girl had done to cover up herself, she seemed to be a hurting, lonely, lost, abandoned child, and Willy's heart turned over for her. He reached down to the sleeping face that the lamp light illuminated and gently pushed a mass of hair away from her face. He whispered, "Only Christ Jesus can heal the inside and make a new person. I pray that you will know Him someday." Willy was whispering this really more to himself and God, for he knew she wasn't listening. Then he turned and scribbled a note on the hotel notepad.

Meet me at the Shoney's two blocks over at 9:00 a.m. Here is money for a taxi. Sweet dreams.

Willy

Willy then left his business card and laid a sucker next to it. He took one last look at this heartbreaking case and then turned and looked in her purse. Rusty raised his eyebrows, wondering what in the world he was doing. Willy found the desired item: her wallet.

He looked through it until he found some identification. *Christy Henson.* Then Willy put back all the contents he'd taken out and laid the purse on the end table. He hated to invade in people's private space, but this called for breaking the rules. He needed to know what name to give the front desk for a wakeup call. He thought she'd need one. Then he turned out the light and closed the door and left.

Rusty didn't need to ask; he laid his hand on Willy's shoulder and prayed. *L*ORD*, help this girl to know You in some way. May she find a good night's sleep. May she meet Willy in the morning.* L*ORD, open her heart that she may see You in Willy as they meet. May Your name be glorified. And, God, thank You for Willy's heart. He encourages me so much. I'm so glad that You found the perfect guy for our tour. We praise You. Help us be faithful in all our ways. Amen.*

Willy had a lump in his throat. He was so touched by Rusty's heart. He said a gravelly, "Thank you. I needed that."

Everyone was up, seated in the common area living room, waiting for the two to get back. If curiosity killed the cat, they would've had a travesty on their hands. Willy was headed for bed. It was late or early, whichever way you wanted to look at it. And he didn't want to be late for his arrangement with that girl. He was almost to his bunk when he walked backward up to the front, and stopped in front of Sky Blue.

"Can I use the jeep in the morning, say from eight-thirty to noon or so?"

"Sure."

Willy thanked him and proceeded to his bunk.

Sky Blue grabbed his arm. "Hey there. Not so fast."

Willy turned to see everyone looking at him. "What is it?"

Cookie and Jordie both at the same time said, "We're waiting to hear 'what is it' from you."

Willy looked into each expectant face. It dawned on him that they wanted to know what happened. "Just another hurting chick needing some TLC. That's all. Really, that's it. Now I'm going to bed."

Willy was waiting on a bench, praying, when a taxi drove up. Christy stepped out. Obviously, she had no other clothing to change into, but she looked refreshed, her purse and coat hung over her arm. Willy knew this would be awkward, but he had spent the morning praying over her and this meeting, asking God for the right words. It was her all right. She looked like a frightened kitten.

Willy jumped up, "Good morning, Christy. How did you sleep?"

Christy jolted at the question, realizing he must be the person who left the note, the business card, and the sucker. She was scared about the note and business card because she couldn't remember a thing about last night. All she remembered was fighting with Kevin. She almost chickened out, but curiosity got the best of her. So she had showered and fixed her hair best she could, ironed her clothes with the in-room iron, and called for a taxi before she lost all nerve.

They were headed inside. Willy hadn't stopped outside for fear she would bolt. She certainly looked as though she was going to jump ship at any moment.

Willy held the door open for her and then waited to be seated. When the hostess came, he said, "A private seat for two if you have it, please."

Christy took a step back and looked the crazy guy in the face. She wasn't sure what he was up to, but she wasn't taking anything from him.

Willy did some quick reassuring. "It'll be okay. Trust me." He was smiling, and that seemed to bring out the tiniest smile from her as she nodded her head.

Christy had a killer headache, and she wasn't able to hide the dark circles under her eyes; but, as with most mornings, she just didn't care, especially lately.

"I," they both began. They looked at each other, and then they both said, "No, you go ahead," at the same time. That brought laughter from both of them.

Willy normally let ladies go first, and he planned to, but first felt the need to lay some groundwork. Willy looked at this pitiful girl who desperately needed to know Jesus. "Okay. I just want you to know that I don't have any personal agenda or ill intentions. I'm above board, and please feel free to ask me anything you wish." He made sure she understood and then said, "Now, ladies first."

"Humph. Some lady I am." She was twisting her napkin. She looked up but away; she couldn't meet his eyes. She was nervous. Tears were welling up. "How did you know my name?" she asked nervously.

Willy snickered and smiled. "After last night's encounter, how could I forget?" He was looking intently at her when he realized his mistake. Her eyes were huge.

She put her hand over her mouth and gasped. She was shaking her head back and forth. "Please don't tell me—"

Willy put his hands in the air, waving her down. "Hey, hey. That's not at all what I meant."

She gulped and then put her hands on her hips, her chin jutting in the air. "Then tell me, Mr. YoYo, what *did* you mean?"

Willy laughed out loud at what she called him. But laughing only made things worse. It wasn't going very well, and Willy prayed for a rescue. He sorely needed one. "Well, I was hoping you would do the talking," Willy said, trying to get her to open up as to why she was lying in an alley roadway late last night.

Christy had a hangover that was out of this world. She'd never had one quite this bad on the morning after. She rubbed her head, her hair falling in her face and a grumpy expressing claiming her lonely features. "That's just it. I, uh…I…" She rubbed her temples again. "I, uh…I just can't seem to remember anything." Then the tears that had been held back breeched the dam and came in torrents. She put her hands to her face and put her face down to the table in shame.

Willy wished to comfort her by a touch but wisely refrained. He simply yet powerfully prayed for her until he could hear her trying to speak.

Through the gasps of air and hard crying, she asked, "I just…I…uh…I just…need to know…uh…did we…uh…?" She kept crying. "I'll never forgive myself if I gave that away." She sobbed. "I just can't remember—"

Willy caught on quickly what she was saying and could certainly help her out on this one. "Hey, hey. Now shh. Shh." Willy reach over and briefly patted her arm. "It's okay, Christy. I can assure you," Willy said with a chuckle and all sincerity, "that nothing of that nature happened between you and me."

That caught her attention, and she looked up, not minding the tears that streaked her face.

"What? What did you say?"

"Listen, Christy. I don't know what all happened to you last night. I can only vouch for what happened when I was with you. And I had a witness during all that time." Willy pushed his plate back. "And actually, you were asleep the whole time."

She tilted her head in the cutest way and wrinkled her nose. "I was?" She was even more baffled. She cleared her throat. "Um, I think, Mr. YoYo, that you better tell me everything."

Willy leaned his head back and let out a big laugh.

"This is no laughing matter!" she said with hurt feelings at his insensitivity.

"I know it isn't. But you keep calling me YoYo." He chuckled. "My name is Willy. People just call me YoYo Willy."

"Oh. I see," she said, thinking that was strange. She had to ask, "Why do they call you that?"

Willy tried to briefly explain. "Because they said I brightened people's day. So they got in the habit of saying, 'This here is YoYo Willy, bringing you up when you're down.'" He was giving her the smile he gave everyone, melting her heart just a bit.

"I can see that." She actually cracked a little smile. Even being with him this little bit of time had made her day. "So you kept the name YoYo Willy?"

"That's right." Willy smiled. He realized he'd been drumming on the table so he put his hands in his lap. "So when I found you last night, you were passed out in the alley over on Baxter Ave." Willy wrung his hands together. "Actually, I tripped over you, nearly falling down as I was carrying a heavy load." He looked at her to see if she was processing all this. "That was around eleven or so. How long you'd been there, I don't have a clue."

Pain washed over Christy as she remembered leaving the party and buying a bottle of cheap champagne. She wondered if he knew. "Then what?" she asked just above a whisper, not sure if she could take anymore.

"Well, my buddy and I put you in our jeep, took you to the hotel, took off your coat and shoes, put you in the bed, and covered you." Willy shook his head at remembering. "I couldn't believe it, but all that time, even when put in the jeep, you didn't wake up. You only groaned twice."

"And that's all?" Christy snidely asked. She just couldn't believe this story. There were no such gentlemen in the real world, only in fairytale land.

Willy looked her dead in the face. "Yes, and that's all." He was stern. "I did look in your purse in order to get your name so that I could tell the front desk when ringing for your wakeup call. I wrote you the note, left my card and a sucker, then we left."

Christy looked away and was contemplating the situation. She just didn't trust anyone, much less men. She tilted her head the other way. "But why? Why would you pick me up off the street and put me up in a hotel for the night if you didn't want something in return?" She jutted her chin in the air while tapping her nails on the table, clearly waiting for an answer.

That was when it was hard for Willy. He so wanted to say the right words to honor God. So he opted to answer her with a question. "What would you've done if we had been in opposite shoes?" He raised his eyebrows at her.

She was thinking.

"Would you have just walked on over me and not tried to help me?"

This seemed to take the fire out of her. God used it to establish the lifeline that Willy so wanted to hand out to her.

She leaned back with a great sigh. "Then, Mr. YoYo Willy, I should be thanking you," she said as a single tear slid down her cheek. "I thank you from the bottom of my heart." She then looked at him with all the thankfulness she possessed at the moment, which was a lot, thinking about other possible outcomes. Had some of her high school classmates found her, they wouldn't have had such an honorable story to tell this morning.

Willy nodded. "Now, as to how you got in the alley, I don't know." He said this more as a question than a statement.

That did the trick; she uncorked and let it all out.

"I just needed to get out of there. I, uh…it was just too much. It hurt too badly. And to top it off, when I saw Kevin with Aubrey, and I mean *with her*, I mean they just should have gone to the private room sooner. I got so upset that I did something I've never done before, and that was drugs. The pain was so great I just wanted to escape. So when it came by, I took a snort. Then, when I watched the two of them go off to a room, I left. I ran as hard as I could. I didn't know where I was running. My heart was just so broken that I had to get out. And then I found myself at a liquor store and went in for my normal lonely fix. But I had no clue how the two would interact. And that is all I remember."

Willy let out a low whistle to himself, holding his tongue lest she hear it. *Wow!* he thought. *This is it, Lord. This is who You came to save. I hold this desperate child up to You. Hold her close to You,* he prayed. Willy licked his lips. "You probably passed out shortly there after, and that's where I found you."

She really wasn't listening. She was shaking her head. "I'm not…I refuse to give that up. It's mine, and I will decide when, where, and, most of all, who." She shrugged her shoulders, continuing this one-sided conversation. "I don't know why I was so upset. I had already told him no several times, so I guess he gave up and went on to a better offer. But it still hurt to know he doesn't love me more than that."

Willy sat listening, hoping his bottom jaw wasn't on the floor. This was a hard one. She was down, and the only way up was Jesus.

She looked up and put her hand over her mouth. "Oh gosh. I'm just rambling. I bet that was just an earful."

Willy, not sure what to say, decided to mention Peter's wedding. "Well, my cousin just got married, and I'd say they're both glad they saved themselves for each other."

She tossed her head in anger. "Well, I'm not planning to get married, but that wouldn't make any difference to me." She banged her fist on the table. "It's not about purity, but about the only thing I've ever had that was mine. My parents have controlled everything in my life, but they can't have this. And I'm not about to give away my only control so flippantly."

Now Willy did let out a low whistle, thankful they were in a private booth. "Well, one thing is for sure. Drugs and alcohol don't mix."

"You got that right!" Christy was shaking her head.

Willy went on. "I have to be honest. I've never been in that kind of heartache, but I have to come clean with you, Christy."

"I knew it! What now?"

Willy watched her roll her eyes.

"I think I have something that will give you cause to think long and hard." Willy looked to be sure he had her attention. "It's something very dear to me. As a matter of fact, I'd lay my life down for it." He paused. "And that is Jesus Christ."

Christy flipped her hand forward at him. "Oh yeah, I know. Well, everyone knows that. But from what I've seen, it don't do 'em any good. I gave up on that a long time ago." She wasn't angry, but cynical. "It might be good for you, but I'm way too messed up for God to do anything with."

"Well, I have a tract here if you should desire to know just how wrong that statement is and want to know more. Also, if you need someone to talk to, call that number on the back bottom of my business card. Don't hesitate to call. She's a great listener," Willy said with all the hope in his heart that she would call.

She'd kept the card in her purse. She had looked it over several times. "Thank you, Willy, for everything," she said sincerely.

"You, my lady, are very welcome. Now, if you're finished, I'll be delighted to take you home." Willy, smiling at her, picked up the bill and left a nice tip for the privacy.

They exited, and Willy opened the door to the jeep for her. "Sorry it's not a limo ride, but if you saw my other car, you would be thankful for this one." He laughed, thinking about his car back home.

"Hey, a ride is a ride. Thanks." She had him take her to an old friend's house across town from her place on Rodeo Drive. "You can just drop me here. Thanks." She then leaned back into the window. "And I do mean thanks." She stepped back so he could leave.

He hated to just drive off, but what else could he do? She seemed confident to be on her own, and she certainly was strong willed enough to take on a tiger, should he show his stripes.

CHAPTER 4

Willy had shared the morning's events with the crew. They prayed for her right then, and Willy knew they'd continue to do so daily. She put a face to the many unnamed lost people they prayed for on a regular basis.

They'd done the Saturday night gig, two different churches on Sunday, and then had been asked to stay and do another gig at a different high school.

Right after lunch, they set up a portable stage on the school's football field. This time, Cookie shared his testimony and they did six songs. They weren't allowed to mingle or share the gospel. But Willy always stepped in and told them about the skateboard shindig before signing off. He never tired of hearing how God had changed Cookie's life on the bridge of disaster.

But today, Willy was in for a bizarre surprise. After most of the kids had cleared out, a young girl Willy recognized right away came toward him. She was in stonewashed jeans and a white V-neck pullover shirt with a blue hoodie. He was surprised and delighted all at the same time.

She was smiling as she sauntered over. She tapped the stage. "Hey there, Mr. YoYo," she teased. "You didn't tell me what the beat of your heart was." She had her hands in the back pockets of her jeans. She rubbed her fingers over the business card he had left. She had kept it with her like a treasure, reminding her that someone in this world really cared about her. "Here I was thinking you made old granny rocking chairs, only to find out here you are, a drummer for this really cool band, and, I might add, a spectacular one at that."

Willy had come over to the edge of the portable stage and squatted down as she'd approached to be more personal. He smiled his special smile.

Ignoring her teasing, he looked deep into her eyes, and asked, "How are you?"

She nervously switched her weight from one foot to the other. Instead of telling the truth, she lied and said, "Great after that concert! Wow! You guys really know how to *rock*!"

Willy chuckled.

"And was that man for real who shared his story, or was it all made up?" She was trying to see Cookie around Willy. "I was just sorta blown away at how much he said God had changed his life. That doesn't seem real, or at least all I've seen around me." She shrugged her shoulders.

Willy's heart just melted. *Oh, Father, she's searching. Show Yourself to her,* he silently prayed. "No. I can vouch that Cookie's testimony is for real and that his love for what God has done in changing his life is expressed every moment of every day he lives," Willy said sincerely. He knew she was thinking hard on all of it.

Most everyone had cleared out, and she was getting nervous about being late for class. "I need to go, Willy. I've skipped classes too much already this year, and this is my last year. Then I'm out of this place for good."

"So you'll be graduating in May, I take it?" Willy asked, sizing things up.

Her chin went up in the air. "Yes, sir, I am. I worked hard to get to where I am, and I plan to walk across that stage with pride."

Willy smiled at her words, so like a child at times yet so confident at others. "What do you plan to do after that?" Willy asked, curiosity getting the best of him.

"I don't know. But I know this much. Whatever it is, I'll be as far away from here as I can get."

Willy wondered just what would make a person so unyielding about staying in the place she lived. It must be something in her home or personal life, Willy assumed. But there wasn't the time to ask her. So he had to just let it go.

"Well, Christy, have a great year. It will be one to be remembered." Willy said one more thing that remained with Christy: "Every day is a memory in the making, and memories will still be there when the alcohol and drugs wear off." He then brushed her cheek with the back of his hand and stood up to watch her leave.

She did exit on that note, thinking, *This guy just can't be for real!* She turned around halfway across the football field and waved.

Willy was still watching her and waved back.

He turned around to help the crew, though most of the work was done since they weren't allowed off the stage to mingle. It wasn't many hours until school let out and the skateboard shindig would happen. But Willy was in much need of just spending some time with his Father. He went to his bunk, got out his Bible, and started reading the book of Mark. He hadn't made it very far when this verse jumped off the page at him: "'Come, follow me,' Jesus said, 'and I will make you fishers of men'" (Mark 1:17). He plopped his Bible down and cried out to God. *Oh, Lord, You've called me to be fishers of men, but, Lord, the fishing can get so hard and weary. I want to do Your work and save every fish I hook. I know that is wrong to demand You to do our bidding in the salvation of souls. Help me remember my job: to simply cast the net and You will bring them in. I am simply to cast out the gospel message, You change the lives.* On he prayed for Christy, his family, personal needs and the crew; he prayed about everything on his heart. Then he continued to read the entire book of Mark, listening to what God wanted him to know and learn as His fisherman disciple. In no time at all he heard Chet calling for him to get up or he was going to be left behind.

Willy didn't need to be called twice. He hopped up, got his skateboard and Bible, and headed out. Everyone had asked about his wrap-up distraction after the gig earlier. And to everyone's amazement, Willy told them that this was the alley lump he had tripped over. Even Rusty was in disbelief. Willy told them he was pretty wowed himself.

On the way over to the other side of the empty parking lot they'd chosen for the shindig, Willy was in deep thought. Why he hadn't thought about this earlier, he didn't know; but looking back, he thought it a bit odd that Christy went to this high school when he'd dropped her off on the other side of town. Willy scratched his head. Another mystery question that he'd probably never know the answer to. He shrugged his shoulders, hopped on his skateboard, and did a few tricks on the way over. He certainly didn't want to waste brainpower on figuring that one out.

It had taken some doing, but Willy finally convinced Sky Blue to let him purchase a small, portable half-pipe ramp, along with a few other ramps. So they actually set up a cool area, including using cones and things to grind and jump over. They had purchased a few extra boards too for those who didn't have one to use. As part of the routine, a couple of youth ministers had already met them there with huge water coolers full of ice-cold lemonade and water.

Chet and Jordie were skateboarding today too. Sky Blue wouldn't come near a board. And Cookie, though very supportive, would rather talk to people, though he did carry a skateboard, and he even put it on the ground under one foot and moved it back and forth while standing still. It was, of course, just for looks, but it did the trick. Cookie was the cheering squad and peer pressure guy that got people over there and started, though he never really rode one.

Jonas loved watching this from the bus. He would set a chair outside and watch to his heart's content, and he was also the prayer warrior; that was his job in this evangelistic shindig. Rusty and Sky Blue hung around, mingling, getting to know the kids, seeking open hearts to speak to. Even Kenzie came out and hung in the backdrop. Because they learned early on that where there are boys, there will be girls. So when the girls began to filter in, she would mingle with them and pour her heart out among them in sharing the gospel, praying, or just listening, and even sometimes crying with a broken heart.

Willy had been doing several half-pipe moves, showing a few guys how to do it. He'd worked up a sweat, as usual, but he loved it. He used a bandana to keep his hair and the sweat out of his eyes. He soared with wings of ease all over the place. He was a very accomplished skateboarder. It was then that he noticed a small commotion in the corner of the watching zone. He did a quick look so as to not lose balance. Sure enough, it was Christy. Only, she wasn't alone. There was a guy behind her, putting his arms around her waist and trying to pull her close and whispering or something in her ear. But she'd already removed his hands and moved away twice, but he had followed her, being very persistent. This caused Willy to flinch. He had to be careful and loving. The guy held Christy much like a spider does the bug that flies into its web, with no intentions of letting go.

Willy skated over to her, popped up his board, and said, "Hey, since this young lady obviously wants to be left alone, why don't you join me for a spin?"

The guy gave Willy a look. He actually thought about it since there were several others out there. But his pride got the best of him, and he said, "I need to get to work. Don't got time for wheels today." He walked off, downcast and defeated. He seemed just as sad and lost as the lady he desired to devour. His downcast, angry eyes said he needed the Lord. And Willy's heart went out to him. He was searching in all the wrong places for fulfillment.

Cookie, sizing up the situation, went over and talked with Kevin for well over forty-five minutes. They made a connection, and God planted seeds that Cookie cast on Kevin. He shook Cookie's hand and thanked him for talking to him and said that he would really think about the things he'd shared.

Willy thought you'd have to be blind not to see that Christy was an attractive girl. However, Willy couldn't stand to see any kind of intimacy disregarded in such a flippant, disrespectful way. Not to mention that any attempt to take advantage of a woman was wrong. Not many things got under his skin, but that one did. But God still won out in his heart and gave him love and compassion for the offender too.

Willy had skateboarded back into the group immediately, not even checking on Christy. He wanted to be there for everyone. He had freed the chick from her snare, so he went on. They were there another two and a half hours before calling a wrap-up. There'd been some open hearts, and there were always those who hadn't even been soft, but that was all part of it. You never knew where a seed would land. That was God's part. But He asked them to cast seed, and that was what the skateboard shindigs were about.

What had amazed Christy the most were Willy's eyes when he'd spoken to Kevin. She'd seen compassion in them, like he really cared about Kevin. Christy was so taken back that she nearly broke down on the spot. Willy was a fabulous skateboarder. But she just couldn't shake how he'd handled Kevin. And at the same time, he'd obviously come to her rescue. She'd lived so long without letting love be part of her life that when she saw it in any form, it nearly made her run. She was so frightened of the intensity of the emotion that she couldn't handle it. She'd been a loner for as long as she could remember. After living in a home absent of love for so long, she became calloused and had built walls so thick that nothing could penetrate through, or so she thought.

Willy popped up the board and grabbed it just like he'd done all afternoon. It's second nature to a skateboarder. He smiled at Christy and said, "I'm assuming that was Kevin?"

She nodded.

"My heart goes out to him," he said. "He's looking for happiness in all the wrong places."

Christy noticed that same compassionate look again. She was disturbed about it. But then Willy was asking her a question.

"Want to take it for a spin?" He was holding out the skateboard.

Christy was hesitant. "I don't know. This is one thing I'm not very good at." She looked up at Willy.

"It's not as hard as it looks," Willy said, smiling. And then gave her a few pointers and encouraged her to try it.

"Okay. I'll try it as a thank-you for getting Kevin off my back."

Willy laid the board down and opened his arm as an invitation. "There you go, miss. It's all yours."

She barely moved, but she tried and actually stayed on the board. But she dared not try any tricks or ramps. Then she came back to him and handed him the board.

"Thanks," she said. Then she switched her feet back and forth. She had her head down, and then she looked up. "I've been thinking a lot about what you said to me the other day, and then the music and its message, and then Cookie's testimony, and just watching love walk all around this parking lot." She paused, "I just don't know if I can let down my guard to love. I'm scared of love, to love or be loved. And from all I hear about this Jesus who died because of His love for me and these people who are loving others right here and spending their time free of charge to do a gig and then to spend their afternoon in a parking lot for horrible people like me…" She had to look away. There it was again, love. She paused. A few tears streamed down her cheeks. She shook her head. "I just don't know…I just don't know if I can take it." She looked up into Willy's compassionate eyes and said, "I'm afraid love will ask more than I'm able to pay." She looked so sad at that very moment.

Willy was compelled to respond. "I can promise you that love does cost." Willy pulled her chin up, for she had dropped her head. "I would be lying to you to tell you that a life of love doesn't have its times of pain. Following Jesus Christ will cost you all you have, but you will gain all that really matters in this life."

She had a confused look on her face. "Why does it seem so real here, yet when I go to my world, it's though they speak of an entirely different God?" she asked. She didn't even wait for an answer before going on. "And besides that, He'll change His mind after He finds out how bad I have been." She crossed her arms, clearly about to bolt.

Willy could see he was about to lose his audience, so he said, "He already knows."

Her head spun around. "What do you mean?" she spat. "Did you tell Him?"

Willy had to suck in his cheeks, for he was about to chuckle. "Christy, Jesus is in heaven." He didn't think this was the right time to try to discuss the Trinity with her and add to her confusion, so he did the best he could. "He sees and knows everything. Nothing is hidden from Him, not even our thoughts."

She gasped and put a hand over her mouth. "Oh my." Her eyes got big as saucers. "Now I know He'll never love me."

Willy shook his head. "Oh, my dear Christy, you are so wrong. In the Bible, it says that no one is righteous, not even me. All of us here are sinners, what you might call bad people. But it's not about how bad you are but about how good God is. God is in the business of making the bad good, the unrighteous righteous, the unholy holy, the condemned cleansed, just like the song 'Changed' we sang earlier." He took out a pocket pad and wrote down two verses:

> But God demonstrates his own love for us in this: While we were still sinners, Christ died for us.
>
> Romans 5:8

> This is love: not that we loved God, but that he loved us and sent his Son as an atoning sacrifice for our sins.
>
> 1 John 4:10

"And if you want to really see what this Jesus that we speak of looks like, then get a Bible and read the book of John. It's toward the back." Then, seeing her dismayed look, he asked, "You do have a Bible, don't you?"

"Uh, yeah. Well, maybe." She looked up. "Well, if I don't, can I check one out at the library?" she asked in all sincerity.

Willy, thinking most people would laugh at her if she were to check out a Bible, almost laughed himself at the picture. Willy held up his finger. "Wait right here." He skateboarded back to the bus and brought back a Bible for Christy. They had a stash of Bibles for this very purpose.

"Hey, here's a Bible to keep." He put the note with the verses at the beginning of the book of John and raised it up. "Christy, I'm telling you the truth. I lay down my life for you in saying all your answers are in this book." Then he gave it to her.

Christy said, "Thank you, Willy. I'll never forget you." She turned and left before the tears began.

CHAPTER 5

Willy sat with his Bible open on his leg. It was Wednesday night and his turn to lead the Bible study, prayer, and worship time. It felt weird to teach older people, but he wanted to pull his share of the load even in this area. He leaned over with his hands together and began with what had been on his heart.

"I was reading in the beginning of Mark, and Johnny Boy took me by surprise. Turn, if you will, to Mark chapter one." He began, reading at the beginning for context, Mark 1:1-9. Then he began to share about these verses. "The first part is about John the Baptist and his assignment."

"He is a great example to us about staying focused. That's for sure." He was tapping his foot and really getting into the message. "I mean, wow. To be called to be the forerunner of Christ, well, that is…that just blows my mind. Can you imagine being asked to go prepare the way for the Messiah to come through the world?" He took a breath. "I, for one, have questions. Did he ever waver? Did he lose heart? What kept him going when the hard times came? Did he ever have his own desires? Did he ever take a vacation? What did he do for *fun*? How did Satan attack him? Where was he weak?" Willy paused, putting his head down for a moment. "I know he wasn't perfect, but do we really pursue holiness like Johnny Boy"? Willy went on to describe John the Baptist. "I mean, truly, when I read this passage and description of John the Baptist, the word *weirdo* comes to my mind. He was definitely different. I don't think he was trying to be different to be separate from the world, but just the opposite, that his mission made him so focused that he didn't concern himself with the things of this world so much. Willy went on. "I mean, this dude, he dressed really strange, certainly not a fashion bug. And his happy meal consisted of locusts and honey." Willy snarled. "Now, I can handle the honey. Ain't nothing like putting a piece of fresh honeycomb in the old pie hole, as my mamma calls it, and savoring the rich sweetness. But locusts, now that is a different story altogether."

The crew laughed at Willy's antics.

"I bet he probably used the honey to dip the locusts in. Some things just go together, like French fries and ketchup, chips and dip, tacos and salsa, fish and tater sauce." He licked his lips subconsciously. "You get the picture. But can you imagine honey and locusts?" He made a disgusting grunt. "And who knows? Maybe he liked it."

"But I do feel like Scripture tells us he wasn't worried about where his next meal came from because there was always good ol' locusts and honey. What was his message?" He looked around. "It was simple and sweet, kinda like the locusts and honey, huh?" He chuckled at his own analogy. "But on a serious note, his message was 'repent, for the kingdom of God is near!'" He read verses 7 and 8, which stated the very answer:

> And this was his message: "After me will come one more powerful than I, the thongs of whose sandals I am not

worthy to stoop down and untie. I baptize you with water, but he will baptize you with the Holy Spirit."

"And in Matthew it tells us his simple message," Willy said.

> In those days John the Baptist came, preaching in the Desert of Judea and saying, "Repent, for the kingdom of heaven is near."
>
> Matthew 3:1-2

Willy went on. "We must be clear and not compromise the truth. I wonder if he was well received. I mean, that's not exactly an easy-on-the-ears message, if you get my drift, which then again points back to God, that He has to draw the heart, open the eyes of an individual." Willy licked his lips. "But how will they hear without someone telling them?" Willy closed his Bible. "I want to challenge us all to be Johnny boys. Let's focus less on ourselves and the world's cares and care for the people of the world more."

Willy ended with, "Let's spend some gut honesty before the throne of grace."

They were near the end of the Ocean Praise West Tour when Jordie and Chet both asked Willy to stay on for another week. "Hey, Willy. I was wondering if you wanted to stay on, get a place in Malibu. The three of us can split the rent and catch some waves."

Kenzie walked by and rolled her eyes and sarcastically said, "You mean catch some babes."

Chet put his hands on his hips. "Hey, wait a minute." He pointed at his chest. "I can't help it if I'm cool *and* good looking."

He combed his hair and stuck his mega comb in his back pocket and then strutted around, acting all cool.

Everyone laughed out loud.

"Hey, why is everybody laughing at me?"

It was true that Chet thought himself to be on the handsome side, but he didn't intentionally try to get chicks; it just happened that way.

Willy really did want to learn to surf. It had to be similar to skateboarding but out there in the ocean. That just seemed to be the coolest thing he'd seen yet. "I'm in, as long as we are not baywatching but surfing," he teased, but he made his point that he was not interested in getting into temptation's way.

"Man, Jordie, I sure hope you know what you're doing." Willy had just taken the surfboard that he'd rented under his arm and gone to the water's edge. Willy had to say he was extremely excited yet, at the same time, scared out of his wits. He was about to turn back, thinking that perhaps he couldn't do it after all.

"Come on, Willy. If you can skateboard, you can do this. That is, unless you can't swim." Jordie knew he could do it.

"I can swim like a fish. I just don't want a shark to think I'm a tasty one." Willy gave him a skeptical look.

"Man, just don't be the last seal," Jordie said seriously.

"What does that mean?" Willy asked with a disgruntled, confused look.

Jordie laughed. "Basically, it means this: sharks love seals, so if you are dressed up in a wetsuit, swimming with the seals, and they take off, you better boogie." He paused for dramatic effect. "The slowest seal loses." He said it so dramatically that he could hardly hold his laughter.

Willy's eyes were so big Jordie thought they were going to pop out.

Jordie jabbed him in the side. "Gotcha!"

Willy let out a sigh of relief.

"No. Really, they're not too much trouble. For one, you're not in a wetsuit, and I usually make sure I surf where there are other surfers stirring up the water." He smiled at Willy. "Hey, come on." He nudged his friend. "Let's hit the waves." He grabbed Willy's arm and pulled him into the water. "Just follow me and do what I do," he yelled back over the crashing waves.

Willy plunged in with all his heart, just like he did everything else.

After a half a day of trying, Willy made it up on the board and rode a wave. His face was red when he came in to shore, where he met Chet and Jordie, who were both taking a break, enjoying some juice from their cooler.

"That is so gnarly, man! Like nothing I've ever done!" Willy said as he jumped around in excitement. "That makes skateboarding look like an aircraft carrier in a bathtub!" He then let out a loud, "Yahoo!" Before going back out, they ended up in a great game of volleyball. Many of the big city beaches had nice boardwalks on which you could walk, skateboard, ride a bike, etc. And in the sand, they had several volleyball net setups. There was even a sand sculptor that had made several life-sized dolphins, mermaids, and other sea creatures out of the sand. *They really did it up nice*, Willy thought. The coast was so different than his little country world. He loved the sand and ocean, and all the more thinking that his Creator made it.

By the third day, Willy had tanned up nicely and could stay up on his board. It was a blast. They were only going to stay for two more days and then each head home. Even though there had been many a girl turn her head, none of the crew took the bait.

><

Willy stepped ever so slightly on the grass. He was sneaking up to his mother, who was in the garden, picking green beans. It was hot work, but she loved having her garden. Willy was light-footed when he wanted to be and had accomplished his task. He grabbed his mother at her sides, nearly scaring her to death.

She turned around. "Oh, Willy! You're home!" she said. He grabbed her, and instantly they were in a bear hug. When they pulled apart, there were tears in her eyes.

Willy waved his hand. "Oh, Momma, don't cry." He walked her back to the house.

"Who's crying? Not me. That was *sweat*, honey," she said. She wiped away more *sweat* with the hem of her skirt, displaying her garden bloomers.

They were arm in arm when they went in the back door. They entered the house only to find that everyone had known Willy was home and watched the whole scene with excitement. Even Doug had played along.

Wilma waved her dishtowel at them all. "You bunch of rugrats," she teased.

Wilma served everyone iced tea and cookies as they sat around the living room, listening about Willy's tour. He had been home for Peter and Lilly's wedding, but it was just for two days; and with those days full, they really didn't have much time to visit.

After dinner, all went back into the living room to hear more. They wanted to know all about California. The older girls as well as the younger ones were on the edge of their seats in expectation of weird and wonderful stories from another land.

Willy stood up and yawned an exaggerated yawn. "Well, it's time for ol' drummer boy to hit the hay. I guess you all will have to wait," he said as he began to leave the room, only to be tackled by all his sisters.

Willy peeled them off and turned around. "Well, I just wanted to know if I was missed."

There were cheers that couldn't be denied that Willy McCollister had been missed incredibly. Willy tried to bring them to San Francisco to cross the Golden Gate Bridge with him. He tried to bring them to Jade Cove and see the beauty of the sea nestled in the bluffs, the splash of the crystal water, footprints in the sand, and the sound of crashing waves. Still, he said that descriptions and pictures didn't near do justice to being there. He openly, with tears, shared his experience at Sand Dollar Beach before Almighty God. He then went on to share in detail the last week of surfing. He tried to get the girls up on a surfboard, but words just were inferior to the experience.

Then Willy shared the beat of his heart. He had gotten very serious, which caused the room to literally stand still. Even though it was late, all eyes and ears were on Willy. They knew that they were about to be blessed in hearing Willy's heart.

"I just can't tell y'all what it's like. When I did the radio, you could hear my heart and I was very evangelistic, and I really have a heart for the hurting, or so I thought. But, man, let me tell you, I had no clue. This tour has really challenged me to put feet to my DJ days. This tour has put faces on all those songs." He moved up to the edge of his seat, his hands moving with passion. "Mom, Dad, you just can't imagine what it's like to see the faces of hurting kids and young adults who come to a gig looking for answers. When we do the skateboard shindigs, it kills me to see such messed-up teens with such deep problems, and I have the only hope that will ever change them." He had a few tears streaming down his cheeks. "It's such a mission field. I just can't tell you all enough to pray for us. I'm still taken back by the eyes that mirror a soul that is destined for hell. The looks of hopelessness have haunted my nights. There are so many. It's true; the field is ripe unto harvest." He got up and walked around a bit as faces swam through his heart.

He was passionate as he poured his heart out to his family. He turned. "I'm so blessed! I've had such a fabulous home life, sisters, parents, and friends. This is an altogether different world." He went back over and sat down. I do think God has placed me where I am with a heart for the lost. I just…uh…I just had no idea what being thrown into the sea with thousands of them would be like." He took a long sip of tea and just rested his head in his hands. Then his head came up with a chuckle. "I actually tripped over such a case just a few weeks ago in Los Angeles."

"What?" came Wilma's concerned reply. "You know you are going to gray me completely." Willy went on to tell how he'd met Christy Henson.

No one in the room needed to be asked to go to God on behalf of Willy, and it was a sweet time in prayer. Not an eye was dry when heading off to bed.

><

Peter and Lilly came over the next day, and for Lilly, it was like Christmas all over again. Willy pretty much told a repeat of what he'd shared with his family the night before, with the exception of the tripping incident. Then they did some worship and singing, like old times. This brought tears to Lilly's eyes. How much she had missed Willy.

Lilly and Willy took a walk in the afternoon.

"So, how's married life treating ya?" Willy asked.

A big grin spread across her face. She looked at him. "I'm loving it," she said with passion. "I must say it's more than I ever dreamed possible."

Willy had fallen in love with this enigma of a girl the first time he'd met her, and now all the more watching her and Peter together as a couple. *Who would've ever believed a story like theirs?* he thought.

"So, Willy, when are you going to tie the knot?" Lilly was teasing, but she wanted to know if he'd found a special someone. She looked back at him with a smile. "I highly recommend it."

"I bet you do." Willy leaned his head back and roared. "As far as the first question goes, when I find the beat of my heart, and not a moment sooner." He then shrugged his shoulders and continued. "And really, Lil, I'm not in any hurry." He kicked a rock down the road like a soccer ball and then turned backward so he could face her as they walked. "I'm having the time of my life."

Lilly knew that to be true. She could hear it in his voice when he called to retrieve his messages. And there was no doubting that it was true after seeing him in person.

"Like I shared earlier, it has its hardships, but I love playing the concerts, the gigs, and even the Sunday worship services. I think it's real cool the variety of what we play and how we minister with music, not to mention all the lives we talk with off stage."

They were headed back home.

"Well, you sure are getting some interesting calls," Lilly snickered. "What do you do with them?"

"Well, so far, I've been calling and checking on them every week or two, depending on their response. I don't know if I'll be able to keep up forever, but I'll keep on as long as I'm able." Willy smiled. He loved people.

"What do you do when people call you? And how many have you received?" Willy asked her in return.

Lilly was looking up, trying to count up the number. "Well, let's see. I don't really keep count, but I'd say since it has only been two months, about five people have called. Do you pass out my number to everyone?"

"Anyone who shows any interest in giving me a moment of their time, I usually give them one. But I don't pass them out like gospel tracks, though I have handwritten the number on tracts a time or two as well."

"It must be magnificent yet overwhelming all at the same time."

"You betcha! I recently taught about John the Baptist. Just thinking about his job makes this one look easy, but I do take it very seriously. And it's been neat to see the crew take my suggestions and run with them. You should've seen Sky Blue's eyes when I suggested that we buy a portable half-pipe."

Lilly giggled and acknowledged that it must have been a hoot. They were almost to the house when Willy asked, "Has a girl by the name of Christy called?"

Lilly tilted her head in the most adorable way. "Hmm. I don't think so. I don't recall anyone by that name." Then she looked over at Willy's disappointed look. "Why? Is she someone special?"

Willy smiled. "Not exactly."

Willy then went on to tell Lilly what had happened when he tripped over Christy.

Willy looked over at Lilly several times as he shared, her heart being read in her eyes. She so had a heart for the lost.

It must just crush her sometimes, he thought as they entered the house.

Peter called from the couch, "Hey, what's this? Stealing my lovely bride out from under my nose?" he teased Willy. Peter patted the seat beside him for Lilly to join him.

Willy grinned as he shut the door. "Well, I must admit we were just discussing how long it took to get the rice from *your* wedding out of *my* car."

Peter gave a glare. "I should have just watered it down and it would've cooked."

It had been a hilarious trick to play on Peter, and now he could be teased about it; but at the time, well, that was a different story.

They had a wonderful weekend at the Barnabus House B&B. It was awesome for everyone at church too, as Willy did some songs on Sunday before heading back out on tour.

CHAPTER 6

Noel slammed the front door on her way out of the house after another heated argument between her and her mother. She jumped in her pink Camaro and squealed out of the driveway. She needed out. She needed to get away.

She hit the steering wheel. "They're never going to understand me!"

She let the tears flow since she was alone and no one would see her crying. She couldn't let her guard down in front of others. She always had to play the part. But when she was alone, she really fell apart, especially when she fought with her mom and dad, which seemed to be more and more these days.

She went over in her mind what her mom had said: "Noel, I just don't get it!" she screamed at her daughter. "We give you everything! And we've tried to establish for you a good, promising acting career, and you just spit in our faces!" She set down her wine glass and asked, "What's not to like about Hollywood?"

Noel, known to everyone else as alias Christy Henson, rolled her eyes, and let out a disgusted grunt. Furious, she retaliated with, "I want more to my life than switching bed partners, kissing different lips, scrambling to the top, and manipulating everyone in order to stay there. But most of all, I hate being someone you're not every day," she spat out.

Ericka reached over to slap Noel's face, but she'd stumbled and grabbed the counter instead. She stabilized herself. "How dare you say those things about our careers!" she spat out. "You witch child!"

She was coming at Noel, and Noel wasn't sure what was about to happen. It looked like they were going to get into it in a bad way.

Noel sneered as she moved around the island in the kitchen. "You don't even know who you are anymore, do you? Hmph! You've played the part so long that the *real* Ericka no longer exists."

Noel was moving fast. Her mom chased her to the piano, and around they went, glaring at one another.

"I knew by letting you go to the city school you would get messed up! You were the cutest little girl! Now look at you!" She took her fists and banged them on the piano and went crazy and just kept banging and yelling. "And all you want to do is play music!" She screamed as she banged. "Ha! It won't get you anywhere!"

Noel left her mother sitting there, screaming and banging her fists on the piano. She didn't know what to do, but she had to get away. She was at a red light now and didn't even know where she was headed. While she continued to drive, she glanced up at the most popular sign in the US, the HOLLYWOOD sign sitting up on the hillside, not but a few blocks from her home in Los Angeles, California. It let the entire world know they were in the land of the stars. But Noel knew different. What people saw on TV was *not* reality. She lived this reality every day. She'd grown up in the studios. She'd been doing parts since she was a baby. She finally quit about four years ago and absolutely refused to do anymore; no more lies.

She'd seen Hollywood destroy her parents. They each had their own careers. Both were only married for convenience of keeping the news cameras off their backs. Both had been in other relationships many times. They were only interested in keeping up and being on top at anyone's expense, including their only daughter,

Noel Franklin. Things were so messed up that she didn't know what *real* was anymore.

She braked hard for another red light, and her purse spilled on the seat beside her, causing Willy's business card to fall out. She picked it up and fingered it. She'd thought of this YoYo Willy guy a lot. She'd even read the verses and Bible portion he'd asked her to. She still didn't understand what it had to do with her life. She was so confused. She looked down at the bottom, at the number Willy had mentioned if she needed to talk. She *was* desperate, so she pulled into a gas station that had a payphone. She just couldn't chance having her friends know she was in this kind of trouble. She dialed the number.

Lilly had her hands in dish soap, so she ran to phone, and caught it on the fifth ring. "Hello. Hands to Hearts, Feet to Friends Ministry. This is Lilly. How can I bring a smile to your face?"

"I just don't know if you can. Things are so, um…so out of control. Willy said I could call you if things got too bad." Tears threatened to spill over as Noel slid down the phone booth box and sat on the floor.

Lilly's heart was pounding. She hoped that the girl on the other line couldn't hear the beating of her heart. "Yes, that's right. Um…it would be a mite easier to converse if you could give me a name." Lilly always tried to get a name and a phone number to keep in contact if possible.

"Oh sure," she said between sobs. "It's Noel. Noel Franklin." She forgot to use her alias. But she was tired of living a lie. Knowing what could happen, she still decided to be for real from now on.

"Hi, Noel. I'm so glad you called. What's going on that you've actually picked up the phone to gain an ear to hear?" Lilly coaxed.

Lilly never knew what would happen. At times, the other person hung up on her. But she had prayed many times and just trusted that God would give her the words when they were necessary. It was definitely a ministry that required trusting in God.

"I don't know where to begin," she mumbled through her tears. "I just had another"—she laughed at the thought—"another fight with my mom. She just doesn't care, and my dad doesn't either. All we do is fight." She then said, "I feel so hopeless."

Before Lilly could say anything, Noel went on, as though she were talking to the air.

"My boyfriend is pressuring me. My grades are slipping." She ran her hands through her hair. "I mean, my life is a mess. I don't know what to do." She paused. "My boyfriend, he just makes it miserable if I don't give in to him. And I have tried to get him off my back, but he's persistent." She wiped away tears. "I mean, this is my senior year. It's supposed to be the happiest time of my life, and it's the most miserable." She slapped her knees. "I have everything money can buy but happiness. Things just keep getting worse and worse." She finally quit crying. "I just don't know what to do."

Lilly prayed for God to help her. She began by asking a few more questions. She found that usually this did some more uncorking. "Noel, do you have any brothers or sisters?"

"No. Thank God for that. I'd hate to have anyone else be put through what I have had to grow up with." She snorted.

"Noel, you said you live with your parents. What do they do for work?"

"They are the biggest liars in town!" she screamed back.

This was a bit out of Lilly's ballpark, but she went on in faith and in love for this girl calling for help. "What exactly do you mean?"

Noel didn't think it really mattered to this lady, so she told Lilly about her parents. She wouldn't know them from a man in the moon, so she opened up. "Well, what if I told you that my parents are Burt and Ericka Franklin?"

Lilly did a quick think. She thought the names were familiar. Then she remembered, her mom had watched them every day, about four hours of them. So every summer, Lilly caught up on all the lives of the soap operas. And, of course, primetime was always on. So in that time frame, Lilly became very aware of who's who in Hollywood.

Lilly opted to try for the truth from Noel instead of making a wrong guess. So she asked, "How is it that your parents make a living at being liars?"

"Girlfriend, are you for real?" Noel asked, astonished. "I thought everyone knew who Burt and Ericka Franklin are."

"Well, I recall those names from the TV when I was younger. But I'm not sure I can place them. Maybe you can help me out." Lilly was fishing, for she really hadn't kept up with the Hollywood stars of recent.

Noel opened up. "It's hard to be the child of a star. Eyes are on you all the time. I hate it. I just hate it." She paused. "You live your life in a glass house. Everyone expects so much from you. And it's all about parties, dinners, movies, moving up, what you look like, what you do, on and on. It's the most wretched life." She began to cry again. "I don't even know who my parents are anymore. The audience of the world has taken them captive from me." She cried. "I just want to be in a normal family."

Lilly's heart just broke for this hurting, lonely child. Lilly cleared her throat. "Noel, the only hope is Jesus Christ. I don't know how much you know about Him. But unless you believe that Jesus is God's Son and that He came and died for your sins, then there really is no hope for you. Not only is your life now going to be miserable, but your life after this will be really bad."

Noel had become *very* quiet. "Oh, you mean hell?"

"Yes, that's exactly what I mean."

"Yeah, Willy said something about that. But I just don't believe in all that make-believe stuff. I'm a reality girl living in a Hollywood body." She laughed. "Not much gets by me."

"Well, Noel, I can't convince you of the love that Jesus has for you in His death on the cross. He will have to do that. All I can do is tell you that He does love you. He loves me and has changed my life, and that is why I tell people who need help that the only *real* help is Jesus. I care about you and want everyone to have this hope that is inside me."

"Yeah, it's the love thing that gets to me," Noel said.

Lilly, sensing the need to pray for her, asked, "Noel, can I just pray with you a moment before hanging up? And I was wondering if we could perhaps talk again."

Noel felt a lot better after talking to this woman, and it just couldn't be for real that she would care, but she couldn't deny her tender words and listening ear. "Yes, I'd like that," she agreed.

"What's a number that I can get a hold of you at?" Lilly asked.

Noel didn't want to give out her family number but did anyway. She told Lilly that if she didn't call by a certain date that was set for two weeks from then, she could call that number. Otherwise, she wasn't to use it.

After they'd made their call-back arrangements, Lilly prayed, *L*ORD*, You know how this sweet Noel is hurting. Father, I ask that You make Yourself real to her. Father, her whole world has been a fairytale land She needs something real, and You, oh L*ORD*, are the real thing. L*ORD* God, can You show Noel what Love is? Help her to not be afraid of love and not to run. L*ORD*, help her deal with her parents as best she can. Also, L*ORD*, help her be strong and not give in to the pressure of* *her boyfriend's demands. Lord, protect her. Make her Your own if it be Thy will. Amen.*

Then they hung up the phone.

The tour actually ended in Charlotte, North Carolina, so Peter, Lilly, and all of Willy's family drove three hours to see him in concert. They got special seats for the night so they would have a bird's-eye view of Willy in action.

Thanksgiving was the week after the concert, so with Willy that close, he just went home after the last concert. It was a sweet Thanksgiving, all having quite a different story to tell this year than last year. And the annual bonfire, hot dog roast, and hayride were a sure delight.

It was during the first two weeks of December that a winter jam tour took place. They didn't do those every year, but when asked, it was better to do them than say no and let some other group get the slot, at least that was what Sky Blue thought, and he was the boss.

It was during that mini tour that Willy checked in with Lilly to get his messages.

"Hello."

"Hey, ragmuffin! How are you?" Willy asked.

He had to pull the phone back from his ear a moment as Lilly let out a squeal of delight.

"Is that you, Willy?" Lilly laughed, "How are you?"

"I'm fine, Lil. You act like you've not seen me for months. I was just home not but a few weeks ago." Willy laughed.

"Yes, sir. But a lot can happen in just a few weeks." Lilly's smile was huge as she laughed over the phone.

"Okay. Out with it, ragmuffin! What is it?" Willy knew something was up, and he wanted to know now.

Lilly sounded dreadful. "Well, Willy, I'm afraid that you are going to have to move out your equipment to make room for a baby crib."

Willy jumped up. "Wahoo!" He slapped his leg. "Are you kidding me?"

Lilly giggled. "No, I'm not kidding you. Well, I guess I am kidding you. A kid really is on the way."

"Oh, Lilly, that's so wonderful!" He pictured her heavy with child, and shook his head. "Hey, I'll be glad to move out when I get home next week. That's just such grand news, and right here at Christmas, when we are thinking of the Christ child."

"Oh, Willy, I just couldn't wait to tell you, but I wasn't serious about your moving out. It'll be a long while"

They went on to discuss how Lilly made the announcement to Peter, and Willy got a kick out of that. Then he retrieved his messages. Two gals had called for him from church. They were both sweet on Willy, she thought. Willy was always a perfect gentleman and was a delight to be with, so she didn't fault the girls for falling for Willy, as he would be a great catch for whoever caught him.

Willy asked about the Noel girl but didn't get her number. He asked about others who had called and retrieved numbers that he planned to check on. That was always his connection to home, and he treasured his calls to Lilly.

CHAPTER 7

They were three days from Christmas, and all were in a flutter. Lilly had made sure they spent some time at her Aunt Maureen and Uncle James's house during the time they were off from school. That was where Lilly had lived when she first arrived in Shelbyville, North Carolina. Her aunt had been saved at Christmastime last year and remarried her husband in February. So she was very close with this aunt. It had been Lilly's delight to watch Aunt Maureen grow in the Lord. She and Peter had been having a Monday night Bible study at her house for well over a year now. Aunt Maureen was ecstatic about the baby. She just couldn't contain herself. At church, all she did was talk about the new baby. She would be like the grandma, even though she was really the great-aunt. It'd be a special Christmas for all this year.

———

Noel was in the limo, coming home from a New Year's party with her parents, when she told them her plans. "Mom, Dad, I just wanted to let you know that I'm going to visit a friend for a week. I leave tomorrow. I will be back in time for school to start."

That took them by surprise. They were always concerned about what the media might pick up.

So her dad asked, "Just what will you and this friend be doing?" He wanted to know what he might be reading in the paper next week about his daughter. She'd many times caused disgrace to them and put their careers (image) in jeopardy. But not all of the episodes were her fault, or even true for that matter, as the news media can be cruel. But nonetheless, he wanted her to be careful, and she obviously didn't hold the same interest in carefulness as her parents.

Before she could answer, her very sloshed mother piped up, "If you're going to sleep around, don't get caught, and that means in more ways than one."

"Oh, Mother." Noel groaned. She was so disgusted with the way her mother thought about such things. But then, of course, her mom had a very real reason to think that way. As a baby would wreck a Hollywood career, she had a strict contract that would not allow for such *accidents*. But Noel shuddered at the thought that her mother would even consider an abortion just to keep a part or a show. Noel had no such plans of anything that was evidently going through her mother's mind, so she wasn't worried about it.

"You just never take anything serious, do you?" Ericka snarled back.

She was ready to fight, and Noel could tell; however, she wasn't going to tonight. They'd just had a fight Christmas Eve, and it was so bad that for her birthday she asked for a peace treaty for the day. She begged to have just one day where there were no arguments. And she was delighted that they'd granted her that wish on her birthday, which was Christmas Day.

They had given her a large amount of cash, which she was using for this trip. She also got some clothes and an expensive purse. She didn't want to appear ungrateful, but she just didn't care that much about expensive clothing. She wanted to be in style but more along the lines of everyday people's styles, like the seniors she went to school with, not the party life of Hollywood styles with their long evening gowns accented with diamonds, studs, and other flashy stuff costing hundreds of dollars. She just hated it. But she didn't want to hurt her parents' feelings for their gestures.

She rolled her eyes at her mother. "I know what I'm doing, and I'm not a kid anymore! I don't need you breathing down my neck like a dragon." She paused. "I don't intend to get into trouble. It's not like I go looking for it." She was so irritated that her parents didn't trust her more than that.

"We just want what is best for you. That's all," her dad intervened.

"Yeah right," she mumbled under her breath. She thought, *You only want what is best for you. It just is a nice day when what is best for me is the same as yours.* She was silent after that, hoping for no more questions. It seemed that their worlds were worlds apart.

Peter put his arms around his wife's waist, hoping to feel the baby.

Lilly giggled. "It's much too soon for that, Mr. Collins."

He was disappointed. "But it's not too soon for this." He kissed her neck.

Lilly turned around. "You, mister, are incorrigible." She smiled and put her arms around his neck and said, "Thank you for letting Noel come here and taking me to pick her up from the airport. It really means a lot to me." Lilly moved away from him and walked to the living room. "I can't believe she's really coming."

Lilly was nervous; Peter could tell.

Peter went and sat in his overstuffed chair and patted his leg. He wanted her to come sit in his lap for a talking to. She obeyed. Peter rubbed her back as he spoke.

"You know I love you deeply, and a big part of your heart is spilled out for others, and I delight in that for you. But please, Lil, don't forget the little ragmuffin you are carrying. Take your rest. Don't overdo it, or I will step in and help you readjust your commitments. Do I make myself clear?" Peter was very stern.

That was the part of her husband's character that she liked the least, but Lilly took the clue that her husband meant what he said. Then Lilly, needing a distraction from his sternness, said, "And what if I push your buttons?"

"Do you really want to find out?" Peter raised his eyebrows.

"No," she said as she gave her husband a hug. Then she jumped up to freshen up before leaving for the airport. She said as she readied, "It's too bad that Willy had to head back out to tour. I'm sure he would've liked to have spoken again to this Noel if he remembered her. He says the name doesn't ring a bell, but he admitted that he talks to a lot of people. So I guess it's likely he doesn't remember her at all." She brushed her hair. "But, knowing Willy, it wouldn't matter if it was the first time. When they were done, she'd know he loved the Lord."

Peter agreed, knowing his cousin and former roommate well. "Willy certainly is one of a kind." Peter put on his shoes. "I actually thought the two of you would've made a great pair." Peter surprised her by saying.

"That's not possible when I only have eyes for you."

Lilly said that she'd hold up a sign that said, "Mistletoe," and that would be her cue that it was Lilly. So she waited at the designated gate, and it wasn't long with Noel's flight on time, in which a young lady, a brunette with red highlights, slightly curled, came toward them. She had worn a red dress and heels and had fashionable nails and makeup. She wasn't sure what to wear but decided a business attire would be best since she didn't know these people. She wanted to give a good impression. Her smile was captivating. Lilly wanted to hug her right away. But Peter had warned her, knowing his wife's heart, that not all people, especially people in such need, are that open to begin with. So not wanting his wife to have her feelings hurt, he'd warned her not to expect too much at this first meeting.

Lilly stuck her hand out to shake Noel's. Lilly said with a smile of her own, "Hello, Noel. It's so nice to finally get to meet you."

Noel returned the handshake like a seasoned politician.

"Noel, this is my husband, Peter Collins." Noel was surprised to see a husband, but she greeted him with the same delightful business professionalism. One wouldn't have known she was still in high school, much less scared to death, behind the mask of professionalism she'd learned early on was a great cover up to the real person.

Peter spoke up. "Ladies, this way to retrieve luggage." He placed his hand on Lilly's back and turned her around, and the threesome went to the baggage claim area.

Peter pleasantly seated both ladies in the car, stowed the luggage and began the drive home. He looked in the mirror and could read fear in Noel's eyes, though she was looking out the window. Peter's heart went out to her. "Noel, now, do tell me you are not a Christmas child?" he asked, already knowing the answer.

"I hate to disappoint you, but yep, that's me." She looked away. "Every mother's nightmare, to have a baby born on Christmas Day!"

Peter replied with compassion, "Well, if I have anything to say about it, there's not a more special day in my book than Christmas Day. Therefore, having a baby on Christmas Day would be double the pleasure."

Noel thought that was kind of him to say.

"So you just had a birthday. How old are you?" Peter continued.

"I just turned eighteen."

"Have you heard Willy play?" Lilly asked.

Peter was watching in the rearview mirror what he saw was a huge smile and pink cheeks.

"Yes, I have. He played at our high school back in August." She paused and then said, "He's an exceptional drummer." After thinking a moment, she asked a question of her own. "And how are you and Willy related?"

Peter spoke up. "Willy, that ol' crazy Willy, is my cousin. I might add a much-loved cousin."

Noel almost laughed out loud, and Lilly thought she heard a snicker, so she said, "Yes, I know what you're thinking, Noel. These two are as different as night and day." Lilly laughed, releasing Noel to do the same. Lilly then added, "I've known Willy for almost a year and half, and during that time, they shared an apartment together. And let me tell ya, it was a hoot. The two of them kept me rollin'."

That seemed to do the trick. It was obvious to both Peter and Lilly that Willy was the sure connection for Noel. She seemed to speak about him with such fondness, and that one subject brought a smile to her lonely features.

Noel said with a quiet laugh, "I just bet you have the stories to tell."

That was how they spent the entire ride home, Peter and Lilly taking turns telling stories, giving Noel the *Willies*. It made the ride home great and built the much-needed bridge between Lilly and Noel. It put everyone at ease, almost like they were old friends.

At the apartment, Peter let both ladies in and then explained about the arrangements. They only had a two-bedroom apartment. They had one bedroom, and Willy's studio took the other one. So since it was late, Peter said, "Noel, we have just a small place here. This is the apartment that Willy and I shared before Lilly and I married in August. We have allowed Willy to leave his stuff here, so that leaves us without a bedroom for a guest, much less even a bed." Peter had put his hands in his pocket and raised his eyebrows. "What we have planned is for you to sleep here for the night due to the late hour, and then sometime tomorrow, Lilly will take you to Aunt Maureen's for you to sleep, but you'll be here during the day." He was looking at her to see what she thought.

Noel smiled. Though she didn't like the thought of going to another unfamiliar place, she shrugged her shoulders. "Oh, whatever is fine with me." She was looking around the place, wanting to hide her sea of nervousness. She could really use a drink right now to calm her nerves, but that wasn't going to happen, at least not tonight. Noel asked, "Um…where do I sleep?"

Peter and Lilly chuckled at the same time. Lilly did the honors.

"Well, we will let you have Willy's old bed." She walked over and picked up the decorative pillow on the couch. She patted a cushion. "This is it. I know it's not much, but it's all we have." She looked up to disappointed eyes. Lilly's heart sank.

"You mean…you don't mean the couch, do you?" Noel stuttered, letting her real thoughts out. She'd never been reduced to such sleeping arrangements before, except at her friend's houses or at parties, but even then, she at least had a bed, even if she had to share a room.

Lilly began to apologize for not having anything better, but Noel interrupted. "Please don't be sorry. I'm the one to apologize for my rudeness. This is just such a different world for me. I'm grateful for anything you have to offer," she ended up saying.

The only sad thing about it was that Lilly saw a shield go up, and she knew that Noel had just slid into a role of professional happiness, taking her heart with her to the safe place where no one could see it.

Lilly looked at Peter for a rescue, but Peter was without an answer, so he said, "Noel, we didn't think to ask whether you had eaten any dinner. I was going to make a sandwich. Would you like one too?"

Noel did the cutest thing. She tilted her head and put her index finger to her cheek, thinking. "Um…yes, I think I will," she said. She hadn't had anything since her bagel and fruit that morning in LAX airport.

Lilly planned a special breakfast the next morning. She tried to stay in her room, Peter too, until they thought that Noel might be up. So Lilly finally slipped out and into the kitchen and had already made the coffee and was well into bacon and French toast when Noel had climbed off the couch bed.

Lilly giggled. Noel was a sight. She might rather meet a bear than this Noel first thing in the morning.

"I know. I'm a sight, aren't I?" Noel spoke.

"Well, we all could use a little waking up," Lilly said to ease the scene while trying to ease the queasiness in her stomach as morning sickness from the pregnancy tried to overtake her.

"Well, I probably look better than I often do on the weekends and holidays," Noel said, still half asleep.

"Why is that?" Lilly asked.

"Well, I've learned that alcohol dulls the pain. So as long as I don't have to get up for school, I usually hit the bottle and drown my sorrows." She smiled a wobbly smile. "But it makes for a grumpy morning. But then, usually, there's no one there to care, so what difference does it make? Only that for a time, the pain is gone."

Lilly didn't really know what to say, but her heart broke for this girl. "Well, that is the disappointment with manmade fixes; they only fix temporarily. God has the only permanent fix."

Noel had nothing really to say. She only rolled her eyes, wondering if she was going to be able to handle hearing about religion all weekend.

Lilly sensed that but decided to remain quiet about it. "What do you normally like for breakfast, Noel?"

"Oh, really something light like fruit and a bagel or fruit and a piece of toast. Usually something quick," she said.

While Lilly continued to cook, she asked Noel questions and Noel uncorked. "Well, my parents want me to be somebody, so since I quit pursuing the acting career, they've made me something different at each party, it seems." Noel huffed. "One time I'm a businesswoman, the next a doctor, the next a veterinarian, the next getting a doctorate in archeology, and on it goes." She was disgusted with her parents. "I just can't seem to please my parents unless I become the *somebody* they want me to be."

Lilly had set the table, finished the cooking while putting the last piece of bacon on the plate, and called Peter, who had showered and dressed for the day.

"So, Noel, what do *you* want to do?"

Noel bobbed her head. "I want to be in music."

All was quiet, and Lilly and Peter looked at one another and smiled.

Noel missed the glance and said, "I love to sing. It's the blood in my veins." She was tapping her fingers. "My mother made me take piano lessons when I was five. I hated it at first, but then the music began to be a haven of escape. And for a long while, it pleased my parents tremendously to have an accomplished pianist. We have a huge baby grand in our living room dance hall. But when I began to show interest in singing, they were against it. But I snuck out anyway and took lessons on my own. I've been doing that for years now. I also learned how to play the guitar by ear."

They were all seated, the food getting cold, but no one really cared.

"Let's pray. Then we can eat and you can tell us more about the beat of your heart," Peter said.

Noel was full of energy. But she quieted down, embarrassed at the mention of prayer for the food. She knew that people did this as a religious custom but had never been around anyone who did it. But then she remembered the breakfast she had with Willy. He had bowed his head for a few moments. She wondered if he'd been praying too. She listened to Peter's prayer. It seemed weird to hear him talking to the air, but that was what he was doing. But then he included her in his prayer, thanking God for her and thanking Him that she could come and be with them for this time. She'd stopped listening and was a stunned Noel when they opened their eyes.

"Are you okay, Noel?" Lilly asked.

Noel cleared her throat. "Um…yes. Um…I'm fine. Thank you."

Both Peter and Lilly noticed her quietness as she began to eat. "That was the best French toast I've ever tasted!"

"I think so too, my love." Peter winked at Lilly, kissed her cheek, and got up to help clean the kitchen while Noel took a shower.

They were side by side, washing dishes. "Are you okay?" whispered Peter.

Lilly looked up. Peter could read her heart. She'd always carried her heart in her eyes. And right now, her eyes told Peter that she could cry a river for that girl.

"Yeah. I'm doing fine. She's just so special," Lilly whispered back.

Both knew that this wasn't the time to talk, as the object of their thoughts could walk in at any moment.

Peter decided to spend the day at the college, in his office, to give them time alone. He had classes to prepare for anyway. Lilly hadn't made any special plans; only dinner at Aunt Maureen's was on the schedule.

After Lilly had gotten ready for the day, she walked out of her bedroom only to see the back of Noel. She was standing in Willy's studio doorway, just staring. Lilly wondered what she was thinking. She joined her and said, "Go ahead. You can play. It's okay."

"Really? You mean it?" Noel stared at Lilly.

Lilly really didn't know what to do. That had never been a problem, and Willy didn't leave any instructions about his equipment, so she didn't think he would mind. "Yes. Go ahead," Lilly encouraged.

Noel began to back up. "No. I better not. It's not mine." She was having second thoughts, though she longed to touch the guitars he had in there and play the drums, though she didn't know how.

Lilly turned her around. "Really, Noel. Go ahead. I want to hear you sing something," Lilly encouraged.

Noel gave her a skeptical look.

Lilly pushed. "Really. Go ahead." She motioned her back into the room.

"Okay. What do you want to hear?" she asked incredulously.

Lilly, realizing that their taste of music were probably quite different, opted to say, "How about your favorite song?" After a pause, she asked, "You do have a favorite, don't you?"

"Yes, I suppose I do, but it's hard to choose."

Noel was smiling as she went over and picked up a guitar. She played and sang the most beautiful song. Lilly knew it, as it was an oldie. Even though that wasn't Lilly's genre of music these days, she still knew the song well. But what took her more by surprise was Noel's voice. It was the most beautiful voice she'd ever heard.

"Wow! Noel, that was beautiful! Sing another!" she urged.

So Noel sang another pop rock song. Lilly knew that one too. Lilly leaned on the doorjamb and said, "Another."

And then Noel did another song. Before long, they'd spent two hours doing just that. Though Lilly didn't encourage secular music, it was Noel's world and one Lilly needed to step into to reach Noel's heart. Besides, what did one expect from the world but to hear the world's music?

"Noel, I'm absolutely stunned by your talent," Lilly said as she put a hand on her shoulder. "You have the most beautiful voice I've ever heard."

"Yeah? Do you really think so?" Noel smiled, surprised by that compliment.

"Really, Noel. Your parents are missing out," Lilly said.

"Well, they really don't care about anything except to be sure I keep up their image of what they want me to be," she said sadly.

Lilly thought this was a good jumping-off point. The rest of the morning and into the afternoon, Noel bore her heart. She shared about her boyfriend and school problems and her family situation. Lilly mostly listened and asked questions when she wasn't clear. Lilly only had four days with Noel. One included Sunday. She hoped to get her to come to church before she was to fly back to California.

Later they went to Aunt Maureen's house for dinner. She and James had put out a feast. They welcomed Noel with open arms. Maureen soon had a very shy Noel at ease with her country charm and deep Southern accent.

The next day, Lilly shared her own story, which had a great impact on Noel. It really got her thinking. She still just could not believe that Jesus was for real and forever. But Lilly's story was a miracle even to Noel.

Lilly asked Noel if she would join them for church the next day. She was hesitant, yet she didn't want to leave Lilly's side.

She felt safe and loved there, at least the closest to love she'd ever allowed herself to be. And besides, she was watching Lilly and Peter both to see if they'd mess up and forget this God thing. Surely, she thought, they'd tire of it.

They had to bring her along on the bus route. Noel was curious, as she stepped on the bus knowing Lilly's story. Noel could picture Lilly as an abused and unwanted kid who loved riding the church bus. She could see Peter befriending her. It was obvious that riding the church bus had changed her life. Someone had evidently taken her in and poured lots of love into her. She could only imagine how horrible it must have been to be snatched from the bus people and church as her mother took her away.

Noel giggled, but it must have been a hoot for Lilly to show up in Peter's English class in another state altogether. Noel could certainly see why Lilly and Peter still worked in the Bus ministry. Noel found that she liked it. Later she sat in a pew next to Lilly, listening to the sermon. She loved the singing. Though she didn't know the songs, they still stirred her heart. It seemed weird to her that the people were singing songs to a God they couldn't see.

Then a man in a suit and tie preached from the Bible. She listened. He was talking about a new year and a new life, putting away the old and living in the new. But only in Christ could one really do that, the preacher said. He went on to explain what "in Christ" meant and that it wasn't enough to just be a good person. Noel listened intently, but not much of it was believable. Yet all those people around her were listening too. But how did she know they weren't just like everyone else she knew back home who did their own thing but went to church sometimes?

Then they were singing another song, and then Lilly grabbed Noel's arm and took her back to the bus as the kids were getting on. It wasn't until they were home and had eaten lunch that Lilly asked Noel what she thought about the morning.

"Well," she said as she tilted her head, "it was very interesting. I enjoyed the music, for sure, but then, that's easy for me to do. But what was weird about it, I must admit, is that everyone was singing to a God who wasn't even there, or at least I couldn't see who they were singing to." She paused. "I wasn't sure exactly what the man meant by being in Christ and about being a good person." Then she shuddered and made an ugly face. "And I didn't like it at all when he talked about hell. That made me really uncomfortable." Then she smiled. "But I did enjoy the bus ride and the children, all the more after hearing your story yesterday, Lilly."

"Noel, if you don't mind, I'd like to comment on your observations, if I may," Peter said kindheartedly. "Noel, the people who were singing today were singing to God, and you are right in that you cannot see Him; yet He is everywhere."

Noel gave a tilted-headed, quirky look of total confusion.

Peter went on. "God is Spirit, so you cannot *see* Him, but He is Creator and King of this universe, so you see His handprints all over the place. For instance, in creation you see Him, for He created the world, the birds, animals, the air we breathe, the flowers that make it beautiful. He even made you and me."

That alone seemed too much for Noel. "What happened to the shotgun theory?"

Peter chuckled. "Satan wants to keep you from believing in God, so he's made up all kinds of false stories and delusions to keep you from seeing the real God. It's like the wind. You can't see the wind, can you?" He waited for her to answer. "But you can see where the wind goes, you can feel it on your face, you can see it fly a kite, and so on, right?"

Noel nodded, and then she really began to understand. "I think I see what you mean." She paused. "But it still seems strange that they would love to worship someone who doesn't do anything for them in return."

"Oh, my dear Noel, God has done so much for us. That is why you need to read the Bible to find out. Then perhaps you will understand more why they worship a God who has done everything for them."

Noel asked, "Then what do heaven and hell have to do with God?"

Peter raised his eyebrows. Lilly was fervently praying for them both as he shared.

"Well, heaven is where all those who believe—truly believe in God—will go when they die. Jesus made that possible with His death on the cross. He paid your way." Peter paused to see if she was taking this all in. "And hell is where a lake of fire and damnation is, where all those who don't believe will go when they die and stay forevermore." Peter stopped with that. It was a heavy enough load for the time being.

"Well, at least I don't have to worry about that. I'm a good person. I mean, I, uh…you know, I uh…drink too much sometimes, but I'm nice to people unless they make me mad, and I don't steal or murder anyone like that."

Peter looked at Lilly. She had tears streaming down her cheeks.

"Noel, as much as I like you and think you're a sweet young lady—and I do believe you are a good person—but there are a lot of *good* people in hell." He said this with all the love he had in his heart.

Noel's eyes were huge.

"You see, it's not about whether you are a good person or not. If you want to use the term *good person*, then we have to say *good* by God's standards, not yours or mine. But it's about your need for a Savior, realizing you are a sinner and destined to hell already. You were born that way. Only those who repent from their sins, ask God to save them, who escape those flames, those same people trust in Him and live in a daily relationship with Him, allowing Him to change them into His likeness."

Noel wiggled in her seat. "You certainly have given me something to think about. Just being with the two of you and your aunt and uncle has given me much to think upon when I go home. I haven't ever been with real people much before. I mean, I'm at school, and I am so thankful I was adamant about getting away from tutoring by the time I was going into the seventh grade, or I wouldn't have had that reality either." She looked down at her polished nails, and then she looked up with silent tears running down her cheeks. "I just can't thank you both enough for letting me be a part of a real family. It means more to me than you'll ever know."

They spent the rest of the afternoon chatting, and at times, Peter read Scripture to Noel about different things she'd asked about. Lilly shared too. They went back to church that evening, and then they had the usual pizza night afterward. Noel had more questions about what she'd heard in the sermon, so over bites of pizza, Peter and Lilly tried to answer her the best they could.

On Monday morning, Peter noticed that Lilly was scooting her breakfast casserole around on her plate. Noel silently watched this interchange between husband and wife.

"Hey, ragmuffin. Not eating this morning?" Peter asked as he put his arm around her shoulders.

Lilly looked up into his sweet face. "Uh, no. Not really. I'm not into it this morning, I suppose."

"Is it really that bad?" Peter asked.

As answer to his question, Lilly jumped up, knocking her leg on the table, and ran from the room with her hand over her mouth. All heard what she had tried to eat come up in the bathroom. Noel looked at Peter. Peter was smiling and shaking his head.

Lilly soon came back. She stood at the table's edge. "If you two don't mind, I will sit on the couch until y'all are done."

Peter wiped his hands on a napkin and looked over at Noel. "I think we're both finished. It was a delicious meal, my love. Yes, you go over and lay on the couch. I'll get you a cold, wet rag and slice of lemon, and then I want you to stay there with Noel. I'll clean up."

Lilly smiled. She knew it was a command and didn't try to talk her sweet husband out of it.

When she looked over, Noel's mouth was wide open in astonishment, not believing what she'd just witnessed. "Wow!" She didn't think she could take any more surprises. This couple was different from any she'd ever met.

"Lil, it looks like you got some explaining to do," Peter said as he grinned at his wife while collecting the plates.

"Come, Noel. Sit here beside me while I rest a bit."

Noel sat down and then watched Peter bring a rag and a lemon and smiled into his wife's face. There it was again, this thing called love.

"I'm sorry about the disruption, but I'm in the first stages of pregnancy and have been pretty sick and queasy." Lilly sighed. Just talking made her want to head back to the bathroom.

Noel popped out with the first thing that came to her mind. "So is that why you two got married?" She looked back and forth at each of them, waiting for an answer.

Peter had been listening as he worked in the kitchen and wondered how Lilly would answer.

Lilly hadn't thought how it might look to an unregenerate person. *Lord, help me!* Lilly prayed before answering.

"No, Noel, it's not the reason we married," Lilly sweetly answered, "but the results of the joy of being married. You see, we did not…" Lilly was fighting hard for the right words. "We both valued saving ourselves for marriage. So this baby is just a result of God blessing our marriage." Lilly stopped and looked over at Noel. "Does any of that make sense?"

Noel let out a disgruntled sigh. "Humph! Not from my world. Number one, I wouldn't have felt the need to marry just because I got pregnant. And number two, as my mom is always telling me, too many abortions can do some real damage, so be careful." Noel said what was true from her world, but she had no idea what it was doing to the other two people in hearing distance.

Lilly really needed God to step in and give her words, for she was lost on what to say, so she just sucked on another lemon slice.

"Noel, this again is an area where, as Christians, our views would be very different than yours." Lilly spoke gently. "You see, in the Bible, it speaks of sex outside of marriage as sin, so we do what we need to in order to keep ourselves pure. We abstain from fornication, sex before marriage, and adultery. This is very important to God. He speaks seriously about it." Lilly resituated herself so she could see Noel's face better. She knew she might be overloading her, but she couldn't let it go. "And for the Christian, babies are a blessing, not a curse or an inconvenience. As a matter of fact, in our world, abortion is considered murder, and God hates that."

Noel chuckled and rolled her eyes. "That would blow my mom and dad out of the water."

Lilly's heart just squeezed at the thought of what the girl had grown up with.

"I haven't had to consider abortion, but at least in my thoughts, I don't think I could do it." She wiggled in her chair. "I'm not sure why, but it just makes me sick to hear my mother talk so flippantly to me about my not getting caught and that nothing can get in the way of her career, much less an unwanted baby. But what irks me is that she thinks that I'm the same way, and I'm not." Noel ended by saying, "I mean, I don't know about the murder thing, but I just can't seem to get past not giving the kid a chance in this world. I mean, who am I to take that choice away from it?" Noel had thought this through many times, and that had always been where she landed her own values about abortion.

"We are both so excited about this baby." Lilly grinned. "It might be uncomfortable being sick, but we're so delighted to be blessed by God this way."

Peter had made his way over with his Bible. "Noel, I just wanted to share some scriptures real quick so you know we aren't just making this up." He simply read the verses, got up, and left the two of them alone.

"So you believe all that?" Noel popped up.

"Yes, I do! Every word!" Lilly said with zeal.

"I have a lot to learn. I just don't think I could read that whole book and remember to do everything." Noel got up and moved around the room.

"That's the beauty of being His child." She pointed up. "He gives us the desire to learn about Him and the strength and the power to obey His commands."

Noel came abruptly and sat down and gushed out, "What if you don't want to do what it says?"

"Well, as a believer, that is called sin." Lilly smiled. "It simply isn't an option when the Holy Spirit, which is the form of God that lives inside of me and every believer, teaches us or convicts us about something in Scripture, which is the Bible. We are to obey it; otherwise, it is sin."

"So what's the big deal if you sin?"

"Noel, I love God with all my heart, and when I sin, it makes our relationship rough," Lilly simply said. "It breaks the sweet fellowship with Him that I desire above anything in this world." Lilly licked her lips. "Because of my love for God, I do all I can to please Him, and that wouldn't include any kind of sin. But I don't want you to think I don't sin, for everyone sins. But I don't want to, and it breaks my heart when I do. That's the difference. Has any of this made any sense?"

"I'd be lying to say I'm not on overload." Noel laughed. "It's a lot to grasp. I mean, this whole visit knocks my socks off." Noel looked at Lilly. "Don't get me wrong. I've loved every minute of it. It's just a lot to think about, and I wonder if I'll even be able to remember all this when I get back home." She seemed downcast at the very thought. "I dread going back home. I mean, here, I'm so safe and loved."

"You know what I think?" Lilly reached over and took her hand.

"No. What?"

"I think God is already working on your behalf by having you meet Willy and by you picking up the phone and calling me and by bringing you here. So perhaps you can hold onto that thought when you go back home if things get rough," Lilly said with hope in her eyes.

It was obvious that Noel hadn't thought of that.

"I'll be praying for you. I've seen God already answer prayers on your behalf." Lilly squeezed her hand.

CHAPTER 8

It was well into February and cold outside, but that didn't dampen Willy's spirits any at all. He loved the tour every bit. He'd grown closer each day to the guys. When he called Lilly, he was thrilled that more people had called. She told Willy that the girl Noel had actually come for a visit and that she felt as if God was really working on her. She stated that it had been a most interesting and challenging visit all in one. Willy was ecstatic to hear it. That God would even think to use Willy as a vessel for His purpose was overwhelming to him. He wanted to be about seeking the kingdom of God first in his life, and God was blessing his effort.

He was now in the payphone booth, calling Lilly to retrieve messages once again.

"Hello," came her soft voice.

He recognized it, but today it sounded sad.

"Lil, what's the matter?" Willy was concerned, his heart jumping in his chest.

Lilly couldn't even answer. She burst into tears.

"Hey hey, sweetie, shh. Tell me. What's the matter with my ragmuffin?"

Those words brought more harsh sobs. Willy was worried.

Between harsh cries and gasps of air, Willy heard, "We lost the baby."

Willy's heart broke. He didn't know what to say or how to comfort her. She was sniffling and blowing her nose.

"When?" Willy quietly asked.

Lilly went on to share about the details of the painful miscarriage, the helplessness of watching it happen, the D&C, the overnight hospital stay, the emptiness that remained, and the struggle that she was somehow defective, and the disappointment she felt she caused for Peter, which started Lilly's tears afresh. Willy had gathered that this had happened less than two weeks ago. Obviously, it had happened since the last time he'd called.

Willy prayed out loud as Lilly cried into the opposite receiver. It took some time, but Lilly eventually ran out of tears for a time and was actually able to give Willy his messages. She even asked how the tour was going. Out of respect for Lilly, Willy cut the conversation short, expressed his sorrow and his love for them, and said he'd be praying and hung up.

By the weekend, it had snowed so beautifully in Knoxville that they took a break to enjoy it. Willy was thinking, *Boy, a big bowl of snow ice cream would be perfect.* He was licking his lips when Chet bumped into him.

"Hey, wanna fight?"

"You bet!" Willy jumped up to get ready, Jordie right behind him. The three *rascalteers* jumped off the bus and could be seen making snowballs and throwing them, making a big snowman, and playing fort like a bunch of little boys. Cookie had gone to his bunk to write his wife and kids. Rusty had gone to town to get the cream, sugar, and vanilla because Willy had told him he needed to make the specialty snow ice cream.

Jonas was at the wheel, which gave him optimum view of the three rascalteers. He had given the three guys the nickname from a combination of *Little Rascals* and *The Three Musketeers*. It fit so perfectly the rambunctious mischievous threesome.

Sky Blue stood and leaned on the edge of the seat looking at Kenzie. "You want to go out and play with them? You can." His voice was sweet. His eyes held understanding.

"No, not really. Maybe if I was at home, where it would be easier to deal with the soon-to-be wet clothes and a fireplace to warm up at." She smiled at the thought and looked up at Sky Blue.

He came over and sat next to her, very closely she noticed, their arms touching, and watched the guys out the window and laughed at the entertainment. Sky Blue was very comfortable and enjoying the closeness to Kenzie and the smell of her hair. He also noticed that he loved her laughter. Kenzie had much the same thoughts about the man next to her. She'd not seen him this way very often and not ever like he was actually spending time with her that might possibly mean more than friendship.

The Prairie Praise Tour at the Grasslands had ended, and Willy had gone home for the month of March. He spent a lot of time with Peter and Lilly as they continued to struggle with the loss of their baby. Willy thought that, though still fresh and painful, God was healing them. And even through tears, he knew they were following hard after God. He also spent time practicing for the coming up last leg of the tour that he'd not been on yet. And, of course, he filled in his parents and sisters on all that had gone on. It seemed like the more he was away, the more his love and appreciation deepened for his family.

⨯

They were in New York City, and Willy thought he'd already seen it all on the West Coast. But boy was he in for a surprise. Man, the city was jammed full of people. Jonas, being good at what he did, meandered the bus through the big-city traffic right to the back door of the coliseum stage, so they unloaded and prepared for the concert to come in just a few hours.

⨯

"That's a wrap, guys," Willy said.

It was the end of the concert. He stood up and began to disassemble everything and carry it out to load the bus. That was the routine. He'd just burst through the back stage door with a heavy load only to be met by a flying yellow yoyo. He followed the yoyo back to its owner, which had him face-to-face with the eyes of Christy Henson.

Willy's smile stretched off his face.

She said with a mischievous grin, "YoYo Willy, bringing you up when you're down!" She said all this as a greeting. "Just wanted to make sure you didn't trip over me again."

Willy was speechless. He moved out of the way for Rusty, who was coming out with more equipment. "What are you doing here?"

"I came to hear Mercy Seat Rockers' coolest drummer," she said, smiling at him. "And, I might add, that was an awesome concert, mister."

"How did you know to find me?"

She slyly turned her head, and pointed to the bus.

"Kinda gives it away." She laughed at Willy's expression. "Plus, I know a backstage door when I see one. Been there, done that."

"Well, it's sure a nice surprise. But you didn't come all the way from the West Coast to hear me chop some sticks." Willy smiled.

"Oh, well, actually, I came to see a cousin who lives here when I saw the marquee." She pointed to the big flashing sign that had their concert information on it. "So I just had to come and hear you again."

"That's really cool," Willy said. He knew he needed to be helping. It wasn't fair for him not to pull his weight. "I need to help load. Can we meet tomorrow?"

"For sure," she immediately said.

"Well, I have the morning and into the early afternoon free." Willy quickly said, "I've always wanted to see the *Abbey Roads* of New York, so to speak. Would you like to join me?"

She agreed, so they made a neutral meeting place then she left and Willy went to finish loading with a spring in his step.

Willy arrived ten minutes early the next morning, in bad need of a cup of coffee but was excited about the day. They'd chosen to meet at a café, and Willy was extremely thankful for the mocha sitting in his hands as he waited for Christy to arrive. She came walking down the sidewalk not too much past the meeting time.

Willy smiled at the sight of her. She was in jeans, a white sweater pullover, and her black coat. It was cold outside, but they didn't seem to care.

"Good morning, Mr. YoYo," Christy teased. Then she got up close to his face. "Hey, are you awake in there?" She was full of energy and smiles.

Willy's eyebrows went up, though he was chuckling. "Yeah. Man, am I wiped." He took a large gulp of coffee. "Can I get you a mocha or something?"

She tilted her head in the most adorable way. "That would be great. A white chocolate, double-shot espresso mocha, please," she said as she sat down. Then she turned. "Oh, and have them put caramel and chocolate on top of the whip cream, if you don't mind."

"Coming right up," Willy said as he gave her a smile and went up to the counter.

He came back with just what she wanted. She took off the lid and ate all the whipped cream, caramel, and chocolate syrup.

"I have a car just down the way. How about I give you the tour of the town, sir?" She stood with her arm open. "I'll take you wherever you wish." Then she made a small bow and curtsy.

Willy hopped up, ready to leave. "Okay. But how in the world do you know your way around this crazy place?"

She gave a quick smile and led the way. Off they went walking in downtown New York City, along with throngs of other people. It was loud with cars honking, music blaring, and people walking and talking.

"This place is nuts," Willy commented.

"You haven't seen anything yet, drummer boy!" She laughed over her shoulder.

It was all Willy could do to keep up. She then got into a BMW and unlocked Willy's door and he hoped in.

Willy let out a whistle. "We're not in a stolen car, are we?" Willy was checking it out. It was a fine piece of machinery. His eyes matched his smile, both huge.

Christy laughed as she pulled out into traffic. "Why, yes, we are, Willy. It's how I make a living." She was sucking in her cheeks to keep from busting out laughing. She tapped the steering wheel.

"And you can see I'm quite good at what I do." Then she turned to look at him. "You won't tell anybody, will ya?"

If she thought Willy's eyes were huge, they were about to pop out of his head. And for that matter, she thought he might just open the door and jump out. Christy, sizing up his thoughts said, "I wouldn't if I were you. This isn't the best part of town, and you'll get run over. And maybe by eleven tonight, the traffic will be slow enough to get your mangled body off the street."

Willy took some deep breaths. *Okay, Willy. Think hard...* Willy was saying to himself, trying to calm down.

Finally, Christy had mercy on him. She busted out laughing. "*Gotcha,* didn't I?"

Willy didn't know what to think of this mystery woman.

"Yeah, I'd say you took the string out of my yoyo!" He wagged his finger at her. "You, missy, are gonna get it. You were about to make me jump," Willy teased.

They both laughed together.

"No, really. Where do you want to go?" Christy asked.

"No, really. Where did you get this car?" Willy asked.

Christy thought he wasn't going to enjoy the ride until he was told about the car. "It's my cousin's car. He let me borrow it," Christy said as she maneuvered through town.

"Wow!" Willy whistled again. "What does he do for a living?" Willy asked in disbelief.

"He's a studio owner."

"What? You got to be kidding me!" Willy let out a, "Yahoo!" yelled, and hit the dash. "Well, that beats all!"

"No, I believe you beat all. Remember? You're the drummer boy," she said, laughing.

Willy finally put the pieces together a bit. "So that's why you know your way around this crazy place. Am I right?"

"That about sums it up. I've been coming here every summer and pretty much every school break since I was thirteen. I love it here, at least down where the studios are."

Willy was thinking about the last time he saw her. She had a nagging boyfriend. "Does Kevin miss you while you are gone?" Willy asked, changing the subject.

She put her hands up, and then slapped them on the steering wheel. "I don't know what he does. I don't really care," she said. She was quiet for a moment. "Well, that's not exactly true. I guess I do care, but things are just such a mess." She paused, not really sure what all she wanted to tell Willy. She had intended to keep things low-key about herself and just give Willy a thank-you tour. She knew he'd love the fact that she could get him in any studio he wanted. Christy, glad for the distraction, said, "Here we are," as she pulled up to the curb. "New York's *Abbey Roads*, here we come," she challenged. She turned off the ignition. "I figured you didn't know your way around, so I thought I'd take you to the best studios in town."

Willy was so wowed that he didn't know what to say. Christy thought Willy looked like a kid in a candy store window, drooling to get just a taste of anything in the store. Willy looked all around, his mouth open, walking backward, trying to see to the top of the sky rises. He bumped into a few people, only to apologize and do it again.

After he turned around three times in amazement, Christy had pity on him. "This way," she said as she led the way to a door. Christy had it half open when Willy came to his senses and grabbed it from her.

"Here. Let me get that." Willy had finally come back to earth only to be wowed again on the inside.

Christy got Willy into the studios and into the back places the public wasn't allowed. How she did that was a mystery to

Willy. Like a roller-coaster ride, it just kept coming and coming. Christy introduced Willy to producers, owners, everyone she knew. It was all done very professionally, which really had Willy's head spinning.

That happened all morning long. They went from one to another. Christy thought she was going to have to use a napkin to wipe the drool from his chin. She just laughed. She was enjoying doing for someone else. And she loved the studios as much as he did, so it was easy. She even went to her cousin's studio, introduced Willy, and toured him all around. It was the most fabulous day ever since starting the tour, Willy thought.

At one o'clock, Christy said, "I know of a cozy Greek sandwich shop. Are you hungry?"

Willy put his hand on his stomach, like it was going to answer him.

"Come to think of it, I'm famished." He didn't know about the Greek thing, but he could eat a cow at the moment.

Christy drove them over, parked, and went to the door with Willy trying to keep up. He did manage to get the door this time. They were seated at a table for two. Christy looked over her menu and then made some suggestions to Willy, who was looking all around and hadn't even ventured to pick up his menu.

"I'll have a mango paradise iced tea," Christy told the waitress. She looked over at Willy. "They are very good if you like tea."

"Make that two," Willy said.

The waitress left to get the drinks.

Willy looked at the menu. "I better get with it, or you might just leave me here, and I don't know where in the world I am."

"I doubt that." Christy laughed and then made the food suggestions again, seeing that he was about to drown in the unfamiliar choices.

Willy folded up the menu. "Yeah, that sounds good. That's what I'll have." Tapping his thumbs on the table, he said, "So, Christy, I just can't believe you are, like, this New York City licensed tour guide." He took a sip of the tea. "Wow! That is delightful. So why do I get the feeling there's a whole lot more to you than I'm seeing?"

Willy leaned forward, clearly expecting a complete explanation. He was about to be disappointed. Christy only smiled as she took a sip of her ice-cold mango tea, her eyes shining at Willy.

"So, tell me how you got on tour with this singing group of yours." Christy didn't want to talk about herself, and she was curious about that and much more.

She spent the rest of the time in the restaurant listening to Willy's crazy way he got on with the group. It was a delight for Christy to be out of her world of problems for a change.

"Willy, it's two thirty. I think you said you needed to get back to the bus by three. We better hit the road."

Willy looked at his watch and let out a low whistle. "Time flies when you're having fun."

Christy was delighted to hear that comment. She reached over to grab the bill.

"I'll take that." Willy reached over and took it from her.

"If I recall, you paid for the last time we ate together," Christy protested. Then she spoke softly. "I wanted to do this to say thank you for caring enough to take me to safety and paying for my breakfast while I cried and talked your ears off."

"No. It's my turn to say thank you. This was a spectacular day. And you are not going to pay for lunch. You've already spent most of your day driving me around, taking me to studios, and introducing me to all kinds of people." Willy paused. "It is definitely I who want to thank you." Willy looked at her most sincerely.

Christy grabbed her purse and got up. It was getting way too personal.

Willy was laughing on the way out to the car. "And who would've thought I'd ever see you again?"

Willy chuckled as he lay in his bunk that night. He shook his head. He could hardly believe that he had spent the day with the same girl he had picked up in the alley, drunk as a skunk. If he hadn't known it, he would've never guessed they were one in the same person.

CHAPTER 9

Lilly held Noel in a tight embrace. Then pulled back and looked at her. Noel had come for a short visit after leaving New York. Then, all of a sudden, Noel popped up with a gift. It was in the shape of a jar, so she knew it was a jar of something. "For the baby," she said with a huge smile. It was wrapped in cute tissue paper with a matching ribbon.

Peter was watching the scene and his heart broke for his wife. He wondered if either one of them would ever be the same. The loss of the pregnancy was still on their minds and hearts, and often, he'd found Lilly crying.

Lilly hated to dash Noel's kindhearted gesture, but she needed to break the news to Noel. She hadn't mentioned the miscarriage in their phone calls. Lilly said, "Thank you, Noel. That was so thoughtful of you." Lilly actually sat down and carefully unwrapped the gift right there in the airport. She wanted to show her delight at being thought of, and it was neat to see Noel thinking of others. Lilly laughed. "It's a jar of pickles!" Lilly turned the jar around, it was from the store, but still, the thought meant so much to her.

Then Noel watched as the bright, cheerful Lilly crumbled. Her face went all red and scrunched up, and then she began to cry.

Noel didn't know what to do. Peter stepped in and put his arms around his wife. Noel finally sat down in a chair next to the couple.

Peter spoke over his wife's head. "Noel, there was no way of your knowing this, and this gift is so special to us. That you thought to bring us a gift will ever be in our hearts. But Lilly miscarried about seven weeks ago." Peter paused so she could take it all in. "It still upsets us, and Lilly still cries, especially at situations like this. We wanted that baby so much."

Noel was without words. She was so taken back by their deep sorrow over what her mother and other women from her world would be rejoicing over. Noel finally put her hand on Lilly's shoulder and said, "I'm sorry."

Those simple words meant so much to Lilly. She finally cleared her face. "I'm sorry I broke down like that, and right here in the airport, of all places. Not to mention what a dreadful greeting that was." Lilly took the jar of pickles and looked at it again. "Thank you so much, Noel. Baby or no baby, I'll devour these." Then she paused. "Welcome."

"It's good to be here." Noel smiled.

―✕―

Noel had settled in, and Lilly, knowing it was Good Friday, told her, "Noel, Peter and I are planning to go see a play of sorts this evening and wanted to invite you along."

"Oh sure. I'd be happy to join you." They'd had a good time catching up. Noel told them about the church she was going to. She'd gone to the one they had suggested. She was glad it was so huge because she could just slip in. She mentioned she'd signed up to go to some classes. She said, "I think they are called Sunday school classes, and they have a youth group, and I have actually done a few things with them. I was thinking of going to a Friday night Bible study, but Kevin is furious with me about Sundays, so I don't know if it is worth another fight. But then, on the other hand, maybe it would keep me out of trouble." She had said all this as though she were talking to herself.

Right after dinner, they got in the car and went to church. When they got out, Noel said, clearly confused, "I didn't know they did plays at church."

"Yes, sometimes they do. This is a very special play. It will explain a lot about what we've been sharing with you," Lilly said.

"Well, that's good. I need all the help I can get."

They went in and took a seat in the third row from the front.

During the beating of Jesus, Noel moved to the edge of her seat, her eyes moving back and forth. She was clearly disturbed. She was moving her lips and quietly saying, "Stop it! Stop it!" Then, when they hung him on the cross, she put her hand over her chest and began to sob. "Make them stop it!"

Lilly let the Spirit move in Noel. She simply took Noel's hand and held it. She cried through Jesus's burial. Then she thought the play was over but was surprised to see no one rising to leave, all eyes still on the stage. So she glued her eyes there too. And to her amazement, she saw the man Jesus come back alive from the grave. She said out loud, "He's alive, Lilly! He's alive!" She was shaking Lilly and crying, totally captivated and moved by the moment, not caring who heard her.

Lilly wasn't embarrassed that she was talking out loud. Noel didn't even notice. And if the excitement that was moving Noel made her talk out loud, then bring it on, Lilly thought. Lilly just prayed.

They were a quiet threesome who left the church building that night. Noel didn't speak to anyone but headed straight for the car, Peter and Lilly not far behind.

When they got into the apartment, both Peter and Lilly sat on the couch, and Noel sat on the floor. She leaned over and spoke.

"Could you explain all that to me? I'm, like, totally *lost*."

Lilly and Peter looked at each other, knowing that her words meant more than she knew.

"Sure, Noel. We'd be happy to," Peter said with a smile.

Peter got out his Bible and turned to the book of John. He read of Jesus's last supper with his disciples, about Judas, and about the arrest and the trial. He explained what was going on at each section as plainly as he could.

Noel held a face of horror. "But why? Why would Jesus allow the people to kill him if he was innocent?" Noel was shaking her head in confusion. "I mean, from all I could see in the play tonight, He was a really cool guy and everything, you know, like a nice guy," she ended, waiting for an answer.

"Well, it actually all goes back to the Old Testament and before time began. But that's a lot to read and comprehend in the short time you are with us, so I'll try to explain a short nutshell version."

Noel nodded her head for him to do so.

"In the beginning, God created everything. God created man as an immortal being with one condition that mankind would abstain from eating from a certain tree. Adam and Eve, who were the first humans God created, disobeyed God and caused sin and death to enter the world," Peter began.

"Wow! That's scary! I didn't know that!" Noel interrupted, her eyes wide open. "Then what happened?"

"God demanded death as the payment for sin, and the whole world died spiritually and began to experience physical death. God then made a covenant with His people Israel, which demanded complete, perfect conformity to its system and instituted an animal sacrifice when broken. However, the animal sacrifice was imperfect because in Hebrews 10, the Bible states, 'The law is only a shadow of the good things that are coming, not the realities themselves.' For this reason, it can never, by the same sacrifices repeated endlessly year after year, make perfect those who draw near to worship. If it could, would they not have stopped being offered? For the worshipers would have been cleansed once for all and would no longer have felt guilty for their sins."

Peter went on to explain the scripture he had just read. "For this reason, a perfect voluntary sacrifice had to be found. However, the problem was that the world was corrupt; under God's judgment; and there was no man or beast that was uncorrupted, sinless. So God sent His Son born of a virgin to be God incarnate, to live a perfect life and then voluntarily take all the sins of the world upon him in a voluntary death, death on the cross. That, Noel, is what you saw." Peter ended quietly. "You saw Jesus making payment for my sin and yours on the cross through his shed blood and death so that, believing in Him, we may have eternal life with Christ Jesus."

"But then it looked like Jesus had come back to life." She motioned with her hands. "What was that all about? Are we gonna come back to life too?"

Peter chuckled. "Yes. Because of sin, all of us die. However, we are all eternal beings, meaning that we live forever. The question is, where will we live forever, heaven or hell?"

"You've got to be kidding. There's no such thing as hell, is there?" Noel scoffed.

"That, my dear Noel, was the whole reason for the need of redemption, so that we could be snatched from hell. His resurrection and ascension is the proof of this." Peter was serious yet loving.

Noel was slow in saying this, her face as serious as they'd ever seen it. "So that means I'm going to hell because I don't believe in this Jesus?"

Peter hated to do this. This was the hardest thing, yet he believed it to be the most loving thing people could ever be told. Peter said softly, while nodding his head, "Yes, Noel."

Noel slouched, defeated. "Is there no hope?" she asked quietly.

Lilly spoke up, grabbing her hand, "Oh yes, there's hope. Believe in the Lord Jesus and you shall be saved." Lilly quoted a verse. "Noel, cry out to God to save you, repent of your sins, and ask God to be Lord of your life."

"Thanks for explaining it all to me. It's all much clearer now. I have a lot to think about. Sorry I kept you both up so late. I'm sure that wasn't easy to tell me." Noel got up saying good night.

Both Peter and Lilly rose so she could go to bed on the couch. Due to the late hour, they didn't bother to take her back over to Aunt Maureen's.

"If you have any more questions, please don't hesitate to ask us, even if you need to wake us up. Okay?" Lilly said.

Noel nodded.

><

Lord God. Man, this is weird. I am actually talking to the air. But, God, Lilly says You are real. And Peter and Lilly believe in You. They act like You are their Father, and I believe them. I just don't know how to do this praying thing. But I want what they have. I'm so sorry for the bad things I've done. And now I know that it separates me from You. Wow! This is just too much for me. Lord, save me from hell. I do not want to go there. I want to be with You. Change me, I cry to You. Make me Your daughter." Noel started crying harshly, *Lord, I have done so many bad things. Can You ever want me? I'm not good like Lilly and Peter. Can You love me? I'm Yours...*" and Noel fell asleep a daughter of the King.

Peter wiped the tears that fell on his chest from his dear wife. Both had heard the cries of Noel's heart asking God to save her.

There was a knock on their door early the next morning.

"Come in," Peter said.

Both he and Lilly were in their robes, sitting up against the headboard, reading their Bibles.

Noel opened the door, her hair a complete mess, and said, "I was just wondering if I could borrow a Bible and if you could tell me where I can find the family rules. I asked God if I could be His daughter last night." She broke into tears. "And I want to do everything right for my Jesus." Her head was down, and she whispered, "My Jesus," again like it was the most precious words she'd ever heard, and that was, indeed, the way she felt.

Lilly knew this but jumped up and ran to Noel put her arms around her. "Oh, Noel, that's the most important thing that can ever happen. I'm overjoyed with you." Lilly had to wipe away a stream of tears too. "And by the way, it's not about rules so much as finding out what pleases God, your heavenly Father, and doing it."

"How come I get the feeling this love thing is going to crush me?" Noel rolled her eyes.

Peter got up and hugged her too. He gave her his Bible. He said, "You might try the book of Ephesians. It's a good place to start. Also, Lilly would tell you to read the Gospels, and I agree with her. Any of the four will give you a glimpse of the life and love of Jesus. And to get a good start on how magnificent our God is, start at the beginning. I usually like to read in both the Old and the New Testament at the same time to keep focused on today with the encouragement and examples of yesterday."

Lilly took the Bible from Noel, and they went to the living room. Lilly gave Noel a quick rundown on where to find all the places Peter had just mentioned. She showed her how to find both the Old and New Testaments and how to use her table of contents. Also, she highlighted the four Gospels. Then she handed her the *words of love* back to Noel and said, "Feast on His Word and you'll never go hungry!" She squeezed her arm and went back to her room to get ready for the day.

For Noel, the day sped by. She spent most of it on the living room floor, engrossed in the Bible. She would ask questions when she didn't understand something, so Lilly and Peter hung around. Being with a new redeemed heart was refreshing. That evening, they made it over to Aunt Maureen's place for dinner.

Sunday morning, at the end of a dynamic Easter service, when the invitation was given, they watched Noel leave her place and go up to the pastor, as did several others, and some to pray. After a time, he closed the invitation and began to share. He called Noel Franklin forward. He gave the microphone over to Noel to speak.

Her knees were shaking, and her voice was gravelly. "I just want to say, more like shout, that I'm a daughter of the King. I've asked God to snatch me from the pit of hell, and He has done that. And if He can do that for me, He can do that for you. He is now Lord God of my life. My every breath I give to Him." She then turned to the pastor and said—and all heard her since the mic was still on—"I would like to be baptized now."

The pastor's eyes got big. He was doing some quick thinking. *We usually don't do it this way.* But he said, "Uh…uh…you mean now, as in *right now?*"

The congregation watched this entire episode with great interest.

"Yes, that's what I read yesterday, 'Believe and be baptized.'" Noel nodded her head. "Is there a problem?" She waited a moment. "Don't you got no water?"

Lilly was covering her mouth, holding in the laughter and tears. It was quite out of the box. Not only that, but Noel was dressed in her red dress, high heels, black coat, with heavy makeup, which she had already cried through. She looked a mess, and some would say she looked ready for street work.

Noel's innocent eyes were the pastor's undoing. "Uh, yes. Let's do it."

He called Erma to come help Noel to the baptistery, and then he followed behind. The pastor was so excited see her zeal that it gave him joy to step out of the box. The band played some songs while waiting for the baptism to be ready. Then, up in the baptistery, the pastor appeared, and then Noel.

He asked, "Noel, do you proclaim Jesus as your LORD?"

"You bet! Now let's get wet!" Noel didn't hear the laughter at such an interesting confession, for she was immersed under the water. She came up and, turned, facing the audience, and put both hands up and sang in the most beautiful voice, the chorus, *I love You* LORD, with tears streaming down her face, her eyes closed as she worshiped her God of less than forty hours. She had learned that chorus at the church she'd been attending, but she didn't understand its meaning until that moment.

When she finished, she looked up to the ceiling and said, "I love You, Jesus. Thank You for dying for me." Then she walked out of the baptistery into a completely new way of life.

There was much hugging and tears at the airport the next morning.

Lilly pulled back and removed a stray hair from Noel's face. "Remember, I'm praying for you." She laughed. "And probably more than just me."

They'd already gone over what she might spend her time reading in the next few months. So with one last hug, Noel boarded the plane back to Los Angeles, to the land of make-believe, but this time with the God of reality in her heart.

CHAPTER 10

Noel was living a nightmare. Anything but fun was what she was having. This Christian thing was a lot tougher than she ever dreamed. Yet when she laid her head on her pillow at night, even if it was soaked with tears, she cried out to God, *her* God, to help her be the daughter He wanted her to be. It seemed the closer she got to being the daughter that God wanted her to be, the farther away she got from the daughter her parents wanted her to be.

She'd gone home from the Easter weekend with such joy. She immediately told her parents of her decision to follow Jesus Christ and be one of His disciples and that she was a Christian now. Then she even went on to share what she'd learned concerning Jesus, God, heaven and hell, for she was sure her parents were *not* Christians. And this really burdened her heart now that she understood so much more about life and death.

But her parents would hear none of it once they saw where she was headed; and had made, in their opinion, a stupid decision. They accused her and her friends, Peter and Lilly, as no good. Thus began a wedge that just kept getting bigger and bigger. Noel didn't push her religion on her parents. She tried not to talk about it unless she had to. But she began to go to church more and more. She hummed the tunes she learned from church around the house without thinking. But what bothered her parents the most was her kindness.

They still argued, especially over the areas of career and lifestyle choices. On more than one occasion, she and her mother went to bat over the fact that Noel didn't like to wear revealing clothing so much anymore. Not that she was telling her mom not too, but just her convictions alone seemed to condemn her parents. But Noel had read in the Bible that she was to honor her mother and father, so she tried. It was a reversal from what most teenagers and parents argued over. Noel wanted to be more conservative against her parents' wild lifestyle requests. She was encouraged, though, as she saw God work in her mightily, but she still failed at times.

Added to her problems with her parents, Kevin was still pursuing her, and he didn't understand this new Christy. Not only did she still not give in to him to go all the way, but now she didn't allow much more than simple hand-holding and light kissing. When he persisted past a certain point, then conflict would arise, and it usually ended with Christy leaving. Kevin was definitely not happy about how much time she spent going to church. She was even spending a lot of their party weekends doing something at church or with people from the church, and that really got under Kevin's skin, and they often fought about it. Kevin didn't want anything to do with church.

She had kept in contact with Lilly at least every two weeks, sometimes every week if she was having a hard time. She didn't want to drown her sorrows in alcohol, but in Jesus. So she often called Lilly to get the support she needed.

Finally, the last week of school, just before she graduated, she told Kevin it was over.

"Hey, Kevin." She switched her feet back and forth. She was so tired of his nagging her. She was confused in what she wanted in her life, and she told him, "I'm the kind of girl who laughs at my mistakes, so pardon me if I laugh in your face." She then turned and walked off. She turned not a few steps away. "It's over, Kevin. Just get it through your head. We just weren't meant to be together."

Kevin hung his head, spit on the ground, turned in anger, and left sputtering words Christy didn't want to repeat.

Surprisingly, Noel's parents attended their daughter's graduation, though they wore sunglasses to disguise themselves and couldn't believe that they had to actually sit outside on bleachers for the ceremony. They didn't know that not only did Noel graduate, but she graduated with honors. But what really knocked them off their feet was before the ceremony began.

The principal announced, "All rise for the national anthem." Then he turned to face the big flag that had been raised for the occasion, and then the most magnificent voice sang the beloved song. It actually had tears streaming down Ericka's face, and Burt had a lump in his throat. Neither had heard such a strong, clear, lovely, yet passionate voice singing the national anthem before. When it was over, the principal said, "Thank you to our very own senior, Christy Henson." Noel waved a flag as the crowd roared in applause, and then she went off the field to get into her cap and gown. Her parents couldn't see their daughter from where they were seated. Because they had refused to hear her sing all these years, they were stunned by the announcement of the soloist.

There was a gasp from Ericka as she grabbed Burt's arm, "Was that our daughter?" she whispered.

"I think so," Burt replied sadly. He then wondered just what they had missed.

⤬

Noel was in a pay booth and had slid down the wall not two weeks after graduation, waiting for Lilly to pick up the phone. Lilly finally picked up.

"Hello. Hands to Hearts and Feet to Friends. How can I cheer you today?"

"Hey, Lilly. It's me, Noel," she said, and then began to cry and tell Lilly all that had happened. She shared about her parents' lack of enthusiasm for her graduation, the big fight with her mom and dad, the break-up with Kevin, the continuous disunion, and the rejection from her friends for being a Christian. It was all too much for her. She paused a minute. "I was wondering if I could come and spend the summer with you and Peter. I'm not sure what I want to do or where I want to live, but I thought this was a good time to come and learn under your tender love and care. I just need some TLC for a bit." Noel was afraid of rejection, but things had gotten so bad that she had to take the chance, for she was desperate and about to go crazy.

"Hey hey there. Shh. Shh. Remember, God is in control," Lilly said. "I'll talk to Peter and Aunt Maureen, and you can call me back in two days for an answer. I don't see a reason to say no, but I need to ask Peter first and see if James and Maureen can put you up. You understand? But my heart goes out to you, sweet Noel."

They talked a bit more, and Lilly prayed with her, and then they hung up the phone.

CHAPTER 11

Peter and Aunt Maureen had agreed to let Noel come for the summer. She stayed over at Aunt Maureen's a few days and then at Lilly's a few days. She'd even thought about getting a summer job to help out. She was at Lilly's when Peter called saying that he had a flat tire and needed Lilly to come with her car to help him.

So Noel told Lilly that she'd be fine at the apartment alone while she went to help Peter. Lilly knew she'd been eyeing Willy's studio since she'd arrived, itching, Lilly was sure, to get in there and play, so Lilly knew she'd be fine for a while without her.

Lilly was exactly correct in her assessment. As soon as she left, Noel hit it. She wasted no time in getting in the room with all the fun stuff in it! She was well into a song on the drums, not that she knew how to really play them, but was doing her best to make some awful racket. She'd even put on the headphones so she wouldn't hurt her hearing. She was so into it, singing and playing some of her favorite hits, that she didn't notice when someone unexpected walked in.

※

Willy had finished the tour, it was his month off, and he'd gone to the apartment for something, used his key, walked in, tossed his keys on the table, and went directly to the sound of the racket coming from his studio room. That was one thing he did not like, someone playing his instruments. He marched in, his anger flared immediately. *Where in the world are Lilly and Peter, and who is this burglar who can't play worth a hoot?* He stopped short at his studio door. There was a female banging on his drums.

The girl had dark, black, straight hair, only it had jagged edges all around, including the sections framing her face. She caught his movement and his anger and stopped playing. Immediately jerking off the headphones, she jumped up off the seat, knocking over the stool she'd been sitting in. She backed up to the wall behind her, almost tripping over one of his electric guitars as she slid sideways down the wall. Her hands behind her, tracing the wall, while she mumbled, "I'm sorry! I'm so sorry!" She was about to burst into tears. As soon as she got close, she bolted through the doorway in which Willy was standing.

Then he turned to look at her in the living room, wondering what in the world was going on in his cousin's apartment. He scrunched up his face and asked, "Christy?"

Right at that moment, Lilly walked in. "Noel!" She noticed something was wrong. Just as she was about to ask her, she spotted Willy. But the angry, stunned, strange look that was on his face stopped her in her tracks. She looked from one to another and then back again.

But before Lilly could say anything, Willy piped up, looking at the mystery burglar, and slowly asked, "You're Noel?" He walked toward the couch and sat down, shaking his head, and then he looked at her. She'd changed her hair color and style to something drastically different, and so was her makeup. He continued to stare. He'd never expected to see her again, much less in his cousin's apartment, and he certainly didn't expect to find her banging on his drums. But it sure did look like Christy, only this girl looked frightened and white as a ghost.

Willy scratched his head and asked, "Christy, is that you?" He said it in such bewilderment that Noel was afraid to answer.

Lilly interrupted the scene, thinking she could help out the situation by clarifying some things. She said, "Willy, this is Noel, not Christy, and she is staying here with us. I wasn't sure you'd remember her since you see so many people on tour. But we've become close friends, and she's been to visit us twice before coming this time. She's going to spend the summer with us, and just at Easter—"

Noel had put her hand up to stop Lilly. Both Willy and Noel had locked eyes during this whole speech, Willy's speaking fire and Noel's speaking fear.

Then Noel spoke. "Lilly, if you can wait a minute, I need to do some explaining before you go on." She paced the floor and then looked at Lilly and put her soft gaze on Willy. She was wringing her hands, wondering just how she'd landed in this mess.

Noel turned to Lilly. "Lilly, I am Christy!" And then she turned to Willy. "Willy, I am Noel!"

Both sported a lopsided grin and a look of total confusion, so much so that Noel chuckled. She then looked at Willy. "Willy I never meant to deceive you. But due to my parents' profession, I grew up with an alias name, of which you are very familiar, Christy Henson. But when I called Lilly, I didn't want to play the acting role any longer, so I gave Lilly my real name, Noel Franklin." She paced some more and wrung her hands. "And since I never spoke to either of you about any other name than the one you knew me by, neither of you would've known."

Lilly turned to Willy and spoke slowly. The situation dawning on her, she pointed a finger. "So this is the girl you tripped over?"

Willy slowly nodded his head up and down and said, "One and the same." He sighed, stood up, and ran his hands through his hair, shaking his head. He then turned to Lilly. "So do you mind if I take Christy out for a bit? We have some talking to do," he said sourly.

Lilly couldn't help it. She needed to lighten the mood. "No, you can't," she said smugly.

Willy's head whipped around. "What do you mean I can't?" Willy paused. "Don't tell me she's got a hot date."

"You can't take Christy, but you can take Noel." She laughed. She had a lot questions for the lady in question herself, but she knew they'd have to wait, as Willy needed to find his answers first.

Willy picked up a pillow and threw it at her. But she felt better that at least Willy had calmed down.

"If you are going to be real late, you can drop her off at Aunt Maureen's," Lilly said.

"If we run close, I'll drop her off over there," Willy said dryly.

All this had been said without consulting Noel/Christy at all. And she was none too happy about it. She put her hands on her hips and asked, "Is anyone going to ask me?"

"Since I'm not sure who to ask, I didn't bother," Willy said snidely. Noel gave in and grabbed her purse, gave Lilly a hopeful look, and went to the door. Willy followed her, opening the door for her. No matter how irritated he was, he was still a gentleman.

Noel wanted to protest, but she did care about Willy, even though she was seeing a not-so-lovely side of him at the moment. But much of that evaporated when she saw him go to a car she hadn't seen before—not only not seen there but hadn't seen the likes of anywhere.

Noel had to put her hand over her mouth, holding back the laughter. She'd never quite seen the likes of this piece of work Willy drove. She wasn't sure how old it was, but she did know it was old. She thought it might be a 1970 or so four-door Chevy Nova. It had an old tennis shoe on the driver's side mirror and a Coke can on the antenna, upside down. It was rusted in more places than not. And there was a pink-with-purple-trim hand mirror for the passenger side mirror that someone had glued on and let the glue drip down the side, whereupon it had dried permanently.

"You drive this thing?" she questioned as she walked completely around it, staring at the unique pile of junk on wheels.

She was giggling so hard that Willy's mood lightened some.

"Quite different than your cousin's BMW," he said dryly. He jerked open her stuck door. "If you're not too embarrassed to ride in this chariot treasure, then I'd like to take you out so we can talk. It seems like there is a crisis of mistaken identity. And I want to know who you really are."

Noel nodded and quietly said, "I will answer all your questions if you'll tell me where in the world you found this, um…um… unique treasured chariot."

"It's a deal." Willy chuckled.

Noel noticed that some cute towels, though unmatched, covered the torn seats. And the air vents were twist-tied open. He had a miniature drum and sticks that hung over his rearview mirror, along with two guitar picks on a string. Noel didn't think she could hold in her laughter. She said the only thing that came to mind. "Mr. YoYo, this is so you."

"That it is, but I must say, I don't get very many dates this way." He really was in no mood for her antics, but he tried to be nice.

"This is certainly probably not the nice car you are used to in the sunshine state, but it does fine for me."

Noel let out a whistle, and then she said, "This here is YoYo Willy, bringing you up when you're down."

He glared at her.

"How am I going to bring you up when I forgot my yoyo?" She was trying to get him in a better mood but didn't know how.

Willy decided to take her to the Round the Corner Restaurant for some heart-to-heart conversation. They were quiet as they entered and were seated. They both looked over the menu, only Noel was not really seeing the words; they were muddled with the tears gathering in her eyes. She hated that Willy was cross with her.

"Do you know what you want?" Willy finally asked.

"Just get me whatever you are having," Noel said as she laid down her menu, her voice sad and wavering.

He could tell she was on the verge of tears.

Willy put down his menu and looked across the table. His heart melted, yet he felt he'd been duped, so he was dealing with a lot of mixed emotions. But mercy won out over judgment. He reached over and slipped a sucker under her hand and then laid his hand over hers and said, "Hey, I'm sorry. I've not considered your feelings and shown you kindness in this upheaval of my day." Then he removed his hand, leaving the sucker as a peace offering.

She looked at the simple sucker. "What's this for?"

"It's just something I learned from Lilly, and I've used them to brighten faces when people feel suckered in by the circumstance of life." He grinned, looking at her smile as she turned the sucker around in her hand. "And apparently, it works."

"Thanks for the sucker," she said, trying to control her tears. "I am sorry that I'm the cause of your unpleasantness." She so easily went into acting to cover her hurt.

"I wouldn't call it unpleasantness; just surprise." Willy took a sip of his tea. "I have to admit, I've got a few questions for you." He chuckled. "I've been crazy out of my head the past thirty minutes trying to figure you out, or rather who is the real you."

"Yeah, it seems I came into the world a surprise and I just keep on surprising people." She was getting down just thinking of her parents.

The waitress came and took their orders. Willy didn't want to order for her, but it seemed that she wasn't going to do it, so he ordered something he thought she might like. Then he picked up the conversation, thinking he needed to take this slowly and not just fire at her with a round of questions.

"What did you mean by that?"

She knew she could be honest with Willy, but she was nervous about what he thought of her. "Willy, did I ever tell you what my parents do for a living?" she asked while twisting her napkin.

"No, I don't believe so." Willy wondered just what in the world she was going to tell him, asked, "What do they do?"

Noel was hesitant, and then she rushed on. "My father and mother are both very famous movie stars." She let that sink in.

The change of looks on his face was comical. But she noticed that he got them under control immediately.

"Really? That must be interesting," he said, hoping she'd share more.

"Well, most people think it's heaven on earth to be one of Hollywood's top one hundred paramount stars." She snorted. "But what I see is that Hollywood is a trap that slowly strangles the life out of you and you don't even know it." She went on to tell Willy the major parts, movies, and soap operas that her parents had played in. "I was a surprise to them at birth and have continued to surprise them often. The only problem is they hate surprises."

"What do you mean by that?"

"Oh, let's see. First, they were pleasantly surprised that it was to be a family affair. As a newborn, they put me in shows, parts, contests, you name it. They had all the connections. Really, as a little tyke, I felt like a new century in-color version of Shirley Temple. I did the cute things they wanted me to. But the acting took its toll on me, and I just wanted to play. So as I got older and more bored, well..." She snickered, and her eyes twinkled. "Well, I got into more trouble. Hiding, playing in the sets that were unused—well, it really is a fairytale land with lots to play with. Only I was lonely. My parents didn't have time for me, and I was at the studios most every day after tutoring for shootings. Then, when I was much older, I saw the truth in all the make-believe lies. I soon learned that nothing is for real in Hollywood. At least in my world, the world of movies and TV shows, the film just keeps rolling even after you leave the set. It's really sick. Before you know it, life just becomes one big film. You never really know the heart of someone because they are always playing the part." She paused and looked down and then away as a single tear slipped out.

"I just wanted to have an ordinary family," she whispered, "not one with dinner parties, stage lights, and cameras, not this constant running from the news media, the infidelity, alcohol, drugs, and depression that comes with climbing to the top." She was quiet. "I hated being in the spotlight and having to keep up the look of what everyone expected of me. There's never any letting your hair down, so to speak."

"Wow, that had to be rough!" Then he went on to say, "So that is the reason for the alias Christy Henson."

Noel nodded. "The one thing I never budged about was using the alias, as it was the only help of privacy available." She took a bite of her burger. "By the way, Willy, this is a wonderful burger. And the fries are the best. Thank you for bringing me here." She licked her lips clean. "The alias was extremely handy when I rebelled and went to public school, which is what everyone knows me by. And actually, I have done the role-playing so long that nobody really knows what my parents do or that I have no financial need and are better off than probably most in my entire high school. But that's just it. I don't want them to know." She sighed. "I want to be normal like everybody else."

Willy nodded, more understanding coming. "So why did you tell Lilly your real name?"

"I never dreamed I'd even meet her, much less become so attached to Lilly and Peter. But I was so upset and so out of my mind that I just wanted to be real to someone, and since I thought it was safe to do so, I did it."

Willy nodded again. That made sense to him. Curious, he asked, "Does Kevin know?"

Noel was shaking her head. "No, he doesn't." She looked right at Willy, "I don't want someone to love me for my money, my fame, or because I'm the daughter of a famous movie star." She paused. "I went to school to be normal, so I've really ended up being the star anyway in hiding my true identity in order to do that." She huffed, realizing for the first time that she was really a first-rate actress to have been able to pull that off the past six years. Her success didn't please her, but only at what it had allowed her: a view of the normal world.

Willy could see her wheels spinning. She was thinking about a lot of this. It couldn't be easy. Willy opted for wits. "So no wonder you've never seen the likes of my car. What do you drive, a Lamborghini?" He smiled, teasing her.

She liked to have choked on her Coke. "No. My dad has one, and my mom has a Porsche. I didn't want to embarrass my parents by having people ask questions, so I opted for a flamingo-pink Camaro!"

Willy let out a low whistle and shook his head. "And you actually rode over here with me!"

She sat back and threw a French fry at him.

Noel let out laughter that was sweet to Willy's ears. He was sure learning a lot about this mystery woman. Willy got back to the questions. "So why did you call Lilly?"

Noel played with her remaining uneaten fries, a sad cloud coming over her eyes, "Well, partly because of you."

Willy pointed to himself and shrugged his shoulders.

"Yes, you, because you'd left such a strong impression with me that you and your friends really cared, that when I became desperate, I reached out and picked up the phone." She continued. "And, boy, I'm so glad I did. It was scary at first, not knowing Lilly and all, but like you said, she's a great listener. So I kept on calling every two weeks or so, and then I came out here last January, the day after New Year's, but I guess you had gone back on tour and we must have just missed each other."

Willy nodded.

"Then I actually came here from New York the day after our studio tour drive." she smiled at the remembrance.

"Why didn't you tell me?"

"Well, it was your day, and I didn't want to do the talking," Noel stated simply. "And if I recall, you were quite taken with all your surroundings." She giggled.

Willy was bobbing his head up and down, smiling around a bite of burger, remembering he was dazed like a kid at a candy shop window.

"And really, I didn't think I'd ever see you again, so there was no need."

"So, why are you here?" He looked into her eyes, hoping to gain a *real* answer from the *real* girl who had certainly taken him on a wild trip.

"Ah, it's a long story, drummer boy. Are you sure you want to hear it?"

Willy noticed that the food had been devoured, so he made another suggestion. "Hey, it's still light outside. I know of a nice little park. Would you like to go for a stroll and we can continue our talk?"

"Sure. If you have the time. But I thought a famous drummer like you would have better things to do than to take a walk in the park, listening to my life's sorry story."

Willy beat his fingers on the table in a drum roll just before moving to get up. "If life's not about people, then there wouldn't be any songs, my lady." He hopped up and put his arm out. "After you," he said, and they left.

Willy hadn't gone far when he wheeled into a thrift bakery store. "I'll only be a minute, but you are welcome to come in."

So she did.

She stood and watched Willy in his element, which meant people.

"Hey, man." Willy raised his hand to high-five the cashier. "What's up, Justin? How's it going?" He waited for the guy to answer. It was obvious to Noel that Willy knew this guy and cared about him. He then asked, "How's your wife?"

They talked a bit more. Noel was trying not to eavesdrop but was again touched by Willy's caring heart for those around him.

Willy then grabbed five loaves of two-day-old bread, real cheap, and a couple of dessert Danish items and paid for them and turned to see if Noel was ready.

"Did you want anything?" he asked, smiling.

"No. I'm ready when you are."

They got back in the car only to be disappointed at the dead whine it gave when cranked. Willy put his head on the steering wheel, and then Noel watched him get out and pull the drumsticks from his back pocket. She noticed that he carried them everywhere. Then her eyes got big. She watched him play a rendition on the front hood, put the sticks back in his pocket, get back in the car, and start it. It didn't start on the first try, but then, after some sputtering, it cranked over on the second try.

"What was that all about?" Noel asked incredulously, looking at him in sheer astonishment.

Willy looked over at her while backing up. "That, my friend, is God's mercy." He went on out into traffic. "A lot of times after it sits while I'm on tour, it gets lazy and doesn't want to start."

"And the drum roll thingy? Isn't that like taking things a bit too far, drummer boy?"

"It might appear so, but the things of God can't always be seen by the eye. The playing only gave me time to pray to God for it to start," Willy explained.

"Does God always answer to the beat of your sticks?" Noel was thinking she sure had a lot to learn.

"No. That's why I said it was His mercy." Willy snickered. "For there are times that He chooses to make me push. But then, that is His prerogative. He is God." He paused, wondering just how far he should go with this. "But then there are times like this that He chooses to have mercy."

"It sounds like you are just a puppet on a string," Noel said, perplexed.

"Not at all. Just a thankful servant," Willy tried to explain.

Noel let it go. She would ask Lilly about it later. "So where did you buy this rare beauty?" Noel asked, rubbing her hand on the back of the seat.

Willy laughed out loud. "The junkyard, silly. I've fixed her up a bit and paid about one hundred bucks to get it painted and two hundred to get a new starter, which my dad put in for me. But it has kept up the beat for over three years now."

Noel let out a low whistle. "I'm impressed," she said as she rolled her eyes in mock adoration. She looked over at the shoe on the mirror and just laughed again.

"How come I get the feeling I'm being laughed at?" Willy asked as he pulled into Waller Park.

As they pulled in, Noel figured out just then why the tennis shoe was there. Willy had pulled in so close to the other car that she feared he wouldn't be able to get out. It was obvious the tennis shoe kept him from putting dents in other cars.

Willy opened the door for Noel, something that took her completely by surprise. She wasn't used to being treated like a lady. Willy then got the five loaves of bread out of the back.

"Willy, didn't you get enough to eat?" She shook her head. "I mean, I know you're a growin' man, but five loaves? Really!" She followed him across the plush park lawn covered with huge oak trees.

"Just wait and see." He kept on. Then she watched him slow down by the pond and sit on the bench. She stood off at a distance and watched as he opened the first loaf of bread. Then, out from nowhere, dozens of ducks and geese came flocking to him. He speedily tore off pieces, and Noel watched with fascination as the grubby, fat, feathered friends ate it up.

In no time at all, Willy was on the second loaf. He turned and motioned to her. "Here. Come try it. They love bread." He held out the loaf to her.

She slowly went over to him. It did look like fun, and the birdies were so cute. She took the loaf of bread from him and took out the first slice. She had torn it in two when the little beasts began to squawk and quack, flapping their wings. It frightened her, so she began to back away quickly, but they came after her. She immediately became more scared and began to run, and they chased her, flying up, nipping at her backside. She was screaming, and she finally dropped the loaf of bread and went on an all-out marathon to get away from those monster creatures that had looked so cute.

Willy was laughing so hard because it had been hilarious to watch, though he was sure it wasn't hilarious to her. So he tried to contain himself by the time she'd quit running. He went over and retrieved the fallen loaf of bread and tossed it to the hungry beggars. Then he walked over to Noel. He put his arm around her shoulders. "Hey, are you okay?"

She actually had been frightened to tears, but she was getting them under control. "Yeah. I was just, uh…wow! Those are mean little things," she said with vengeance. She brushed herself off, "They tried to bite me! A good thing I had on jeans, or they might have been better called flesh grabbers."

Willy was leading them back to the bench by the pond.

When she got close, she stopped, "I ain't going nowhere near those beak swindlers."

She was shaking her head, and Willy knew she was scared.

"Come. Let me show you how to do it." Willy took her hand and pulled her.

She was taking baby steps, not so sure she wanted to try this again.

He finally got her to the bench. "Here. Sit down, get out a piece of bread, tear, and toss." He demonstrated. "See. It's easy," he said and handed the loaf to her.

He'd done it so easily, and they seemed so nice to him that she thought she'd try again. And sure enough, they didn't chase or try to bite her this time. She started to smile. *This is fun after all*, she thought.

Willy sat back and enjoyed watching her.

After the bread was all gone, Willy asked if she wanted to walk. She agreed. Noel thought it was so beautiful.

"This park is so beautiful. That is, when you're not being chased by webbed feet."

Willy, having taken the park for granted for years, asked, "What is it that captures your eyes?"

"For one, the grass is so plush and green. Where I live, I go to bed to the sound of *Ch! Ch! Ch! Ch! Chchchch! Ch! Ch! Ch!* She made the sound of the sprinkler system that put her to sleep every night. "If you don't water your yard every day, it will turn brown and crunchy. And funny thing is when the grass is green here, it's brown there. And in the winter here, it's green there." She laughed. "It's like two different worlds, even for nature."

Willy jumped up and turned backwards to see her. "Are you serious?" His hands went up in disbelief. "That's crazy."

Noel went on. She pointed up to the tree they were walking under. She chuckled. "And you wouldn't be walking under any trees. These trees are the most beautiful I've ever seen!"

Right at that moment, a tree squirrel jumped from one tree to the other.

Noel grabbed Willy's arm and put her other hand over her mouth. "What was that?"

Willy chuckled. "That, my dear, is one fat, ferocious, people-eating bat. One bite and you're a goner."

Noel's eyes were huge. Her grip on his arm tightened. "Are you for real?" She was quickly trying to get out from under the tree, all the while keeping a death grip on Willy's arm. "Why? Why, uh…do they let them stay here?"

"I give!" Willy laughed out loud as he held up his hands.

"What!"

"I'm just kidding. Those are cute, well-acorned tree squirrels," Willy confessed.

Noel released her grip and slapped at his arm for making fun of her lack of knowledge. "There it is again, the night and day difference of our two worlds."

"What do you mean?"

Noel laughed, looking again, spotting several of those adorable creatures and watched them chase each other around the trunk of a big tree. She pointed, "I've never seen this kind of tree squirrel. We have ground squirrels that dig holes in the ground and go in them come out for food and then run back in. You can see them everywhere. They're not near as cute as these little fellas." She went closer to the tree, thinking she'd get to actually catch one. "Of course, they don't have trees like these either, so maybe that is why there aren't tree squirrels. They'd have to lower their living status to bush squirrels."

"What? You guys ain't got no trees?" Willy gave her a queer look.

"No. We have trees. It's just that they are few and far between and very different from these magnificent trees here. Even our oaks are called scrub oaks for a reason. I mean, it really is an irrigated dessert." Noel laughed.

Willy was thinking. "Yeah. Come to think of it, I don't recall seeing many trees. I guess I didn't pay that much attention. And it's obvious I've taken these here beauties for granted." He reached up and pulled a leaf off a hundred-year-old oak.

They walked along in silence a bit longer, and then Willy asked, "So, tell me, if our worlds are so different, then why are you here?"

"Ah." Noel sighed.

"You want to sit for a while?" Willy asked, leading them to a bench. "I figure between the webbed-footed criminals and the ferocious bats, you might be getting tuckered."

"Yes, it's been a day. That's for sure. But I'm more worried about you. Didn't you just get in and haven't even been home yet?" Noel inquired.

"Yes, but don't worry about me. I'll be all right. I was just really taken by surprise earlier." He paused. "And I'm still trying to put together the pieces of the puzzle."

"And this one is missing, right?"

"One of the main pieces, though, I'm sure more will come up," Willy gently admitted.

"Well, where did we leave off?" she asked, trying to remember. "Oh yes. I think I told you I made the two other visits here. So when things started getting really bad…I mean I would've never probably called Lilly if things had been good. And I thought things were bad when we first met."

Both were remembering that embarrassing time.

"It was obvious then that my life was a mess." She picked up an acorn and tossed it to a begging squirrel. "But things got so unbearable. I broke up with Kevin for good, and that brought along a whole carload of unpleasantness. But the thing that sent me over the edge was at my graduation."

"Oh yeah! Congratulations!" Willy said, just remembering. "You're all through then?"

"Yep! All done!" Noel bobbed her head. "I wish I could say that my senior year has been a party, but more like a hangover was what I experienced this past year. But no use in crying over spilled milk."

"Tell me what happened at your graduation," Willy said, at a complete loss. "I can't believe that your parents weren't extremely proud of you."

"We'd gone in separate vehicles because I needed to be there early. But I'd told my parents where the school was, how to get to the stadium, and the date and time of my graduation if they wanted to come. I really wouldn't have known by looking around that they'd showed up. There were hundreds of people in the bleachers." Noel said, thinking back to the night, "I bet they just loved sitting on those cold, hard, concrete bleachers to watch all us ruffians walk across the stage."

She looked at Willy and then turned away. "Well, I was selected to sing the national anthem for the ceremony. It was a real honor for me. And though I walked up there on shaking knees and an extremely queasy stomach, all those lessons came to fruition. I remembered every word and note. I was so proud to be an American. I don't know why I didn't expect it, but there was thunderous applause afterward, so I must have sounded decent. It's hard to tell when you are singing what the people are actually hearing. Then to have graduated with honors really made the whole day tops for me. I walked across the stage and received my well-earned diploma." She giggled. "I actually kicked up my feet as I walked off the stage, thinking, 'I am done with these brain-pickin' thieves and fun-suckin' days.' I was so ready to be done. I think the teachers were ready to be done with me too." Noel actually laughed at the memory.

"You can't possibly make me believe you gave the teachers a run for their money." He chuckled.

"You better believe I made sure they earned their paycheck." Then she got serious. "But what upset me was when I got home. It was late since I'd gone to a party." Then she looked at him. "But you'd be proud of me. I stayed sober."

She grinned at Willy and was rewarded with a nod and a handsome smile.

"So what happened at home was *nothing*."

Noel was upset about it, Willy could tell.

"Absolutely nothing. Complete silence. Business as usual. Nothing was said about my singing. Nothing was said about graduating with honors. Not even a mention of the graduation ceremony itself. Nothing. Just nothing. Can you believe how let down I was?"

"Well, are you sure they were even there?" Willy asked.

"Yeah, I'm sure they were there," Noel said sarcastically. "My mom raked me over the coals the next evening about the major public appearance of singing for the ceremony and that I should've been laying low. She berated me by saying, 'It's already a disgrace to have you in public school, and then you go and make a big deal of it.' She never said one word of approval or congratulated me once. She was only concerned about her precious image," Noel said with tears streaming down her face.

Willy couldn't imagine the hurt she must have felt. He put his arm around her and patted her shoulder. "I'm so sorry you had to go through that. That must have really hurt you. How very sad that your parents were so thoughtless and uncaring." He continued to encourage her. "Why, graduating from high school is a huge thing. And you did it with honors. I'm so proud of you."

She looked up and wiped her tears. "Are you really?" She didn't know why it mattered, but it did.

Willy nodded his head. "Sure I am. It's not an easy thing to cram all that stuff into this tiny skull." He banged on his head with his fist.

"So then, I just called Lilly and asked if I could come out for the summer. I just needed to get away. I know that sounds wimpy." She shrugged her shoulders. "I don't know what the future holds, but I just needed a break. They said I could come, and I just arrived five days ago. I actually thought about trying to get a job and helping out since I don't want to ask my parents for any money."

"Well, I wouldn't apply for a drumming position," Willy said with a chuckle, blatantly teasing her. "You were, let's say, um… interesting. I usually call that a drummer who drums to his own beat."

"I will take your advice and not hold my hat out on that one."

Willy, noticing the sunset closing in on them, said, "Well, I better get you over to Aunt Maureen's and get home. Jet lag is coming on fast."

She jumped up and said, "Race ya to the car!"

Willy's eyes were huge, his grin wide.

But before he could tell her she was crazy, she said, "On your mark, get set, go!" And she took off like a streak of lighting.

Willy dropped Noel off at Aunt Maureen's.

She leaned back in through the window. "Thanks for understanding. I had a great time, though I was worried at first that I'd made an enemy. But I think I found a friend?" she asked, more like a question than a statement.

"It might take some getting used to the name change, but it never changed our friendship," he said caringly. As he drove off, he said aloud, "Something tells me this ain't the end!"

CHAPTER 12

Willy gave a courtesy rap on the door before using his keys to the apartment. Peter and Lilly were both on the couch, each engrossed in a book.

"Did you get the answers you wanted?" Lilly looked up and asked with a smile.

"Yeah, and then some I think." He chuckled. "She's one mystery lady. There's a whole lot more to that package than meets the eye." Willy was thinking about all she'd shared.

"She keeps me on my toes, that's for sure." Lilly chuckled. Not wanting to divulge anything that Noel hadn't shared yet, she carefully asked, "Did she tell you about her last visit here?"

"She talked about a lot of things, but I don't think she got that far."

"Well, you'll have to ask her next time," Lilly said with a big smile.

"With me on tour, I don't know that there will be a next time," Willy snickered, ignoring the thoughts that had just overtaken his brain in the car. Then he mumbled, "Of course, she has popped up at the most unlikely of places."

Peter, who'd been quiet, spoke up. "Lilly's been filling me in. Putting together all your encounters with Christy and plus what

Lilly described this afternoon, I'd say your head must be spinning about now."

Willy ran his fingers through the top of his curly head of hair. "Man, it flipped me out. I still think I'm going to wake up tomorrow and find it all a dream."

Peter laughed, having had similar thoughts. He looked at Lilly and said, "Yes, some surprises take a lot of adjustment, but don't miss the surprise while being surprised."

"You would know all about surprises," Willy acknowledged.

"I was worried about you when I walked in. You looked like smoke was about to come out your ears. I don't know if I have ever seen you angry before."

"I'm sorry. Actually, I brought you some Danishes from the thrift bakery for a peace offering. I was pretty heated at hearing my drums being ripped apart by some barbaric hooligan who obviously didn't know how to play worth a hoot."

"I guess you haven't heard her sing yet?" Lilly asked.

"If she sings anything like she played my drums, then let me know so I can get some earplugs." He rolled his eyes, thinking there was no way that girl could hold a tune in a bucket.

Both Peter and Lilly smiled, knowing Willy had some lessons to learn, and they hoped they were around to watch. They both had some interesting thoughts of their own about the harmony these two might drum up together. But they kept these thoughts to themselves, as neither one would appreciate being put on the same music sheet together, at least yet.

Willy opted to not comment any further on the talents of Miss Noel or Miss Christy, whoever she was at the moment. "I got to hit the hay. And you know the family. They'll want to know every detail." Willy shook his head. "Boy, wait 'til they hear about today. That'll get the ol' pie hole dropped open." He picked up his keys. I'll be by on Monday during the day if it's okay to start practicing on some upcoming songs. We're getting ready to do an album, and I really need to stay on top of things while off tour this month," he said as he headed out the door.

"Sure thing," Peter said.

"You know you're always welcome." Lilly closed the door behind him. She smiled at the thought of Wilma and the girls' faces when Willy told them the events of the day.

Sunday morning came quickly. Saturday Willy had spent filling in his family and spending some time with each of his sisters. He didn't have time to practice for Sunday's praise team, so he had to sit out that week, but he'd be able to help out the next few weeks until tour time again.

That's why he found himself sitting by Lilly. Willy had wondered why Noel hadn't shown up. But then again, why would she want to come to church? Her life wasn't one of a godly pursuit, though it seemed that he remembered Lilly telling him something about her asking questions. The service began, and as usual, whether up on the stage or off, Willy worshiped his God. He was refreshed with the songs, challenged, and convicted by them. He was so glad he could worship in complete freedom.

As everyone got seated, Willy situated himself, leaned back, putting his ankle over his knee, ready to listen to the special music. Not a moment later, he was suddenly frightened out of his skin. His mouth dropped open as he leaned forward, his elbows on his knees, his eyes huge.

Lilly leaned over with a huge smile and whispered, "You might want to close your pie hole."

Willy, embarrassed at being caught right out, closed his mouth immediately, sat back, and tried to relax. He was put to shame as he heard the sweetest voice sing "Amazing Grace." He closed his eyes and just let the song wash over him. Tears escaped his lids as he rejoiced that he had been lost but now was found. That was his favorite hymn, and he never grew tired of hearing it. That was the best he'd ever heard it sung, and what he just couldn't get out of his head was that the lovely voice was coming from none other than Christy. Then he shook his head. *No, Noel.* He wondered if he'd ever quit thinking of her as Christy. Not a moment later, Noel come down the side aisle and sat by him since he'd taken her seat by Lilly.

After she sat down, Willy leaned over and said sincerely, "That was beautiful."

"Thank you. It's my favorite song," Noel said as she straightened her skirt.

Willy gave her a queer look and said, "Mine too."

Both stared at one another for brief moment.

Willy said to himself, *This is way too weird.* But he was still astonished by her voice. Plus, the fact that she was allowed up there had his head spinning. *And why is 'Amazing Grace' her favorite song?* He needed to get a grip so he could hear the preacher. He planned to get answers to his questions, but for the moment, they'd have to wait.

The pastor spoke as he got up and situated his Bible and notes. "I can't think of a better person to get up here and sing that song than a fresh convert, one who had been lost and now is found. May we be renewed in our gratitude for our salvation and not lose our fervor for the lost and dying world," the pastor challenged.

Willy looked at Noel, understanding of Noel's conversion hitting him full force. Willy's smile was huge. He grabbed her hand and leaned over and whispered, "Praise You, Jesus!" He squeezed her hand and said, "That is awesome!"

She smiled at him.

Just when I think I have figured out this mystery lady, something else takes me by surprise and I find myself clueless. Willy reined in his thoughts to make them obedient to listen and learn. Now wasn't the time to try to solve the mystery.

After church ended, Willy turned and said, "I was wondering if you'd sing for your dinner." Willy laughed. "No. Really, I wondered if you'd like to come out to my parents' place. I think we have something left unsaid that we need to talk about." He raised his eyebrows with a smile.

"Okay, sure."

Instantly Willy was crowded out by people coming and hugging Noel and asking her all kinds of questions. Willy was pushed aside by the crowd, but he got a full view of all that was going on. He just leaned back on the pew next to him, his feet crossed, arms folded, smiling. He could tell that she really didn't know what to say to all these people. She didn't expect the attention, but she was kind and tried to answer each one, but before she could get through with one answer, someone else would ask another. Willy had all he could do not to laugh out loud.

Finally the people left and Noel turned toward Willy.

He came to her, smiling. "I thought I was going to be a starved man before you got done."

Noel hurried along with him. "I'm sorry," she fussed, "I didn't expect that." She tried to hurry so Willy wouldn't be inconvenienced any longer, but her high heels were rubbing a blister on the back of her left foot. "Where do your parents live?" she asked for a distraction.

"Oh, not too far. About forty-five minutes from here. They live in the country."

Noel had not yet met Willy's parents. She found that she was nervous, yet she didn't know why. Willy wasted no time. Knowing full well they might not have another private moment after his family met her, he plunged in. "I want to say, first of all, that I rejoice with you in your new family heritage. That makes you my sister. Did you know that?"

"No." Obviously, she hadn't considered it.

"I've prayed for you so much. It's neat to see God answer prayers, especially on behalf of someone's salvation." Willy whistled. "That makes all those late nights, crammed living quarters, and skateboarding 'til my knees ache worth it," he said as he patted her hand.

She was smiling. He was getting used to her new looks and thought she looked lovely in her outfit. "I was wondering if you'd share with me just what happened that 'Amazing Grace' is your favorite song."

"Sure. I'd be happy to. But I'm not sure I can do it without tears, for His Grace is so amazing."

She shared about her last visit, about the play at church, about Peter's reading and explanations of the Scriptures, and what had happened. She shared about her conviction and conversion. And she was right; she had shared most of it through deep, passionate tears of gratefulness that God had redeemed her and made her His very own.

"Then, on that Sunday, I went forward and asked the preacher if I could get wet in the Jacuzzi."

Willy put his head back and roared in laughter, thinking just how that must have looked. He could just imagine Noel doing that. He'd be sure to get the exact scene from Lilly later, but even from this view, it was sure funny. "Did you really ask that?" Willy wanted to know.

"Something like that. I just had been saved and wanted to be baptized. I just asked in front of the whole church why right then wasn't a good time."

Willy hit the steering wheel, laughing. "Well, good for you. We can so easily get complacent in the system of doing things that we don't even recognize the movement of the Spirit." He paused. "I wish I could've been here to see it," he said softly.

As they pulled in the driveway, Noel laid her hand on Willy's arm. "Are they going to like me?" she asked with all the insecurity she felt pouring out of those steel blue eyes.

Willy howled in laughter. "I'll be lucky if I even get in a word edgewise after you walk through those doors." He jumped out of the car and went to open her door.

Dinner was ready, and all were sitting in their seats with the exception of Wilma and Doug.

Willy began the introductions. "Mom and Dad, everyone, this is Noel…" Then he turned to her and laughed. "You know what. I don't know what your *real* last name is." He was embarrassed, to say the least.

"Franklin." Noel quietly supplied the missing information, and Willy tried again.

"Mom, Dad, everyone, this is Noel Franklin, and she has agreed to sing for her dinner." Willy laughed.

But Noel had turned ten shades of red and elbowed him.

He exaggeratingly grabbed his stomach and said, "Well, since we don't want dinner to get cold, how about singing for dessert?" he asked Noel in full tease.

"I think I'm suddenly diabetic." She rolled her eyes with a smile.

"Welcome to our home, Noel. We are delighted to have you." Doug shook her hand.

Wilma took Noel into a warm embrace. She could tell the girl in her arms was stiffened with fear, but Wilma hoped to dispel that before she left. "We are so glad you're here. We've heard so much about you from Lilly and Willy both, and it's an honor to have you here."

They moved to sit down at the table. Willy pulled out Noel's chair, and she clumsily sat down, her skirt catching under the chair. As she scooted up, she hit the table, nearly knocking over her glass of tea.

Noel was embarrassed, but nothing was said. And to cover her clumsiness, she began to babble her thanks. But all was quiet at the table. Then she began to wonder why everyone was looking at her.

Then Willy leaned over and whispered in her ear, "Dad wants to say grace."

If it were possible, Noel would've slid under the table.

She covered her mouth and said, "Oh," and then bowed her head.

Willy looked over at his dad with a smile and a shrug of the shoulders. Doug gave Willy a knowing smile and thanked the Lord for the food and their special guest. Noel was overtaken by Doug's prayer for the food and for herself. She just didn't think she would ever get used to people praying for her, even though she'd seen the power of their prayers. It was still all so new and awesome.

"I am going to tell you the name of everyone who pesters me, starting over there," Willy said, pointing to the twins. "Those two, Daisy and Susan, are double trouble for a guy like me. They force me to eat all their cookies at their tea parties, and they always let me win at checkers. With those girls, trouble follows you everywhere."

Both girls were giggling at Willy's antics.

"I bet you miss him while he is on tour," Noel simply said as she spooned up some mashed potatoes.

Both girls chorused together their agreement.

"Next to Daisy is Hannah, who was sweet sixteen and is now sassy seventeen, and all she does is pilfer my razors only to replace them with dull ones."

"Drummer boy, it's hard for me to believe that. It don't look like you've seen the sharp side of a razor anytime recently," Noel teased him without mercy.

"Hey!" Willy said, looking at her indignantly.

Noel had everyone laughing.

Then Willy introduced the oldest of the girls. "And on my right here, is Olivia. She drives me crazy, is always on my tail about my hair. Instead of having night crawlers, she has night callers, keeping me up all night, making me lose my beauty sleep." Then he put his hand up to his hair, mocking a girl fixing her hair.

Olivia, good at sparing with her beloved brother, waved her hand at him. "Hogwash. I gave up on your unruly hair a long time ago. There ain't no helping that head of curls all wanting to go in different directions like a bunch of sailors jumping ship."

Willy threw her a glare, but she went on.

"And as far as beauty sleep, even a coma wouldn't afford you what you need." She chuckled.

The table roared. They teased each other often, but their love ran very deep.

Finally, everyone settled down to finish the meal. Noel was fighting some big-time feelings. It was so different than anything she'd ever known. It was what a real family was like. Not only did she have unusual circumstances, but she was an only child; thus, she didn't have a clue what it was like to have a sibling.

"Noel, how did you learn to sing like that?" Doug asked.

Noel didn't know what to answer. So she opted for honesty.

Noel looked at Willy, and then she realized that Willy didn't know the answer either. She cleared her throat and blurted out, "Well, to my great delight and disgrace, it was through absolute belligerence and disobedience to my parents that I could get up there and do what I did this morning."

Willy had been drinking his tea and about had it come out his nose. He choked a bit. "Uh…could you explain that?" He had noticed the shocked looks on everyone else's face.

"When I was young…" She stopped, turned to Willy, and asked privately, "Do they know about my parents?"

"Uh, yes. A little bit."

"When I was young, my parents wanted a new-age Bach and proceeded to make me into one. I did several years of piano lessons and hated it at first. But it opened up a world of music to me. I began to fall in love with it. It was a place of peaceful escape for me. But when my parents saw that I didn't want to be a Bach but instead wanted to sing, they shut me down and turned completely against it. So I still played the piano for another year or two. I still play, for that matter, but not around my parents. But what they didn't know was that I have been sneaking out twice a week for the past six years for voice lessons." She took a sip of tea.

There was a hush at the table. Even Willy was without words.

Finally, Wilma cut the silence. "Well, I can see why your instructor wanted to teach you year after year, for he probably loved hearing you sing as much as we did this morning." Wilma smiled at her and began to pick up the plates. Then she spoke again. "And as far as singing for your dessert, we will serve it in about an hour in the living room, so you better get ready." She winked at her.

Willy looked over Noel's head and gave his mother a grateful smile and wink for coming in and saving the moment. Everyone began to get up and clear away the dishes. Noel just stood back and watched all the girls. Willy and Doug gave Wilma a hand, and in no time at all, everything was clean and put away. She'd never witnessed anything of the sort. Even when she was at her friends' house, they didn't usually eat together, and it was a whatever-you-can-find-and-eat-in-your-room kind of thing.

Noel schooled her features and followed Willy into the other room. Doug had made a conscious choice each week to ask his family what they had remembered and/or learned from the sermon that morning, so he proceeded to do just that, and he started with Willy.

Willy looked at Noel and smiled and then looked at his family and said, "That grace is amazing." He explained no further.

"Noel, would you like to join us in this time of sharing?" Doug asked. "You don't have to, and we'd think nothing of it, but we wanted you to feel welcome."

Noel was still reeling over Willy's comment, yet she wanted to share. "Well, I, um…" She was hesitant. "I, uh…since I'm a new Christian, I don't know very much. So just call me sponge because I feel like I'm just in great need to soak up everything so I can be a good Christian."

All the hearts broke in the room. She didn't understand that she didn't need to be good but that good would flow out of a heart changed by God.

Noel went on to say in a quiet voice, "The part about the rich young ruler really touched me in that he loved his riches more than he loved God. That it's not really about keeping a list of rules so much as loving God and people." She licked her lips and, in a soft whisper, said, "Money can't buy everything." With a tear running down her cheek, she said, "The most important thing in life isn't for sale, yet it cost Jesus everything."

"That is something we need to hold close to our hearts and not forget. Thank you for opening up and sharing that."

Doug went on to each one in the room. It was such a wonderful time of sharing and seeing others' hearts and reinforcement of what was taught that morning that Noel was glued to her seat.

"I think it's your turn," Willy said as he elbowed her.

"I already shared," she said with a disgruntled look.

"No, not that. It's your turn to sing for your dessert!"

Noel rolled her eyes. Surely they weren't really going to make her do this. But they were all getting up and moving to the little piano in the corner. Willy motioned with a hand wave for Noel to come over to him. She reluctantly did so.

She'd been learning the hymns since becoming a Christian and had picked up a chorus book; thus, she knew a few.

Willy said, "Play and sing something for us."

Noel looked at him like he'd grown five heads. "Look. You only said I would have to sing for my dessert, not play for it too," she said teasingly, dead serious.

Willy clapped his hands and roared in laughter along with everyone else. "You're right. Would you rather have Olivia play for you?"

"Yes. That would be great." She hoped Olivia would pick something she knew.

She got up from the piano bench, and Olivia sat down. Wilma turned to *Sweet Hour of Prayer*. "Do you know this one?"

Noel studied it for a few seconds. "Yes, I think I can do it."

So that was what they did, but by the third verse, all quit singing so they could her Noel's clear, sweet voice ring out.

She finished it out, having learned not to ever stop in the middle of a song. "Why did y'all quit on me?" she asked as soon as she finished, completely unaware of the reason.

All were silently grinning. She looked from one face to another and then looked at Willy for an answer. He was standing close beside her as they all huddled around the piano.

He smiled warmly into her face and leaned over for her ears only. "Because we wanted to hear you."

Her ears turned red along with her face.

They did this for over an hour before Wilma said, "Okay. My dessert isn't that great. I give in. Let the poor girl alone." She waved her hand as she backed up from the group to the kitchen to prepare the dessert.

The little girls went to help Wilma with the desserts while the older ones riddled Noel with questions. Willy sat back with a huge grin and watched. Doug also sat back and watched his son, all the while telling himself not to go down that road with his thoughts.

After dessert and more fellowship, Willy asked Noel, "I usually go to praise band practice when I can. Do you want to join me?"

"Sure," Noel said, getting up from the floor where she was playing a game of checkers with Susan.

"Willy, she hasn't even had time to relax, much less to get out and enjoy the country," Wilma piped up, entreating for more time.

But Willy wasn't giving in. Willy smiled his infectious smile at his mother. He turned and glanced at Noel. "Well, I guess that means we'll have to do this again. See ya later." Willy kissed his mom and patted his dad on the back.

"Thank you for having me. Dinner and dessert were great."

Both Olivia and Hannah hugged Willy and then Noel.

Olivia punched Willy on the arm and said, "Be nice to her, and bring her back. We barely got to know her."

Hannah joined in on the bandwagon, badgering him.

Willy rolled his eyes. "It wouldn't matter how many times I brought Noel over. You two would still find words that needed using," he teased his sisters. Then he looked at Noel's surprised face that showed her thoughts.

They want me to come back like a friend, and they're not rejecting me.

That melted Willy's heart. "I'll see if I can drum up a few more reasons to bring her back out here to the sticks," he told his sisters as they parted.

CHAPTER 13

Noel sat on the front row, tapping her nails to the beat on the back of the pew. She was so enjoying watching the praise team/band practice, cut up, play, and sing. She was watching Willy play his heart out on the drums, and then before too many songs went by, he and the guitarist switched places and Noel was again in admiration of the many talents of the crazy, skateboarding, curly-headed, laugh-a-minute yet compassionate, fabulous guitarist and great singer she called drummer boy.

She continued to smile, watching him play. She noticed he couldn't stand still. She wondered how he ever managed to remain seated while playing the drums, but then she realized that was probably why his arms flew and his hair was everywhere when he played.

Noel found herself humming along. After a bit, the leader of the group hopped down off the stage and gave Noel a stack of the songs they were singing. He said, "Hey, anytime you want to join us, feel free. We'd love to have you."

"Thanks." Noel flashed him a beautiful smile. She, however, did not get up there. She way was too scared. But she was having more fun just watching and worshiping. It didn't compare to anything her old life had to offer.

Willy's eyes often strayed to Noel. He felt responsible for her, at least until Peter and Lilly got there. He was delighted to see her smiling. It looked like she was really enjoying the music. But what he didn't expect was that his eyes were not the only ones looking her way. He wasn't saying that anything was wrong with some of the other guys looking at Noel. She was beautiful, and more so every day with Christ becoming more and more precious to her. They were probably just curious. He couldn't blame them. She was a curiosity to even him.

It wasn't long before they finished practice for the night. Willy needed to go deplete the two RC's he had swigged down just before arriving at practice. So he jumped off the last two steps of the platform, walked swiftly to the back, his hand hitting every pew, jumped over the last one, and let out a loud, "Woohoo!" This was often how he went around the auditorium. He wasn't showing off; just being crazy Willy.

Noel just shook her head. *That Willy*, she thought.

When he came back to the auditorium, he noticed that Noel didn't need his company, for Rob was chatting with her. So instead of going her way, he just went and talked with the fill-in drummer about some changes.

Before long, Lilly came up and tapped Noel on the shoulder and said, "Howdy, stranger."

Noel turned and smiled.

Rob took his cue with a smile. "Well, I better get going. Maybe we could get together sometime."

"Yeah. Sure." Noel flashed him a warm smile. "It was nice to meet you, and I had a fabulous time watching practice."

He put his thumbs up. "Glad you did." Then he walked off.

Noel got up and went to sit with Peter and Lilly. Church was about to start.

Having finished, the praise team went to their seats. Somehow, Noel had expected Willy to sit by her. She was crestfallen when he gave her a smile but kept on walking past her and went to the back center section and slid in with a pile of youth. The girls who sat on each side of Willy were apparently good friends. She didn't know why she was disappointed, but she was.

Of course he has lots of friends. He has been at this church for many years, and he's a people person, Noel consoled herself. But that she was bothered at all really bothered her.

Lilly knew it was Willy when she heard the rap on the door and then keys rattling, so she didn't move. She was at Willy's doorjamb, listening to Noel sing while playing one of his guitars. Willy was furious at the sound, knowing someone was playing his guitar. However, all anger drained from him as he stood next to Lilly, watching Noel play his guitar beautifully and singing her heart out. He was spellbound.

Lilly turned to him and smiled. She knew exactly what he was thinking.

When Noel noticed they had company, she immediately stopped, put down the guitar, and began to crouch away, saying, "Oh, I didn't know you'd be here. I didn't hurt anything. I promise." She tried to leave, Willy's silence putting bars of condemnation around her.

"No," Willy said sternly.

Noel's eyes jerked up.

"Play it again," he said softly.

Noel stared at his eyes, trying to read them, but she couldn't define what she saw there. She looked away. "No, I don't think that's a good idea. I might pop a string on your precious guitar."

She said snidely as she brushed between the two of them and headed for the front door.

Willy turned and knew that he couldn't get to the door fast enough. He bellowed, "Please don't go!"

Noel had her hand on the doorknob, her back to the room. She paused.

"Face it. Don't run from it," Willy challenged, hoping Noel wouldn't run out on him.

She actually surprised herself by praying briefly. *Lord, I can't do this. I don't want to be hurt. The pain is too much. I so need their approval. Help me handle it if I get no one's approval but Yours.* Then she turned back around and leaned on the door and looked Willy square in the eyes.

Lilly had discreetly gone to her room to give the sparring couple more space.

Noel said with fire in her eyes, "I'm facin' it all right, but I don't like the looks of it." She had the meanest face Willy had yet to see.

Willy knew it was a serious moment, but he was about to bust a gut in laughter. "Hey, I took a shower this morning. What is it? Do I have a big ol' booger on my nose or what?" his antics revealing his "what's not to like about me?" mock attitude.

Noel cracked a small laugh. Though she wanted to stay mad at him, she was having a hard time with his sweet craziness. "No. What I'm facin' is a guy who's more afraid that someone will bugger his guitar than the booger on his nose."

Willy immediately swiped at his nose, wondering if indeed there were unaware stragglers. Noel had to cover her smile.

"I've known guys who have said, 'Mess with my girl and I can forgive you. Mess with my guitar and you better leave town.' But I didn't think I was that bad," he said as he scratched his head, fearful of her answer. He turned to the closed door, where he heard

Lilly beat Noel to roaring laughter. He looked at the closed door and then at Noel and slowly asked, "Am I?"

"Let's just say you give that guy a close run for his money," Noel said after she stifled her giggles.

Willy hung his head.

"But if you want me to keep you accountable to not become like that guy, then I'd be happy to play your chops and strings every day just to see how mad you get."

Lilly stuck her head out the door. She just couldn't resist. "Just look at his ears. They are a great gauge. If they're real red, you better back up and call the fire department, for that means he is firehouse mad." She giggled and then ducked back into her room and shut the door.

Willy reached up and felt his ears. They were hot. And he looked at Lilly's closed door and then at Noel, who was looking at his ears. And he could feel them getting hotter. He stomped to the kitchen, got out an ice cube, and rubbed it on the edges of his ears as he sat down on the couch.

"Siss." Noel let out a teasing sizzle. "As hot as those things are, you might need a whole ice tray."

"Okay, okay! Yes, I admit I have a problem." Willy raised his hands up. He was still trying to chill out his ears. "But I want to change," Willy said with cold ears but a warm heart. "So to keep that change ever before me, you are welcome to play in my room anytime you like, Miss Noel." Then he added, "Just use a tissue if you plan to leave any boogers, will ya."

Noel crossed her arms. "I promise I'll be careful as though they were my very own."

Willy motioned with his head for her to come. "How about right now? I really did want to hear you again." When she didn't move, he repeated, "Really, Noel. Please."

She finally gave in and headed back to the studio room.

Lilly had come out with a white hankie. "All clear in here?" she asked as all three crumbled in hysterical laughter.

Both Willy and Lilly stood in the doorway and watched Noel do the song again.

Willy was mesmerized. He let out a low whistle. "That was super!" He crossed his arms as he leaned on his doorjamb. "How about another one?"

Noel nodded. Then she did another, and that really got Willy's pie hole open.

Lilly leaned over. "I tried to tell you."

They both listened for another hour. Then, discreetly, Willy moved in to sit on the extra stool and sang along with her on ones he knew. After a few of those, he subtly went to the drum set and quietly played along with her and sang too. Lilly was then the one with the open pie hole problem. She thought they were a perfect blend. She hadn't ever heard better harmony. She thought it symbolized more than music. But she better keep that number to herself for now, but she just couldn't wait until Peter came home to tell him all that her heart was singing about.

They ended up spending the rest of the afternoon doing just that, singing and playing together. Willy tried to sing songs she knew, and he taught her several new choruses and worship songs and helped her with the ones she was struggling to learn. They really were spectacular on songs that they both already knew. Willy had so much fun. And Noel was floating.

It was such a delight that Willy happened to show up the next two days in hopes of a repeat. He bopped in the first day and said, "I was hoping to check out how well I'm doing with someone else pulling my strings." He winked at Noel. He had talked with Peter and worked out a practice time plan.

Again, Willy was amazed at Noel's talent playing the guitar and singing. "You really play great. You know that?"

"It's the beat of my heart!" Noel shrugged her shoulders.

Willy's head spun around at her choice of words.

"I just wish my parents thought that," Noel said sadly.

"I still can't believe they don't know how beautiful you sing or that you can play Jordie out of a job. It's sad that they don't share in any of your interests."

"Well, they don't." Noel sighed, putting her hand on his arm. "That is why I can't tell you how much jammin' with you has meant." Her voice was quivering, trying to hold back the tears that threatened.

Thinking she needed a rescue, Willy said, "I was wondering if you wanted to come to the house tomorrow after we pluck strings and hit the chops." Then he paused. "You can jam tomorrow, can't you?"

Noel laughed at his presumption and leaned toward him. "You silly Willy. I don't have anything else to do, so I might not have bread, but I can always jam."

Willy laughed. He was finding that he enjoyed her company as much as her playing. She certainly was a match to his wit. And she was like a perfect glove fit as far as singing together.

"Back to what I was asking. I thought I'd ask today so that you can bring what you needed from Aunt Maureen's when you come tomorrow. Then, after our jam session"—he leaned over toward her and smiled—"we can go out to the house and you can stay the night and just ride with us to church. What do ya say?"

"Okay. Sure. I don't see why not. It sounds like a totally cool idea. And it'll give Peter and Lilly some time alone."

"Whew," Willy said, wiping at fake sweat on his forehead and letting his hands fall limp. "The girls have been relentless in hounding me like a dog to get you back over. So it'll be like a slumber party for you girls." He slapped his knee. "And that leaves me out." He puckered his lip. "I guess I'll have to be the lonely hero."

"A lonely hero? What's that?" Noel scrunched up her nose.

"Well, I'll be a hero to my sisters for bringing you to stay over but lonely since I'll lose my jam partner."

"Well, here now. A hero does have its drawbacks." Noel put on fake sympathy, shaking her head.

Then they began some warm-ups.

"Even Superman couldn't have the best of both worlds."

Willy helped both his sisters into the saddle, allowing them to place their foot in his joined hands as he hoisted them up. Then it became awkward with Noel. Willy really didn't have any issue, but Noel did. She was not about to have him help her. She shivered to think of her foot being in his hands and her behind in his face. She turned several shades of red just thinking about it. She decided she'd just get up there herself. So she tried but couldn't make it, as the horse was taller than she remembered horses being. She tried three times with miserable failures and was about to just say never mind and go back to the house when Willy walked over.

Willy had his hands on his hips, a smile spread across his face, sweat pouring down from it. "Can I help ya in the saddle?"

"Uh…um…no. I can do it. I just needed to catch my breath," Noel said. "You know, it's much hotter here than I'm used to, and the humidity is quite suffocating. Maybe I should just go back to the house and wait for you all to get back. I don't mind." She was stepping away from Willy and the horse as she gave this declaration, which was delivered with a bundle of nerves.

Willy put his hand out and grabbed her just before she bolted to the house and chickened out on the horse ride altogether. "Hey, wait a minute. Come back here." He pulled her to stand in front of him. "Now, a gentleman always takes a lady at her words, but something tells me though all you said might be true about the temperature and humidity, but I think there's more going on here."

Willy watched Noel very slowly nod her head yes.

With a brief touch, Willy tipped her chin up. With his eyebrows up, he asked, "What did we say about not running from your problems but facing them?"

She gave a quirky smile and crossed her arms with a stubborn attitude. "Yeah, but that don't mean I have to like what see."

Willy leaned toward her face. "Just what are ya seeing that has you wanting to run like a wild bull on red carpet?" Willy was trying to be kind, but it wasn't helping her situation.

She snorted just then in frustration, and both ended up laughing at just how much she sounded like a frustrated bull. With that, she broke down her defenses.

"I just don't want you to help me get up on the horse, and I can't do it, and the heat and miserable humidity is making feel like a walking sauna and one dismal person to be around. She rolled her eyes. "And no breeze to boot. We always have a breeze in California, no matter the temperature. Here, you'd starve if you owned a kite business."

Willy was soon laughing. Then he said, "Hey, listen. It's not a problem for me to real quick like boost you up. We sure would like you to join us. It's one of our favorite things to do, even when it's hot. My mom will have fresh lemonade when we return," he said with an entreating voice.

Noel found herself agreeing to put her shoe bottom in his joined hands for boosting her up. "Where is the Germ-X when you need it?" she mumbled under her breath, only to watch him walk away brushing his hands on his denim jeans as he went to his horse and mounted it. She shook her head and said to her horse as she patted its mane, "Yep! Two different worlds, all right!"

She fell in behind the two girls. She hadn't ridden horses much but knew what to do. She just hoped that this little adventure wouldn't require any tricks, for if it did, she was sure to come unglued. They ran the horses through the fields and trails, all of which were absolutely beautiful Noel thought. The camaraderie was doing terrible things to her heart, though. Being part of a family sure makes love take risks. And she was very quickly falling in love with this one.

Sure as Willy had promised, "Fresh lemonade anyone?" Wilma asked as she came out carrying a fresh pitcher of the inviting liquid. She had already set down a tray of cookies.

Noel's cheeks were redder than normal, so she put the cool glass up to them. When she looked over at the smiles that were watching her, she plopped in the nearest chair. "I know. I'm a baby." She sipped her drink. "But this heat just kills me. Man, if it got up to eighty degrees, it was a heat wave. Most people don't even have air conditioning unless they live inland. Boy, on a hot day like today, you'd find me at the beach, cooling down in the surf. On the occasion it does warm up, it's only that way for about five hours in the middle of the day. Here, I've noticed its hot when I get up *and* when I go to bed. I guess if I were to live here long, I'd have to become a night owl to enjoy the cooler weather."

All laughed at her comparison.

Wilma stood back and in her sweet, motherly voice said, "Now don't mind us. We're just enjoying your rosy cheeks. That's all. I'd imagine it's a culture shock to the body to have such drastic differences in temperatures and humidity."

"Yeah. I'll probably go back and freeze." Noel snickered, but the words *go back* made her shudder, for she was so comfortable here. She loved both Olivia and Hannah and the twins, for that matter, too. She also let her thoughts go so far as to think that Wilma and Doug were the best parents she thought ever existed.

"Are you going home soon?" Wilma asked as she poured more lemonade. "It seems like you just got here."

Noel didn't really want to think about leaving. She just wanted to erase it all from her memory and have a great summer before heading back to the dreadful home life she'd left. She began to get nervous, twirling her cloth belt around. She attempted an answer. "I, uh…really don't know what's ahead. But I know I can't just live with Peter and Lilly forever, even if I get a summer job to help out. It's only for a time." She let out a big sigh.

All the hearts in the room broke at her dismay.

She looked down as a single tear slipped down her cheek. "I'll probably go back home and gather my things and move to some quiet place and try to start a life. I don't really have any skills, so to speak, but I am a quick learner and a hard worker." She then smiled at Willy. "At least I can *act* like it enough to get a job." She let out a small laugh. "I like California okay, but my home really holds nothing for me." She then turned her face away so no one could see how much she was hurting right at that moment. What she didn't reckon on was that all did see; her turned face hid nothing from those around her.

Willy thought his heart would break for the girl. No one really knew what to say. That is except Wilma.

"You're always welcome here, Noel," she said sweetly as she made eye contact with Noel so that she understood her offer.

Noel was about to come completely unglued. To keep from just blubbering all over the place, she nodded her head, her eyes saying, "Thank you for rescuing me."

Willy, not really knowing what to say, turned to leave the room. A thought formed, but just as it did, he literally shook his head, thinking, *No way!* He slapped the couch back on his way out and said, "I need to hit the sticks. Noel, you're welcome to join me if you wish." It was getting way too intense for him.

Noel ended up not joining Willy at all. She helped the girls clean up some, and then she played with the twins, helped with dinner, and simply enjoyed watching everyone, Willy momentarily gone from her thoughts. Therefore, when he came in through the living room many hours later, Noel jumped out of her skin, for he did a drum roll on her head with his sticks. He thought her scream was a bit off beat. She didn't think it was funny, but then, after seeing his goofy smiling face, she couldn't help but laugh. She figured he probably did that to his sisters all the time.

She put her hands on her hips. "Just what part of tour practice was that?" she asked as a comeback for being scared to death.

"I guess to see how far I can push buttons," he quipped and headed for the dinner table with a mischievous grin.

It was the following Sunday, and Willy was driving Noel to his parents' house after the morning church service.

"Willy, I don't know why you wanted me to come back to the house with you," Noel said, completely lost as to what was up with Willy. She crossed her arms. "I mean, I don't want your mom to get sick of me."

Willy was grinning and tapping the steering wheel to a morning tune but had otherwise been quiet on their ride. Noel was getting frustrated and wanted to get to the bottom of this.

"I've been thinking," Willy said, "that you'd really be a great addition to our praise team at church and wanted to personally ask you to join us, and if you said yes, then I'd teach you some of the songs this afternoon, and then we could go back together. It saves you a ride. "So what do you think?"

"I'm not sure what to say." Noel gulped. "Do you want me to play or sing?"

"To sing with that beautiful voice, of course," he said with a smile.

She began to shake her head wildly. "I don't know. I mean, I don't know these people, and I don't know the songs." Clearly, she doubted her ability and was very unsure of herself. "Not to mention, I don't know how long I'll even be here."

Willy, expecting that answer, replied, "Well, then you must not be the lady that just stood and sang the national anthem without a single missed note." He looked over at her open mouth. He held up his hand. "Have you forgotten I've heard you sing, my sweetheart?" He was pulling into the driveway. "As far as how long you'll be here, they'll take you one week as well as a hundred. Have you forgotten that I'm only here a month at a time?" He smiled with raised eyebrows.

Noel knew he had a point. How could she refute? "If you think it's a good idea, I'll give it a try," she said. "As a matter of fact, I do think it's a good idea, but if you are unsure, then perhaps our time this afternoon will convince you." He smiled and took her by the elbow and escorted her to the door.

CHAPTER 14

Noel looked longingly out the airplane window. It was hard to believe she'd been gone for just over a month. The time had flown faster than the jet she was now on. All there was to see at the moment were soft clouds floating freely by, so opposite her torturous thoughts. She closed her eyes and leaned her head against the window. She didn't have anything against clouds, but right now, her heart was anything from peaceful and calm, and the clouds seemed to mock her, so she just shut them out.

But as she closed her eyes, the last week in Shelbyville assailed her with such intensity that she shivered. She reflected on the luncheon that got her in the seat she was sitting in. She recalled every word. They were sitting down, having lunch, and the conversation was about one of Peter and Lilly's bus kids and a situation of forgiveness. Peter and Lilly talked and shared scripture. Willy interjected as well.

It was at that very moment that Noel spoke aloud these words: "I have to go back."

All at the table fell suddenly quiet and stared at Noel. She repeated herself, her body stock still, as silent tears ran down her cheeks. Before anyone could say anything, she got up and went to gather her things. Everyone looked at each other, and then Lilly went to her.

Noel was crying as she quickly gathered her things. When she saw that Lilly had followed her, she said, "I'm so sorry. Do you mind taking me to Aunt Maureen's so I can get the rest of my stuff?"

"Sure, Noel. I don't mind. But what's going on in your heart?" Lilly looked straight into her eyes. "What just happened?"

Both Peter and Willy were listening to the entire exchange.

Noel said, "When I left, I said such unkind things to Kevin. I have to ask him to forgive me, or he'll never see Jesus. I don't want his blood on my hands. Look at what all Jesus has done for me." Noel was sobbing. "I have to tell them, with my words and my heart." She was thinking of her parents too. As she finished packing her few items, she wiped away a few more tears. "No matter the response, I'm going back to show them the love of Jesus." She paused. "If I can't forgive them, then they won't see the forgiveness that Jesus offers from the cross."

Peter, Willy, and Lilly were all so astounded and touched that they didn't know what to do or say.

Finally, Willy said, "Here. I'll take you to Aunt Maureen's."

"Noel, will we see you again?" Peter stepped forward to carry Noel's things.

"I don't know where my life will go, so I can't say for sure." Then she patted her chest with her fists and, in a husky voice, said, "But I will always have you here in my heart." Then she hugged both Peter and Lilly and looked into their eyes. "Thank you for everything. I'll never forget you." She turned then and walked out. She didn't want it to be any more painful.

Willy told Peter he'd book her flight and get her to the airport. With a big grin, he said, "Yeah. I somehow think you'll for sure see her again."

Both Peter and Lilly wanted to question him, but he was out the door.

Noel was quiet as they drove to Aunt Maureen's, and Willy just let her alone. He had his own things to work through, and the silence was what he needed as well. It was time to act on that nagging thought that had pestered him for some weeks.

Willy got Noel inside, turned her to face him, and spoke gently. "I'm going to book your flight. I'll call later to tell you when I will be picking you up. I'll try to make it as early as possible, sensing your urgency to get back. But I think you need to rest tonight." He squeezed her forearms for emphasis.

She nodded.

"One more thing. I want you to read Psalm Twenty-seven before I pick you up. You might find several of its portions a comfort, especially verse ten."

Noel agreed.

Willy tapped her on the nose lightly, and said, "Everything will be all right." He then forced himself to turn and leave.

Noel explained as best she could and thanked Aunt Maureen and James for their hospitality. She then bathed and turned in early for the night, having received the call from Willy that it would be an early flight in the morning. She now lay in her comfy pajamas under the light covers with her Bible open.

Oh, LORD, how will I do this? I'm so scared. I'm afraid I'll let You down. Truthfully, I'm afraid of the conflict that is sure to come. Oh Father, my Father, the One who saved me, I'm forever indebted to You, LORD. I know You are asking me to go back and tell them, rather, show them Your forgiveness through me. Father, can You take my fears and turn them into something useful to You? LORD, please give me the words to say to Kevin, my parents, and my friends. God, whatever You have for me, I will do it.

On Noel prayed, and then when she was prayed out, she turned to the passage Willy had told her to read.

Noel laughed; it was just what she needed.

The Lord is my Light and my salvation—whom shall I fear? The Lord is the strong hold of my life—of whom shall I be afraid?

One thing I ask of the Lord, this is what I seek: that I may dwell in the house of the Lord all the days of my life, to gaze upon the beauty of the Lord and to seek Him in His temple.

Though my father and mother forsake me, the Lord will receive me.

I am still confident of this: I will see the goodness of the Lord in the land of the living. Wait for the Lord; be strong and take heart and wait for the Lord!

"Wow!" she said, "How did Willy know what I needed to read? That Willy, he's something else!" She was talking out loud again and went back to prayer, thanking God for these scriptures and how they'd strengthened her. She didn't sleep well and was up early, which was why she was drifting off to sleep along with the good-byes she'd been through. She had missed saying good-bye to Willy's family. That was hard on her, but right now, she just wanted one of those soft, fluffy clouds to take her away to sleep.

She was aroused sometime later to the landing gear letting down. She disembarked in the Chicago O'Hara Airport for her two-hour layover, walked through the crowds to her next terminal gate to wait to board her next flight.

She'd been sitting there for about twenty minutes when she heard the familiar drum roll of drumsticks on the seat behind her. She jumped up and turned so fast that she nearly lost her balance. Sure enough, she was looking Willy square in the face. He was standing with one foot in the chair, a huge smile on his face. He tapped the drum roll again.

"You don't miss a beat, do you?" Noel asked, her hands on her hips.

"Nope." Willy shook his head with a huge smile, and then he jumped over the seat and sat next to her.

To say that Noel was flabbergasted was an understatement. "What are you doing here?" she demanded, forgetting they were in public.

"Seems to me that this is a public airport. Do you have a problem with that, Miss Franklin?" Willy replied, loving the surprise on her face.

"Well, of course not. Uh…" Noel babbled. "I guess it's not my business what you do." She crossed her legs and turned her face.

Willy got up and left. Noel was not only hurt by this action but very confused. He didn't even say good-bye. *But then,* she argued with herself, *he owes me no explanation.* She picked up a magazine in order to distract her torturous thoughts. It did the trick; she was deeply absorbed in an article when a coffee cup slid down between her face and the magazine. She looked up, following the hand into Willy's cheery face.

"Thought you might need a pick-me-up since my drum roll didn't do the trick," he said as a peace offering.

Noel was humbled by the act of kindness. She was so touched that she didn't know what to say. He had even gotten her favorite mocha blend topped with whipped cream with caramel and chocolate drizzled on top.

They enjoyed their coffee for a few moments before Willy spoke up.

"You better drink up. We'll be boarding in less than fifteen minutes." He winked at her.

"What do you mean *we?*" She gulped loudly. She was more confused than ever.

"Well, I just thought that maybe you could use a little company when you go back so that you're not overwhelmed." Willy smiled.

"What do you mean?" Noel's eyes were huge. She just couldn't believe her ears.

Willy chuckled. "It's simple. I was to fly back the end of next week to begin the Ocean Praise West Tour that starts right in your backyard anyway, so I thought I'd just go back a week early so I could be there for you if you needed anything. I know it'll be hard for you, knowing the situation that you left." He shrugged his shoulders as though it were an everyday event to rescue a girl like a knight in shining armor.

"You mean you'd do that for me?" She placed a hand on his arm and looked into his eyes.

"Why not?" He laughed. "Besides, I'm afraid of where we might meet next," he said, teasing her, thinking of the bizarre ways they'd met so far. Then he added, "That is, if you want the company."

"Oh yes. Of course!" she exclaimed. "That's not a problem. I'm just so, so touched." She got serious. "But I must warn you. My parents will probably *not* like you."

They soon boarded the plane, and Noel sat by the window with Willy next to her.

After takeoff, Noel asked, "So your mom knows you're going with me?"

Willy nodded.

"Is she angry with me for taking you away early?"

"First of all, my mom doesn't anger easily. Secondly, you didn't take me; I wanted to come." Willy smiled. "And my parents, though they didn't get to say good-bye to you, did ask me to tell you they are praying for you and they all send their love."

"It's like saying good-bye without the tears." That did wonders for Noel. "I was so dreadfully sorry that I didn't get to see them before cashing out of North Carolina."

"They understand and just made me promise that I'd make a way for you to see them again."

"Did you promise?"

"Sure I did. Do you know what it's like to be tackled by four girls all at once?"

"I'm not sure you should have." Noel sighed. "I'm at a time in my life where I need to make some decisions. I can't just keep on running. I need to settle down into something, some kind of way to make a living. I don't think I can stay at my parents' forever. Even if I did, I'd still feel the need to pay my way, though they lack nothing."

Willy wondered just what lay ahead.

Willy leaned over to catch his breath. Then he looked up at the most magnificent house he'd ever seen. He was on the cobble-lined driveway ensconced in a fancy, manicured lawn. Willy had just gone for his usual early morning run. The house he now stared at was adobe, and it seemed to go on and on in different directions. There were huge windows everywhere, and he was looking at the most unique and ornate front double doors he'd ever seen. The grounds, well, he'd never seen anything like it—bushes shaped like dolphins and other exquisite yard decorations here and there. Willy scratched his head. Even his mom's yard didn't hold a candle to this one.

Willy said out loud, "And this is simple?" He'd already been down the street and many blocks over to know he was out of his class many times over.

Many of the things Noel had told him were beginning to make sense. "No wonder she didn't want me to know where she lived when I took her home a year ago," Willy said to himself.

He had no more than closed the door quietly when he heard voices coming from the kitchen area. He moved deliberately but remained hidden, as to not interfere with the conversation, or rather argument.

"So who is it this time?" came the seething question.

Willy figured that to be Noel's mother.

Noel tried to explain but was interrupted.

"Listen, Noel. You just waltz out of here, not a word from you. Now you waltz back in, only bringing a guy with you," Ericka remarked snidely. "What am I going to do with you?"

Noel finally gave up her defense and let her mother rage on. She had learned that she was going to anyway. In her old life, she'd interrupt and argue, but she wanted to be different. And besides, that never worked either.

Ericka went on. "Do you realize how hard it was for me to cover up for you?" She waved her hands. "It's not easy to keep those camera wolves off our backs about our daughter's debut into the adult world," she spat. "Do you think you can sit still long enough for us to set a date for your debut? You just can't let us down, Noel. After all we have done for you, can't you just act right and do this without embarrassing us?"

Willy so strongly wanted bust in and rush to Noel's defense. But he remained silent, jaw clenched tight. Willy heard Noel's sweet voice.

"Whatever you wish, Mother. I'll be available for you. Just let me know the date and plans." Noel hadn't asked for a debut but decided that she could honor her parents in that way. Before her mother could get away, Noel changed the subject back to Willy. "So, Mother, is it okay for my friend Willy to stay here for a week or so?"

Ericka threw up her hands. "You mean boyfriend. And why bother asking? You never have before." She growled, "You know I don't care just so long as you keep yourself rid of unwanted results. I just can't have you parading around pregnant. I'm trying to get on with a movie contract, and bad publicity means everything."

Noel was stunned, though she didn't know why. That was always her mother's big concern. Not ever about morality or the unborn; it was always about her image. She was trying to control her anger and form a reply that would honor Christ when she was rescued by the very object of their conversation.

Though Willy had to admit that wasn't how he wanted to meet Noel's mom, after his morning run, but he felt he must come to help Noel.

He cleared his throat, surprising both women with his stride entering the room, going straight for Ericka, his hand stuck out. "Good morning, Mrs. Franklin. It's so nice to meet you. I've heard so much about you." Ignoring her open mouth, he shook her hand firmly only to hold ice-cold ones limp as rotten asparagus, not returning the gesture one iota. Not one bit of that was missed on Willy or Noel for that matter. Noel was embarrassed.

Willy ignored the disgust on her face. "Sorry about my appearance. I was just out on my early morning run." He knew his hair was wild. There wasn't much he could do about this first meeting. "Thank you for having me in your home. The name is Willy McCollister. Most just call me YoYo Willy."

Ericka hadn't moved a muscle. She still held a horrified face.

"Yes, another admirer. Can't you see we want to live our lives in private?" were Ericka's first words after meeting Willy. She then turned to Noel with clenched teeth. "Why did you give away your alias?" her mother demanded. "It's there for all of our protection. That was a stupid thing to do." She threw her hands at Willy and snorted. "You don't know this kid. Why, he might be a stalker for all you know."

Willy chuckled, ran his fingers through his wild hair, and spoke. "Let me just set a few things straight." He looked at Erika. "I'm neither an admirer nor a stalker. Without offense, Mrs. Franklin, I've never seen any of your work, so an admirer I'm not. As far as the accusation of a stalker, well, nothing could be further from the truth. I'm a good friend of Noel's." Willy thought he would plunge in and make some more things clear. "And I do mean *friend*. I have no intimate intention with your daughter. I slept in the guest suite, as I'll do each night while here, unless you need the room. Then I can sleep in the garage." He then looked at Noel. "I do care deeply for Noel, but we're just friends." Her smile in return to his was all the thanks he needed. Willy then went the extra mile. "And for the voice of unborn children, they never asked to be created."

A door just off the kitchen burst open. "What's all this racket in here?" the voice boomed. Burt Franklin, Noel's father, looked around the room. When he spotted Noel, he went to her. "Well, Noel, you're home!" They hugged quickly, as Burt didn't want anyone too close to him. "Where have you been these days? Certainly missing the cameras. No one has found you, and we keep close eyes on those camera mongers." He was babbling on when he spotted Willy. He pointed to him, "Who's this carpetbagger?"

Willy ran his fingers through his hair again. Noel tried to talk, but as usual, her parents steamrolled over her.

She was about to introduce them when her dad boomed again, "Noel, if I've told you once, I've told you a million times! No strays, animal or human!" He turned his eyes on Willy with venom and began to leave the room, mumbling something about food and peace and quiet, neither of which he got.

Before he disappeared, Noel went after him. "Dad, this isn't a stray. He's my friend. Please come back in here and meet him," Noel pleaded. "Please," she entreated again.

He growled but turned around and moved back toward Willy.

Willy took the open door and grabbed his hand and shook it. "Nice to meet you, Mr. Franklin. You have a very talented daughter here." He looked over at Noel with a smile.

Burt rolled his eyes and slapped his leg. "Oh great! Someone who wants to nab your pocketbook, Noel! Just how you manage to do this is all I want to know." He was shaking his head. "You really know how to pick 'em."

"No, Daddy." Noel jumped up. "This isn't someone after your fame or fortune, nor mine." She quieted down. "He's really just a friend. I promise."

"What party did you pick him up at? And how long is he going to sponge off us?" Burt asked right there in front of everyone.

Noel smiled and looked at Willy for a brief glance. "Well, how we met is a long story, and you said something about eating. Maybe one day, if you have more time, I'll tell you. As far as staying here as our guest, less than a week and he'll be gone." Noel smiled a sweet, begging smile at her father.

"Okay, okay. He can stay," her father begrudgingly agreed. "But if makes one bad move, he's out of here."

Willy wasn't sure he should say anything but felt bereft at what these people thought of him. He had the strong desire to defend himself. "I can assure you both that I'm not what you think of me and only want the best for your daughter." He then turned to Noel. "If this interrogation is over, could you show me the shower and some towels? Maybe if I cleaned up, they'd think more of me."

Both of her parents had confused looks.

"Oh sure, Willy. It's this way." She led Willy back to his room and led him through another set of double doors, which Willy had clearly missed.

Noel smiled at his blunder and turned to go. "Thanks, Willy. When I'm at Peter and Lilly's, I forget what it's like here. This morning was hard, yet I must stand firm in the battle and pray for love, huge mountains of love to be poured out on them. It's just so easy to get rumpled." She slumped her shoulders. "And I just got here."

She turned the knob to leave, and then Willy took her hand.

"Hey, why don't we pray right now?" He began, and both prayed.

Noel was in tears before she was done pouring her heart out to God for her parents and her own hard heart that didn't want to love in all situations.

Just before Noel slipped out the door, she said, "There is food in the fridge. Just help yourself. We sorta all get our own stuff. Quite different from Wilma's kitchen. As a matter of fact, you'll probably find everything here night and day different than what you are used to. I'm sorry."

Willy lifted her chin and tapped her nose. "Don't be sorry, sweetheart. I knew it would be different."

"You're terrific. Did you know that?" She smiled into his face. "By the way, I'm going to spend some time reading my Bible. I need it. Then I'm going over to Kevin's. I'll be going unannounced, so he might not be home. But I'm anxious to see him." With that, she turned and left.

Willy watched her from his window, not more than an hour later, pull out of the driveway in her hot pink Camaro. He let the drapes back down and got on his knees in earnest prayer for her. After some time, he got out his own set of wheels and hit the pavement.

Willy said to himself, "There's nothing like California weather." In no time, he was flying down Los Angeles's most expensive Hollywood stars' sidewalks. He didn't think he'd know a star if he saw one, but he wasn't going to waste a day inside that insane museum Noel called home while he had a skateboard and a lovely day. He weaved in and out of people, his blue jean shirt unbuttoned and flying in the wind, showing his white t-shirt. Willy was having fun. He even stopped when prompted to talk to people and give them a gospel tract. He really didn't have much time to himself on tour, so he felt like a free bird. He got the tour of his life. Those were definitely the houses of the rich and famous, he deducted. He'd never seen the like. But then, that was what Noel's parents were. He had to laugh. *So unlike her,* he thought.

Willy spent most all the morning skateboarding. Then he went to the beach. Though not dressed for surfing, he did make plans to return to do just that. He thought he'd take advantage of being close to the ocean again. Though not as beautiful as the beaches up north, any ocean was an amazing sight to him.

―――✕―――

Noel opened the front door at about 7:00 p.m. Willy had chicken on the grill, had made a fancy pasta, sautéed fresh French green beans, and had picked up some dark-honey bread loaves from the bakery. Willy had found all the needed things to set the table and had everything prepared.

"Noel, you can close your pie hole." Willy chuckled.

"I'm just so…wow." Noel was speechless. "Willy, this is all so very nice of you." she looked around, complimenting everything, her surprise and appreciation evident. "I had no idea you were so talented in the kitchen."

"Like living in a house full of girls and a momma who loves to cook, I could escape learning a few tricks of the trade."

"Well, I'm indeed honored," Noel said. "My parents should be here any moment and will hopefully be pleased."

"How did it go with Kevin?"

She looked away, as she was trying to get control of her emotions. "I'll tell you about it later."

"I'm sorry. It's really none of my business. I know this is very personal," Willy said.

"Oh, not at all. I'm just emotional these days. Maybe later we can sit on the veranda and I'll tell you how my day went." Then she actually giggled. "And I'm dying to know what you did all day."

Right at that moment, the front door opened and Burt and Ericka came in.

Burt sniffed. "Ah. Now I remember why I love having you here, Noel." He then went straight to the dining room.

Noel went quickly to put away her things and returned to the dining table, where all were seated. Still, not a word from Burt and Ericka to Willy had been spoken.

Willy bowed his head, and Noel followed suit. Burt dropped his fork, and Ericka clanged her goblet glass against her plate. When they had finished praying silently, they looked up into the seemingly ashamed faces of her parents.

Noel broke the silence. "Thank you again, Willy. Everything looks and smells wonderful."

Ericka ate a few bites and dismissed herself. She put her satin napkin over her plate. "I just can't eat another bite. It's way too fattening for my figure. Do excuse me." With that, she left the table, no thanks, no gratitude, just offense.

Noel gave Willy a longsuffering look.

Burt, on the other hand, was enjoying his meal very much, though he was quiet. When he finished, looking at Willy he asked, "You cooked this?"

Willy nodded with a smile.

"Keep this up and you can stay another week." Then he left the table. Not exactly a thank-you, but better than her mother had done.

As they finished up, Noel asked Willy about his day, so he told her about it. They laughed. Actually, Willy had Noel in tears she was laughing so hard. Then Willy got up and began to clean the dishes.

"Oh, if we just put the dishes in the sink, the housekeeper will do them tomorrow," Noel said. "We just need to put away the food and wipe everything down."

"Well, in all appreciation for my mother, I ask you to join me as I wash the dishes and clean the kitchen," Willy said with a bow.

"Do you know how long it has been since I washed dishes?" Noel asked, her hands on her hips.

"No. Probably the last time your housekeeper was sick," Willy said, thinking she was going to say never.

"I'm disappointed in you, Willy." Noel stuck out her bottom lip in fake pouting. "Why, just two days ago at Aunt Maureen's!"

"It must have been a culture shock for you the first time you went to North Carolina," Willy said as he started the dishwater.

"I've done a lot of growing up this year. But all along the way, I've tried my best to remain unspoiled. But I'm sure I seem very pampered to you, and I guess I am. That is one of the reasons I insisted on going to public school. I wanted to be like the rest of the kids. And I tried to be like a chameleon with my friends so I could blend in and be normal."

Willy looked over at her as he passed a plate. "You're so different from your parents. I see where you live and know how famous and rich your parents are, but you're not that way. You're polar opposite of all they represent. That makes things very difficult. I can see they want a different life for you than what you want. You'll have to love and respect them, all the while living differently. That, my dear, is no small task."

"Boy, do I ever know that. I've always strived to be different after I saw what this Hollywood disease did to my parents, but not always for the right reasons. Now it's not about what I want but what God wants for me. I just hope they see a different me in the same differences we've always had. Does that make sense?"

Willy blew suds her way. "Yes, it does. We'll just pray our way through," he said as he let the water drain out. "By the way, I got ice cream for dessert. Care to join me?"

"Totally!" Noel got out some bowls. "I scream, you scream, we all scream for ice cream," she jabbered the old saying as she got out the ice cream scoop.

They settled on the back slated veranda, which was covered with wild wisteria. It was breathtaking. It wasn't dark yet. It was just perfect for the sunset and ice cream.

"My mother would envy this courtyard setting," Willy said.

"What most don't understand is that everything comes with a price," Noel said sadly. "Give me a yard full of weeds and a family to help weed it any day to this manicured masterpiece that someone else tends to and is seldom enjoyed by its owners."

Willy didn't really know what to say, so he chose a change of subject. "So how did your day go?"

"Oh, Willy, and I thought this morning was rough. It was a piece of cake compared to the rest of the day," Noel said with a full heart.

"I take it Kevin was home."

"Yeah, he was home, all right." Noel put aside her ice cream bowl. "I knocked on the door. I figured both his parents were at work, so if he was home, he'd answer. And he did." Noel was slow in recounting the day, as it was painful.

"He swung it open and said, 'Yeah? What do ya want?' Then, when he saw it was me, he was lost for words for a moment. Of course, the reason why he was speechless came bopping to the door, a girl from school, and that I had interrupted them was obvious. It was an embarrassing moment for all of us. The other girl finally said she was leaving and went to gather her things and then busted out the door, telling Kevin, 'Later.'"

Willy wasn't sure he wanted to hear anymore but encouraged Noel to go on. "That I had messed up his good time was obvious by the way their clothing looked, or rather the lack of clothing. He invited me. He asked why I was there as he prowled around. I figured he was probably high, but still, I had to take the chance. He then began to berate me, scream at me, call me every name in the book. I actually was scared for a while because he was so angry. But I remembered the verses on fear you just had me read, so I let him rage at me. He's really messed up right now, which, of course, he blames all on me. He said that if I'd never broken up with him, he wouldn't have done more drugs and wouldn't have lost his job. His parents are threatening to kick him out, and his new girl is giving him a hassle. All because I up and left him high and dry. Oh, Willy, I was so unkind to him when I left." Noel was crying now. "That's true, but it's not my fault. Yet he's so convinced that it is that I don't know if I can ever get through to him to show him Jesus." She put her hands to her face and sobbed.

"It'll be okay, Noel. What else happened?" Willy shushed her and patted her leg.

"He paced around like a caged animal, and then he came to me and jerked my head back by my hair and began forcing himself on me, kissing me roughly and saying all kinds of vile things. I tried desperately to push him off. But it was some time before he quit fighting me. Then he berated me, saying I was better than him since I didn't want him. Oh, it's just such a mess. Why did I ever think coming back here was going to be easy?"

She continued when she could control her tears.

"Then I told him in no uncertain terms that he wasn't to touch me again uninvited, that if it happened, I wouldn't come back. I told him that I wanted to talk and I hoped to rebuild our relationship. Though I knew what he was thinking wasn't going to happen, it did the trick to get his attention. I knew that today was obviously not a day to tell him about Jesus. I did finally get to apologize for the unkind words I said and the way I left and asked him to forgive me." Noel actually made a small laugh. "He didn't know what to say. He was so dumbfounded." She balled her fist and hit her lap. "I've got to remember that Jesus came for Kevin and can save him just as He did me. That was so hard to remember when he was being so forceful and violent." She then looked up as the sun set. "And I guess a part of me does really care for him. I was surprised that there was anything left between us, not that I would encourage it." She laughed at her confession. "We're not compatible, even if Kevin cleaned up a bit. I don't know if it's in the Bible or not, but I think it'd be a mess to continue a close relationship of that nature with a non-believer. I'm only asking for more heartbreak, aren't I?"

Willy didn't want to interrupt or change the subject, so he said, "Actually, there is scripture that speaks to that. Maybe we can go over it tomorrow."

Noel nodded.

"So how were things when you left him?"

"I'm hopeful." Noel smiled. "He said we could get together and talk about where I'd been and why I left. So with that, Jesus will come into the picture. It's because of Him that I do what I do. And just maybe after a few days, Kevin will actually start listening to me. I kissed his cheek and made plans to meet again tomorrow." She ended feeling very relieved that she had shared.

Willy was so overwhelmed that he didn't know what to say. "Well, let me know if I can help in any way. It's hard to think of him hurting you and me not being there. But I also know that he probably wouldn't be open if I were there, at least not at this time." He looked over at her. "By the way, I am inspired by your heart and obedience. This is a hard path for you. But you're walking down it. Now, let's pray for Kevin." He leaned forward and prayed for Kevin, his family, his heart, his problems, and for Noel and their future meetings. "That was a beautiful sunset," Willy said as he gathered the dishes to go in.

Noel got up behind him.

In the kitchen, he said to her, "Hey, I know it's late, and I don't want to disturb your parents. But I was wondering if somehow you could jam with me in the morning before you leave?"

"Sure. It's the least I can do for my own personal lifeguard." She laughed. "I just don't know what I would've done without you." She paused then whispered, "Thank you."

The next morning, Noel woke to a simple yet lovely breakfast. Willy had already done his morning run and had fixed scrambled eggs, bagels, and cut up fresh fruit. He set out yogurt and juice to complement the meal. Willy, Burt, and Ericka were sitting at the table when a very sleepy Noel came in the room.

She sat down and said in a grumpy voice, "I guess I'm in a real need of some beauty sleep."

"Well, my dear, I can send over my makeup girl, and she can take care of that for you," Ericka said, wishing her daughter would do more with herself. She then turned to Willy. "Uh, William, Willy, whatever your name is, you don't have to cook for us, and you're welcome to stay here without working. I'll not have my guests working for their room and board. We try to keep a reputation here, you know."

"The name is Willy, and I'm not working for room and board. I'm cooking because I want to please others," Willy said, shocked at her attitude.

She didn't know what to say to that, so she got up to leave, but before she left the room, she told her daughter, "You have an interview tomorrow at ten a.m. at the studio portfolio complex. Please, Noel, let my girl do you up for it. Then there is a party Friday night I'd like to ask your attendance to." Ericka was trying to be nice so that Noel would come. "And as far as the debut, July twenty-eighth is planned. Will that work for you?"

"Uh...yes, ma'am. July twenty-eighth will be fine. I'll be at the interview as well." She slowly asked the next thing. "Um...would it be a problem if I bring Willy to the party?" She cringed to think of her answer, should her mother deny her request.

"Sure, honey. Bring whoever you want to," her dad jumped in. "Just be there and socialize like we taught you."

"Then yes, we will be at the party too. And I'll have Ginger do my makeup and hair for both."

Ericka did a double take. She was so surprised at Noel. "It sure seems like you are different," Ericka said with a strange look on her face, not sure what to make of her daughter. And from all she could tell, this guy hadn't laid one hand on her either.

"Thank you, Mother. I am different."

Ericka then left, and Burt left shortly behind her. It was time for the famous couple to leave for their careers.

Willy went to the piano bench and patted the seat next to him. Noel went straight to him, sat, and began to sing and play.

Ah, Willy thought. *She plays and sings so beautifully.* He decided in his heart that while out today, he'd contact Sky Blue about what had been nagging him for a month.

Before they knew it, two hours had passed by.

Noel said, "Oh my. Look at the time."

"A hair past a freckle?" Willy, who hadn't a clue, said as he looked at his watchless wrist.

"I certainly don't need Kevin mad at me." Off Noel went to freshen up and get her purse.

When she returned, Willy was leaning up against the formal foyer column, his feet crossed at the ankles, smiling at her. She was cute to watch when in a hurry.

"What are you laughing at?" she asked as she scampered to the door.

"Why, you, of course."

"What is so funny?" Noel asked, backing up.

"Oh, just you when you're in a hurry."

"We'll discuss this later," Noel said.

Willy got serious. "I did want to ask you a question."

Noel stopped and looked at him. "I know this isn't a vacation for you, but it's the last of mine before tour starts up again. I was sorely wanting to hit the waves some. Any chance of you taking me? Or if there's another way to get there, I'd be happy to do it. A taxi every day will begin to add up, I'm afraid." Then Willy added, "If only I'd brought the beast." He snapped his fingers in mock seriousness.

"Then my parents would surely have denied you sponging off them and parking that thing anywhere near their palace."

Both laughed.

"I'll see what I can do," Noel said as she left.

"I'm praying for you," Willy called after her.

Noel couldn't shake just how good looking Willy had been that morning nor how it made her feel to sing with him again. It had been a few days since they'd done that, and it just seemed different.

Willy and Noel were sitting on the couch late that afternoon, having a Bible study. Willy was showing her what he'd promised about being unequally yoked with a non-believer. However, Willy thought this was a good way to spend time with Noel and perhaps what she needed most outside of prayer. He decided that a book of the Bible might be a good addition to what he was already doing with Noel during jam practices.

"Hey would you like to do a study in First John with me?" Willy asked. He thought it might help her if she got the chance to share with others around her.

"Oh, I'd love to." She smiled. "I have so much to learn, and being here is so different than in Shelbyville, where I can ask most anyone I'm around a question."

They were nestled shoulder to shoulder on the plush couch in the informal living room, with the Bible open between them.

"I guess I'll go back to the church I went to a few times before. It seemed all right to me. Though I'm finished with high school, they'd probably still let me do things with the youth. What do you think?"

"Well, I don't really know. I mean, I can't really say, having never been there." He looked at her. "But I do think you need to go somewhere for learning and encouragement." He winked at her. "Or, like my momma said, you could always move back East."

"As much as I'd love to do just that, I have a mission to accomplish here. I'm not going to run, even if it means I'll stand alone."

"Hey, what am I, chopped liver?" He jabbed her.

"Oh, Willy, you'll never know what coming here has meant to me. I so needed the support to stand firm." She looked sad. "I'm sure I'll cry buckets when you leave."

"Well, then let's get to studying so I'll feel like I've at least equipped you the best I could before hitting the road again."

With that, they went into a deep study of God's Word. That was the scene that Ericka walked in on. She just stood there and stared. Both Noel and Willy shoulder to shoulder, sock feet on the coffee table, with a book between them. They were discussing something that was foreign to her, but she couldn't take her eyes off the couple.

Finally, the couple looked up.

"Oh hello, Mrs. Franklin. Dinner will be ready shortly. How was your day?" Willy asked, all from his comfortable spot on the couch.

Ericka wrinkled up her nose and shook her head. "What are you reading?"

Noel jumped up nervously. "Oh, we were just, uh…we were just reading the Bible. That's all."

Ericka shrieked, "The Bible! Why in the world would you do that?" clearly seeing it a waste of time. She wondered what was wrong with her daughter.

Noel looked over at Willy for a rescue. She was as nervous as a cat on its ninth life spooked on Halloween night.

Willy held up the closed Bible and tapped it gently. "This is the reason for your daughter's changes, Mrs. Franklin." He looked over to see if Noel was okay with him sharing. She gave a slight nod of the head. Willy leaned forward. "See, your daughter has chosen to believe everything written in this book. She came to a point in her life where she saw the gulf between God and herself. She's learned that the only way to get to God is through His Son, Jesus Christ. She saw her need for a Savior, and she has chosen the One and Only Jesus Christ to save her from her sins, so that she may escape hell's judgment and live forever with God."

"Oh, well, I don't have to worry about all that stuff. I don't sin." Ericka waved her hand and spoke as she walked away. "But Noel, on the other hand, could use a little help, I suppose."

Noel was about to come unglued but bit her tongue.

"Oh, I guess it's all right for her to read the Bible so long as she doesn't become a Jesus freak or something weird like that." Ericka turned to go when she heard these words.

"I am a Jesus freak." Noel was soft and respectful yet firm.

Willy got up and put his arm around her shoulders. "Me too, Mrs. Franklin."

The couple just stood there, strong in their beliefs and made even stronger by standing together.

Ericka tossed her head and growled as she left the room. Noel collapsed into hysteria after she left. Great sobs soaked the front of Willy's shirt as he pulled her to him in a loving embrace.

She finally pulled back. "I just couldn't let her talk about my Jesus that way." She was shaking her head violently. "I just couldn't." She cried some more but was calming down. "Thanks so much, Willy, for standing with me."

Willy thought his heart would melt. He brushed the back of his hand along her cheek. "Anytime." He took her hand. "Hey, let's go out to the veranda and pray."

They went out and knelt on the cold cobblestone and prayed their hearts out for her parents.

After that, they went to prepare the last parts of the meal. When all was ready to eat, Burt came to the table, but they noticed that Ericka wasn't present. Noel gently knocked on their bedroom door. When there was no answer, she went hesitantly in. She found her mother asleep, a vodka bottle nearby. Noel wanted to break down and cry again, but she didn't. She quietly tiptoed back out of the room and closed the door. She went to her room and pulled out some pretty stationary and wrote her mother a simple note saying, "I love you, always. Your daughter, Noel." She then discreetly went back into her mother's room and laid it on her vanity, where her mother would find it in the morning.

When Noel sat down at the table, Burt asked, "Is your mother coming to eat? Is something wrong with her?" His mouth was filled with spaghetti at the time.

"No, Dad. I think Mom is just tired today. She's had a hard day. Maybe she'll be hungry for a midnight snack. I'll leave some chocolate out for her," Noel quietly answered.

Burt looked at his daughter. She was acting strange. But then he really wasn't around her much, so what did he know?

"It was good. Thanks," Burt said and excused himself for the evening.

Both Willy and Noel looked at each other and smiled.

"I can't believe he said it was good." Noel was so excited at the small glimmer of hope.

"God is good all the time," Willy said as he sucked in a long strand of spaghetti.

"You're crazy. Do you know that?"

"Hmm. It seems like I've been told that once or twice."

They cleaned up the kitchen and then went to the beach to watch the sunset. They walked along the shore, the wind doing wild things to their hair.

"So how was your day with Kevin?" Willy asked.

"I wish I knew why I was so attracted to him. When I think clearly, which is when I'm not around him, I can see that from the world's viewpoint, he's a real jerk." Noel bent and picked up a broken shell. "But it's just like this broken shell that seems crushed by the weight of the ocean. I see Kevin broken by the weight of this world. I think his actions are only a lashing out of the turmoil inside. He's had a hard time of it, and he turns to everything to fill that hurt inside. I know. I've been there," she whispered. "But the sad part is that it only makes things worse, not better. All of his addictions and his constant need for sexual fulfillment are just his way of dealing with the pain and emptiness." She paused. "How do I tell him that only Jesus will take the pain away?" Noel's passionate voice prevailed.

Instead of answering her, he did something *Willyish*. When he didn't answer, she watched him. He began to pick up broken shells. In just a few minutes, his pockets were full.

"What are you doing?"

"Why don't you help?" Willy asked.

So she slowly began to pick up broken shells too. When she had a handful, Willy motioned them over to a huge tree that had washed up on shore probably many years ago. He got there and fell to the ground on his knees. He began to take the shells and spread them out on the tree log. Noel followed suit, still wondering what in the world he was doing.

When he had emptied his hands, he looked at Noel. "Noel, I don't have the answers you seek. But I know God does, and He wants Kevin to have salvation more than you do. All these shells are the Kevins of this world, and the Erickas and Burts and…"

Noel caught on and began to give every shell a name, a name of a person she knew, her parents, their friends, family, Kevin, her school friends.

When she was done, Willy said, "Let's pray for each shell."

Willy began. He picked a up a shell and prayed for it by name. When he ran out of names he could remember, Noel took over. Both were fixated on bringing those broken lives before the Lord. People walked by and gave them strange looks, but neither noticed. They were fairly covered with sand by the time they were done, but neither cared.

Willy turned and leaned his back on the tree and entreated Noel to join him. She jumped over and slid down next to him.

Willy pointed to the sunset, "May the Son set in each heart we prayed for."

Noel didn't know what to say and didn't want to spoil the moment. The sunset was spectacular. She wondered why she hadn't done this more often. She shivered as the temperature dropped.

Willy put his arm around her and rubbed her arms to get them warmer. As soon as the sun finished setting, Willy hopped up, helped Noel up, and led her to the car.

"Thanks for bringing me. I can never get enough of the ocean," Willy said as he opened Noel's door.

"Well then, you'll be pleased to know I've set up a time for you to come back tomorrow. Here's the plan. I have my interview and will leave early. We might have to do our jam time in the evening. Then I'll come home and change. Then we'll leave to pick up Kevin and eat at our favorite burger place, In-N-Out Burger. Then we'll go to the beach and stay until you're ready to leave. Kevin and I will do our talking at the beach." She was moving through traffic so easily, but Willy had white knuckles. "How does that sound?" Noel then noticed his tense face.

"Uh…how does what sound?" Willy asked.

"Did you not hear a word I said?"

"I just want to know one thing. Is this why you dye your hair?" Willy asked between clenched teeth.

"That's a bizarre thing to ask. What's it to you what I do with my hair?" Noel asked, confused at what in the world Willy was asking.

"Well, if I lived here, I would too, because in a matter of just a few months, I would be gray." Willy's eyes were wide, and he was still holding onto the dashboard as though it were a life preserver.

Noel busted out laughing. "You get used to the traffic. Really, you do."

She repeated the plans, and Willy tried to pay attention.

Willy was ready for bed when they got home. They both went down the hall and at the end went into their separate wings.

Willy turned and smiled with a thumbs-up at Noel. "Everything's gonna be all right," he said before exiting to his room.

CHAPTER 15

Willy popped up his skateboard and went into the telephone booth. He leaned against the glass frame as the line rang. He sure hoped Sky Blue was home.

"Yo. This is Sky. Whatcha got?"

Willy laughed at the way he answered his phone. "What I got is something you gotta hear, man."

"Willy, is that you?"

"Yep." He did a drum roll on the mouthpiece. "The one and only YoYo Willy."

"Whatever your excuse is, the answer is no." Sky Blue wasn't happy. "Being part of the band means every tour, no exceptions." Sky Blue was used to his players calling just before tour, wanting more time. Not that he blamed them. He did too. But that wasn't part of their life. It wasn't that it happened every time, but it did happen.

"Man, I'm already here. What are you talking about, dude?" Willy wanted to know what was up with his attitude.

"I'm sorry. What is it that you need, man?" Sky Blue asked as he chilled out.

Willy switched his feet back and forth. He was nervous. If his plan didn't work out, it could mean heartbreak for those dear to him. But he felt this was something he needed to do. "Hey, man! I found your girl!"

"What?" Sky Blue was at a complete loss.

"I found your girl. You know, the lead female vocalist to partner with you."

"Whoa, whoa, whoa! Now wait just a minute." Sky Blue laughed. "Just where did you find this girl, and how do you know if she is good enough? How do you know if she'll complement my style? And even if all that were perfect, can she handle road life, especially with a bunch of extreme guys like us?"

Willy knew he wouldn't be easy to convince. "I think she's the one. I tell ya. I've listened to her for almost a month now. She's the one." Willy was being bold, he knew. But he felt he had to in order for Sky Blue to even give Noel a chance.

"I don't know, man. I've been looking for some time now. This isn't an easy fill, ya know," Sky Blue said despairingly.

Willy knew that a bargain was in order. "Hey, listen. Just give her a try. I'll tell you what. Why don't you come early next week, and on Wednesday, we can meet at the Waffle Queen in Los Angeles on Mapque Avenue, say at nine a.m. Breakfast is on me. What do you say?"

"This sounds very familiar," Sky Blue said slowly. "Should I fear wearing syrup again?" Sky Blue was remembering just a year ago, when he'd first meet Willy. Sky Blue shuddered as he recalled that sticky breakfast when Willy had made a deal to bring a replacement drummer, only to find out he was the deal. In his excitement, he used Sky Blue as a napkin. He convinced him to listen to him audition. But of course, in the end, he was happy it had worked out so well.

"Um…well, you might be safe. I'll order something else." He knew what Sky Blue was thinking. He hoped it turned out to be the same ending that his first breakfast with Sky Blue did.

"You're killing me, dude!" Sky Blue said.

"Seems to me the only thing you have to lose is a nice, hot breakfast."

Sky Blue didn't want to do it, yet if he really did want to add a front stage female singer to the group, why not start with a suggestion. "Okay, okay. But I ain't promising anything."

"All right, all right. I just asked if you would give her a chance." Willy had his hands up in the booth. "I wouldn't expect you to keep someone you don't like."

They finished meeting plans and hung up.

Willy clapped his hands and shouted, "Yahoo!" right in the street as he popped down on his skateboard and headed back to Noel's. She'd be home soon from her interview. "Now," he said, "for the next step, to ask Noel without getting her hopes up. This might prove harder than asking Sky Blue," he said out loud.

Willy let out a whistle when Noel walked into the house. She was sure done up to the hilt. It's not that she was unattractive; Willy was just not used to seeing her so different. Her outfit was left at the complex, so she was in her jeans and a t-shirt, but you could tell by her haircut and style, her make-up and nails, that her dress wasn't something Noel would normally wear. Noel rolled her eyes at him.

"Ready to go?" she asked, assuming his big grin was that he was thrilled to go surfing.

"Yep! You bet! "You wanna drive?" She offered to toss him the keys.

"No way. Are you kidding?" Willy put up his hands and shook his head. "If I could get there on my skateboard, I would.

"So tell me how the interview went." Willy asked.

"Ah, well, just like they always do. I've been well trained in how to avoid answering questions, how to smile and play the part. I most often feel like a politician; lots of smiles and waving, and the rest is just lies." She continued to drive smoothly, only with millions of other cars. "Of course, everyone wants to know what my future plans are." Noel paused. "You know, today wasn't about me or the interview; it was about Jesus. Because I'm learning, though the hard way, that honoring my parents brings honor to my Lord. So, though I don't like interviews, I don't like publicity at all, but my parents thrive on it. I wanted to do this for them, so I tried to answer the questions with what they might want to hear. It actually became easy, even to have my hair, make-up, and nails done and to be squeezed into pantyhose and that fancy dress. It's all worth it, if it pleased my heavenly Father."

Wow. Willy didn't know what to say. He was touched by her attitude. "That's my girl!" popped out of his mouth.

Noel looked over. "Since when did I become *your* girl? Am I missing something?"

Willy put his hand through his hair. He didn't often stick his foot in his mouth, but when he did, he stuck the whole foot, shoe and all. "You're right. I forget at times that you're taken. Bad choice of words. I'm sorry." *Whew!* He wasn't sure he was going to make it out of that one.

"Taken?" Noel said. "Taken by whom?"

"Kevin, of course."

"I'm not taken, nor am I up for grabs. I'm not going to say that, at times, I still yearn for Kevin to hold me, and I long for that intimacy we once shared. But I know that's wrong. Therefore, I must crucify that part of my flesh until it is submissive to God's will, though it's not easy when I look into his eyes or he touches me. I don't know if it's him or my own issues of wanting to be loved. And that's the only way I understand it, coming from a

Hollywood viewpoint. Passions can get very carried away when you're not a Christian, and there is no reason to hold back."

Willy was thinking it was a very odd conversation and getting way too personal.

"But now, as a believer, I feel I don't have the right to just do whatever I want in that area. Maybe you could show me some scriptures on that later tonight?"

Willy was thinking, *That's the last subject I want to discuss with you!* That wasn't what he bargained for. "Uh…yeah…uh…"

"There are rules about such things, right?" Noel looked over at him.

"Yes, there are." Willy knew he had to be blushing.

"Good. Because I want to obey in every area. I'm so glad you're here. You've taught me so much already. What am I going to do when you leave?"

"Come with me!" Willy blurted out. And then he covered his mouth, but it was too late. He had messed up. Though he planned to talk to her, that wouldn't have been the place.

"What are you talking about, drummer boy?" Noel demanded.

"Oh nothing. We can talk about it later."

"I want to know now," Noel said, curiosity suddenly overtaking her good sense.

"I don't want to talk about it right now. Maybe later or tomorrow would be good."

"Okay, later. But don't forget." Noel didn't want to drop it but felt like she had to.

"Oh, I won't forget."

Noel wondered if she'd make it all day without the suspense killing her.

They pulled into a pretty rundown neighborhood, and a few more turns put them pulling into Kevin's driveway. Kevin came out right away, tossed away his unfinished cigarette butt, and jumped in the just-vacated front seat.

Willy's heart went out to him. He sure hoped Kevin wasn't getting into the water with all that metal on. *He'd surely sink to the bottom,* Willy thought. He pushed on his shoulder. "Hey, man. It's good to see ya again."

"Good to see you too if it means you brought my girl back," Kevin said as he reached for the radio and turned it on to a hard rock station. "Yeah, it just isn't the same without you, Christy."

Willy locked eyes with Noel in the mirror. Willy had forgotten her alias. He'd become so used to calling her Noel without a care. He was sure going to have to be on his *p*'s and *q*'s not to mess it up for her. It was important.

"She came back on her own free will, and if I remember correctly, you were the reason." He didn't want to raise Kevin's hopes, yet he wanted Kevin to know he was cared about.

"Well she's here, and that's all that matters." He was caressing her shoulder. "Hey, babe, ya going to get a six-pack, aren't you?" he asked.

Noel looked in the rearview mirror, licked her lips, "Hey, Kev, I don't think so. It's one of the changes I've made in my life."

"Well, does that mean *I* can't have a beer or two?" Kevin asked indignantly.

Noel, not really sure how to field that one, said, "Well, no. But I thought that since we were going to be talking, you would want to be thinking clearly."

"I hope we are gonna do more than talk," Kevin said suggestively.

Willy had to suck in his cheeks not to laugh at the kid.

"Kev, please. You know what we agreed to," Noel pleaded.

"I was hopin' you'd changed your mind."

Noel gave him the death look.

Kevin put up his hands. "Okay, okay. We can talk."

Willy just sat back and prayed.

It wasn't long before they were at the burger place. They ordered and tried to find a seat, but the place was packed.

Sitting outside, Willy was rewarded with the best burger and fries he'd ever had from a fast food place. He slapped Kevin. "Good choice, my man." He took another bite of burger and looked at Noel. It seemed from the short time Kevin had observed Noel and Willy that there was some chemistry sparking between them.

"Looks like the two of you are an item," he said with a hint of jealousy.

Willy stole a glance at Noel, wondering what she'd say, but she didn't look eager to jump on that one. Willy tapped his thumbs. "We're just good friends."

"Yeah right!" Kevin said and took up his tray.

"I guess he's ready to go," Noel said quietly as she got up with her tray too, leaving Willy with a messy table and a heavy heart.

Willy helped carry stuff to the beach. He had made two trips while Kevin just carried his towel and radio. Noel had overloaded herself, and Willy removed a few items

"I don't mind. I'm used to it," she said.

"But I do. And no lady is going to overload herself as long as I'm around." Willy smiled.

Noel laid out the big beach quilt, and then Willy helped set everything out while Kevin walked off for a cigarette.

At least he's being polite, Willy thought. When all was ready, he said, "I'm going in to catch a wave. By the way, you should join me sometime. The surf is great."

Noel just smiled and waved. Willy then took his wetsuit and found a changing place, then he rented a surfboard for the afternoon. The crashing waves were calling him.

Noel watched him go. He was certainly a special guy. She'd never met anyone like him.

Kevin plopped down and turned on the radio. He had on his sunglasses, but that didn't dim his view of Noel's curves and legs. She was in cut-off jean shorts and a t-shirt with the sleeves rolled up to her shoulders for a better tan. She was on her knees, facing him. Kevin was glad he had his sunglasses so he could take in his fill.

Noel watched the people in the water, hoping she would actually see Willy up on the board. And she was taking the time to pray before talking with Kevin.

"Kevin, could you turn off the radio for a bit?" she asked when she felt ready.

"What, don't you like my music now that you're strung up with this drummer boy?" Kevin was hot tempered.

Noel dropped her head in irritation and then raised it. "No, Kev. It's not about your music. I just wanted your full attention. That's all."

Kevin lay on his back, with his hands under his head. "It's not like it's hard to give you attention."

Noel was getting exasperated before even starting. "That's not the kind of attention I was talking about."

"Hey, I'm all ears," Kevin said and added to himself, "and eyes."

"I guess, Kevin, I want to tell you what has happened to me," Noel began. "I know I tried to tell you when all this began to take place back in the spring, but I don't think you understood. Then I was so unkind when I left after graduation. I can only imagine you were confused as to who was the real me. But I want to share what all has been going on." Noel could tell that Kevin was nervous, but she didn't let that deter her. "All my life, I've been searching for answers. Then, in high school, things began to be unbearable and I tried to fill my brokenness with everything. I immersed myself in alcohol to dull the pain. Do you remember the night way back when we were at that party? We'd just had a big fight earlier that day, and I saw you with another girl, messing around? That was the night I took drugs; got drunk; and ended up in an alleyway, left for dead. That's what my life had been reduced too. Do you hear me?" Noel was passionate as she relived her story.

"So what happened?" Kevin asked.

"My life was a mess, Kev, a real mess. Someone picked me up from that drunken alley and told me about hope. They told me that Jesus Christ was the only way out of my mess. Then, as I made trips to see this lady and her husband, they taught me much about the Bible and God and what His Son did for me. So God worked on my heart and showed me just how wicked living for myself was. These people were so different, like none I had ever been around. They lived out what they believed.

"So after seeing a real Easter story in the spring, I finally understood my sin and my need for a Savior. I had never even thought about hell and that I already carried with me, as a birth certificate, a one-way ticket straight there. But I repented and asked God to save me, and He did." Noel was both crying and smiling.

Kevin was glad he had on his glasses so she couldn't see the queer look he was giving her.

"So I've traded all my addictions for an addiction to the things of God." She wiped a tear. "I can't tell you what joy fills my heart. Oh, by no means, Kev, is it easy, especially when I'm faced with my past. But I long to please God with my life. I read the Bible to find out how He wants me to live. I'm strengthened by what I read. I just can't believe that He'd have me." She quieted for a moment. "And that's what I so want for you." She pleaded, "Kev, are you listening?"

Kevin sat up and pulled off his sunglasses. "If going to church with you means that much and you'll come back and be my girl, I'll go." With that, he put back on the sunglasses and lay back down to watch her.

Noel felt utterly defeated. "It's not about going to church." Noel didn't even know what to say, but she avoided the getting-back-together offer. Noel reached for the suntan lotion for a distraction.

Kevin jumped up on his knees, taking the bottle from her. "Here. Let me help you." He was rubbing it on her shoulders and becoming very close and intimate, saying seductive things in her ear. She could feel his breath on her neck. She was losing her grip when up walked a dripping, smiling, all-dressed-in-black seasonal surfer, Willy.

Kevin backed up from Noel. "Dude, you are like a big, ugly wart, always showing up when you're not wanted." Clearly, Kevin didn't take kindly to being interrupted.

That scene was doing all kinds of things to Willy's heart. For that reason alone, Kevin's comment went unheeded. Willy didn't know why this bothered him. *Is my protection of Noel really jealousy? And if it is jealousy, why is it there?* All that went pounding through his heart.

"That was a nice thing to say," Noel said snidely as she jabbed Kevin.

"I just came up for a break and a drink," Willy said, opting to just ignore the scene. He put his board down and sat on it, not wishing to get Noel's blanket wet.

Kevin had gone back to his laying-down spot. "I'd like to say we have something good to offer you, but we ain't got no beer today," Kevin said this to irritate Noel.

Noel got out a water bottle for Willy. He swigged it down and said, "Ah. Nothing like water to quench a thirst." Willy didn't need to ask how things were going; he'd summed up the situation pretty well. "Thanks, Christy. That hit the spot. I'll just rest a bit and then ride some more waves." After catching his breath, he asked, "So, Kevin, do you surf?"

"Not if I can help it," Kevin said dryly. "I don't care to be fish food. Thanks."

"Well, if it's my time to go, then I can't think of a better way than riding in a wave with the setting sun at my back." Willy chuckled.

"Well, in my world, there ain't much to live for," Kevin blasted.

Noel's heart broke for him, as did Willy's. That was the heart of his ministry, broken people with broken lives, but how could he really reach out to this guy when he'd never worn his shoes? But he had to try.

"Oh, Kevin, you're so wrong," Willy said with compassion and zeal. Willy had leaned over as close as his wetsuit would allow. On his knees, he pleaded his case. "Kevin, you're right on with the fact that this world doesn't have much to offer you, and what it does is fleeting and will go up in smoke one day. But God changes everything. I can't tell you just how much he has changed my life. I love Him so much. Man, if He can save me, He can save you."

Kevin sat up. "But you don't understand. You've never been a bad boy like me, strung out on drugs, alcohol, and sex. You name it, I've done it. The man upstairs ain't interested in the likes of me, only choir boys like you."

Noel sat still and prayed her heart out. She didn't want to interrupt, so she put her head between her knees and put Kevin on the altar for God to work in him.

"Kevin, you're so wrong about yourself and me. You see, it doesn't matter how bad or good you are. Both are destined for hell. But while we were here sinning all over the place—that is you and me, man—Jesus died for us. He made a way to cover our sin so we can escape hell's eternal punishment and live forever in heaven with God."

"Wow, man. You got to be kidding. Why would a guy die for me?" Kevin asked, intently listening.

"Because He loves you."

"So if the guy already died, then I should be good to go. I just need my angel wings. Woohoo!" he said as he flapped his arms.

Willy quoted John 3:16. "'For God so loved the world that He gave His only beloved Son, that whosoever, believes on Him shall not perish but have eternal life.' But *believe* is key here. Kevin, you have to realize you've offended God and that not believing in Him is the greatest sin there is. So you must believe with all your heart, soul, mind, and strength. You must repent, man, which will produce a turning from your wickedness. Confess your sin to God, and ask for His mercy on you. Ask Him to save you and be your Lord and Master forever." Willy bent his head down and looked Kevin in the eye, "He'll honor a broken heart and prayer like that, but it must be sincere."

"Thanks. That gives me a lot to think about." Kevin was stunned.

Willy hopped up and picked up his surfboard, put his thumb up at Kevin, and said, "Anytime, man!" He then jogged back out to the water.

Willy spent several more hours in the water before calling it a day. He was worn out, or he would've surfed into the sunset. They stayed to watch the sun sink into the ocean and then left.

In the car Kevin asked, "So, YoYo, man, where are you staying?"

"Uh…uh…," Willy fumbled from the back seat.

"He's staying with a friend," Noel supplied.

"Cool. If you need a place to dive, you can come to my place," Kevin said.

Willy tapped him on the shoulder. "Thanks, man." Willy hoped he wasn't being too forward but asked, "Hey, Kevin, would you like to study the Bible with me? I mean, I can show you the things we talked about and you can get a glimmer of this God we speak of."

"Well, it's not like I got much else to do, so sure, man. That will be cool," Kevin replied wryly.

They went ahead and set up a time to go to Kevin's place.

Kevin turned to Noel. "Christy, you coming?"

"Sure. I'd love to."

He rubbed the back of her head and said, "That's my girl." They were in his driveway, and he hopped out and went around to Noel's window.

She rolled it down.

He leaned in very close to her face and said seriously, "Thank you for sharing." Then he leaned as though he was gonna lay one on her but kissed her lightly on the cheek instead and went into the house.

Noel put her hand up over where he had kissed her. She had a lot to think and pray about. But that was sure a positive sign that he listened and even thanked her.

"What a day!" Willy said as he hopped up in the front seat.

"I just can't believe he agreed to have a Bible study," Noel said in a husky voice as she hit the steering wheel. "I'm so excited about tomorrow. Thank you, Willy, for helping me out. I'd been sharing with him, but he hadn't really been receptive."

"Yeah, and you got me out of a big one too. I knew you didn't want your parents' home revealed, but I wasn't sure what to do."

"This is when the whole alias thing stinks." She sighed. "I feel like I need to tell Kevin because I'm convicted more and more of the lying it makes me have to do, like tonight. Thankfully, Kevin didn't push the issue. I've always evaded where I live and just gone to his place or met in parks and such. But it's getting harder to do." She tilted her head. "But I still want to honor my parents. I guess this is the consequence of disobeying them and coming out of that covering even with Lilly and Peter, and then the problems with you it caused, not to mention that all the folks in Shelbyville only know me as Noel."

"Well, you never know when a change of events might change some of that." Willy was thinking about what he needed to talk to her about.

Noel thought that was a queer thing to say but let it go.

They were quiet for the rest of the way home.

When they pulled in the garage, Willy said, "Hey, Noel, I know it's late, but I was wondering if you'd sing with me. I'm missing my chop time."

Noel couldn't see his face, but she could *hear* his smile.

"Sure. I'd love to. Let me heat something up in the microwave, and then we can play in my room. It's the farthest away from my parents' end of the house. I don't want to wake them if they're sleeping, which, I'm sorry to say, leaves out the piano."

They ate and went to her room.

Willy looked around. What he saw was very *not* pink and *not* teenager. It wasn't really girly at all. It felt strange to be in her room, but he understood the reason. There were pictures of old-fashioned people done in huge, oval, Victorian-style frames, a nice touch to her Victorian themed room. "Well, I guess we can just sing. And, well, you know me, I can use anything for a drum." He went to her fancy desk and did a drum roll. "Hey, is this you?" He picked up a picture of a little girl much like Shirley Temple.

"Yeah, that's me. I don't recall the movie, but it's a shoot from it. It's one of my mother's favorites, so I framed it."

Noel put up her finger to her lips, signaling for Willy to be quiet. She got on the floor and reached far under her bed and pulled out a guitar.

Willy's smile was huge, and he was shaking his head and wagging his finger at her surprise.

She brought it to him and whispered, "My mother doesn't know."

Willy took it and began a song they both knew. She joined in like old times. When they looked at the clock again, it was midnight.

"Oops," Noel said. "That was fun, but we better get to bed or I'll turn into a monster."

"Yeah right! You scare me!" Willy said dryly. He decided not to tell Noel that night but in the morning.

Noel make a mock roar at Willy and then said good night and put her forbidden guitar away.

Willy knew his days with Noel were almost over. Today was Friday, and before they left to go to Kevin's, Willy planned to talk to her. But first things first, he prepared breakfast, with Noel partnering him in his efforts. She liked the new concept of eating as family. Then after breakfast and her parents were gone, Willy plunged in his attack.

"Hey, sunshine. How about some bench time?" Willy asked as he threw the dish towel her way to hang up.

"What do you mean bench time?" Noel spun around at a complete loss.

Willy crooked his index finger, beckoning her to follow him. She did so, curiosity getting the best of her.

Willy walked to the piano and opened his hand for her to sit. "Bench time. I want to hear you play and sing," Willy coaxed.

"We just jammed last night." Not that she minded playing; she loved music, and especially loved singing, but Willy was acting strange, like something was up.

"Please," Willy begged, his smile pleading his case.

"All right. If it makes you happy." Noel slid on to the bench and began playing and singing some of the songs they'd learned together in Willy's bedroom studio.

Willy didn't join her. He was mesmerized by her crystal-clear, strong voice. When she made eye contact, she gave Willy one of her winning smiles. Willy thought she was beautiful. Just watching her was doing things to his heart that scared him.

After some time, Noel inquired, "Why don't you join me?"

Willy very softly returned, "Why don't you join *me*?" He was inviting her to join the Mercy Seat Rockers.

"What do you mean, Willy?" Noel's hands immediately stopped on the keys.

Willy had been leaning over the piano, facing her, but now, he moved around to the bench. She scooted over to allow room for him.

Willy took Noel's hands. "I want you to come with me." He looked into her dazzling eyes. Willy licked his lips. "I mean, I don't know if it'll work out, but what would you think of the possibility of hitting the road with me next week?"

She blinked three times. The silence was like a knife. Then she withdrew her hands and jumped up like a hurt child and backed up against the wall. And through tears, she said, "Willy, that is a horrible thing to do, teasing me. You know how very sensitive I am about music and my singing. How could you? How dare you!" Noel was crushed.

Willy jumped up. He went to her, though she turned her head away. He reached over and turned her chin toward him. He then reached up and wiped a tear from her cheek. "Sunshine, I wasn't teasing you," he said softly.

Their eyes locked for a moment before what he had said sunk in. The closeness of the moment made Noel gasp for air. Willy's face was so close to hers, the closeness was making it hard to breathe.

Willy let go of her and stood back. "I mean, maybe you don't want to do that, but I knew that we, or rather Sky Blue, has been looking for a female vocalist. And I thought of you. I mean, as I much as I'd like to say join me, it's not really up to me, though I personally think you're a perfect fit." Willy grinned at her astonished look. He ran his hands through his wild hair. "Noel, you might want to close your pie hole."

Willy chuckled as he watched her hand come up over her mouth.

"You are serious, aren't you?"

Willy nodded his head.

"I just, uh…I just don't know what to say." A thousand thoughts were going through her mind at once.

"I was sorta hoping you would say yes."

She jumped up and put her hands together over her mouth to control the joyous sobs. With tears, she said, "Yes! Oh yes!" and she went over and hugged Willy, nearly knocking him over. When she finally cleared her head and settled down, she had a bazillion questions that she rattled off.

Willy did his best to answer all her questions. He told her that for some time, the group had been writing songs that included a female voice. Everyone in the group thought it was a good move to bring in a partner for Sky Blue. "We just hadn't found anyone, then you came along, tripping me up."

Both smiled at the way they'd met.

"A lot has changed since then," she said softly. Then Noel squealed, jumping up and down. "I just can't believe it."

Willy raised his hands. "Hold on. I didn't know how to ask you about this without raising your hopes up. But if you weren't interested, then there was no need to get Sky Blue involved. So just realize that Sky Blue is a tough nut to crack, and not only do you need to have a great voice, but one that will complement Sky Blue's, and he has to like you; you'll have to blend in and be able to handle road life, which isn't always easy."

Noel was nodding her head in understanding, some of the thrill leaving her.

Then Willy tapped her on the nose, "But I'm rooting for ya!" He moved away from her. "We better get over to Kevin's. We don't want to be late." On the way out the door, Willy casually said, "By the way, you're meeting Sky Blue next Wednesday morning at nine."

Willy meet Noel's eyes. They were big as saucers.

"So do I need to drive?" Willy teased.

Noel shook her head no, and got herself together before hopping in the car.

Willy let out a low whistle and shook his head. "My, oh my. You're gonna turn heads tonight. I don't know if I can handle the competition," Willy teased.

Noel was dressed in a party dress like Willy had never seen. It was sheer red, sleeveless, and had a low-cut v neck and was bundled at the waist with a huge gemstone belt. It was thigh length, and the material came down in triangle layers. Noel was glad that her mom hadn't made her wear something more revealing. Willy knew she was uncomfortable, as it still was showing more skin than she cared to, but she had let her mom pick it out, so she'd endure it with a smile, not to mention that her mom's hair dresser had come and done Noel's make-up and nails and wisped Noel's hair up into very attractive French twists of types, leaving ringlets, in all a very becoming evening dinner hairstyle. Willy had never seen her hair done that way, but he rather liked it. It certainly made her look like a lady of fame, fashion, and wealth. Willy was getting another glimpse of what it must have been like to grow up in Noel's shoes.

Willy had never known anyone rich, much less famous. It was no wonder her mother had rented a tux for Willy so they wouldn't be embarrassed. Ericka, in no uncertain terms, gave Willy the lecture about using only their alias names and that he'd better not slip up. That made Willy nervous, as he was so used to calling Noel by her real name, not her alias, Christy. He'd even slipped up a few times at Kevin's that very day, but he didn't notice.

Noel giggled as Willy preceded her out the door. "Hey, what is so funny, Miss Henson? What has you cracking up on your way to your own debut into adulthood?" Willy tried her alias last name.

"Well, I'm not sure if it's your skateboard shoes with the black-and-white tuxedo or the puka shell necklace that you put on top of your bowtie." Noel stifled another giggle. "Not to mention that every time you take a step, your drum sticks puff the tails of your suit like a rooster. But what really turns my giggle bucket over is the uncomfortable waddle dance you're doing. You look like a penguin out of water." She knew he was very uncomfortable in the suit, but her mother had insisted, and since it was a special occasion, she had implored Willy to comply with her parents' wishes, which landed him in a very tight, uncomfortable tuxedo.

He turned and, putting on his most ferocious face, growled, "I'm only doing this waddle dance for you, my dear. Not to mention all that goop Burt insisted I put in my hair to *tame* it, he said."

Willy did another low whistle, to Ericka's dismay, when the black, shining limousine pulled up. The white-gloved driver got out and opened the door first for Burt and then Ericka and then Noel. And Willy, who wanted to just open the door and hop in, waited patiently, wondering all the while what a long night it was going to be as he swished his uncomfortable legs before climbing in beside Noel. Her parents were in two compartments ahead of them, the dim glass separating them.

Willy thought it odd. He leaned over and asked, "Do your parents always sit separate from you?"

Noel's answer was to nod her head for fear of tears. Willy had to look out the dark window in order to gather his own emotions. How could parents orphan their kid like this? It was so wrong.

Willy took Noel's hand into his and began to pray. *Lord, God, our Abba, I come to You on behalf of my dear friend Noel. She desperately needs You this night. She needs to feel Your presence as she goes into a godless environment. Lord, I ask that You give her ways to please her parents tonight. Make them proud of their daughter. I pray that You will protect Noel's heart from breaking, should her parents find any displeasure in her. Father, just seeing the orphaned at home, may I be more and more used of You for this orphan and those You bring into my life. Use this for Your glory, and use this in Noel's life to make her more like You. May You take all the rejection and hurt and make something beautiful out of it tonight. I pray You pour out Your grace upon her as she greets and answers questions, that her kindness would stop people in their tracks. Lord, give Noel the words You would have her speak when it is time for the spotlight to be on her. Amen.*

Noel's face was wet when Willy finished. "Thank you, Willy. You really are my knight in shining armor."

Willy just shrugged it off and slipped a sucker into her hand. "Every princess needs a sucker on her special night."

Willy was overly stimulated in the ballroom social cove. He tried to be nonchalant about his gawking, but Noel had to elbow him in the side a few times to get him to pay attention as her escorted guest, but the whole thing just fascinated him. He loved to people watch, and it was certainly the place to enjoy doing that to its fullest.

Willy thought she was a picture of grace, smiling her best. Her eyes dazzled as she greeted each guest and made them feel special by telling them a cherished memory. She looked into their eyes, showing true appreciation for each one. Willy noticed that many of them walked away mumbling something about how nice she was and how much she'd changed. Willy kept praying for her.

Not too long after that, Ericka ushered both Noel and Willy into the formal dining room, where they were seated at the head table. Willy loosened his tie, which seemed to be choking him. He wasn't sure he could eat a bite with all that fancy stuff. Then he nearly choked when he was finally seated and he noticed all the silverware. In all his life, He'd never seen so many forks and spoons for one meal. He glanced over at Noel, who was chuckling as she smiled at him, knowing just what he was thinking. She put him at ease with a wink.

He leaned all the way across the table in a low voice. "Are all these for me?" he asked, pointing to the dinnerware.

Noel giggled and nodded.

Burt then got up and thanked all the guests and gave evening instructions and then sat down to be served. It smelled delicious, but Willy had a sudden loss of appetite, nervous that he'd spill something on his penguin outfit. He glanced over at Noel, who then led him in what fork, what food, and how to eat a meal with the rich and famous. Willy gave her a grateful smile of relief. When he was finished, it was all he could do to keep his seat. He really wanted to high-five his eating partner in the success of the meal. He didn't think Burt and Erika would appreciate that demonstration of success.

So he sat back and looked onto the huge projector screen they had on the wall, where all kinds of family photos were cascading down, most of which were Noel's. They had even gone through the trouble to have little blurbs of her life's milestones flash through the pictures. It was very nice. Though Willy thought they could have easily had her singing in the background, instead they chose some classical instrumental arrangement.

After the meal was over and every one had had their share of fine wine and social fish tales were compared and swapped, Burt got up and shared very kindly about his daughter from her birth through graduation. He was very formal, due to the crowd, but there was no mistaking that he was proud of his daughter, at least at the moment. Then he asked her to come and give her speech about her future and to thank her guests.

Noel was a bundle of nerves. She adjusted her mic. "Tonight is a very special night in my life. I can't think of a finer way to spend it than with each of you. I hold you all very close to my heart. I want to thank each one of you for the role you've played in my life and for the valued influences you've had in making me what I am today." She then looked over at her parents. "I know at times I have disappointed my parents, much to my regret. I enjoyed my younger years on stage and have had a lot of fun making films with many of you." She smiled and named several films, names, and parts. There were smiles and laughter around the room. She then honored her parents. "Mom and Dad, please stand up." She waited for them to do so. "Thank you. Please, everyone, give my mom and dad applause." She was smiling and clapping hard for her parents. She so wanted to please them, yet she must speak of her Father. When the applause died down, she finished up by saying, "I do not know what my future brings, what I will pursue, or where I'll end up, but this I do know: I will live every day following Jesus, who loves me so." With that, she blew a kiss to the audience and left the platform in an uproar of praise and applause.

Both Burt and Ericka stood up and bowed several times. Then Burt went back to the platform.

"That's my girl!" He smiled. "Now let's forget about all that jazz, and let's boogie on into the dance hall for some tango."

Willy placed a quick kiss on Noel's cheek. "That was a magnificent twirl of words for someone who's been through all you have."

"God makes beauty out of ashes, doesn't He?" Noel flashed Willy a bright smile.

Willy whistled and then stepped back and did an exaggerated look up and down Noel. "I'd say so!" He then put out his elbow. "Miss Henson, may I have this dance?" She put her hand through his, and they walked onto the dance floor. Willy whispered, "Hey, by the way, I've never danced before, so watch your toes." Noel giggled.

Willy wasn't so sure he liked this. Having Noel so close to him was causing extra beats in his heart. His face was flushed he was sure, for he was getting hotter by the moment.

As they gently whirled away, their eyes locked for just a moment. Neither wanted to look away.

Then Willy suddenly got a tap on the shoulder. He turned and asked, "Yeah? This here's YoYo Willy. Whatcha got?" He held out his hand for a shake only to stare into the bewildered look of a dashing young man in perfect formal attire, it was obvious Willy sincerely didn't know what he wanted.

The guy raised his nose a bit, looked at Noel, and snidely said with a bow, "I wish relieve this beauty out of the grips of the likes of you." Then he continued. "As well as to have a chance to dance with our gorgeous guest of honor." He gave Noel a ravishing look-over.

Willy hated to leave her. He rolled his eyes. "Gorgeous is right." He smiled at her. Then he turned to the guy. "Enjoy your dance. It's your only chance." He looked over the guy's head and said to Noel, "I'll be back," as he gave her a wink.

As they began the dance, Noel watched Willy over the guy's back. She saw him take out the drumsticks from his back pocket, tapped them together, and do a drum roll in the air and flash a great smile just for Noel and then turned back around and left the dance hall. As it was, Willy didn't get to dance with her again. She had a continuous long line of offers, so Willy spent his time praying for her and people watching. Quite the night, he thought. He even wondered what it would've been like had Kevin been there as Noel's guest. Before he knew it, he was getting back into the long limo. Noel laughed. Willy's jacket was over his arm, his tie lay loose midway down the front of him, his shirt was untucked, and his shoes were in his hands.

"What is it?" he teased.

"Oh nothing. You're just so funny. That's all." She scooted over for him to sit and took the unwanted things from him.

He looked over at her. She was so beautiful, even at that early morning hour. "You were brilliant tonight," he said softly as the moonlight bounced off her cheeks.

"Thank you for being here. Your courage gave me the strength to remember who I really belong to." A single tear ran down her cheek. She pointed up. "He was spectacular tonight!"

Willy put his arm around Noel. "Yes, He sure was!" Willy laughed. "God has never let me down, but He has left me in some rather humorous predicaments, like having dinner with the rich and famous and having so many forks to choose from."

He squeezed her shoulder in thanks for helping him out. But then he just left his arm there, and she was content to stay in the safe arms of the man she was becoming so attached to.

CHAPTER 16

"Chill out, sunshine. You're going to wreck. Look. You've been chewing your lip all morning," Willy implored.

They were on their way to meet Sky Blue, and Noel was a bundle of nerves. Willy had to stifle his amusement when Noel came to the breakfast table. For the big day, Noel had dyed the tips of her hair blue. And then she put tiny rubber bands around the tips. He supposed she had ten of those rubber bands at the end of her hair. She wore a pair of jeans with boots and an untucked blouse. Her parents didn't say anything, and it was unusually quiet, due to Noel's nerves, Willy guessed. He knew that her parents didn't know what she was doing. There was no sense in upsetting her parents if she didn't make the cut.

Sky Blue was early that morning and sitting out on a bench, waiting for Willy and the chick he was sure would *not* work out. About fifteen minutes later, he saw a pink Camaro drive in and park. His eyes got huge as Willy stepped out of it. He didn't even notice the girl, as his eyes were on Willy and the set of wheels.

Willy came up and punched Sky Blue on the shoulder. "Hey, man. So good to see ya!" Willy gave his smashing smile into the face of skepticism. "Why don't we go in," he said, leading the way.

Sky blue turned to follow Willy and the chick inside. He got a semi-private booth. Willy and Noel sat on one side, across from

Sky Blue. After they were settled, Sky Blue gave the chick a closer look. He was not impressed with what he saw. He doubted that things were going to improve. He was quiet for some time as he scrutinized Noel.

Then his expression changed and he said, pointing a finger, "Hey, wait a minute. Don't I know you from somewhere?"

Before Noel could answer, the waitress came to take their orders. Willy was so thankful, as was Noel, for all she'd managed so far was mumbling.

"Shall we order?" Willy said for a distraction. Then he took a moment to flip through the menu and then spoke to the very patient waitress. "I think I'd like biscuits and sausage gravy." Then the rest ordered.

After the waitress left, Sky Blue cut to the chase. "So tell me, Miss, uh…whatever your name is, a little bit about yourself." Sky Blue then sat back to listen with a closed heart written all over his face.

Noel was more nervous than she'd ever been in her life. She looked over at Willy, who nodded for her to go ahead. "Well, uh…I, uh…well, um…" She wiggled in her seat and looked up. "Well, uh…what do you want to know exactly?" she blurted out.

Sky Blue let his exasperation be known. He speared Willy to the booth and slapped his hand on the table and was about to get up when Willy saved the moment. He hoped to distract his unyielding boss and give Noel some time to gather herself together.

Willy smiled as he wiped his gravy clean with his last bite of biscuit. "Umm…sure good like momma makes." Then he looked at Sky Blue. "Hey, man, how was your break? Did you go see family or interview for a wife, or rather, better asked, did you scare some unsuspecting female into filling the role?" Willy was being his usual jokester self, and it did the trick.

It usually made Sky Blue mad whenever someone pointed out that he was still single, for he wanted a wife, but that was proving to be a difficult thing to come by. He gave Willy a low growl and the eye and said, "That's none of your business."

Noel cleared her throat and took both men by surprise. As she began, Sky Blue shook his head in disbelief. She couldn't possibly be the same girl who just did a ballerina dance over her words just a minute before. Willy sat back and just stared. She sat up straight with a totally professional air, her shoulders squared, her voice clear and concise.

"First of all, I want to thank you for coming here. Thank you for taking the time on my behalf. You can call me Noel Franklin, but my life runs after a different beat. I'm an above-average graduate of Regehetti High School. I've been playing the piano since I was nine years old. I've perfected my music ability greatly over these years of tedious practice. After some time on the ivory, I began to hit the strings. This is more of a love for me. I'm a self-learner, and it came to me naturally." She was so serious and proficient.

Both guys still had dumbfounded looks on their faces.

She finished by saying, "I've been singing since I was in diapers. I took choir all four years in high school. The instructor commented that my voice needed no extra training and that it was of professional quality. It's obvious that God has ordained that this voice be used to bring Him glory. The question is, will that be with the Mercy Seat Rockers or not?" She finished and waited for an answer, clearly no longer intimidated.

Willy let out a silent whistle. Not many people got away with talking to Sky Blue like that. Willy rolled his eyes, thinking she'd done well until the end. He looked over at his boss. Clearly, he was without words too. But what shook him up the most was how quickly she went into acting to pull this off and how good she was at it. Willy saw it for what it was, and it concerned him.

Sky Blue came to attention, realizing she'd not shared anything about her personal life. He cleared his throat. "Well, all that might be true, and let's just say that it is. Bus life isn't easy. You can't bring along a husband or easily maintain a relationship. You've only a tiny area to sleep in, and the schedule is very demanding. You really have to sacrifice a lot to do this kind of work and ministry. As well, we are a close-knit group, and I won't have anyone upsetting that, not to mention that having a mixed band is difficult at best, and our reputation is to be upheld at all times. Even if you can sing great, it doesn't mean that you and I will blend. You have to be just the right fit." He was frowning, just thinking about that blue-tipped, wild haired Thing singing with him.

Noel listened, taking in all he was saying. She knew she could do it. She didn't have anything to lose and had no plans for her future.

"So, where did you two meet?" Sky Blue asked.

Noel and Willy looked at each other. Willy could see the sudden pain and fear there. He knew what she was thinking.

"Um…hey, Sky Blue. Can I have a word with you for a moment?" Willy scratched his head as he moved to get up.

Sky Blue didn't look like he wanted to get up. He looked to the girl and back at Willy, sighed, and said, "Sure."

So both men went outside and left a very vulnerable Noel sitting in the booth, shivering.

Sky Blue leaned up against his car, not having a good feeling about it. He crossed his arms and demanded, "Let's have it!" He knew something was up.

Willy was nervous and switched his feet back and forth. He smiled and began. "You just wouldn't believe it if I told you how we met." He was stalling.

"Try me," Sky Blue challenged dryly.

He knew he had to get it out, so he plunged in. He ran his hands through his wild hair. "Now don't freak out on me when I tell you this."

"What are you gonna tell me," Sky Blue retorted and threw his hands up, "that she was running from the law and crashed into your car?"

"No, nothing like that exactly." Willy waved his hand, "Um… well, actually"—he laughed. "You just won't believe it." He switched his feet again. "Do you remember the girl I tripped over, Christy Henson?"

"Yeah. What does that have to do with anything?"

Willy paused before he dropped the bomb. "Well, this girl Noel and her are one in the same." He plugged his ears, waiting for the blast.

He didn't have to wait long. Sky Blue had been casually leaning against his car. He jumped forward like it was on fire and got in Willy's face. "You got to be kidding, man!" He slapped his leg. "There's no way that's the same girl!" He paced around the car and then came back. "And if that's true, then it's totally out of the question!" He slashed his hand down through the air. "No way am I going to get on stage with that kid you found in the street as a singing partner. Just no way!" He was about to get into his car.

"You know you said that this band has a standard, and it is to be held in high regard as followers of Jesus. Yet, right now, you are using a double-standard. You're not even willing to give her a chance but made a decision without even listening to her sing." Willy was desperate, but he also was a man of justice, and he didn't want to see prejudice toward anyone. He knew he was possibly stepping across the line, but for the love of his friend, he wanted to point out the inconsistency in his life.

Sky Blue slowly closed his car door and turned toward Willy, his voice calm and his demeanor contrite. "Thank you, Willy, for reminding me of an area I struggle with. You are right." He paused and groaned as he looked around and got back in Willy's face. "It's just that the last time Cookie brought me 'the perfect girl,' she was a real kick in the ear!" He walked around in deep thought. He then turned back. "I mean, what do you even know about her?"

Willy let out a low whistle and a chuckle. "Well, I know that she's had a rough life. But, great news, she got saved in the spring. She's zealous for the things of God, yet I think she'd be so relatable to those we minister to at our concerts. I wouldn't have brought her up for a suggestion if I didn't think she was the perfect fit, not only for you but for the good of the band. She's a hoot to be around, yet she is kind and fun loving. She'll bring a challenge to us all if we have in any way fallen into complacency." Willy didn't think he should divulge her parents' profession. He wanted to leave that up to Noel.

Sky Blue couldn't believe he was actually doing this, but he was agreeing to let her audition for him. Willy followed Sky Blue back into the restaurant and to the booth where Noel was about to leave because they'd been so long in coming back. This was so much like what he'd done just a year before, when he picked up Willy for tour, and that had turned out perfect. Would he be so lucky as to do it again?

They were back at the table, and Sky Blue cleared his throat. "Well, it seems to be in the mix for you to do a couple songs for me. Is this a good time, and do you mind coming to the bus to hit some notes?"

Noel looked at Willy and smiled a huge thank-you. She then turned to Sky Blue. "Sure I can. We'll follow you to the bus." She then placed her hand on his arm and said softly, "Thank you, Sky Blue, for giving me a chance."

At the bus, Jonas greeted her but didn't recognize her either.

Sky Blue took charge. "Okay. Sing something," he demanded with a cold heart.

Noel, not really liking how Sky Blue was handling things, did as she was asked, only mockingly.

She began, "Twinkle, twinkle little star, how I…" She sang this in a baby voice as one would've sung in preschool.

Sky Blue attempted to speak, but she cut him off.

"I'm not sure how it is, sir, that I have offended you by my very existence, but I do not wish to be patronized by you, or anyone, for that matter. You've treated me as a lesser person, and I'll have you know that if you are contemplating us working together, I demand your respect. If I'm not a real consideration, then you're just placating me and I have better ways to spend my time."

Sky Blue was taken aback by her clear description of his heart. He nodded his head. "Okay. You're right. I owe you an apology."

Something that the crew all knew was that Sky Blue did have a kind side and he was fair.

"Thank you. Now, if you'll hand me a set of them there strings, I'll put you out of your misery momentarily."

Willy handed her Cookie's guitar.

She played the first of their hits and was well into the second one when she opened her eyes to see the face of Sky Blue. It was so stark that she quit playing and singing. "What is it? Did I hit a wrong note?"

"No, no. Go on, go on. You're doing fine." Sky Blue shook his head.

"You sure?"

"Oh, yes, I'm very sure," he said with a huge smile of satisfaction.

So Noel picked up where she left off, and then she played three more of their songs before stopping and asking Sky Blue, "Well? Am I gonna make like a puzzle and fit?"

"Well, you sure have a voice. And I *do* think it will complement what I have need for." He paused and then spoke, clasping his hands together. "How about you coming back tomorrow and doing some sheets I give you, and then if that works out, we can talk details, contracts, and business."

Noel wanted to squeal, but she squelched the urge. "Thanks. What time do you want me here?"

He told her the time. As she left, he called after her, "Hey, Noel. Sorry I misjudged you." Though he still couldn't get past the hairdo and the bright green fingernail polish, she did have a fabulous voice, and she seemed to have a sweet heart. But the best part was that she didn't drool on him as many girls did. She respected him as a person, which was strange. *It was as though she understood the stardom aspect and let me be myself.* He shook his head as she departed. *Just maybe Willy was right. She just might be the one. And I'll have to get over the looks.*

"No worries. I'm used to it." She waved her hand in the air and then stepped off the bus.

After she and Willy got into her car, she let out an ear-piercing scream of excitement.

Willy covered his ears. "What was that for?"

"I'm so excited, Willy. It would just be tops to sing in your band." Noel was driving carelessly as she tried to talk.

Willy laughed at her display of excitement. "What are you gonna tell your parents?" He hated to bring her down, but he wanted to know.

"I don't know." She landed quickly. "But I better wait and make sure after tomorrow." She squealed again.

Willy wanted to confront her on the acting that she'd done so well with Sky Blue, but he decided to let it go for now. Instead, he questioned, "So, are you going to tell them about your parents and your acting career?"

"Well, there's no need to do that before an offer is made either. So I guess we'll wait and see." She was contemplative, and then she suddenly spoke. "I wonder what Kevin will say." She sighed. "Well, I can't live his life for him, but this might be a big letdown for him."

Willy thought she still had a strong attachment to Kevin. For someone who broke up with the guy, she sure thought of him a lot. "You seem to be very attached to Kevin."

She tilted her head as she weaved through traffic. "I guess he'll always hold a special place in my heart." She gasped. "Oops. Speaking of, I forgot that we were to meet him thirty minutes ago. Can we take a spin over there?"

Willy chuckled at the sudden change of events. He was learning that nothing was normal with Noel. He said, "Sure." He'd picked up his Bible that morning, so he was set for whatever God sent his way.

Willy had just cleaned up the dinner dishes with a quiet Noel at his side. He knew her wheels were spinning. So he left her to her thoughts. He put up the towel and said, "I think I'll take a run on the beach. See you in the morning." He then tapped her chin with the back of his finger and went for the door.

She grabbed his arm as he turned to leave. "Thanks, Willy," she whispered, and then she got on her tiptoes and place a sweet kiss on his cheek. She wanted to somehow convey her gratitude for all he'd done for her. She didn't see the raised eyebrows or the smile on his face as she went straight to her room.

Now he for sure needed that run.

※

As God would have it, Sky Blue decided to give Noel a try. She had a great interview, and all the guys liked her. Even though she blew them all out of the water when she told them of her parents' fame and wealth, they all cheered her welcome. Both she and Willy told of the very eventful reuniting that they'd experienced just over a month ago. All had huge eyes and much laughter.

But the laughter was quickly snuffed out as she sat down at the table with her parents that evening and told them she was leaving. Both were walking on the ocean edge, letting the waves crash over their ankles, reliving the conversation they'd just had.

They were in the middle of the meal, and Noel couldn't eat a bite. "Mom and Dad, I have something I want to share with you. I'd love to have your blessing."

They lifted their heads and speared Noel to the chair with their dagger eyes.

She put her hands in her lap and spoke softly. "An offer has been made to join Willy's band, and I've accepted it. Right now, it's on tour. It tours eight weeks on, four weeks off all over the country. So I'll be leaving in the morning for two months. I hope to make you proud." She smiled at them.

"I can't believe you! You betrayer! How could you?" Ericka spoke in a voice of terror, scooted back her chair, and left the table.

Burt simply looked at his daughter in disgust. "We bent over backward to get you opportunities to pursue an acting career, and you've done nothing but spit in our faces." He sighed. "We've given you everything that a kid could ever want, and this is what we get!" He then spit his food out and left. On his way to his room, he turned back and said, "When you leave, don't bother to come back."

Noel was crestfallen. She buried her face in her hands and blubbered out of control. Willy just patted her back until she finished crying. Then he asked her if she wanted to join him for a run on the beach. She nodded slowly, and they left. Those were the torturous thoughts that swirled like the angry sea through their heads as they walked silently along the shore.

Noel placed her hand on Willy's arm. She looked him in the face. "Should I have stayed? I mean, is it wrong of me to join the group when my parents are so against it?" She was about to spill over in tears again, he knew she was very upset and wanted desperately to have her parents' approval. Then she asked before Willy could say anything, "Have I let God down?"

Willy hesitated to answer, for he really didn't know what to say. He wanted to be careful with Noel's heart, yet he knew she looked to him for spiritual answers, but this was a tough one. He let out a huge sigh and ran his fingers through his wind-ravaged hair. He began to walk again as he tried to answer her. "Noel, you're in a tough spot. Yes, Scripture tells you to honor your parents. And obeying them when you are young and a teen is what God expects. However, as an adult, though you are still bound to honor your parents, obedience takes on a different hue. Whereas you still honor them, you have to become independent of them. At this time in your life, you are making your own decisions, and, thus, you are making your own consequences. The honor comes in how you treat your parents, how you talk to them, how you respect them, how you love them. It's not about doing everything they say, as it is time for you to break away and become your own family. That's not to say that your parents don't have wisdom to impart to you as mine have me, and I listen and learn from them. But in your case, with your parents not being believers, you're going to be hit with persecution, which I think is what's going on. And many times in these types of situations, no matter what you do, they'll not see it as honoring them because you have dishonored them by becoming a child of God. So I think if you've prayed about this and you feel that God is not telling you no, then you haven't dishonored your parents, no matter their response, for choosing this career that God has led you to." He paused. "As far as disappointing God, well, I don't think so, but only He can answer that one. So ya might just want to ask Him."

Willy looked around and found a small cove of rocks and led Noel there, and he sat her on a boulder. He knelt in the sand in front of her and said, "Hey, my sunshine, let's just go to our Father right now."

Willy took Noel's hands and prayed his heart out for this girl. He'd held his tears in check while praying, but they leaked out when he heard Noel spill her heart out before the Lord Almighty in simple childlike faith of a broken and contrite heart. Her desire to please the Father was so evident that it touched Willy's heart in ways he didn't know was possible.

After they finished, the sun was setting and they turned around and leaned on the rocks and watched it dip into the restless sea. It was a quiet couple who left the beach that night for the last time.

Willy jumped out of Noel's Camaro beside the bus. "Hey, I'll be praying for you. I know this won't be easy. It's times like these that I focus on Jesus, and it makes my situation seem easier." He smiled and patted her arm. "By the way, welcome to Mercy Seat Rockers. I expect this to be a wild ride with you along." He then turned to let her go. She had a mission today: saying good-bye to Kevin and her friends. Plus, she was going to reveal her true identity to them. For soon enough, it would come out all over the place because she was *not* planning to use her alias on stage. "See ya later!" He waved off and hopped on the bus.

Willy waited up that night. Privacy for them would now be reduced to about zero. And he had to find out how it went with Kevin and her friends. So when he heard the car pull up, he exited the bus. They leaned on the side of the big rig, and Noel filled him in on the events of the afternoon.

"My three closest friends were all jazzed at me when I told them about my true identity. Even more jazzed when I told them about how we meet at Lilly's and about out jam sessions, and then I told them about you coming here early and then about the interview with Sky Blue." She chuckled. "They were all jealous and squealing like young teenagers." She laughed. "Yeah, they think it's easy being a star. Whether it's media or music, it's not easy, and the public tends to steal the privacy away from the very people they love and admire. But not me. I mean, it's great to be with the group, more than you know, but I'm not worshiping anyone in the group but my Jesus."

Willy was thrilled to hear that. He even laughed at the description of the girls. He could help but ask, "How was it with Kevin?" That, he knew, was going to break his heart.

It was dark, but he could see her tears by listening to her sniffle as she recounted her last encounter with her high school sweetheart. "He was surprised to see me but welcomed me in. His parents were gone, and it was just him. He was concerned, seeing how serious I was." She was slow in recounting it, as it was tearing her heart out, but she reiterated verbatim what happened. "'Hi, Kevin. It's good to see you. How are you doing?' I asked him. He answered about how he'd been and the questions he was struggling with about the Bible. It really delighted me that he was actually reading it. Then I said, 'I have something to tell you.' He was instantly alert. 'I've been taken on with the Christian music group that Willy is with. Do you remember they came to the high school way back when? They've asked me to join them on tour. I leave in the morning. I'll be back in the area in a few weeks. Look me up with the group and come see me, will ya? I'll never forget you.' He had tears in his eyes when he lifted his head to look at me. He said, 'You're for real, aren't you?' I nodded. He was quiet. Then I said, 'I also have something else to tell you. This is harder than the first, but know this: I never meant to hurt you. I'm really not Christy Henson but Noel Franklin, the only child of the famous Burt and Ericka Franklin.' I told him of the works my parents had done, and he connected the dots. His mouth was wide open, and he was speechless. I finally closed it for him. I shrugged my shoulders. 'It's just something that when you're famous, you have to have an alias for protection. But I'm not going to use it anymore, and you were the first person I wanted to tell. As it spreads, I didn't want you to be left in the dark or feel resentful at my duplicity. I pray for you every night.' I paused. 'I have to get to the bus now. Good-bye, Kevin. I'll keep in touch.' My last words to him were, 'Read, Kevin. All your answers are in the Book, all of them.' He nodded his head, and I walked out." She was crying by the time she finished recounting her day.

Willy put his arm around her and pulled her close. "Shh, shh. It's going to be all right. There are new mercies every morning." He held her until she was quiet and her eyes were dry. Then he took her into the bus, where everyone converged on her to welcome her to the group. Kenzie then showed her where she was to sleep. Then all crashed like waves hitting the seashore.

As they began the tour, they went north to San Francisco and Sacramento, California, on the Ocean Praise West Tour. Sky Blue scheduled several day shows in mega churches so that he and Noel could practice some serious stage scenarios and blend their voices together in a bigger atmosphere than the bus offered.

They'd been through one song when Noel hit a wrong note and Sky Blue slashed his hand down. "It's a cut, guys." And all the music immediately stopped. "I thought you knew this one! You can't make that kind of mistake on stage! It'll ruin us!" he bellowed at her, coming across so angry that she cowered backward.

Willy wanted to jump to her rescue, but that was where she had to stand on her own.

"I'll try to do better. I'm sorry, Sky Blue." She blinked her eyes and whispered.

He rolled his eyes and started the band up again and began the song over. That time, Noel did it without a hitch. Afterward, she yelled to the top of her voice, "Yahoo!" She twirled around with her hand up, wanting a high-five from Sky Blue. But after holding her hand up and realizing he wasn't going to play along, she was embarrassed. "You're a mean one, Mr. Grinch," she said, and Willy did a drum roll and Jordan his repetitive victory scale.

Sky Blue wasn't happy and turned to scowl at them and found big grins smiling quietly back.

But Noel was not a quitter. She simply had to find a way to lighten up Sky Blue. So she came in early on the next song on purpose.

Sky Blue slapped his leg. "You're early!" he yelled.

She smiled a saucy face at him, "Seems to me you're late."

What happened was entertaining, so much so that the entire rest of the band stood stock still and had their mouths open, watching. Noel and Sky Blue went toe to toe, nose to nose, eye to eye in a heated argument.

After feeling like she won, Noel said, "I just wanted to see how you handled mistakes, and if I'm not mistaken, not very well." She giggled. "But now that you're loosened up, maybe we can hit it off better than we started out." She turned and said, "Hit it, guys."

She'd no more than turned around when Sky Blue flared up. He was pointing to his chest and talking angrily to her. "Nobody, and I mean nobody, gives the cues around here." He then turned and said, "Hit it, guys."

He shot fire out of his eyes at Noel, but she just giggled.

That time she really got into the song, letting everyone and everything that hindered her fall away. She looked at Sky Blue as though she'd known him a lifetime and had been singing with him for years. Though Willy could tell she'd slipped into her acting roll, she did it so well you would've thought they were a couple, not a sparring, unlikely pair who'd never sung together before. She even got a tiny smile out of Sky Blue.

It was decided that they needed to do that every day for a month or so and that during that time, Noel would only come on stage for three songs, the three she knew the best. She had two days before her first concert night. She could hardly wait, yet she was so nervous.

Later that evening, they were all on the beach, enjoying some down time, when Noel kept trying to catch up with Sky Blue, who really wanted his space and didn't want it to be shared with the blue-tipped, nagging, wild thing. It had been a hard day, and he'd been with Noel most all afternoon, and the last thing he wanted was to spend more time with her. He wanted to take a walk on the beach with a female for sure, but Noel wasn't who he had in mind.

He kept increasing his pace when she'd get close to catching him. She tried to talk, but he ignored her. Finally, when she got louder, to keep from a scene, he stopped with his hand on his hip, and the other he used to air his frustration. He looked around with a sigh.

"Do you ever let up? You've been after me since my feet hit the sand. One thing you're going to have to learn is that living in a bus demands some space, so when I increase mine"—he spread his hands wide open, indicating the space of the beach—"I don't want you filling it!" Sky Blue was so exasperated by the situation.

That crushed Noel. She tried to fight the tears, and she was successful in not allowing them to fall, but they were flooding her on the inside. "I'm sorry you detest my presence. I just came to apologize for the argument at the church today. That was unkind of me. And to see if there was anything I needed to work on. Apparently, it is invisibility."

That was Sky Blue's undoing. He ran his fingers through his hair and let out a sigh and looked around before looking down at her. "Hey, sorry. I was out of line. We can talk in the morning when I lay out some more music for you. Right now, I just need space."

She nodded.

He then patted her shoulder and said, "Really, Noel, I'm glad you joined us. You're a great singer." Then he continued down the beach.

Kenzie, watching from the bus, wondered just what was in store for those two. It tore at her heart to think of Sky Blue seeing someone else. She'd thought there was a chance for the two of them, but suddenly she wasn't so sure since the arrival of Noel.

But the closeness that the two singers would now share made Kenzie shudder.

Someone else was also watching the sparring couple from a distance, and that was Willy. He'd found himself watching Noel often. He had become very protective of her, yet he didn't know why. But whatever the case, her joining the band had him seeing Noel in a whole new light. It wasn't the sweet jam sessions they used to have. Now he had to share her with others—most of all his boss, who was looking for a wife. It made Willy shudder at the thought of those two, so much so that he went in the bus to get a hoodie. Kenzie was aware that he was there. She had watched him hop on the bus. She knew there were tears on her cheeks but just didn't care. Willy stopped in his tracks when he went by the common area, where he spotted her. She didn't turn on her normal bright smile in greeting him. But the reflection told everything. Willy could see her tears and sadness in the window reflection. Though he didn't think that Kenzie knew she could be seen, he still had to stop.

In his sweet concern, he scooted in beside her. "Hey, Kenzie, what has got your smile turned upside down? Why are your eyes watering your nose?"

Kenzie turned and smiled a wet smile at Willy. "Sometimes, I just wonder if there's more. I mean, I knew the touring would be hard, and I was willing to sacrifice for what God had for me. But I wonder if He'll ever have it for me to be a wife and a mother." She laughed softly. "Why am I telling you this? Willy, you're so special and easy to talk to. I'm sorry I just unloaded on you like that. I'm okay. Really I am." She gave Willy her best smile.

"Just call me forklift Willy, taking the load off a heavy heart." He smiled at her.

She giggled at his name. "You know, you're gonna melt some girl's heart, and she'll make your forklift spin its tires," she teased back.

Willy looked out the window and watched a lonesome figure walk along the edge of the water alone. It seemed to him that she needed forklift Willy too. "Sure you're okay?" he asked Kenzie once again.

"Go have fun!" She nodded and shooed him off and reached for the book she had been reading.

He left and made a beeline for Noel. When he caught up to her, sure enough, he noticed tears. "Hey, sunshine. There's already enough water in the sea. No need to add more."

She kicked a broken seashell and looked out over the ocean. She hated being so vulnerable to anyone, especially to Willy. She thought if she spoke, the dam holding back her tears would burst and she'd soak them both. But his concern for her was so touching.

"Want to tell me why, with an ocean of water next to you, you felt the need to wet your cheeks too?" Willy prompted again.

Noel didn't really want to talk about it. But Willy deserved kindness, so she tried to answer him. "I just don't know why it bothers me so much to have Sky Blue's approval, but it does. I mean, I can't seem to please the guy." She was sobbing again. "My very existence seems to be the bane of his," she blurted out.

Willy just listened. He figured there was more to come, and he was right. She threw her hands up. "I mean, for him to be every girl's dream catch, he's my living nightmare. Who'd know such a gorgeous-looking talented guy could be such a toad?"

Willy had to suck in his cheeks to keep from laughing at her description of Sky Blue. Willy wasn't sure what was really going on. She could have a crush on Sky Blue for all he knew. But he did know how one was to react, and that was with the grace that has been given us, so he said, "Hey, listen. I'm not sure what is going on, but, Noel, you have to give grace to Sky Blue no matter what he does to you or how upset he makes you. This is the example Jesus gave us when He said, 'Follow Me.' Scripture makes it very clear that vengeance is the Lord's. And that should give us comfort that God will make all the wrongs right one day, and He'll do it in a manner much more effective than what any of us will do."

On Willy exhorted Noel about her actions and attitude. Not long thereafter, her tears were stemmed and she felt better.

Her smile told Willy that she was ready to take on the world. He thought, *Sky Blue better watch out!*

CHAPTER 17

It was Sunday morning, and they'd just set up in the scheduled church auditorium when Sky Blue hoped up on the stage and flung a newspaper at Noel. His eyes shot fire in her direction. Everyone had stopped their warm-up at that scene.

Sky Blue was pacing back and forth in anger. Finally, he walked back over to her. "What's the meaning of this?" he huffed. "Just what in the world did you tell them?" He slapped his hand down. "What gave you the right?" He walked off.

Noel could see the front page of the Sunday Gazette. It had a picture of the two of them in their first concert together on Saturday night. The snapshot showed what Noel wanted to accomplish. They looked like an item, though that couldn't be further from the truth. They were looking at each other in a particular song as though they'd been doing it for years. Noel was good at acting. She'd done it all her life. And Sky Blue just reacted to her role-playing, so the camera captured a nice picture of the teamwork between the two of them. Actually, Noel thought the picture was a good one.

"What's the big deal?" she asked as she fixed a stray hair. In a mocking voice, she said, "I think I rather look good, but you, on the other hand, could use a different hair color." She was trying to lighten the mood, and if it had been another time, the team would've had a hoot on it.

"This is no time for jokes!" Sky Blue walked over and hit the bottom of the paper. "Read what it says!" He huffed and went back to his angry pacing.

Noel quickly scanned the article. She'd been interviewed that day, as had Sky Blue, for the occasion of a new addition. However, what had been written wasn't true. They'd flat out lied to make it a hot-off-the-press article. Not only did Noel's true identity of her being a daughter of famous movie stars come out, which she thought would happen sooner or later when the camera hungry wolves found her, but they said that she and Sky Blue were engaged with a possible wedding soon. Right there in print for the whole world to see was a newspaper *misprint* of a lifetime. She was a *miss* and planned to stay that way. How they ever got that she and Sky Blue were an item, she didn't know. The item that paper wrote about was no item at all.

She slowly looked up, dawning hitting her like a ton of bricks. "You think I did this, don't you?" She snarled at him. "You think I planned this whole thing to hook you, don't you?" She walked over to him, put her hands on her hips, and tapped her toes in an angry beat. "I'll have you know that there are a whole lot more fish in the sea that I'd rather be falsely accused of than the likes of you."

"Yeah, you don't have a thing to lose. But I do," Sky Blue retorted.

Noel nodded viciously and went back at him. "You're right about that. When I joined you, I lost everything!" With that, she turned and ran from the stage to the bathroom. She sank down against the wall, put her knees up with her head between them, and cried her eyes out.

Sky Blue let out a disgruntled growl and raised his hands up in the air. "What? What have I ever done? Why me? Why do I have to deal with this?" He was walking around in a daze.

Willy was just glad it all happened in the privacy of the group. Willy walked up and picked up the paper Noel had thrown when she left. He scanned the article and looked at the glaring picture. He too thought it was a good concert picture of the group, especially of them two. It was like Noel said; it was supposed to look like that. But after scanning the article below, he knew why Sky Blue was so upset. They really said most all untrue statements and attached true names to it.

Willy knew he needed to stand up for Noel this time. She'd been fighting her own battles, but this one was not fair. He walked over to where Sky Blue was leaning on the backdrop banister, his hand covering his face. "Hey, look. Sky Blue, I realize this is none of my business, but it seems that you're blaming Noel for something she didn't do. I'd lay down my life on the fact that she had nothing to do with the wrong information in this article. I know you don't know her very well. And it might appear as a setup, but I'm telling you it's not." He was soft spoken. "She didn't do this." He paused. "As a matter of fact, if I recall, they interviewed both of you separately. How does she know that it wasn't you who gave the misleading information?" Willy knew he'd gone way out on a limb with that kind of questioning, but he was sure it wasn't Noel's fault.

Sky Blue gave a sharp you-better-watch-yourself look to Willy.

Willy finished by saying, "Hey, man, you ought to know by now that the media can be vicious. Noel is used to it. Why, she probably doesn't even read the paper because she'd spent her whole life avoiding it. Give her a chance, man. I think just as the snapshot said, getting her on will boost the crowd and add a new dynamic to our clientele. The best thing you can do is get some more interviews to correct this poor, misguided journalist. Or better yet, get a wife, and real soon." Willy gave a wink and a big smile, and then he went back to his drum set. He figured that Noel was in the ladies' room, and he wasn't about to go in there, even if the place was on fire. Plus, if he knew Kenzie any at all, Noel was the reason she wasn't at the piano bench. He left a grumbling Sky Blue and began to look over the song arrangement.

As it happened, Kenzie couldn't convince Noel to come back, and there was no time for Sky Blue to make amends, much less do anything about the situation. As God would so deem it, Sky Blue performed without Noel. And he wasn't through the first song when he felt the full brunt of his reckless angered accusation. He couldn't believe, in just one performance, how much he missed her. He'd not realized how much difference having her up there made. She was very show savvy and poured her heart out to the audience. She had a way of showing respect to Sky Blue as a singer, all the while worshiping. It was her spirit he missed so much. She somehow had the captivating connection with the audience that he didn't have.

Sky Blue usually spoke a bit about what God was doing in the course of a concert, whether in church or a coliseum, when he introduced the group. Today he said, "I was reminded this morning that the only truth you can be sure of is the Word of God. The Bible is true and can be trusted. Not everything you read is true." He laughed. "And not much of it can be trusted." He turned around and said, "Let's hit it, boys!" And on the mini concert went. He didn't feel the need to say anything else. He just hoped and prayed that Noel would forgive him and come back. At the moment, he wasn't sure where in the world she was.

※

It was really no surprise at all where Noel was. She was in a phone booth on the floor, leaned up against the glass, talking to Lilly. She'd been greeted by Peter, which started her tears afresh just hearing his deep, caring voice on the phone. Then she thought she'd not be able to stem them when Lilly got on the phone. After she cried hard for a bit, she was able to get through the story.

Lilly had all she could do not to get personal between her and Willy, yet she was Noel's friend, and her friend needed a listening ear and godly counsel. And that was just what the doctor ordered. It was more than an hour later when a joyful Noel hung up the receiver and walked down the street to hail a cab.

Because of the fact that the group was snagged right away to go to lunch with the pastor, Noel and Jonas had peanut butter and jelly together, and then, after reading psalms from the Bible to each other, Jonas challenged Noel in a game of checkers. He didn't try to engage Noel in conversation about the morning's events or the fact that she'd missed the performance. He just went for being a friend where a friend was needed.

Thus, she was in a much better mood by the time the door opened and the group piled in. It was quiet as soon as Noel was spotted, all waiting to see what was going to happen next.

Sky Blue, in his deep voice, said, "Noel, I'd like to see you a moment by the jeep"

She slowly got up, dread heavy upon her. But then she remembered God. She remembered that she didn't have to be afraid, because God casts out fear. She smiled a wobbly smile and walked off the bus behind him.

Outside, Noel was having a hard time looking Sky Blue in the eye. He took his index finger and turned her chin to face him. She still averted her eyes.

"Look at me, Noel," he demanded.

She helplessly complied.

"I am so sorry about this morning. I was wrong to accuse you. I was wrong to react in anger. Can you forgive me?" He had both hands on her upper arms.

Noel was shocked speechless. Sky Blue knew a moment of terror when she didn't immediately respond. He dropped his hands and his head and sputtered, "I can really understand if you can't. I just—"

Then he heard her whisper, "Forgiven."

He looked back at her. A single tear ran down her cheek. He wiped it away and said, "I was so worried that you were gone for good." He stuck his hands in his jean pockets. He looked away for a moment and then looked her straight in the eyes. "I found out this morning that I need you by my side. Your presence was sorely missed." He snickered. "Willy was right. You're a perfect fit."

Noel didn't know what to say. She looked at him, licked her lips, and tilted her head. "I'll be there." She had her thumbs through her belt loops as she rocked back on her heels. Then they sealed the deal with a mammoth hug.

"Now for a little business," Sky Blue said. "One of the things we didn't discuss but is an unwritten rule: no matter what, a show goes on. If you walk out, you stay out. I can't maintain control and run a decent tour if my players can walk out on me like that. I take into account I'm not the easiest person to get on with. But It's true that a captain can't run a ship if all the sailors are diving overboard. So I have a suck-it-up rule. We can take care of the matter later, but people are paying to have us perform. We owe them our best. I know we've had our share of bumps getting started, but I think we can do some smooth sailing now." He tapped the back of his finger on her nose, just as she was accustomed to Willy doing.

Noel played along. She put her hand sideways to her forehead and did the navy salute. "Aye aye, Captain."

Then both went back on board the bus.

Willy never spoke of the event. Actually, no one spoke of it. It was like seeing scripture in action. Willy watched as Noel and Sky Blue became a team. He had to admit they were a perfect fit, only it was giving Willy a fit to watch them. They were so great together. He wasn't sure why the possibility of them being more than coworkers bothered him so much, but it did.

They were on the spectacular Sand Dollar Cove Beach between the northern and southern California tour cities when a hidden sand dollar game broke out. It was a crazy game they were often found playing, kind of like Marco Polo and hide-and-seek all wrapped up in a beach motif, except you had to find the person with a sand dollar in their pocket.

They'd been running hard when both Willy and Noel backed into each other. They turned immediately, Willy grabbing her so she didn't fall. Willy was breathing hard from running. He was so close she could feel his breath on her face. She looked into his eyes. It was an intense moment, and she couldn't look away. Willy searched her eyes. He wasn't sure what was happening, but something told him he needed to get out of this private cove. There was some kind of chemistry brewing, and he was scared of the combination.

"It seems you are desperately looking for something." He looked at her lips. They looked way too inviting. He whispered, "I have what you are looking for." Willy couldn't believe he just said that. What did he mean? He wasn't even sure.

"You do!" Noel yelled. She grabbed in his pockets, found the wanted sand dollar, came out of the cove, and hollered, "Got it! Got it!" Over and over she screamed, waving it in the air, until everyone came out and converged upon her, congratulating her as the winner.

Willy was slow in coming over, not sure what had just happened and that the hidden sand dollar was the farthest thing from his mind when he'd spoken to her. Obviously, she had misunderstood him. He'd lost the game because of it, but had he lost her?

On the way back to the bus for lunch, both Chet and Jordie pegged Willy.

"Hey, man. What's up with the chick?" Chet asked.

"I don't know what you're talking about," Willy innocently replied.

"Come on, man. Yeah, you do," Jordie challenged. "I've been watching you!" He laughed. "Don't need no glasses to see you got it for Noel."

"Oh, we're just friends."

"Yeah right. Just friends. And you're just friends with Kenzie, but you don't look at her that way!" Chet burst out laughing.

Both showed no mercy on him until Cookie and Noel passed them on the way up the stairs.

Noel turned around, hands on her hips. "What are you three up to?"

Both guys about doubled over in laughter.

Willy said, "Well, let's see. With Jordie's five feet nine inches and Chet's five feet seven inches, combined with my six, hmm…I guess we'd be up to seventeen feet and six inches." He grinned and kept on walking up, passing them all. When he reached the top, he didn't get on the bus but waited, leaning over the rail for one last look at the emerald sea below. He didn't ever think he'd get the beauty of this place out of his mind.

All filed into the bus, some still laughing as they passed Willy. He gave them the look, which only increased their laughter.

Noel came and stood beside him at the railing. She said in a hushed voice, "It's beautiful here, like nothing I've ever seen." She was watching the waves crash on the big boulders.

"God is like those mountain boulders, strong, magnificent, stable, never changing; a mighty tower of rock is our God. The waves are constantly crashing against it, but it's not moved from its purpose. It boggles my mind to think upon the power of the ocean, yet it's just an eyelash to what God is really like," Willy said.

It was then that they spotted Sky Blue and Kenzie walking together on the beach.

"They make a charming couple, don't they?" Noel smiled.

"That doesn't make you upset?" Willy implored.

"What?" Noel was confused.

"The couple part of the two of them."

"Well, Mr. YoYo, first of all, I don't know whether they are a couple or not, but I think they'd be great together." She looked at him. "Secondly, as much as we might blend our voices together, he's not my type of guy."

"Could have fooled me, the way you two are." Willy's big eyes showed his jealous heart.

"Then you don't know me at all!" Noel told him and then darted away.

Willy's hand came out of nowhere and grabbed her wrist. "Not so fast, lady."

Noel didn't like being detained and said as much with her facial expression.

"Not to bring up the subject, but I spent the first tour knowing two ladies with a different name, but the same dame."

Noel chuckled and finally smiled.

Willy continued. "So I must admit there are times I'm still figuring out the beat of your heart."

"That makes two of us."

"So if Sky Blue isn't your type, who is?" He knew it was personal and that he stood the chance of severe damage, but he needed to know if he could even be in the running, though he wasn't sure if he wanted to even put on running shoes.

"Sky Blue is way too serious for me, not to mention quite a bit older. We don't have any interests the same other than music and Christ, which is okay, but, well, we just don't seem to hit it off in that way." Then she quietly spoke. "I think when it happens, my heart will keep beat with his and it'll just stick."

There was a good space between them, and they both knew that they had onlookers, just as the couple below them did, so they just looked at each other, neither sure what to think. Finally, Willy looked back out at the ocean, and Noel followed suit. Willy finally broke the silence.

"I love this place. Its beauty is beyond description." Willy breathed deeply the salty air, closing his eyes to get the full aroma of the ocean breeze. "I feel like I can literally see the face of God here when I go down to the water's edge with the mountains surrounding me, my hands raised, praising God. My favorite place to talk to God is at the ocean edge, with the moonlight shimmering over the water. It's like a secret place just between God and me." He paused. "I just can't get enough of it." But he said to himself, *I'll have a lot to pray to Him about tonight.*

Noel was taken in by the beauty of the place and the serenity of the conversation. She spoke softly. "Yes, I can see why you love this place and why you feel so close to God here. It's like the cove is the arms of Jesus holding you and the wind is His breath on your face as He holds you close to His heart." She inhaled, as Willy had, the salty air. "I still can't believe there is so much of California I've never seen, and I'm so ashamed to say I've been here all my life and never known of such places." They were soon interrupted by the very couple who had begun their conversation. All went to the bus for some grub, the moment lost.

That night, they had a fire on the beach. It was unusual that they got that opportunity, but on this tour, they always tried to make time because this section of the coast was like no other. It was their secret hideout. Of course, it was all new to Noel. Willy was humming and playing with a stick in the blazing fire when Sky Blue piped up, "Hey, Noel, we'd all love to hear your testimony. I mean, I've heard it on the interview. But this is the perfect place for all of us to hear it, not to mention that you'll be called on to do this really at any time I ask. I find the best way to share the gospel is through our own personal testimonies of what God has done in our own lives. So could you share how God has changed you, please?"

He then put his arm around Kenzie and got comfortable around the fire.

Willy interrupted before Noel could begin. "Hey, Sky Blue." Then Willy put both of his thumbs up. "Glad to see you took me up on one of the options I suggested not long ago," he yelled across the fire and above sound of the crashing waves, but Sky Blue heard him loud and clear.

Kenzie turned her head up to the man holding her. "What is he talking about?"

"Oh, nothing really. Willy just made an incredible suggestion not long ago, and I've decided that he was right and have sought out to do it." He smiled at her delighted to no end that his interest hadn't been denied.

"What was the suggestion? Maybe we all should do it," Kenzie said, not satisfied to let it go.

Both Willy and Sky Blue roared in laughter.

"No, I don't think so!" Willy shook his head.

It was obvious that it was between the two of them, and everyone else around the fire just watched with amusement.

"I'll tell you later." Sky Blue squeezed her shoulder.

That contented Kenzie and then Noel began to share. To say that Noel had a sudden case of nervous was an understatement. She looked at Willy.

Willy couldn't take it. He put his arm around her and leaned into her and whispered in her ear, "Think of it like you are sharing with Kevin. Just share from your heart. If God saved you, then you definitely have something worth saying." Then he leaned back into his place, ready to listen to her.

She looked at Willy with total sweetness. "What would I ever do without you?" She just stared at him a moment. Then she plunged into the task set before her like a bulldozer on a road crew.

She looked at the faces around the fire. She couldn't contain herself. Her tears began. "Really, God used all of you in my life, in showing me there is a difference, that there is a real God. You showed me love through your hands and through the heart of Jesus when you loved me in a very unlovable state. Who would've even stopped to pick up a drunk off the street? I had to have been a sight for sore eyes."

She looked over at Willy for conformation, but all she got was a smile. It was as though Willy didn't see her in that light. It touched her heart in ways she couldn't understand. She went on to share in detail how God had redeemed her and made her His very own.

"Wow, Noel. What a work God has done and is doing in you," Sky Blue acknowledged, and everyone one joined in confirming and encouraging this truth in Noel. "You're the poster child, of why we do what we do." He moved his hand around the group. "We pray and pour out our hearts for orphaned people just like you. So now it's an honor to bring into the group a product, if I can say, or better yet, a result of earnest prayers to represent just what a changed life that we sing about can be."

Noel didn't know what to say. She was so touched by it that words escaped her, so once again, Willy came to the rescue, jumped up, and had everyone pile on her in one great big group hug. After the cheers died down, still huddled together, Willy started praying for all the Noels and Kevins out there. When he exhausted his prayer, Cookie started, and then someone else, and so on, the first real experience of many that Noel would be involved in, the passionate praying, the pouring out of hearts for the lost as everyone in the group cried out to God. She now understood how they had prayed for her. It was an experience like none she'd ever known.

Later that night, Noel wondered about the conversation she'd had earlier as she watched the silhouette of Willy leaving the bus, she presumed going down the staircase to the bottom to be with his God. She prayed, *Lord, I pray for Willy right now. You know how very special he is to me. Lord, I wonder at times if there's something there, if there's interest on his part. But I'm scared that if it's not or if it falls apart, we'll lose the precious friendship that we have. But I know that's really a lack of faith on my part that You can't figure out who I am to spend the rest of my life with. Father, help me to trust completely in You for my every need, including a husband, if You have one for me at all. Amen.*

Willy did just as he said he would, though he ran the length of beach that was remaining from the tide, five times. Then he raised his hands in honor and praise to his God. *Lord, I praise You. I love*

*You. You are Almighty. You are King of kings and L*ORD *of lords. You are Holy. You are worthy of all my praise. Help me adore Your every Word, desire with all my heart, soul, mind, and strength to worship You in all purity and holiness. Father God, I need to know if Noel is the one. When I'm with her, my heart does funny things. I feel like I want to be with her every moment. Is that love? L*ORD*, help me know. Help me to be gentle. I don't, above anything, want to displease You or hurt Noel by losing the precious friendship we have. I need Your guidance in this like never before. Is she the beat of my heart?*

CHAPTER 18

Willy got up wobbly as usual after a late night, his hair looking like the Los Angeles freeway, but as typical, Willy didn't care. He was in search of some food but was out of luck since he had slept past breakfast time. He had a grumpy face, but when he saw Noel sitting by the window, looking out in wonder, his grumpiness dissipated. He slid in the seat next to her and leaned to peer out the window too. He whispered, "It's awe-inspiring, isn't it?" He paused. "Absolutely breathtaking."

She waved her hand in front of her wrinkled-up nose. "You're right. It's breathtaking all right. Do you ever brush your teeth?" She was trying to be serious, but she was about to crack up looking at his expression.

Willy covered his mouth. "Well, yeah. When I go home, I go through a whole tube of toothpaste to make up the difference." He teased back, then got serious. "Is it that bad?"

"I'm just kidding." She laughed. "But your hair, on the other hand…" She shook her head. "Where do you keep it?"

"Keep what?" he asked, confused. He raised his hands as he stood looking around.

"The pitchfork you use to comb your hair." She had to cover her mouth to conceal her loud laughter.

"You just wait. I'll get you for that one!" Willy wagged his finger at her. He raked his fingers through his bundle of wild strands. "It takes me over three hours to tame this head topper, and I didn't want to miss the scenery," he exaggerated, defending his appearance. He puckered his lip in fun. "But if I'm not wanted here, then I'll go back to bed."

Noel grabbed his hand, offering him a seat. "Not sure which scenery is most interesting, this one or this one." She pointed out the window then the pointed at Willy's hair. "But sure. Join me. Both are worth it." She didn't look his way, or she would've seen a big grin on his face.

They were driving down scenic Highway 1, where you have the mountains on one side of you and the ocean bluff on the other. It was obvious with Noel's nose to the windowpane that she'd never seen anything so magnificent. She said, "Sure beats anything Hollywood puts out! Much of the time, it's just backdrops and video art that make the movies. What a fake compared to what God created." She was quiet after that, thinking about how much her parents had missed, not seeing the Creator in creation. When you look through the eyes of a new creation, it changes the way you see things.

Not long thereafter, they pulled into a parking area on the bluff.

"What are we stopping for?" Noel asked.

"Just you wait and see. Come on." Willy smiled, grabbed her hand, and snagged his camera.

"What in the world is that noise?" she asked, just two steps off the bus.

Willy pulled her hand and literally ran down the pathway and leaned over the rail and pointed. "Those are elephant seals!"

Noel clasped her hand over her mouth. Her eyes spoke the words that were lacking. "I've never seen something so big! And it looks like there are thousands of them!" she listened and watched.

They were making an awful rooting noise like the sounds of a sick animal. But when that many were talking at once, it sounded crazy, like nothing she'd ever heard. But then again it was nothing she'd ever seen. All on the stretch of sand were literally more than you could count of these creatures. They just covered the place.

"Look. Those are swimming out there. See 'em?"

Noel followed his pointed finger. Then she turned back to the shore, where two elephant seals looked like they were going to go into a boxing match. "What are they doing?" she wanted to know.

Willy leaned one arm on the railing and turned to her. "Those are two guys fighting over their woman, just as we do." He looked into Noel's eyes, wondering what she was thinking.

"Maybe if they just asked the woman herself, there'd be no need to fight," she replied serenely, not taking her eyes from his.

Right at that moment, Chet came up and bumped the back of Willy's knees, which caused them to buckle, and the conversation dropped. Willy turned to see who it was.

"Gotcha!" Chet said, walking past him as he did the victory cheer and fist in the air. He was rewarded with the thanks-a-lot eye from Willy.

"Why are they doing that?" Noel chuckled and pointed.

"Oh, that. They're putting on sunscreen," Willy said.

"No they aren't, you crazy nut!"

"No. Really. That's what they are doing. Course, they're not using lotion. They flick the sand up on themselves to keep from getting sunburned."

Noel just shook her head. That seemed ludicrous. But they were flicking sand on themselves with their tiny flippers. She pointed. "They're so funny to watch move." She did her hand up and down like an inch worm in the air, imitating their movement on the sand. "But they don't get very far until they have to rest. Course, I guess if I was that big, I'd have to rest too."

"There ain't nothing big about you but your heart," he said adoringly, looking her up and down.

Noel was glad she didn't have to respond, for Cookie came up beside them and asked, "What do you think? Cute little things, aren't they?"

Noel elbowed Willy. "We were just comparing sizes, and there ain't a little bone in their bodies."

There was no way that Cookie would've known their previous conversation.

"Except maybe their noses, or rather trunks, might be considered tiny in comparison. Besides size, the miniature elephant trunk, though floppy, must be where they got their name."

Noel and Cookie chatted away, leaving Willy with an ocean of thoughts bigger than an elephant and sealed with the unknown. They stayed for over an hour before returning to the bus. Noel took a window seat and just enjoyed the ride like a kid in a candy shop. Everyone enjoyed watching her.

Noel could hear the air brakes wind down as they pulled into a parking lot overlooking yet another beach. Noel asked, "Where are we?"

"This, my dear, is a wonderful honeymoon place called, Moonstone Beach," Willy answered with a smile. After today, you'll understand why people come here for their honeymoon."

"This was my idea," Willy suggested as they left the bus. "We could do our Bible study out there at those tables. Then I thought we could stretch our legs by a walk on the boardwalk that goes along this scenic beach, opposite the row of hotels and honeymoon resorts." He was watching her face to see if he should go on. "Then, for lunch, there is a great grill joint in Cambria, along with dozens of fun shops to peer into. And I was hoping you'd join me." He was grinning ear to ear.

"Sure. Why not? It's not like there are a lot of options anyway." She shrugged.

Willy was taken aback and gestured so.

Noel, seeing her mistake, tried to fix it. "Oh, that was rude. It's not what I meant."

"You don't have to spend the day with me, Noel. We have skateboard ministry at three in Cambria. Then we have a mini concert on the beach tonight. If you would rather lay low and rest, I can understand."

"I didn't mean to make you think I didn't want to go with you." Noel smiled. "What I meant was that I'd love it because I don't know my way around. And you"—she pointed to his chest—"do. So I'd love to spend the day with you just as you said."

They'd switched from John to Genesis since being on tour and had just finished creation. It had become custom and was very normal for the two of them to bring out their guitars and start singing when they did Bible study together. So just like when they first met, they'd have a jam session anywhere and everywhere there was a pocket of time. Because they'd been studying creation, Willy had taught Noel a new song called "God of Wonders," which exalted God and His creation.

They were sitting of the picnic table, singing "God of Wonders" when Noel jumped up and ran to the railing at the bluff's edge. She was screaming and jumping up and down, pointing.

"Whales, Willy! Look! There is a pod of whales!" She had covered her mouth in awe, trying to contain her excitement.

Willy ran to her and looked where she pointed, and sure enough, Noel's keen eyes had spotted a pod of whales.

"God is so awesome. Can you believe while we are singing 'God of Wonders,' mentioning His creation, that He would care to send us a visual for it?" Willy shook his head and crossed his arms, a huge smile on his face. "That is my God, a God that is constantly sending us messages of His love and care for us, even through whales."

They watched the whales until they were out of eyesight and then went back to put away their guitars and walk on the boardwalk. They had a blast. Noel couldn't help playing with the little ground squirrels that came out begging for handouts. Willy had been right; Noel noted that the boardwalk held a lot of beauty. She could definitely see why it was a honeymoon spot.

They had a great meal at the grill, and Noel did do a bit of shopping, though she knew she was limited by bus storage. She tried to pick up a few things here and there for her friends. Mostly, she purchased postcards of the magnificent coastline to send out.

The town was a cute little hideaway just a ways down from the boardwalk. They did the skateboard ministry, which was totally cool. Noel was surprised at how many kids came out. The concert that night on the beach was definitely different but still a blessing for all who attended. These times of ministry were by far Noel's favorite. Noel let her mind roam over the day as she lay in her bunk. She smiled a sigh of comfort, rolled over and went to sleep to the sway of the bus going down the road.

They pulled into the parking lot at Monterey Bay by lunch. Sky Blue said that everyone was on their own for the day and to meet back at dark for Wednesday night Bible study. Everyone filed out into beautiful sunshine. It was one of the more pristine areas of history and tourism mixed Willy thought the last time they stopped here. They first went past the marina, and then the boardwalk pier came in view.

"Hey, I'm hungry. Will you grub with me?" Willy asked as he grabbed his stomach.

"Sure thing."

Willy put his arm around her, guiding her down the boardwalk to a particular eating joint. "That's *my* girl," he said with contentment.

She looked at him as they walked. He still had his arm hanging loosely over her shoulder. "Why do you call me *your* girl?"

Willy smiled at her. That was a hard one. He wasn't sure how to answer it. He wasn't entirely sure why he thought that way. He was very unsure of how she felt about him. So what could he say? How could he answer that question? Either way, he felt like it would be like jumping off the pier, not knowing what was below the surface. But to ignore the question would be just as risky too.

He chose complete honesty, which he knew is always the best policy no matter the outcome. "I feel somewhat responsible for you, being that I was the one who got you on, and you are young and I feel you need my protection."

Noel flipped from his grip and snarled at him, completely cutting off the rest of what Willy was going to say. "Is that all I am to you, a responsibility?" Noel was unaware of how loud she was or that people around them were beginning to stare. She put her hands on her hips as her face heated up.

She was one fired-up chick, Willy surmised.

"Well, I'll have you know, Willy McCollister, I don't need you. I don't need nobody. I can take care of myself!" She stomped off, tripping over her untied shoelace. She didn't fall, but she hobbled carefully and much more humbly to a bench nearby.

Willy had to cover his laughter at watching her trip over her shoelace of pride. But he didn't want to be caught doing so. So he turned his head away only to see Chet and Jordie snickering, obviously having watched the whole scene. Willy rolled his eyes and was about to lay into them, but they elbowed him, patting him on the back and teasing the life out of him.

"Woohoo! She's so hot. I call that fried *chick*en!" Chet rubbed his middle. "Hey, you lost your lunch date already. Hey, man. We'll join you that is if you're paying. Man, chicks just aren't worth it."

On they jabbed him exaggeratedly, trying to get a free meal.

"Apparently, you have your answer. She obviously ain't your girl."

They hooted and hollered again, all in good fun, of course.

Willy knew he needed to go after Noel and make things right. Willy growled, "You two go take a jump!" Then he left them laughing and made a beeline to find Noel. It didn't take long to find her.

She saw him coming but turned away from him. She was hurt. She'd been crying and felt completely vulnerable.

Willy approached slowly and stood still a moment before speaking. "May I sit with you?" he asked sweetly.

Noel kept her head turned but blurted out a definite, "No."

Willy went to her other side to see her face, but she only turned away again. Willy was desperate, and he hated to see the pain in her eyes, the tear streaks on her cheeks, all because of him. It was more than he could take. He went down on one knee and took both of her hands into his. She tried to take them back, but he overpowered her.

"Look at me, Noel. Look at me. You didn't let me finish." He moved his head so he could make eye contact with her. He then wiped a tear off the tip of her nose. "Noel, when I'm with you, you make my heart skip a beat. You occupy my thoughts by day and invade my dreams by night. I don't know what we have in store, but I'm so afraid of losing what we already have in my conquest. Does that make sense? If your affections lie somewhere else, if a deeper interest from me is unwanted, then you have to speak up. Because I plan to do what it takes to find the answers to our future. Do I make myself clear?"

Noel gave a slight nod of acknowledgment.

"I will try to be careful with my words. The last thing I ever want to do is hurt you." He kissed the top of her hands and then turned them over and kissed the palms. He stood up. "Now I'm powerfully hungry and could just about eat anything for lunch."

Noel looked up at a smiling Willy.

"Will you join me for lunch, Miss Franklin?" He did a courtesy bow. "The most beautiful voice I know, glad or mad." He chuckled at his own rhyme, though it was true.

How could Noel refuse? She was so confused about Willy. She felt like a kid with her first crush, yet she'd just gotten started on the tour. And Kevin still lingered in her mind. And she wasn't sure that love didn't scare her more than being alone did. She took Willy's offered hand and got up. She hooked her arm in his and went back to the pier and into the restaurant that Willy had chosen.

He asked for a private window seat. It was a neat restaurant that sat right over the ocean edge.

The tide was out, so Noel could see the tide-pool animals all out for a ray of sun. She kept pointing. "Is that what I think it is?"

Willy leaned to the glass. "What?" he asked, wondering just what had captured her attention.

"That. That thing right there. What is it?" She asked tapping on the glass.

Willy did all he could not to laugh at the fact that they probably looked like two little kids who'd never been to the ocean before.

"That orange, five-legged thingy right there?"

"Yeah, that's it!" she exclaimed.

"Why, that's a starfish, sunshine. Haven't you ever seen a starfish?"

"You know what kind of stars I grew up with," Noel replied, referring to Hollywood.

The waiter had already taken their order, and all of a sudden, Willy jumped up.

"Hey what are you doing?" She watched him leave the booth, "Where are you going?"

He didn't want her to get up, so he turned and held up a hand. "Stop. Just wait right there. I'll be back." He flashed her a smile.

Sure enough, as Noel looked out the window, waiting on Willy's return, she gasped out loud. She tapped on the window. For down below, a crazy guy looked up, smiled, and waved. That guy was doing strange things to be beat of her heart as well. "That Willy. That crazy Willy," she said aloud.

He tiptoed, shoes and all, through the ankle-to knee-deep ocean water, through the rocks, moss, and sea creatures, to pick up the wanted starfish. Willy brought the starfish right in to the table and used the cloth napkin to set the prized catch on. Noel touched it all over, feeling its bumps. Of course, it had its ocean perfume on, which made Noel wriggle up her nose.

"These things really stink, but you don't smell them when outside, yet there is an ocean full of the same smell. Funny, isn't it?" She continued to admire the creature and even thanked God for it until their meal arrived.

Then she watched Willy get up and take the delicate creation back out of the restaurant, get his shoes wet once again, go back through the tide pool and place the starfish right back where it was.

"He's so sweet," she said to herself as she watched him.

When he came back, she thanked him profusely for his thoughtfulness. He just nodded his head and didn't come up for air until he was scrapping the bottom of his sourdough bowl that was now empty of delicious clam chowder. He leaned back and began to tear apart his bowl. "Sorry. I was starving."

She was still working on her corn chowder as she looked out the window. "Oh, look. It's a seal or a sea lion or something, a woodchuck maybe?"

Willy looked to where she was pointing. He hooted in laughter. "That's a sea otter."

"A sea otter? I've never seen a sea otter before!" Before she realized what she said, Willy had made the move to jump up.

"Oh no you're not! You sit yourself right back down!"

Though Willy was just kidding, it made for a fun time. The sea otter was farther in the water than Willy was willing to go for, at least not dressed properly.

"I don't mind!"

"I know you don't. You're the craziest person I've ever met."

"Does that bother you?" Willy got on a personal level.

"Willy, I don't think there's a bone in your body that bothers me," she whispered.

"I wasn't so convinced of that a few minutes ago." Willy's eyebrows shot up as he took a sip of his iced tea.

Noel looked away and fiddled with the remains of her bowl. "Yeah, well, I still struggle with anger and letting my emotions take control instead of letting the Holy Spirit lead me." She sighed. "I'm sorry. Can you forgive me?"

"Don't know what you're talking about, lady." Willy waved his hands. "But, say, how about a jaunt on the boardwalk? They have the best walking trail along the seashore, or if you're so inclined, they have an awesome aquarium downtown. I went there with Chet and Jordie last year. Or better yet, you can go shopping on cannery row. They have all kinds of unique seaside shops."

"Hmm…" Noel put her finger to her cheek. "I think maybe a stroll to decide would be in order. Besides, I need to work off this bowl anyway."

Willy did his drum roll on the table. "All right, my lady. We're off." He grabbed her hand and led her out of the restaurant.

They'd just landed on the boardwalk trail when they nearly ran into Sky Blue and Kenzie, who were walking hand in hand.

Noel was in her bouncy mood. "Hey, guys. What's up?" she questioned as she put her hands in her back pockets.

Sky Blue rolled his eyes as he slowly turned around. To say that he was irritated was an understatement. He and Kenzie had just gone out for a walk, and he was not planning on sharing this time with those he shared the bus with every day. But obviously, they weren't getting the message.

Willy chimed in with his own questions. "So where did the two of you have lunch?" he asked, thinking what an interesting lunch he just had.

"Nowhere," Kenzie said.

"Kenzie girl, you got to eat. You're gonna blow away like a kite in this wind," Willy joked.

"I didn't say we didn't eat, Willy. I said that we didn't go anywhere," Kenzie sweetly replied.

"You mean you two stayed on the bus together?" Willy pointed his finger back and forth.

"Yes, I wanted to give Jonas some time out. He hardly ever gets time away from the bus, so I offered to bus sit, and Kenzie here decided to keep me company." Sky Blue squeezed her shoulder.

Willy understood all right. "Yeah right, man." He hit Sky Blue in the middle. "I'll have to remember that one," he teased.

Kenzie and Noel were all smiles, though for different reasons.

Noel picked up on the joke, so she said with her hands on her hips, "What did you have, candlelight tuna?"

"I'll have you know," Sky Blue said with a frown, "there was no tuna to be had, but we fared well with a Goober PBJ on old bread, stale chips, and flat soda." Sky Blue wrinkled his nose at the distasteful meal.

"Amazing what you'll eat just to be with somebody!" Willy teased the lovebirds. He punched Sky Blue in the shoulder. "I'm so proud of you!"

Sky Blue was just about to tell them to take a hike when Noel interrupted them.

"Hey." She pointed. "What's that over there?" She was pointing to the surrey that a family was peddling down the walk.

"Oh, that's a surrey cart," Willy answered.

Noel jumped up and down. "Oh, that would be so much fun to ride, wouldn't it?" She looked back over at the peddling machine. "Hey, I have an idea. How about the four of us rent one? It will just be so much fun. What do ya say, Sky Blue?"

Sky Blue was about to explode. He really didn't want to do that, much less spend the afternoon with these two wild cards.

Kenzie elbowed her sweetheart. "Oh, Sky Blue, what will it hurt? You might just like it."

He looked at Kenzie. "If you want to, sure. Whatever you want to do, I want to do." What he said was true; he wanted to be with her but hadn't really wanted an audience.

"Well, I've never been on one, and they do look like fun," Kenzie said.

"Okay then. It's set. Let's do it." Noel jumped up and down.

Willy was already headed to the rental hut. He waved Sky Blue to follow. "Hey, you coming?"

Willy and Sky Blue had the thing rented and turned in the correct direction by the time the girls got over there.

Willy with his hands in his front pockets asked, "Okay, who wants to drive?" He took one look at Sky Blue, and he got his answer.

"I'll do the driving. You two younguns get in the back."

Sky Blue and Kenzie climbed into the front of the four-wheeled death trap for tourists. They'd gotten the simple instructions from the rental man. He made it sound so easy. They had a rough start, but everyone kept their cool. It wasn't as easy as it looked, for the front and back peddles were connected to a drive rod, each side having that setup. Thus, the person in front and the person directly behind them had to pedal in synch. Willy had climbed in behind Sky Blue, and Noel was behind Kenzie.

Everyone was laughing so hard at how ridiculously difficult it was with everyone trying to pedal at his own pace that Willy and Kenzie nearly fell off. Sky Blue had his jaw clinched and didn't seem to find the humor in the situation. It was at that moment that Willy pedaled too rigid and *bam!* the pedal had slipped from under Sky Blue's foot and hit him hard in the back of his leg.

Noel covered her mouth. "Wow, Sky Blue. I've never heard you sing that verse before." She teased him about his colorful mumblings of excruciating pain.

All the while, Willy was apologizing for the mess-up, Sky Blue was trying to escape the entrapment. He moved so quickly that his belt loop got caught. He was hung up there, which made him even madder. He couldn't get loose, so he jerked hard, and rip went the belt loop, but at least he was free. He looked around and realized they'd been the entertainment for quite a few tourists, only they were not on stage and Sky Blue was not singing. He'd never been more embarrassed. Kenzie tried to keep her composure, but it was absolutely hilarious. And Willy and Noel didn't even bother. They were laughing so hard that tears were coming and they had hopped off the cart but could not offer any condolences due to laughing so much.

Sky Blue checked his tucked-in shirt, brushed his pants off, turned his face away from the rubberneckers, and took off walking without a backward glance. Kenzie finally had compassion on him and jaunted up to him. Both Willy and Noel watched as Kenzie hooked her arm in his and they continued to walk.

Willy hopped in the front, where Sky Blue had been, and Noel joined him.

"Humph. Guess they don't want to ride anymore. Wonder why?"

Both burst out laughing again. The two of them waved at all the folks who had stopped for the free entertainment and took off. All went well after that. They enjoyed the ride, though it was work, especially uphill.

Then they walked along the main parts of cannery row, window-shopping, Noel's first lesson in bus limitations. She saw many things she wanted to purchase, but Willy sweetly reminded her of the space on the bus, so she put back the items. But she still enjoyed looking around. It was really a neat place.

They ended up at the aquarium. Everything was so special to Noel. She looked at all the sea creatures and even touched some of them. Then they went out and Noel looked through the outdoor binoculars and zeroed in on the seals. Willy was so close behind her that her hair blew in his face. He surprised himself with the urge to put his arms around her and hold her. That closeness was doing confusing things to his heart, so he backed up and went to another railing, pretending to look out at the beautiful creation. But instead, he found himself praying for the two-legged beauty that God had created that was the beating the drum of his heart.

*L*ORD*, what is going on here? Every time I'm around Noel, I find myself acting a fool. She makes me do crazy things. I do not wish to hurt her, but at the same time, I desire to find out what You may have for us. Help me,* L*ORD*, not to mess up or skip a beat as far as this enigma is concerned.*

The very subject of his prayer came up and grabbed his sides and roared. Willy nearly jumped out of his skin.

Noel backed up with her hand over her mouth, trying to contain outrageous laughter. She said, "I'm sorry! I just couldn't resist!"

Willy, having finally recovered from shock, wagged his finger at her. "You just wait. Payback is coming!"

"Oh, don't bother paying me back. It was at no charge," she teased and walked off with a smile.

Willy was trying to explain a game. They all gathered inside the bus, facing the wall opposite the ocean. Jonas had moved the bus entourage down to the seaside state park area. He was now out in the rocks, hiding the treasure.

Willy explained, "Okay. This is how it works. We pair up in teams for safety and search for this hidden treasure. That is, after Jonas has us run up and down the beach seven times. The first person to find it wins. Each team is given a written clue."

"What do they win?" Noel asked.

"Season tickets to all the Mercy Seat Rockers' concerts," Willy teased.

"What a motive," Noel retorted as she rolled her eyes.

"Hey now. Surely anyone would just love that winning ticket. Okay, okay." He waved his hands up. "The winner really gets a life-sized poster of Sky Blue."

Both cracked up at the sudden growl from the back. Cookie finally gave Noel a break.

"Hey, man. Give the chick a break. If your team finds the treasure, then they get to be duty free in the kitchen for the rest of that tour. So everyone else has to do their kitchen chores." Cookie gave a grin to the wide-eyed newest member, the one who didn't yet understand the doldrums of road life. Then he said, "And I aim to win."

Noel nodded, understanding. Jonas had four names on slips of paper folded and in a bowl. As Rusty, Sky Blue, Kenzie and Noel got off, they each took a name. They weren't allowed to look until after the run. So it was that Sky Blue was disappointed that he already knew that he wouldn't be paired up with the woman he desired to spend every waking moment with. But the good side was that neither did he have to be paired with Noel. So he was glad about that. Not that he minded Noel; they got along great, but she was just such a spaz.

Noel was panting intensely when Jonas was done running them. Then he said after a brief rest, "You know the rules. On your mark, get set, go." And he blew his whistle. The four with slips of paper opened them and found their partners and took off.

Noel smiled as she saw "Willy" written on her paper. She went over to him, and the two of them ran off. He grabbed her into a cove. Breathlessly, he asked, "So what's the clue?"

"Oh," she said and turned over the paper. She read, "The most wanted item on the bus." Noel tilted her head. "Humph. Wonder what that is?"

They began, like the others, to climb the rocks and have fun. It was getting near sunset, but it was well over an hour away. As it was, for a bit, they forgot they were actually looking for something and just enjoyed climbing on the rocks. Willy was taking lots of pictures, as was Noel. The sky was already changing colors. The boulders were magnificent surrounding the tide pools that were like tiny valleys in the mountains of the boulder formations. That alone was a blast.

But then Willy came up. "Hey, the RC that I swigged down just after running wants out. I'll be right back." He then trotted quickly off to the bus.

In no time, Noel saw him returning, and he was shaking his head and rubbing his neck. He spoke when he got to her. "I just don't get it. The door is locked on the bathroom, but I'm not sure anyone is in it." He was looking around to see if he saw everyone.

Noel jumped up with excitement, pointing her finger at Willy. "I know what it is! I know what it is! It's the bathroom key!"

Willy stopped, and you could tell his wheels were turning. "Why, I think you're right!" He was quiet another moment. "That would make sense." He ran his fingers through his hair. Then Willy laughed. "And if you are right, now I really have the motive to get busy. I don't plan on finding out how far I can stretch my bladder."

So they set out to find something small, most likely in a box, they concluded. They'd been searching high and low for about twenty minutes when Noel slipped and hurt her ankle. It was nothing serious, but she sat down and leaned back on the rocks she'd been climbing, instantly Willy was right there, his face inches from hers.

"Hey, partner. You all right?"

She looked up into his face, and all pain seemed to drain away. Willy had the most romantic look on his face. He was breathing hard, but his closeness was her undoing. Willy leaned his head down, and they were just about to kiss when Chet and Jordie came around the outcropping of rocks. Willy immediately moved away, the moment lost. But Noel's heart was beating wildly as was Willy's. They were certainly keeping beat together all right. That wasn't lost on either of them.

"Hey, man. We're not interrupting anything, are we?" Chet asked, teasing the two. He came up put his arm around Willy's shoulder. "I mean, you do have the best-looking partner." He tossed his head back toward Jordie. "No offense, Jordie. But we just thought maybe you two newbies might need some help, but I see you two work quite well together." He winked at Noel and then punched Willy in the shoulder. "Let me give you a clue. You might start looking for the hidden treasure instead of each other."

"Noel twisted her ankle, and I was just checking it out. That's all," Willy defended himself.

Both Chet and Jordie let out a snort of disbelief.

"Oh sure, and my momma is Gladys Presley!"

They walked off, laughing and jabbing each other.

Willy turned his attention back to Noel. He took her hand to help her up. "Hey, do you think you can walk?"

"Yeah. It was just a slight twist I think." She stood and tested her foot. "Yeah, I'll be fine." She at least thought her foot would be. She wasn't sure about her heart.

Willy needed to get the fog out of his head. He couldn't believe he had just about kissed Noel. He shook his head again. Then he tilted his head. But then again, she was a willing partner. All these thoughts plus some were going through his head when he heard a crash. He'd accidently knocked something while in deep thought but was still searching. His hands went frantic to the crashing object. To his delight, it was a small tin box that had been taped shut. And sure enough, it had a metal object inside that clanged when it fell.

Willy raised his hands in the air. "Noel, come." He motioned to her, and then he began to get real loud. "Found it! Found it!" He was jumping up and down with extreme excitement. After several players came over to see the hidden treasure, Willy crossed his legs. "And come to think of it, I need to use it right now." Then he left everyone one in hysterical tears laughing at him as he ran to the bus bathroom.

All got their foldout chairs and came and sat atop the bluffs and craggy boulders to watch the awesome sunset. This one was one of the most magnificent ones that Noel had seen, though her mind was not completely fixed on it but occupied with two guys, Kevin and Willy. She wasn't sure what to do with the dilemma.

She was thinking that in just a few days, she'd see Kevin and her parents. She grimaced at the thought.

Willy leaned over to Noel's chair and whispered, "Hey, sunshine. Foot still hurting you?"

"No. My foot is doing great." Noel turned her foot around a couple of times.

"Well then, what was that look for?"

Noel realizing she'd been caught, she said, "Oh, nothing that the Son won't set straight," making a play on words about the sunset.

Willy let it go. He didn't feel the freedom to press her anymore.

All went in the bus for some grub before hitting the sack. They'd be in Los Angeles by morning.

CHAPTER 19

Noel snatched a swipe of cotton candy from Jordie's tall cone of the delicious cotton sugar that he held away from her when she tried for a second swipe.

"Hey now! Get your own!" He popped another bite into his mouth. "Or better yet, get drummer boy to fetch you some!" Both he and Chet had been teasing Willy to know end.

Seeing that she was going to do no such thing, Jordie asked, "So tell me, missy, what's there to do in this place, and why it's so special?"

They were spending the day at Knott's Berry Farm. And it was an easy pair up. Actually, perfect Noel thought. Sky Blue and Kenzie together, who didn't want any extra company. Naturally, Willy and Noel were together, and Jordie and Chet decided to pal with them for some extra fun. With six being too many, Cookie and Rusty paired up and went off to enjoy the amusement park, just the two of them. And though several offered for Jonas to go while they bus sat, he wouldn't hear of it. It was his job, and he cherished it. That was part of it, and he would enjoy the stories when the kids got back to the bus.

"This is where I played hooky most often. I had plenty of money, so a group of friends and I would come here for the day.

Kevin and I came here a lot too. It was a lot of fun." She was smiling, obviously lost in memories.

Though no one would've encouraged skipping school, they knew Noel probably didn't have the same concerns.

"So tell me, which is your favorite ride?" Chet piped up.

Willy was just taking it all in, listening to the sweet voice of Noel. It was like peeking into a journal or a photo album listening to her prattle on with the guys.

Noel directed them down a lane. "Actually, my favorite ride is over in this section." She waved her arm, inviting them to join her.

They'd just walked under the entrance where Snoopy and Woodstock were in a canoe, tilting back and forth over fake rapids.

"This section is called Snoopy Land, and it's my favorite because I like to come and watch the little kids ride rides. My parents never took me here. And since I missed so much of that, I often would linger throughout this section and dream of what it would've been like to have my daddy or mommy take me on a ride like this one here." She pointed to the Woodstock airmail ride. They stood and watched the life-sized postcard with seven seats in a row on the front bounce up and down while the little ones raised their hands and screamed and waved.

They went to another area, and Noel started up again. "It's hard to decide my favorite. This is the huff and puff and, as you can see, quite the workout."

They all watched as two little girls pumped the mine cart handle up and down. This ride the *rider* supplies the fuel to go up and down.

Willy opted for humor. "Hey, Chet, want try it out?" he asked as he hopped over a railing. Obviously, he'd be too big. Then he turned to Noel and said sweetly, "I guess I'm too big!"

They passed the semitrucks, where a lot of little boys were in line, waiting to drive the big rigs. Noel smiled at the few fathers who had climbed up top to be with their two- or three-year-old sons while they blew the big rig horns. On they went past the huge Snoopy bounce house, and then Willy grabbed Noel's arm.

"Hey, I've always wanted to do that, and in a Snoopy bounce house, well, that would just be tops." Willy had turned the whole group toward the bounce house.

Before Noel knew what was happening, all four of them were in sock feet, bouncing like two-year-olds and having so much fun. Willy went crazy, as did the other two guys, doing summersaults and flips, being careful of little ones of course. But in the midst of jumping all around and upside down, Willy accidently bumped into Noel's chin, sending her down, grabbing her face.

Noel scooted to the door and slid out.

Chet and Jordie, having witnessed the whole thing, grabbed Willy's arm as he started to go after her. "Hey, man. Let her be. She'll be all right. She just might need some time."

Willy still wanted to go to her but thought maybe his friends were telling him some wisdom, so he stayed put.

It was probably about thirty minutes later when Willy figured Noel had had enough time to collect herself. He climbed out and began to search for her. He spotted her not too far away, sitting on a bench, watching the Snoopy bus ride go round and round. She had tears running down her face with a twinge of a smile as she watched the riders laugh and cheer.

Willy quietly slipped his arm behind her as he sat down beside her. "Hey, where has my sunshine gone?" he asked as he wiped at a tear on her cheek.

She remained silent.

He shook her shoulder. "Hey, Noel, did I hurt you?" he needed to know.

After a few moments of hard crying, though not moving her face from the bus ride, she said, "One day...one day, Willy, my kids and I are gonna ride that bus together."

Noel was hurting so deeply that Willy didn't know what to do.

"Yes, yes. Of course you will. Shh. It's okay. It's okay," he comforted her. After another minute or so, the ride ended and reloaded. Willy said, "Hey let's get on with this group." He jumped up and pulled Noel up with him, dragging her behind him toward the bus ride.

"Oh Willy, please," she begged. "This is for kids and their mommys and daddys." Willy couldn't be dissuaded. "You're not going to make me ride by myself, are you?" They were up to the entrance. He pleaded with his big smile.

Her tears were gone, but puffy eyes remained. "Oh, all right." She followed behind him, saying, "Willy, you are one crazy dude!"

They got on the ride and had four chatterbox, hyper kids sitting between them. Willy wasted no time in getting them even more hyper as the ride began. He was totally into making the kids laugh. It brought laughter to Noel just watching him. At one moment, he looked over at her and winked. She was thinking in her heart what a great daddy he would make someday. Both Willy and Noel played like they were scared and screamed when the bus went high in the air and raised their hands. They had a blast with the little kids whose parents hadn't ridden with them. They gave them all a sucker as they dismounted. It brought great delight to the bus riders by emptying his pockets of the suckers he had brought for just the opportunity.

Willy had his arm around Noel's shoulders when leaving the ride. "That was a blast!" He winked at Noel. "Thanks for joining me."

"You're gonna make a great daddy someday." She smiled. She knew that was a personal comment, but she couldn't refrain from sharing her thoughts.

"As you will a great momma," he replied with a grin.

Noel got suddenly still. "I don't want to make the same mistakes my parents did. I know what it's like to be orphaned at home, and I don't want that for my kids. I want them to have fun and explore and to be who God made them to be. I want to make mud pies with them so I can put gummy worms in them to eat. I want to play with Play-Doh for hours with my kids and build forts under the kitchen table. I want hold their hands as we stomp in puddles together." She was crying again. "I want to bring them here and ride every ride in Snoopy Land with them." She dropped her fist and slumped. "I never want them to be alone." She turned and walked away.

Willy was at a loss for words, but he couldn't let her bear it alone. That was what friends were for. He caught up with her. "Hey, I know you're hurting. If this is too painful and you want to go back to the bus, I'll take you. I think the guys will understand."

"Thanks, Willy, but I want to stay." Noel cleared her throat. "I just had a moment of weakness. It seems to overtake me at the oddest of times, and I become very vulnerable and just crumble. Let's get back to the guys. Everything is okay. I'll beat you there. The last one there is a rotten avocado." She took off running and laughing. Knowing she'd given Willy an unfair disadvantage, she arrived the winner but said, "You win since you're such a great friend."

Nothing else was said, and the day was a blast. From there, they took the airlift buckets over to the big kids' part of the park. They'd gotten shaved ice snoopy cones just before entering the ride. So Jordie took off his cowboy hat and put all their cones in it and covered it with Noel's scarf to get on the ride. It worked, and all enjoyed their cone while riding in the air. They goofed off and rode roller coaster after roller coaster. Noel teased Willy about his hair, as it was fit to be tied after the first wild ride. They meandered their way all over the park, including the original Old West town where the original Knott's berry stand was. They even got held up by some outlaws on the train ride, and Chet tried to trade Jordie for freedom.

To end the evening, they were to meet at Mrs. Knott's Chicken Dinner Restaurant at 7:00 p.m. Willy said it was the best fried chicken he'd ever eaten. He commented as well at how country-looking the restaurant was while sitting in the middle of a cutting-edge town, right next to Hollywood itself. After dinner, they went back into the park until it closed at midnight.

Noel had hopped in beside Willy on a corkscrew roller coaster and said, "You know, I didn't realize you could have this much fun and be a Christian too. For some reason, I thought being a Christian was boring and brown."

Willy said as the lady checked seatbelts, "Well, there are times for seriousness, worship, and reverence that wouldn't fall in the so-called fun category, though they are beautiful and needed. But hang on. Being a Christian can turn your world upside down," he said in a roar of laughter as the coaster jerked off at that very moment like a bullet train. All Willy heard was Noel screaming in his ears.

―――

It was Monday evening, and Willy and Noel were on their way to meet Noel's parents. Noel was driving in the crazy downtown traffic.

"Where is this place anyway?" Willy asked, hanging on to the dashboard as Noel easily drove through downtown Hollywood to the other side of Los Angeles.

"Oh, it's not much farther now. Say, maybe twenty minutes, give or take, in this traffic."

"Are you nervous about seeing your parents? Are you sure they will even show up?"

"Well, I don't know if they'll show up. I mean, they might have been busy since I just asked yesterday on the note I left on the door." She paused. "If I say I'm not terrified, I'd be lying. But the LORD will be my strength, and I have to do this."

"I'll be right beside you, praying," he said, as he got out of the car some twenty minutes later. He jumped over to get her door and then proceeded into the nice dinner establishment.

"How many?" the hostess greeted them and asked.

"Umm. Yes, we are to meet a party, the Lanier party of two. Are they here by chance yet?" Noel asked.

The hostess looked at her charts. "Oh yes. Follow me please." She took them toward the back.

"Oh there they are. Thank you," Noel said.

"How did you know it's them?" Willy whispered, confused as ever.

"They always wear wigs and sunglasses when they don't want to be seen, and we have always used this code name for this kind of thing," she whispered back over her shoulder just before arriving at the table and sitting down.

The hostess seated them around a delicate white-clothed table with a candle and fresh roses in the middle.

"Mom, Dad, good evening. I think you remember my friend Willy," Noel said.

Both her parents nodded back their greeting.

Burt spoke first. "Yes, we remember this, uh…Willy guy. He sorta just stole you out from under our noses, if I recall."

"Uh…can you two order? I don't want my meal to be cold, you know," Ericka interjected.

Noel clenched her teeth but answered politely, "Yes, Mother. I'd be happy to." Then she looked over the menu, and both she and

Willy placed a simple order so the waitress could get a move on with the meal.

Noel plunged in and asked how their current movie and scene plots were going, trying valiantly to get into their world. Both Ericka and Burt continued on about themselves until their meals came. Noel, wanting to eat in peace, began to tell them about the coastline she'd just been down.

"Mom, Dad, have either of you ever seen elephant seals?"

"Never heard of them," Burt mumbled, chewing his steak.

"No, I don't recall anything like that," Ericka answered, not much differently. "Hmm. It seems I do remember we used to go up that way for some weekend costume parties at a castle." She was looking into the air, thinking of the name, when Noel filled it in.

"Oh, you mean Hurst Castle?"

"Oh yes. That's it," Ericka said. "Nice place, if I recall. Just my style: luxury to the hilt." She looked at her nails. "Seems to me it was Hollywood's paradise in the hills."

Noel had heard of the place, but they'd chosen not to go there. She was sure that the castle couldn't hold a candle to the elephant seals nor the spectacular sunset and beach cliffs hideaways she'd just seen or watching the waves crash below a lighthouse. What a contrast, she thought. Her parents gravitated to the material things while Noel's heart ate up like candy the creation that she was seeing for the first time through the eyes of a Christian. She shuddered at her thoughts and at the chasm that stood between her and her parents.

Noel fiddled with her napkin. She wanted to get the unpleasantries over with before her mother had too much to drink. She cleared her throat and changed the subject. "So, Mom, Dad, what's up with the lock changes on the house?" She looked at both of them. "I tried my key in every door, and none of them worked. Is there something I need to know?"

Ericka looked at Burt and shrugged. Feeling very uncomfortable, Burt then blabbered, "It's like this. We don't know who you'll be bringing home or what you're doing anymore, so we just felt it necessary to change the locks. You know, to keep things secure." He just stared at her.

Noel blinked her eyes, total disbelief written on her face. "You mean you locked me out of my own house? How could you?" She was furious, yet they were in a public place and she wouldn't disgrace her parents.

"Mind yourself, Christy!" Ericka admonished.

"I can't believe this! I've been kicked out of my own home!" she retorted.

Ericka, getting her claws out, said, "Now you listen here. You were the one who left us for that singing stuff." She snarled and flung her hand at Noel.

"So does this mean you don't have a key for me?" she asked, deciding she wasn't going to rise to the bait.

She felt Willy squeeze her hand under the table to let her know she was doing well. He kept praying for her silently.

Her parents looked at each other.

Burt spoke. "No, I don't think so. We still have the same phone number. If you want to get a hold of us, you can give us a call or call our managers. You know who they are." He shrugged his shoulders. "Or you can just leave a note like you did yesterday. But the more notice you can give us, the better. You just got lucky today."

Noel complied with a sad, "Okay." She began on her salad, but it tasted like gravel in her mouth. Her heart was breaking. *They don't want me*, she said to herself, barely able to hold her tears.

Ericka was well into her meal when she snidely inquired, "This isn't the guy we saw you with in the papers. So how many are there?"

Noel looked at Willy, and Willy just smiled at her.

"You're right. This isn't the same guy, but then, I'm not with that guy either."

"That's not what the papers said!" Ericka snarled back.

"Oh, Mother, you know how vicious the papers can be!"

"Not only that. You looked like you were about to jump in his lap at the concert!" came the accusing retort from Burt.

Noel looked up and said breathlessly, "You came to the concert?" all other conversations draining from her head.

"Yes. Saturday night," Burt replied.

Knowing where Noel's heart was headed, Willy had to intervene so as to ease the blow that was sure to come.

Willy put on his best jovial charm. "Yeah, Noel…I mean Christy." Willy rolled his eyes at forgetting to use the right name. "Christy here, she's been a huge asset to the group. Adding her excellent talent has moved the group ahead quite a bit." He didn't want to give them the chance to put Noel down.

Burt finished chewing his steak. "Yeah, I just bet it has, being she is who she is. It takes a pretty low guy to stoop to using others to get places."

Willy blinked. Surely he didn't just hear what he thought he heard. "Excuse me, Mr. Franklin, but with no due respect, I must take up for my boss and friend. He hasn't in any way done as you have suggested or taken advantage of Christy in any way. Your accusations are unfounded." Willy was kind and gentle yet firm about the rebuke.

Noel couldn't resist. "So what did you think?" Noel asked, begging for acceptance.

Willy's heart sank, knowing the blow was coming.

Ericka tapped her fingernails on the table and, in arrogance, set her mouth free. "Christy, we want more for you than tramping all over the country, singing that junk of yours. We went to one of your concerts. Just don't expect it to happen again." Ericka was tipsy by then. "I mean, you really are a disgrace to us. We've had to answer all kinds of questions since you came out in the papers a rebel to your own heritage."

"Thank you, Mom and Dad, for meeting me here. That was kind of you." Holding her tears, she pulled out a business card. "Since I'm on the road most often, you can reach me at this number. The lady's name is Lilly. Should you need to get a hold of me for any reason." She scooted her chair out to stand.

Ericka shrieked, "You're not leaving now, are you? You haven't even finished your dinner!"

"Oh." Noel sighed. "I'm suddenly not hungry." She went over and kissed each one on the cheek and said, "Good-bye."

Ericka mumbled something that Willy couldn't hear.

And then Willy took Noel out of the restaurant and hugged her in the parking lot before opening the door. "You did great!" He brushed a tear off her cheek.

"That's not what my parents think," Noel replied sadly.

"What did your mom mumble before you left? I didn't hear it, but it seemed to upset you.

"She associated my loss of appetite with me being pregnant." Noel let out a big gasp of air.

"What?" Willy yelled so loud that Noel jumped. "You are kidding me."

"Nope!"

"Your mom is a real trip. We need to pray for them when we get back to the bus," Willy said, shaking his head at how heartless her parents had been.

"My mom has always been obsessed with her reputation, and unfortunately, what I do does reflect on them." She snorted. "I guess I'm glad she didn't see me backstage after the concert. If she'd seen the way Kevin had snuck up behind me, picked me up in a bear hug and swung me around, then that would be number three."

Willy got serious. "Well, if I didn't know you, I'd have questioned your relationship the way he kissed you good-bye and how close he seemed to be. It almost seems like every time you two are together, you pick up where you left off." He was having a hard time with their closeness.

The turn of conversation derailed Noel from her parents hurt and did the trick, but it was wreaking havoc with Willy's heart. Noel looked over at Willy. "Why? Are you jealous?"

Willy simply stated back with a question he was dying to know. "Is there anything to be jealous about?"

"You know that I can't continue with Kevin not being a believer. But he still causes a lot of emotions to run through me, and I care about him deeply."

Willy asked the next question with all seriousness. "Do you think there would be something there if he were to show a genuine conversion?"

Noel was silent for a moment. She whispered, "I pray every day that God will bring into my life the man He has for me and that I'll follow His leading in this area. It's when I take my eyes off what God has for me that I experience the greatest challenges and pain."

Willy leaned up against the bus. He put up his hand for a high-five from Noel. She jumped up and slapped his hand hard.

"Hey, Noel, that was great last night!" Willy was cracking up. "I mean, you had Sky Blue so spun up. It sure puts the fun back into the drudgeries of road life. And you have to admit that he's a great target."

"That he is." She laughed. "But I can only do it so much or he might just end up hating me or firing me." She put her hands in her back pockets. "I mean, I do it really so he'll loosen up some. Let's see. It only took me coming in with the wrong line on three songs before he got mad this time, so he's doing good. Don't ya think?"

Willy laughed. He was going to miss her. He lowered his head and switched his feet. "So, where are you going?"

Noel looked away. Good-byes were never easy for her. "Well, I don't know. I'll figure it out. I obviously can't stay at my parents' place, but I can probably look up some friends and shack up with them." She then shrugged her shoulders. "Then, if all else fails, there's always Kevin's place."

Willy was quiet. He so hated to let her go just like that, but he hadn't bounds to keep her. But he was worried for her. He just had to ask one thing. "You are coming back, aren't you?" he asked in a hushed voice.

Noel caught the tone and the emotion of the moment. "Yes, Willy. No matter what, I'm coming back." She then got up on her tiptoes and kissed him on the cheek and walked away.

Willy watched her until she was out of sight.

CHAPTER 20

The hayride was in full swing when Peter walked over to stand next to Willy, his arms crossed and a huge grin on his face. He'd waited a long time to do this. He began his interrogation. "So, I'm wondering if I have a pry bar big enough."

"Pry bar?" Willy shrugged his shoulders. "What do you mean by a pry bar?"

"Man, I'm not sure I have a big enough pry bar to get your eyes off Noel. They're glued to her." Peter slapped Willy on the back.

Willy averted his eyes immediately, not liking being found out so easily. He asked, "Hey old man, marriage not agreeing with you, or did you eat something bad?"

"Nope. None of the above. I just came over to disagree with you!" Peter's smile got bigger.

"Man, what's with you?" Willy laughed.

"I have waited a long time for the shoe to be on the other foot."

"Man, call me dense, but what in the world are you talking about?" Willy, shaking his head, was as curious as ever.

"You love her, don't you?" Peter simply asked Willy as he looked out toward the bonfire.

Willy's eyes were riveted on the very subject. Noel was standing up, talking to several guys who were sitting on hay bales, her arms going this way and that in a frantic fashion. Willy's smile got even bigger. He knew she was doing her acting and was evidently in a very fiery conversation. Willy could just imagine the entertainment. If there was one thing he'd learned about being with Noel, it was that she was a living act. For the most part, she was fun loving, unassuming, and totally crazy and completely in love with Jesus, all things that Willy loved about her. There it was again, that *love* word.

Willy didn't even know which way was up, so he didn't really know how to answer Peter. Nor did he want anyone prying into his well-protected heart. So he chose his answer carefully. "Yeah, man. You know it. Of course I do. I love everybody." He jabbed his cousin with his elbow.

"Now look here. I have to report to my bride, so just the facts, sir, and nothing else will do," Peter said in his stern voice.

"Lilly put you up to this?" Willy put his hands up in the air.

"No, but I thought I would use her as an excuse because after she sees us over here talking, she's going to be grilling me tonight in bed," Peter grinned.

"Now that sounds like fun!"

"That's not what I mean." Peter cleared his throat. "Now, answer the question, because you two clearly belong together. And as you once told me, if you're not going to claim her, let her free." He paused. "But I warn you, she won't have any trouble getting offers," Peter said, knowing that Noel, though very different from his own wife, would make a man very happy.

"When did you become Mr. Know-It-All?" Willy snickered. "I mean, it sounds like you know all about women all of a sudden."

"No, my man. I just know love when I see it. That's all." Peter grinned and patted Willy on the back. "And after all the teasing you did when I was in your shoes, it's payback time, man."

Willy got it now. Peter was on him like a hound on a hunt. "Whoa, whoa. You can just hold up there, old man. It ain't none of your beeswax." Willy was being funny in how he said it, but he was serious that he wanted Peter to butt out.

"Yeah right. You'll come a-asking, I just know it," Peter said with satisfaction that Willy was a man in love; he just hadn't come to grips with it yet.

"They're calling for the hayride to start. I'm outta here," Willy said to his trusted cousin and took off.

Peter watched as Willy jaunted up beside Noel. They conversed, and Willy put his arm around her as he lead her to the hay wagon.

"Humph. He's in love all right."

Lilly had walked over. "What are you snickering about, Professor Collins?" That was something Lilly had kept up in their marriage when she wanted a kiss.

Peter obliged his lovely wife. "Those two love birds. That's what."

She jumped up with excitement. "Did you find out anything?" She wasted no time before quizzing her husband.

"I got more from watching him than listening to him." Peter smiled and helped his wife up on the wagon. He leaned in close to her ear. "I'll tell you tonight," he whispered.

Lilly rolled her eyes. "Yeah right!"

Willy had led the group in worship songs around the fire, and now he had a surprise. "As many of you know, Noel here"—he lightly touched her arm—"has joined me and the Mercy Seat Rockers. It's been a tremendous blessing to have her, sing with her, and get to know her heart more and more." He looked over at her and smiled. "Tonight, she and I have three songs to sing for you, and then Noel is going to share her testimony. I know you'll be as blessed as I am every time I hear of a heart redeemed and a life changed for the glory of God, our Savior."

Willy got a glimpse of what Sky Blue must feel when he is in concert. It really was like an intimate team when singing together. That he never fell for Noel was simply amazing the way they sang and performed together. Willy had a bongo drum, and Noel played her guitar as they sang together.

Noel stayed standing as Willy took her guitar and set it aside. "May all glory be to God, for He is the creator of anything good in me. Tonight, you might be hurting and going through a really hard time and feel all alone, but let me tell you, you are never alone. You are never forsaken." Noel went on to share her testimony from the night she met Willy right up to the present time. It was very touching and powerful.

Peter gave Wilma his handkerchief. "Thanks, Peter." Wilma blew her nose. She'd cried through the whole thing. "Tell me, Peter. Am I looking at my future daughter-in-law?"

Peter's grin widened as he gave a slight nod. Wilma buried her face. Peter put his arm around her and gave her a squeeze. He knew they were tears of joy, but they were still coming in full force.

In the apartment above the garage, Noel lay with her head against the soft pillow. Tears had been her friend tonight. Her heart was so full that it was sweet release to just let the tears flow. She wasn't sure what they were all for, but she didn't stem them. She lay there with her eyes closed and reflected on the evening. She couldn't get those faces out of her mind. There was fear, loneliness, hatred, abandonment, love, emptiness, and hopelessness in several of the faces that now came to her mind. Those faces troubled and burdened her, forcing her to cry out to God for mercy on behalf of those broken and hurting hearts. She so remembered her own journey to Christ, and she hoped she never forgot the grace that was given her that she, in turn, would pour out her life for others.

Then her mind went to Willy. What fun they'd on the hayride. His laughter was infectious. Even with her eyes closed and wet cheeks, she smiled as she let her thoughts go free about the man who made her heart skip a beat every time he was near. The hayride was obviously bouncy and crowded, and hay was flying. Noel had bumped into Willy several times. Then, in a space of several beats, their eyes locked, their faces close together. All other sounds were drowned out. Willy looked at Noel's lips. Noel couldn't breathe. Then Willy smiled and said, "You have a piece of hay in your hair." He reached up and got it out. There was more bumping into each other, and the moment passed. But Noel's heart could not deny his intentions.

But what she thought about that, she didn't fully know. She felt like she was falling for Willy, yet that didn't mean that it would work out. And more than anything, she feared losing her dearest friend in the world. Not to mention that if things fell apart, they'd still have to tour together. She shook her head. That made her shiver in her bed. She just couldn't take that chance. But...

Her heart told her otherwise as she reflected on Willy's good night kiss. Willy walked her to the bottom of the garage apartment staircase. She became as confused as ever when he detained her. Willy switched his feet and looked up at her. She was on the bottom step and had turned to say good night.

Willy ran his fingers through his hair, "You were remarkable tonight. I never realized the chemistry you and I have when we sing. That was like nothing I've experienced before. I think I'm jealous of Sky Blue. He gets you all to himself."

"Well, if he had his way, he would trade me out." Noel rolled her eyes. "I guess I still have the Hollywood acting in my blood when I want to use it."

Willy understanding her meaning knew just how well at acting she was. He asked quietly, piercing Noel's eyes, "Were you acting tonight?"

Noel hesitated, not sure she wanted to go where this was headed. She whispered, "No."

Willy reached up with his two hands and tenderly cupped her face and did what he'd been wanting to do for some time now. He came close to her face and said with a smile, "I'm going to kiss you, so if I don't hear any objections…" He looked into her eyes. He only heard a gasp, so he kissed her briefly but long enough to know it wasn't just any ol' good night kiss. It had passion and meaning. When he ended the long-awaited pleasure, he simply stepped back and said, "Good night," and left.

Noel now, even as she lay in bed, reached up and touched her lips. The kiss still lingered there. *Where now, LORD?* she prayed, and then she went on to pour her heart out to the LORD—her fears, her desires, and her confusion over drummer boy. Finally, sometime in the wee hours of the morning, she fell into a fitful sleep.

Noel was the last one to the breakfast table, so she entered with a flushed face full of embarrassment that she'd kept them waiting. "Good morning, everyone. I'm so sorry to have held you up." Noel then slid into the only available seat, which just happened to be right across from Willy. She looked at him. He smiled his sweet smile at her.

"Not to worry, my dear. I was just about to send Willy up to wake you, but then here you are," Wilma retorted with a smile.

"Oh please, Mother." Olivia slapped the table. "If you'd have done that, we'd be missing both of them!" she teased the couple.

"Really, Mom. Olivia is right. Sending Willy would've been a mistake, but maybe he'd have gotten her here by turkey time," Hannah chimed in.

"Excuse me!" With a hand on his hip, Willy cleared his throat. "Just what are you girls implying?"

"Oh, nothing. Just that you, um…forget your way around here when you're gone. That's all," Hannah said.

All knew it was normal banter, but Doug had to put a hold on it for two reasons. One was that Noel was beet red and about to slide under the table, and he was hungry. Doug raised his hand and said, "Let's pray." That put an end to all communications except to God, the Provider to which Doug prayed on behalf of all at the table.

There were clanging forks as dishes were passed when Willy spoke to Noel. "Your cheeks are real rosy this morning. You're not feeling under the weather, are you?" He was teasing her, and she knew it.

"Yes. My thoughts could not quiet themselves enough to fall asleep right away," she answered carefully.

"Oh really?" Willy's eyebrows rose. "And what thoughts would those be?"

"Oh, whether or not I want to continue on with the Mercy Seat Rockers." Noel decided to get Willy at his own game. She tilted her head back and forth, "I mean, I'm going home in two days, and, well, I just might decide I just can't handle road life." She glanced over at Willy, who was suddenly quiet and white as a ghost. "I mean, really, it's not an easy thing to wake up to a grouch like you every day. I mean, you're a real bear. Your breath is enough to make one toss their cookies. Oh, but then that's right. No homemade cookies on the bus. Hmm. Maybe I'm missing home more and more." She smiled a satisfied smile toward Willy.

"Oh yes. It must be most dreadful. I mean, you don't have much room. Shopping must be completely out of the question," Hannah joined in the game.

Peter and Lilly had arrived an hour before breakfast, wanting to spend as much time with Willy and Noel as possible.

Peter slapped Willy on the back. "Man, you asked for that one!"

Willy finally understood that it had all been a joke.

"I'll get you for this!" Willy glared at Noel before laughing.

"Sure. I'd like to see you catch me."

"You're on, sunshine," Willy said, thinking of the fun they'd have later.

"Willy, it seems like to me you've been keeping yourself a bit more pristine these days. Any particular reason?" Peter teased. "Or, rather, anyone in particular?"

Knowing everyone was listening, Willy chose his weapons carefully. "I didn't think an old man like you could have that good of vision."

"I might be old, but I'm not blind."

On they went in light banter through the meal. It brought back memories for Peter when Willy was teasing him without mercy about his ragmuffin.

―――⨯―――

Later that day, Lilly and Noel took their much-awaited walk. Their friendship had grown deep. So naturally that was what both looked forward to each time they were reunited.

Lilly wasted no time. "So tell me. How are things with your parents?"

"It seems like the closer I get to God, the farther away I get from my parents." Noel shrugged her shoulders. "I just don't understand. I pray for them every day. But they seem to be more and more against me." She sighed.

She kicked a pebble as she went on to share with Lilly the last meeting she had with them and all that had transpired.

Lilly just listened, her heart breaking for the woman she wanted to protect from all hurt. But Lilly knew that that wasn't the way God worked. She'd learned that pain and suffering will be part of the Christian life. Yet the very nature of the heart wanted to avoid it at all costs. When Lilly thought she was done, she quoted: "'In this you greatly rejoice, though now for a little while you may have had to suffer grief in all kinds of trials. These have come so that your faith—of greater worth than gold, which perishes even though refined by fire—may be proved genuine and may result in praise, glory and honor when Jesus Christ is revealed. Though you have not seen him, you love him; and even though you do not see him now, you believe in him and are filled with an inexpressible and glorious joy, for you are receiving the goal of your faith, the salvation of your souls.' In 1 Peter 1:6-9. 'However, if you suffer as a Christian, do not be ashamed, but praise God that you bear that name,' 1 Peter 4:16. I'm not sure what all God has planned for you, Noel, but you can rest assured it'll include pain and suffering."

Noel nodded and wiped a tear from her cheek. She knew that Lilly was speaking truth, and it helped so much just to be able to talk to someone about her family situation.

Lilly had only scratched the surface of the friendly interrogation, so she pressed on, not sure how much time they'd have. And she wanted to cover all the bases, so to speak. "So how is it going with Mercy Seat Rockers? Are you getting more settled in?"

"I'm loving it!" That brought a smile to her face. She looked over at Lilly. "I would've never dreamed it possible. I'm having the time of my life, especially now that things are going better between me and Sky Blue. It was rough at first, but now I think we're a good team."

Lilly wasn't sure she wasn't hearing that perhaps Noel had a thing for Sky Blue, so she pried a little more. "So have you gotten to be good friends with everyone on the bus?"

"Oh yes. For sure. They all think I'm crazy. But that's okay because most of the time, I think that's true too." She went on to tell Lilly about Monterey, the surrey ride, the treasure hunt, the pranks that they'd played on Sky Blue, and the day at Knott's Berry Farm.

Lilly, feeling satisfied that she was going to be fine, smiled to herself and then went on to other subjects. "So, how are things with you and Kevin?"

"Well, you know we are very close for some strange reason." Noel sighed. "He never could really get over our break-up. But"—she jumped up very excited and grabbed Lilly—"you'll never guess what happened!"

"What? What?" Lilly responded, completely held hostage by the suspense.

"Kevin got saved."

"What? Really? How wonderful," Lilly said as tears began welling up in her eyes. "That's so awesome, Noel. I know we've prayed long and hard over that soul. Tell me what happened."

Noel went on to tell Lilly how Kevin had finally come to see his need for a Savior and had asked God to save him before the last tour had ended; thus, they spent the entire break together, discussing the Bible and the things of God. He had a lot of questions, so she tried her best to answer them.

Lilly thought this was fantastic but was curious about one thing. "So does this mean the two of you will get back together?"

"I don't know about anything these days." Noel sighed. "It seems like the obvious thing to do, but with me on tour, that makes it hard. And it might be that he's not the partner for me at all."

Lilly understood completely, and not that she wished this Kevin any unhappiness, but Lilly was still completely convinced that Noel and Willy made a perfect pair. "Does that mean that you've given thought to someone else?"

Noel was hesitant. She wished she could share everything on her heart, but she wasn't sure herself. "There are times I think that Willy likes me, and then at other times I'm not sure." She looked away.

"Would that be so bad?" Lilly jumped on the subject, not willing to let it go.

"Oh no, but it scares me to death. I mean, he's a lot of fun, and his devotion to the Lord can't be denied. And in truth, I can't find a single negative thing about the dude. But..." She stopped.

"But what, Noel?" She encouraged her to go on.

"I don't know if you can understand this"—Noel grabbed Lilly's forearm—"but Willy means everything to me. I mean, he's my rock, the Jesus with flesh on, so to speak, and I cherish our friendship so much that it scares me to see if there's more in light of losing what we have. Does that make sense?" Noel was desperate for her to understand.

"Yes. As a matter of fact, I completely understand." She was thinking of her Peter and their precarious relationship before marriage. "All I can tell you is follow your heart. Wherever God leads you will be beautiful. Maybe not pain free. But you have to trust God, Noel, even in this. If He so chooses for you to lose this relationship, then let God be God. Though you might not understand, you must trust God completely, especially when things don't make sense. And I can tell you from my own experience that God is true to His Word that He has the best for His children."

They were back to the house, so Noel thanked Lilly and gave her a hug. Then they went in to help with Thanksgiving dinner.

Noel was overcome as she sat, just watching a real family. They'd all helped with the feast and then eaten with such thankfulness that Noel was overwhelmed. Willy noted that she'd been quiet at the table. Then, as tradition dictated, they sat in the living room for their share time.

After Willy took a seat next to Noel, he leaned over and whispered, "Hey, sunshine. Why so quiet?"

"Just a little overwhelmed at being part of a real family." Noel brushed at the imaginary dust bunny on her pants.

Willy nodded in understanding. As the sharing began, Noel was blessed beyond words. When it came her turn, she just looked at Willy and then back at each person in the room.

"All I can say is Thank You, Lord, for letting me be part of this family." She began to cry. "I am truly thankful that God redeemed me and that He showed me what real treasure is."

Willy drove Noel to the airport in his beast. She got out of the car, shut the door, and laughed. "I had forgotten how much character your car had."

Willy took her luggage and waited for her in line. Then he walked her to the terminal and they sat down to wait for the boarding call. Willy spoke up as he leaned forward in his seat to see her better. "You know you don't have to go. My mom would be more than happy to keep you." Willy laughed, knowing just how true that was.

"I can't just sponge off people like that, Willy." Noel looked away and then back at Willy with that sad look. "As much as I hate to leave, I must. Besides, I promised Kevin I'd come home so we could study the Scriptures some more. I can't let him down. Besides, who knows? With it being Christmastime and my birthday, maybe, just maybe, my parents will be more open to listening to me about the Gospel."

Willy nodded his understanding but was silent. He wanted to say, "Tell Kevin you're taken," but he didn't have that surety in this relationship. But what he did say was, "Well, it seems to me that Kevin is a lucky man to be on the receiving end of my sunshine's attention."

"Oh, stop it." Noel waved her hand at him. "We're just friends, and I need to be there for him."

Willy put a stray hair behind her ear and brushed the back of his finger on her cheek. "Let's just hope that you come back the same way." He was looking deep in Noel's eyes, his look holding her hostage.

Neither wanted to leave, but they were suddenly distracted by the boarding call.

"Well, that's you," Willy slapped his legs and stood. He wanted to kiss her. But it wasn't the time or place. Not only that, but he had determined that though he'd enjoyed kissing her, he wouldn't do so again until he was sure her heart was not divided with Kevin or anyone else for that matter. He was certain his heart was way too far gone, and he didn't want to get hurt.

He tapped her on the nose. "See you on the bus soon. Oh, and here." He reached in his back pocket and pulled out a tiny package. "Happy birthday." And then he reached in his coat pocket and pulled out another tiny package and put in her hand. "Merry Christmas too!" He then turned her around and pushed her toward the boarding line. "You can open them on Christmas Day. Now scoot, or you'll be late."

Noel was almost to the line when she turned, ran back, and grabbed Willy by the neck and give him the biggest hug. "I'll miss you more than you know." Then she turned and ran to the door to get on her plane, leaving a smiling Willy in her wake.

CHAPTER 21

"You hold the key to my heart." Noel remembered the words written on the paper inside the gifts she'd opened at Christmas from Willy. She was actually in her parents' living room sometime later when she remembered them. She snuck off to her old room and sat on her bed and took the suckers off the top and unwrapped each one. She found a key in one and a heart locket necklace in the other. And written on the inside of the key gift paper itself was this message: "You hold the key to my heart." On the paper of the other gift was written, "May the picture of whoever captures your heart be placed here. I hope it's mine." Noel didn't know what to think, but it was clear that Willy's intentions were to pursue her heart. He stayed on her mind the rest of the visit. As well, she had a lot to think about on the plane trip back to the tour bus. She needed to decide whether there was anything left in her heart for Kevin that was more than friends. But she felt like she already had her answer. Yes, indeed, no matter the outcome, Willy had completely and thoroughly captured her heart.

Noel's thoughts went to Sky Blue's wedding. Actually, to a particular walk that was taken with Willy the morning after the wedding. Willy had slipped his hand in hers as they took the wooded pathway though the beautiful state park near where Kenzie lived. It was the third day of March, and the sun was beaming, yet there was still the crispness to the air that Noel loved. Noel began to chit chat.

"So, drummer boy, how'd you like the wedding?"

"Hmm. It sure made me less content as a single guy. That's for sure!"

Noel elbowed Willy. "No really. What did you think about the bride? Wasn't she beautiful?" Noel thought that Kenzie was the most beautiful bride she'd ever seen.

"To be honest, I'm not sure."

"What do you mean you don't know? What, did you have your head in the sand?"

"No." Willy laughed. "I just couldn't take my eyes off a certain lady who was absolutely stunning. So, you see, I had no time to look at the bride when I was feasting upon the bridesmaid!"

Blushing to the ends of her roots, she said, "Getting married scares me to death. I don't think I'll know what to do!" she said, talking more to herself. "I mean, Kenzie was so beautiful and graceful and all. I'm sure I won't know how to be a bride."

Her insecurity melted Willy's heart. "Just how do you know the groom will know anything more than you?"

That gave Noel food for thought. Willy hadn't been able to sleep, as his thoughts were so taken with Noel and praying for the right time to ask her to be his bride. They'd come to a stop on the trail, and Willy put his hand up on Noel's cheek and then lowered his head and put his hand through her hair, pulling her lips to his in a kiss he'd remember for a long time.

He hadn't kissed her since the first time, so this was just as special, just as wonderful, Noel thought. In sensory overload, Noel replied after the sweet kiss ended, "I had begun to think that I'd never know your kiss again."

"In case you get worried." He bent and gave her another passionate kiss. "I needed to be sure you were over Kevin before we kissed again, for kissing is something I take seriously between two people." He brushed her cheek with his thumb and then took her hand and continued their walk. He knew he needed to keep his own emotions in check and to not let things get carried away and so dishonor God, not to mention their own integrity.

Noel had subconsciously rubbed her finger over her lips as though she were in his arms again. She was jolted back to reality when Willy set down her mocha. "A single mocha, with caramel and chocolate drizzled over the whipped cream. Leave the lid off please." He set it down in front of the woman he loved so much.

"You remembered!" She beamed at him as she ate the delicious topping.

"I remember every little thing about you."

Noel rolled her eyes, thinking there were some things she'd rather he'd forget about her, like their first meeting.

"Now, missy, what land were you in when I came up just now?"

"Oh, just thinking about Sky Blue and Kenzie's wedding and a certain dashing young man." She winked at Willy.

Willy, feeling sure he knew just what she was thinking about, said, "If we weren't sitting out here on this nice, sunny café sidewalk, I'd think you'd be due for another reminder of my thoughts for you." They were at the same New York café where Willy had met Noel, then, Christy just about that time last year for a tour of studio street. It was a special place to Willy, so he'd asked Noel to join him for a date. They were on tour but had the afternoon off.

"Remember when we were here last?" Noel asked.

"Every moment!" Willy smiled, taking a sip of his hot mocha.

Noel almost choked on her next sip, laughing.

"Out with it. What has your giggle box turned upside down?" Willy demanded, dying to know what was going through her adorable little head.

"Oh, I was just thinking about how mad Sky Blue was when he walked out with Kenzie after their reception and found a surrey instead of his car." Noel burst out laughing.

Willy joined her at the remembrance of their friend and boss. The whole group had agreed upon this prank, and all were involved in one way or another. During the wedding, Willy switched the cars out. He had mercy on Sky Blue and had taken his car only three blocks away. When Sky Blue, anxious to take his bride away, snagged her and went out through the throngs of rice-throwing well-wishers, he stopped dead in his tracks when he caught sight of the surrey with all the cans tied to the bumper, the pompoms tied to the mirrors, and the "Just Married" banner fastened to the top. The band knew to stay way behind the well-wishers but were in clear view of his reaction, for they knew he would blow his stack, and they didn't want to be near the explosion; only watch it. Chet had bought a horn and kept squeezing it for all to hear. But what could he do since everyone was watching?

Noel was in near tears at the remembrance, and Willy was laughing wildly.

"I don't think a more cleverly irritating wedding prank has ever been played than that one. It was so worth it. Though he's still barely civil to us and it's been, what, almost six weeks now."

"Well, that's easy for you to say. You don't have to sing with the guy."

They bantered back and forth every memory of that day, simply enjoying each other's company.

"It's not like I didn't leave a note saying where he needed to pedal to. I mean, that was real nice of me, wasn't it?" Willy said.

They both belted out in laughter again. As it was, they made sure that the newlywed couple made it the three blocks. And really, as mad as Sky Blue was, he could've pedaled to China, they recalled.

Willy had leaned back and listened to Noel. Just hearing her lovely voice was like perfume to the nose; it intoxicated him to listen to her. To say that she was lovely to look upon was an understatement, though she was very different from the girls back home. But every bit what caught Willy's attention.

He interrupted her. "Do you know you're beautiful?" he asked softly.

Noel didn't know what to say, so she just looked at him and then down at her empty cup. After a while, he suggested a walk on the New York streets before heading back to the bus.

Noel couldn't believe how the time had flown touring. It was now July, and they were back in California on the Ocean Praise West tour. She'd been on tour for a year now. Having been to every place, she was now starting over again. Everything took on even more meaning knowing that she was in love with Willy and that he was in love with her. It made everything more special, more fun, more everything. She was enjoying her relationship with Willy, and neither seemed to be in any hurry to end getting to know one another in this deep bond called love. Though he hadn't actually said the words yet, his actions of love couldn't be denied. They enjoyed studying God's Word together, singing together, sightseeing together, and teasing and playing games together. And while their relationship was getting stronger, so were the relationships with everyone on tour growing deeper. There was a bond there like none Noel had ever known.

So it was with that new twist in Noel's life that she met with her parents at a fancy restaurant and talked to them while in town. She actually did that twice. She also invited Kevin to several of their beach days. Willy and Kevin bonded even more now that Kevin could clearly see that those two belonged together. The three of them studied God's Word together and did the skate park ministry. Basically, every waking moment was spent with Kevin and his friends. Putting hands and feet to their faith. It was neat to minister together *with* Kevin not *to* Kevin.

CHAPTER 22

Willy wouldn't have believed it if he hadn't lived it. There it was, the weekend before Thanksgiving and their last tour concert. They had performed a spectacular last concert and then gone to the Barnabus House B&B. Willy had begged Noel to stay through the holiday with him.

He set her suitcase in her room and said, "You were spectacular tonight."

"Oh, Willy, what am I ever gonna do with you?" she teased with her hands on her hips.

Willy grinned and leaned up against the doorframe. "I don't know, but I intend on sticking around and finding out."

Then he caressed her check with his hand, kissed her tenderly, and left. On his way down the stairs, he turned. "You better get some rest. Tomorrow is sure to be a day to remember." She nodded and closed the door. She needed to spend some time with her Lord before going to sleep. Her heart was full, and she needed to unload on the One who knew her so well.

⨯

Willy came up alongside Noel. "You ready for tonight?" It was the night of the annual hayride and bonfire.

"Sorta."

"What does that mean?" Willy asked, concerned.

"Oh, just that I don't like sharing you with all the other girls!" She sighed. "You get quite the attention."

"Come now. It ain't all that bad." Willy laughed.

"Humph." She rolled her eyes. "Yeah right! One thing is for sure: you've no shortage of admirers here."

"But I only have eyes for one." Willy got serious. "And I'm looking at her."

"Hey, let's find a good hay-throwing spot," she said, wanting a distraction as she headed to the wagon.

"Well, be sure and sit far away from Peter then."

Knowing Peter like they did, both laughed as they ran to the wagon just as it was about to take off.

After hot chocolate and hot dogs were served, Willy got up with his guitar, and led the youth in worship songs. Then Willy surprised Noel by having her join him in singing three songs from tour.

"Thank you for coming out tonight," Willy said. "I don't know about you, but I've had a lot of fun already."

There were cheers from the crowd.

"I want to thank my mom and dad for doing this every year. It's one of my fondest memories. Now is the time we have someone share their testimony. They all got comfortable to listen to the speaker pour out his heart. It was a night to remember for sure.

Willy went out the back door when he thought she might be on her cool down and dropped in step beside her. "Have a good run?"

She was breathing hard but nodded her head and smiled. "Yes."

They continued to walk swiftly until she caught her breath. Willy was glad for the moment alone. There wasn't much privacy, and not getting any time alone with the woman of his dreams was maddening, as rules on tour forbade a personal relationship of that nature, and with understanding Willy tried to abide by the rules.

"Hey, there are new baby kittens in the barn. Wanna take a peek?"

"Oh sure. I don't think I've ever seen a litter of the fur balls before."

"Follow me then, my lady. We'll go see these *purrfect* little creatures." Willy led them into the barn.

The smell of fresh hay hit Noel's nose, and she wrinkled up her face at the whiff.

"Where are they?" Noel asked, looking around.

"Most likely up in the hayloft." He stood at the foot of the ladder that went to the top, with his arm stretched out like an invitation. "Beauty before beast!" Noel rolled her eyes and went up the ladder.

Willy was right behind her. He held his finger to his lips, "Shh."

Sure enough, they could hear the purring of the furry creatures, and Willy went right to their nest. He motioned for Noel to come. She complied. Immediately, she knelt down to the floor and took the offered kitten from Willy.

She held it to her cheek and felt its satisfied purring. "They're so adorable!"

Willy just sat back and smiled as she took each one and held it, talked to it, and tried to fix its hair. She would say, "And you'd look better with this style," and, "You there would do better with this color or cut."

After a while, she looked over at Willy. "What are you looking at?"

"Oh, just you!" He grinned. "Just beautiful Noel." He had leaned back against a post.

Noel chose to ignore him and then went back to caressing the kittens. Then she heard more than just purring. She heard, "I love you."

She looked at Willy. He was just as he was, sitting up against the post, tossing bits of hay.

"What did you say?"

"I said, I am madly in love with you!" Then he threw a piece of hay her way.

Noel dropped the kitten she was holding and put her hands up to her mouth in a gasp.

Willy scooted close to her and touched her cheek softly. "You keep me awake at night. You tease me in my dreams. My only nightmare would be that you wouldn't return that love." Willy had spoken all that with deep tenderness while caressing her cheek.

"You are my dream come true. I've told myself a thousand times not to love you, but my heart just wouldn't listen." She licked her lips. "I love you, drummer boy!" She began to cry. "I've loved you for a long time, only afraid of losing you, so I dared not even think you could be mine!"

She was still crying when Willy pulled her to his chest. He took her hand and laid it on his chest. "Do you feel that?" he asked her. "That is my heart beating wildly at the thought of you." He smoothed her hair until she quieted. "You match the beat of my heart perfectly."

He turned her chin up to his face, and with all the love they had, their lips met.

"We better scoot before I act upon my wild feelings." Willy moved to get up.

Noel knew that he was a godly man, such a change from her last relationship. She yearned as much as Willy did, but she too wanted to honor God.

"You're a crazy guy. Did you know that?" Noel giggled.

"Yes, I know I'm crazy. That is, crazy in love with you."

"Did you ever think that the night you tripped over me?"

Willy smiled and shook his head. "Nope, but God did." With that, he tapped her nose and proceeded down the ladder and out of the barn.

✕

CHAPTER 23

At the end of the first week of December, Willy and Noel boarded a plane headed for California. Ericka had called Lilly to be sure that Noel was coming home for Christmas. So she passed the message to Noel, who planned to leave as soon as she could. About seven hours later, they were headed to Noel's parents' place. They were both greeted kindly, which Willy thought a bit odd. They showed them to their rooms, the same ones they'd used before. After he settled in, he went back into the living area and looked at all the Christmas decorations. He was astonished at the drastic difference. This was all so worldly, basically anti-Christ. There was nothing about Christ Jesus at all. It was very sad to Willy, and depressing, he thought, to have a hopeless Christmas. Then he managed to get to the tree. Noel had told him about this, but seeing it was unbelievable. All the ornaments were of movie stars. Glass balls with pictures of the star, their name, and the hit movie etched in gold. And yes, on the top was Elvis, king of rock and roll.

They have the wrong king up there, Willy shook his head.

This was where Noel found him. "I told you it was different."

Willy looked at her and then back at the tree. "Yeah, it's different. It shows just how different you and your parents are, two totally different celebrations from two totally different hearts." He grieved for her parents. "We need to keep them in our prayers."

He wondered just what Christmas Day would be like this year. He was sure it would be as different as night and day.

―――✕―――

They arrived at Cambria by lunchtime, so Willy bought sandwiches at his favorite grill, and then they went to the elephant seal parking lot overlooking the ocean bluffs and rocks where they ate their lunch. *Very romantic*, Noel thought. *It's beautiful here*. They could hear the seals calling to each other. Willy took her hand as they walked to the railing edge and watched the swimming seals. Then they walked down the path to look at the hundreds of beached seals.

After Willy thought Noel had her fill of big fat beach hogs, he suggested a walk on the Moonstone boardwalk before heading back. She was more than happy to oblige. Willy had a plan working in his head. When they got there, Willy drove up to the edge where the trail began, turned off the car, and said, "Hey, why don't you wait here? I want to go down and check out the surf. I thought maybe I'd catch a wave if you don't care."

He was smiling, but then Noel didn't think she'd ever seen him without one.

"Sure. Whatever you want to do."

Willy was happy that his plan was working. So he hopped out and climbed down the rocks to the beach below. He'd parked to where Noel wouldn't be able to see him. As expected, he found some kids playing in the sand. He went to them, squatted down, and said, "Hey, guys. My name is Willy, and I need to ask you a favor." Willy saw their parents approach, so he waited and repeated his first line again then went on. "I need someone to gather shells and write a message for me." Then he looked around and spotted the item needed for the other part of his plan. "Hey, can I borrow this bucket and shovel? I'll bring it back shortly."

"Sure, mister," a little, freckled boy said.

Then Willy looked to the parents and explained what he was doing and what he wanted written with the shells and that he needed it done in about fifteen minutes. The couple agreed, and Willy withdrew a twenty-dollar bill and gave it to them, saying, "Here's for the trouble." The couple took the money and began to get their kids to gather the shells. Willy gave them a thumbs-up and left.

He climbed up the bluff and hopped back in the car.

"So, how was the surf?" she asked, hoping he'd get to go, but the beaches up that way were different than the ones where she lived, so she wasn't sure he'd be able to.

"I'm afraid the waters are too rough. It's a bit windy." Willy shook his head. "So instead, I thought we'd go back to town and get a mocha and roll up our pant legs and take a stroll on the beach. How does that sound?"

"Hmm. You put mocha and beach in the same sentence." Noel tilted her head in the adorable way Willy loved. "What's not to like?"

So they went to town, taking their time so that the kids would have time to accomplish what he paid them to do and find a special shell and put it in the bucket filled with sand.

By now, Willy knew just what to order, and they walked hand in hand back to the car, that is, after Noel ate the topping off hers.

Willy laughed as he stopped her. "Here. Let me help you."

"What?" Noel asked, confused.

Willy leaned over and kissed her upper lip, effectively licking the whipped cream off that she'd left there while eating her topping.

"What was that for?"

"Oh, I was just getting the whipped cream off your lip." Willy grinned and watched her subconsciously lick her lips.

"I guess I better quit eating the topping."

"What, you don't like my kisses?" Willy bantered back, curious.

"Oh yes! But I don't like sharing my whipped cream."

"You're something. You know that?" Willy put his arm around Noel's shoulder and squeezed.

"Off to the sands, my sunshine." He opened the car door to let her in.

They arrived back at Moonstone and parked. Willy went down the stairs to the beach. He scanned for the couple, and the man gave a thumbs-up signal. So Willy steered Noel in that direction. In no time, they were there at the message center; the kids had done a fabulous job. Willy picked up the bucket of sand and slipped the ring into the special shell that was on top. He held the bucket behind his back.

Noel was motioning Willy, who'd hung back some, taking care of the ring. "Willy, come and see!"

"Why? What is it, Noel, that has you so excited?" Willy was trying to act nonchalant. He went up behind her, put his arms around her waist, kissed her neck, and then asked, "What is your answer?"

She twirled around so quickly she almost knocked the bucket over that he'd set down so he could use both his hands. "You wrote this?" Her eyes were bigger than he'd ever seen.

"Yes and no," Willy declared.

Noel had turned back around to stare at the message on the sand. In seashells of all different kinds were formed the words, "Will you marry me?"

Willy put his arms back around her and whispered, "The important thing is, what will your answer be?"

She turned slowly back around. "Oh, Willy, I'm afraid I'm going to wake up and find this all to be a dream."

Willy smiled, just loving every moment with her. "Here. Let me relay that this is not a dream." He bent his head and kissed her with all the love he had. Then he kissed her again. "Are you convinced this isn't a dream yet?" he questioned.

"Um…I'm not sure. Could you repeat that?"

Willy got a big grin, "My pleasure."

So they kissed again, holding each other and expressing their love.

Willy pulled her away to look at her face. "I take it that means the answer is yes?"

"Yes," Noel whispered as a stream of tears rolled down her cheeks.

Willy took her hand and lay it on his chest over his heart. "You, Noel Franklin, are the beat of my heart. I have waited a long time for the woman who would keep beat with mine, and I've found her." He bent down and picked up the bucket and said, "Here. Go ahead. Take the shell and open it. There's something inside."

Noel, with shaking hands, took the shell and opened it. After she finally snapped it open, there lay the most beautiful diamond she'd ever seen. "Oh, Willy. It is…" Tears again. "It's so…I don't know what to say."

Willy took the ring and put it on her ring finger. "You could say you'll marry me tomorrow," he teased.

"Willy, I have you know this is no time for teasing."

She finally hugged him, and he hugged her back, picking her up off the ground and turning around three times before setting her down.

"Something tells me my life will never be boring being drummer boy's wife."

"If you keep calling me drummer boy, you know we'll have to name our little girl Cymbals." Willy raised his eyebrows.

"You, mister, are getting a bit ahead of yourself. And instead of picking out silly baby names, how about picking out a wedding date to begin with?"

"Oh, that's because I already have!" Willy smiled. "And since you didn't like the first choice, I have a second one, June first."

"What was the first choice?" Noel tilted her head, confused.

"Tomorrow!"

"You are too much."

They rolled up their pant legs and splashed in the water as they strolled along the water's edge. As they walked, they planned their wedding. It would be one of a kind, Willy thought as he tried to picture all that Noel had in mind.

They were late getting home, as Willy wanted to take his fiancée out for a fancy dinner at the Chart House. Noel had gotten a key for the day and, thus, they tiptoed in, so as to not wake Burt and Ericka.

Willy walked Noel to her room, kissed her briefly, and said, "Good night, my bride-to-be."

Ericka had planned a big breakfast and the maid help her with it. So it was to an unusual feast that they woke up to that morning. Noel was already seated when Willy came in from his run. He bent over and kissed Noel on the head as he passed by.

"Good morning," he said to her. "Good morning, Burt and Ericka," he greeted her parents. "What a lovely spread you have out. Thank you for allowing me to join in on it." He looked over at Noel to see if she was okay. He was rewarded with a special smile.

Ericka put on her best air of pride and poor manners. "Well, it does seem like you keep appearing with my daughter, so it's not like I can exactly toss you out."

It was obvious that Ericka didn't like him. He wondered if she liked anybody besides herself. Willy actually had to hide his laughter at her rudeness.

Noel caught his snicker and was lighthearted about it.

"Actually, I'd really like to get down to business, Noel," Ericka stated, tapping her perfectly shaped nails on her goblet.

Noel had figured as much.

"Excuse me." Ericka cleared her throat. "But does he have to stay in here while we have this private discussion?" She'd snarled her lip up and pointed at Willy, making the ugliest face.

Willy only smiled back at her.

"It's fine for him to sit in on it, I think. He's not going to hurt anything."

"Very well," came the cold words of her mother.

"Go ahead, Mother and Father. What is it you wish to discuss with me?" Noel had kept her hands in her lap so as to not yet expose her engagement.

Burt nodded for Ericka to proceed. "Noel, darling, there's been an opportunity presented to us that I think you should take a good look at and consider carefully."

"Go ahead, Mother. I'm listening." Noel sat up straight in her chair.

"Now that you have done that touring thing and gotten it out of your system"—she rolled her eyes—"this would be perfect timing."

Noel had to bite her tongue in order not to respond to her sarcastic reference to the tour.

Her mother continued. "Arnold Fitzgerald came to me last week. You do remember him, don't you, dear?"

Noel nodded.

"He has a major role in a primetime series that he said would fit you perfectly. He said they're not even going to have auditions for the majors' roles. They wanted to hand-pick them."

"And he picked you for the female role," Burt chimed in. "Do you realize what an honor this is, Noel? Not to mention it would set you up for a lifetime acting career where you get to do the picking. Why, anyone in Hollywood would die to be in your shoes."

Noel was taking all of it in.

Ericka cut in. "The promotionals are suggesting that the script will be right up there with a possible fifteen-year season. Think of that. This is truly a chance of a lifetime."

"You'd be stupid not to jump at a chance like that," Burt put in plainly.

"What are the details? Where are they shooting?" Noel asked. "How long do they anticipate it taking to get it rolling? And what kind of audience is it targeted for. And who'd be the other main actors?" Noel could see out of the corner of her eye Willy's set jaw. She dared not look at him. She had no intentions of taking the job offer; however, out of courtesy to her parents, she *acted* interested.

Her parents answered her questions, having gathered as much information, knowing Noel would have inquiries.

Ericka then said, "I've set you up an appointment with Arnold at one p.m. tomorrow to discuss the pay for a set like this." Ericka leaned back and tapped her goblet again with a smile. "So what do you think? It's a dream come true, huh?"

Noel opened her mouth to speak and had only gotten out the words, "Why, yes, it's a dream come true!"

Willy leaned forward, his elbows on the table, his face resonating irritation. "I am sorry to disappoint you both, but Noel can't take this job."

"Why the heck not, and what do you have to do with this? This is my daughter's life, not yours!" Burt was furious.

Willy stood up, nearly knocking his chair over backward. He looked both of them in the face. "Noel can't take this job because she's already taken one."

"If you're going to say touring with that band, you're crazy!" Burt rolled his eyes.

Willy nodded and gulped. "You're right about one thing. I'm crazy. That is, crazy in love with your daughter!" Willy switched his feet and glanced at Noel, who smiled at him. "And the tour was not the job I spoke of."

"Well, what is it, for Pete's sake? Spit it out, kid!" Ericka whined.

Willy ran his fingers through his hair. "As my wife!"

Both Willy and Noel locked eyes, completely missing the horrific faces of her parents.

Burt, barely able to contain himself, yelled, "You better explain yourself, boy!"

"Well, it's like this—" Willy started.

"I knew it! When's the due date?" Ericka began to cry and flap her hands.

Willy looked hopelessly at Noel. He raised his hands in the air. "Hey, guys. Just wait a minute. Calm down!" He took a deep breath. "I realize that you really want Noel in acting, as the two of you have pursued. But she doesn't desire to follow in that path. It's time you two honor her wishes to pursue her dreams, as you both have done with your lives. As far as the claim about a date, it's not a due date but a wedding date. And we hope that you both will be in attendance. And as far as setting the record straight, there has never been nor will there be any intimate acts that would allow for that possibility before that date!" He wanted them to know about Noel's purity in this relationship. It was important. "What Noel and I would like is your blessing." He then took his seat.

There was a long silence.

Burt finally said, "Be happy, my daughter. Send us an invitation." He wiped his mouth and left the table.

Ericka was bawling and said nothing as she abruptly left.

Willy took Noel's hands in his. "Are you sure this is what you want? I mean, this is your chance to make it big, and I won't stand in your way."

"I'd rather act as your wife and have a life any day than any act Hollywood has to offer."

"How about a run on the beach?" Willy asked.

"I'm there."

They both got up and left. They ran, and they talked. But mostly, they prayed.

CHAPTER 24

Willy and Noel knocked on the hotel room door.

Noel jumped up and down and gave a quiet squeal. "I'm so excited!"

Willy looked at her wild excitement and said, "I can see that you are! And if you're this excited about seeing my cousin Peter, then I'll have to tie a string on you for the wedding so you'll be still long enough for me to marry you."

Noel knew that Willy was teasing her, but before she could answer back, the door opened. Peter, filling the doorframe, with his arms wide open, grabbed Willy in a bear hug, pulling him in. Next, he came after Noel. Lilly joined then, and all were jabbering at the same time when Wilma and Doug came through the adjoining room door, along with the four girls.

Reaching up to hug her son, Wilma stated, "I thought I heard a ruckus in here. Sure enough, my Willy has arrived." Then she turned to Noel and placed her hands on her face. "And he brought my precious soon-to-be daughter-in-law, Noel." She stared all her love right into Noel's heart. Then she hugged her.

"Hey, what, are you gonna hog her up?" Doug teased Wilma. "Let me hug my son's soon-to-be wife. Do you really know what you are getting yourself into?"

She smiled up at him. "I think so. What I'm worried about is, does he know what he's getting himself into?" Noel laughed.

"Marriage is a wonderful thing," Wilma said, having listened to the exchange. "I knew it would take a special person for our Willy. Many girls have caught Willy's eye, but only you have captured the beat of his heart."

The group had come three days early so they could sightsee a bit. Willy and Noel had actually planned the three days crammed full of Knott's Berry Farm, beaches, lighthouses, elephant seals, a surrey ride, and the aquarium in Monterey before heading to Moonstone, where the wedding was to take place.

Noel wasn't sure which she was more excited about, the days before the wedding or the day of the wedding. Olivia and Hannah were ecstatic, to say the least. The twins couldn't close their mouths, their eyes big with wonder. They tried to cram as many memories into those three days as would fit, including a trip down the sidewalk of the stars, where Wilma insisted that Noel show her where her parents' handprints and footprints were. Noel promised to drive them down Rodeo Drive and point out where her parents lived. Though she hadn't bothered with setting up a meeting with her parents, she thought it would be a useless discouragement and didn't even know if her parents would show up at the wedding, though they'd invited them.

It was the second day, and they were going to spend it at the beach.

Willy had suited up in his wet suit, and he came carrying one for Peter. He slapped him on the back. "Hey, man. This is for you." Willy was about to lose it just looking at Peter's white face.

"You've got to be kidding. You aren't going to get me in one of those things." Peter was indignant. "Plus," he whispered, "where do you even change into one?"

Willy hooted in laughter.

"Well, my man, as you can see, there ain't no bathrooms." Willy smiled. "So use your imagination." Willy tried to hand it to him. "I managed."

"Well, I ain't you, and I will not get undressed out here in public."

About that time, Lilly walked up and put her arm through her husband's. "Why is your forehead all crinkled, honey?"

Peter said with indignation, "My crazy cousin thinks he's going to get me into that tight penguin suit, without a bathroom, mind you, and then he wants me to try to stand up on that skinny, slick thing he calls a surfboard and ride a wave. That's what."

Lilly covered her mouth for fear that she was going to bust a gut laughing. Lilly caressed Peter's back, "It's okay, honey. You don't have to." Peter was just about to calm down when he heard his wife say, "I will!"

She reached past her husband to retrieve the wetsuit Willy had laying over his arm.

Peter stiffened his body. "Over my dead body!" Peter wasn't about to let Lilly do something crazy like that.

Lilly blinked in astonishment. Lilly didn't often do that, but from time to time, they came toe to toe, nose to nose with Peter's overbearing attitude. Lilly put her hands on her hips. "And just why not?"

Willy thought wisely to remain quiet, though he had to suck in his cheeks to keep from laughing, as those two were quite entertaining.

Peter stuttered, "B-because I said. That's why." His forehead was crinkled, his eyebrows pointed.

Lilly began to tap her foot on the sand. "Not a good answer, and you know it," she retorted, holding her anger.

"I don't want you to become shark bait, honey." Peter ran his hand through his hair and tried to calm down.

"She'd be the best-tastin' thing out there." On that, Willy couldn't hold it in, and he snickered.

"Just you wait. Your time's a-coming." Peter glared at Willy. He was referring to the fact that there will be disagreements between husband and wife. And right now, he wanted his way.

"Well, Peter, if you were in the suit, it wouldn't be available for your wife," Willy tried one more time.

Peter growled at Willy. Willy took that as, "I think it's a good time to exit." So he left to find his sisters to see if either of them wanted to give it a try.

Though Lilly didn't get into the water, she enjoyed watching Kevin, Willy, Noel, Hannah, and Olivia surf. The twins played in the sand and collected shells for the wedding, and Doug and Wilma went tide pooling. Lilly found some cute, fat beach squirrels and fed them until they were eating out of her hands. Peter shook his head. Only his Lilly would be worried about the squirrels.

It wasn't long after that, though, that Lilly had a change of heart about animals. She was sitting on a quilt, watching people in the water, when she saw a flock of seagulls come down and attack a bag of Cheetos in a little two-year-old girl's hand. The baby screamed and dropped the treasured chips. All the while, swarms of birds came out of seemingly nowhere and tore open the bag, scarfed its contents, and flew off, leaving a trail of trash and a terrified baby. Lilly ran over to check on the baby. The parents had consoled it and thanked Lilly for her concern. After that, Lilly took it upon herself to be bird patrol. She watched as the same birds flew down and began to tear open a plastic grocery bag that was on someone else's blanket. The owners had walked a ways down the beach and had no idea there were feathered beach thieves. She just had to save their stuff. So she took off her flip-flop and ran over there, beating the birds with her shoe. Peter had been standing behind her quilt the whole time, watching her, his arms crossed and a delighted smile on his face. She was a hoot to watch. It was obvious to him that Lilly had no idea how many birds there were. But to the end, she did that all afternoon, chasing birds, telling them how bad they were and how inconsiderate they were being. She was nearly exhausted by the end of the day from saving the world from seagulls.

They spent the evening around a bonfire on the beach as they'd done many times on tour. They'd brought hot dogs to roast, chips (Lilly was glad they'd kept them in the car), soda, and hot chocolate. Then they sang to the sound crashing waves.

Olivia leaned over to her father. "I can see why Willy likes it so much out here."

Doug winked at his daughter. Then he shared some scriptures and thoughts while everyone watched the moonlight shimmer on the water.

Willy leaned over and whispered for Noel's ears only, "The day after tomorrow and I can kiss you until the sun comes up."

Noel looked him in the face and whispered, "I'll be there."

Willy greeted Noel with a special wedding-day kiss. She had turned from what she was doing, which was making sandcastles in the sand. "What a perfect day to become your wife."

"That was a sweet thing to say," Willy said as he tapped her on the nose before walking back up to the bluff.

Doug, Peter, and Kevin were putting up a huge tent for the reception. The guys from the band were to arrive any minute with chairs. It would certainly be a day to remember.

Three hours later, Peter came to observe how things were going and to check on his wife. As he approached, this is what he saw. Wilma, Noel, Lilly, and the four girls had been very busy and very creative. The little girls had made a pathway lined with bucket sandcastles. The pathway led up to the podium that, in itself, was a lot of work. Then they'd put a shell on top of each bucket sandcastle. The pathway widened at the end. It was long, as there'd be a lot of people and a lot of chairs.

Peter walked up to the girls and complimented their hard work. "You girls have done an excellent job!" He clapped his hands. "I'm so proud of you!"

They looked up, pushing their braids out of the way. "Thank you, Uncle Peter," they chorused together.

Then he moved on. Noel had hired a sand sculptor, who had ridden up with Kevin early that morning. Noel had the sculptor carve four sand dolphins, two on each side of the front pulpit area. He made it look like they were jumping in the water after each other. It looked just like a church on the sand. Peter watched Noel's hand motions as she talked with the sand sculptor. He knew just what Noel was doing. She was witnessing to him. He watched her point to heaven and then put her fist to her heart. He watched her wipe a tear away. There was no mistaking her zeal.

Willy walked up at that moment and patted Peter on the back and looked to what had captured Peter's attention. Willy smiled. "Poor guy. I already shared the gospel with him earlier." Willy's heart swelled so big for the woman he was in love with as she did the very thing that he loved about her: sharing what God had done for her.

Peter whispered, not taking his eyes off the scene. "It's funny that really, though they're from totally different backgrounds and they look totally different, Noel and Lilly's hearts are so similar."

"Yeah. Pretty neat." Willy sighed.

Willy then looked around at how things were taking shape.

Noel had been planning all of it since the day Willy had proposed. Willy had to admit that he couldn't envision it at the time.

But now, looking down on everything as it was near completion, his imagination had certainly done him an injustice. It was nothing like he could've dreamed.

In the four corners of the reception tent, she had a sculpted dolphins standing up. Behind it was a surfboard leaned up against the corner. She had ordered stands made to support four surfboards lying flat to be used as serving tables. That was a really cool idea. Kevin had talked a few surf shops into loaning them along with advertising their shop.

One surf board table held the wedding cake. It was four separate staggering tiers of a drum set. Each round cake was designed as a drum. The knife and server handles were drumsticks. It looked adorable together. All around the cake, on the table, were beach scenes. including a volleyball net, beach balls, sand toys, starfish, beach chairs, sunglasses, etc. Surrounding the edge of the drum cakes were miniature surfboards. It was the most unusual cake Wilma had ever seen, but so like her Willy, she mused. The napkins that Noel had ordered had a tiny drum and sticks in the middle a long with a Bible verse under it. Under that were their names and wedding date, all done in gold embossing.

Another surfboard table held the punch bowl and cups. Noel had a wonderful punch made and floating in the middle was a fresh pineapple top so it looked like a palm tree. She had glass ice cubes in the punch for a nice added touch.

The other two surf tables in between held additional food. One had an abundance of fresh California fruits. In the center was a huge bowl of fresh, mouthwatering strawberries with the best dipping cream. The next table was filled with finger foods of all kinds and the traditional nuts and mints.

It was a spread, all right. Willy let out a low whistle. The bill for it would be a kick in the ear. *We'll be eating beans the first year to pay for this one.* But then Willy laughed. *But eating beans and hav-*

ing Noel by my side, I'd do it again! He shook his head at what Noel had done just two weeks prior. She'd sold her Camaro and cashed in all her savings and bought a barely used motor camper for them to travel in as a married couple so they could have some privacy. Both had witnessed how hard it had been on Sky Blue and Kenzie. Willy had been speechless when she'd gone that morning and had come back with their new home on wheels. Willy had actually put his face in his hands and wept at her sacrifice. He knew she'd given all she had.

Lastly, in the tent area was the guest book table, which was a special surfboard. It was Noel's wedding gift to her husband. Instead of signing a guest book, guests signed the surfboard, along with a message if they so chose to. Next to that was a big sand bucket filled with sand. Inside that bucket were drumsticks. Every guest was to take one home. Noel had printed a verse on each one. That was Cookie's spot, to greet everyone, have them sign the board, give them a drumstick, and direct them to the food line.

―――✕―――

It was nearing an hour before the wedding. Lilly was maid of honor, and Kenzie, Hannah and Olivia, Willy's sisters, were Noel's attendants. They had on a mimic of Noel's dress, which was a sleeveless, pure white dress straight down, nicely framing her figure but not grossly tight. It had tiny sea conches sewn around the waist beltline. It flared at the bottom but stopped just above the ankles in the front and flowed several feet behind her. It had musical notes embossed like a watermark on the material. Her tanned feet hosted a nice pair of white strapless sandals; fresh, soft teal toenail polish that matched the highlights in her hair; two toe rings; and an anklet of gold seashells, something her mother had given her years ago. Her veil was made of tulle and flowed midway down her back. Thus, it covered her bare, tanned arms. She wore a set of beautiful pearl earrings. Each attendant held a drum bouquet. It was actually a bouquet of simple silk flowers arranged in a small, handheld drum like one Willy used. Noel's was a larger drum and floral arrangement, and sticking out of hers were two drumsticks. Also in the middle of her bouquet, you could clearly see a yellow yoyo and a sucker. Willy had put it in the bouquet as a tradition that Lilly had started, and it held special memories for them as well.

Peter was Willy's best man. Sky Blue was his next groomsman, and then Jordie and Chet. They all looked the same except for two things. Willy had drumsticks in his back pocket, and he had on bright orange rubber flip-flops. All were wearing black tuxedos with white shirts, black ties, and cummerbunds and black dress shoes. The only thing lacking from him being an exact resemblance of a penguin was the waddle.

Rusty had set up a battery-operated tape player and battery microphones for use during the wedding. The time had come, and Willy stood waiting for his bride on the sand stage, along with their pastor from Willy's home church.

Music began to play. Both Willy and Noel had shared in preparing the music. They chose praise songs that most all knew and loved. Then it was time for the wedding march. Kenzie had prerecorded it for them, and Rusty now hit the play button.

Kevin leaned over and placed a sweet kiss on Noel's cheek. He then placed her hand through his arm and said, "Are you, my dear, ready to go marry the man who has so captured your heart?"

Noel smiled up at him and said, "Yes, I am." She began her journey down the aisle on the arm of Kevin, who had taken the role of her father in giving the bride away. It meant a lot to her. She looked ahead and saw the beautiful attendants all in their places, the men in their places, and then her beloved Willy standing with his hands together in front of him. She had to cover her laughter when she saw his orange flip-flops. She saw the twin girls with their buckets of sand and shells. They'd done a marvelous job of tossing the tiny shells on the pathway for her to walk over. Everything was just beautiful.

She leaned over to Kevin and said, "Could you pinch me?"

"What?" Kevin did a double-take.

"Yes, pinch me. I want to make sure this is real." She ducked her head to hide the tears. "I just can't believe this. It's all so beautiful, and I'm about to get married." She was smiling and crying; so for a diversion halfway down the aisle, she took the yellow yoyo out of her bouquet and began to twirl it up and down.

Willy watched her in disbelief. She'd already been practically dancing as she listened to the music. Though he had to bite his lip to keep from laughing outright, he'd never tell her what she looked like. Willy guessed it must have been hard to get her down that far without her breaking out in song or snapping or clapping her hands. As it was, Willy could see movement under her dress, and he knew she was keeping beat with more than her yoyo.

When they got to the sand stage, the preacher began the wedding in prayer and then began the traditional question. "Dearly beloved, we are gathered here today to witness these two people, William McCollister and Noel Franklin, in holy matrimony. Who gives this bride away to be married unto her husband?" the preacher asked as both he and Willy looked at Kevin; but before Kevin could say anything, there was a commotion in the crowd.

Burt got up from the back seat, came forward, kissed Noel on the cheek, took her hand, turned, and spoke to the crowd. "This is my daughter, and I desire her every happiness. Her mother and

I give our blessing." He then turned to Noel. "I love you. I hope you're happy." Then he turned to Willy and said, "You better take good care of her or else." And he showed a fist, turned, and walked back to sit with his wife.

Noel gave up on her makeup, for she had already began to cry coming down the aisle, but when she heard her father's voice, she closed her eyes, but that didn't stem the onslaught of tears. That they even showed up was such a surprise that Noel had a hard time concentrating.

They both decided to exchange personal vows. They sang them to one another. But that was in addition to the normal vows and ring exchange. They also insisted that a short but plain gospel message be presented. The band also played a few recorded songs as they knelt and prayed together in front of everyone. If nothing else had not made for a puddle of tears, the praying would have. It really was no different from what they'd done many times on the beach, but each time, it was filled with the Spirit, and thus, it was sweet. This time was no different, only made sweeter by the occasion.

It was finally time to exchange rings. "May I please have the rings?" the pastor asked. He usually held them up as he talked about them and how they represented the unbroken bond that they now would have. The pastor's eyeballs just about fell out as Willy reached in his back pocket and retrieved his two drumsticks and held them out to the preacher. On the end of each one was tied their rings.

They were now down to the last part, the exchanging of their personal promises to each other. Noel went first. She turned to Willy, her voice already so husky from the crying, and the day spent in the wind and sea air didn't make for a quality singing voice. So she took out her yoyo and sang her message to Willy.

When her voice faltered, she spoke. All the while, she twirled her yoyo up and down.

She started by putting her hand to Willy's face and said, "Do you have any idea what this silly yellow yoyo means to me?"

Willy just looked at her, his eyes sparkling. "And do you realize that words can't begin to say all that is in my heart?" Willy gave a slight nod, understanding perfectly.

Noel began her dedication poem to her husband:

CAPTURED BY YOUR SMILE

Left alone to drown in my sin

In an ally full of drugs and bottle of gin

Left to die under the street light

But God had another plan that night

He sent a messenger named Willy

Whom I later came to find quite silly

His love poured out on me so undeserved

He paid for me to sleep in a hotel reserved

He took me to breakfast that next day

I'm embarrassed to think of all I did say

Then I saw him again; he was at my school

Playing in a band and making the girls drool

But I already knew he had a serious attraction

That Jesus was his only distraction

He told everyone about this Savior

Who had changed his heart and his behavior

I noticed that Willy was the real thing

That it was this Jesus that made him sing

Then I met him in a New York café

But God doesn't do things just halfway

He had pointed me to a friend who cared

To this Lilly my heart I openly shared

They took me in when I had no place to go

And sometime later, again, you did show

It was a surprise for you to take

You thought your drums I would break

But after heated words and much confusion

You finally knew Christy was just a delusion

I had not only had an earthly name change

But God had done a heart rearrange

God saved me; why, I will never know

But still I began to quickly grow

After you got over my touching your things

And you found out I could really sing

We began to stick together like jam and bread

Then being separated I began to dread

But this too God had in His design

We would be back together in His own time

He got me the best job ever

And how he did it was rather clever

Now I tour with you on a bus

A few crazy musicians and us

Did God stop there when He had given so much?

No, he added sightseeing, adventure, and such

Sunsets over the ocean, elephant seals in motion

Tide pools, shells, and suntan lotion

My heartfelt love could not be denied

And God chose to have it multiplied

To love is like nothing I have ever known

But to know it's returned and you're not alone

Well it just does crazy things to your heartbeat

Something you can't ignore or delete

Now I am to become your wife

Who would have ever thought that from my life?

All my love, Noel

Willy didn't think he could take any more. What Noel had written was so touching that he wasn't sure he would be able to sing her dedication without breaking down, but he was going to try. Noel sat down at his feet and looked up into his eyes. He had a stool and his guitar brought to him, and he began.

THE BEAT OF MY HEART

Verse 1

I would have never dreamed in a thousand years

That one night I would take a trip and nearly fall

On the woman that would one day be my wife.

I didn't see it then nor would have imagined

Our paths would ever cross again, but God had other plans

How many times have I looked into your eyes

To see you searching the how's, I wonder's, and why's

But now I see our lives completely entwined

Your heart beating so perfectly with mine!

Chorus

I would have never dreamed a love so strong

My love for you will last all life long

I will never tire of seeing your heart

Being man and wife is only the start!

Verse 2

I have waited for you all my life for the perfect wife

For God to show me who you are, a Hollywood ex-star

Who would have ever guessed, but God knew what's best

Worlds apart, but God changed your heart

Saved your soul and made you whole

Now I can hold you forever, our love nothing can sever

Taking life hand in hand as we sing in our band

I will be faithful through thick and then I will love you to the end!

All my love, Willy

By the chorus, he was in full tears. He still choked out the song. When it was over, Noel stood, and Willy said, "I love you with all my heart."

They hugged at that moment, not able to keep from touching each other any longer. The preacher chose that moment to say, "I now pronounce you husband and wife. You may now kiss your bride."

What happened next was no surprise to those watching.

Willy picked up his bride and ran to the water. The whole time, Noel was saying, "Put me down. Oh please, Willy. You're really not going to…Willy…you can't be serious! Willy!"

Willy only smiled and did as he wished. He took his lovely bride waist deep in the ocean and began to kiss her like he'd waited his whole life to do, but he wanted a bit of privacy for the occasion, so he took her to the water. It was a beautiful silhouette. The audience watched as Noel put her arms around his neck, and it was some time before they considered coming back.

Tired of waiting, Chet looked at Jordie and said, "Let's go!"

The two of them took off and ran into the water. Of course, by then, Willy had set Noel down, and a good thing too, for when Chet and Jordie reached him, they dunked him under. All eventually all came out of the water, arms linking behind each other, forming a line of unity between the couple themselves and the band. It was rather splendid to watch. Even Sky Blue was cracking up.

The four of them went to the bus to change clothes and then returned to the receiving line as folks went into the reception tent. Noel was greeted by Willy's parents in a bear hug. Then her own parents came by. Burt hugged Noel but gave Willy his best growl.

Ericka stuck something in Noel's hands, "For the wedding expenses, you know." She waved her hand and then kissed Noel's cheek but clearly didn't want to be hugged or get any deeper than a surface compliment. She said, "Noel, dear, the wedding was, uh…let me say, like none I have ever seen. May you have oceans of happiness, my dear." Then she wagged her finger at her. "Watch your figure." Then she moved on. She wanted to be sure her driver had gotten a picture of everything. She posed for some news crews but wanted her own proof pictures.

After everyone was through the line, Wilma and Doug made a beeline for Burt and Ericka. Wilma came to them and she put her arms around Ericka and squeezed.

She was returned by a cleared throat and these words: "Excuse me, but you are crushing my gown." Ericka tried to repair the damage.

Doug had tried to greet Burt but was met with eyes of steel. Doug said a quick prayer for help, and then the two of them sat down in front of Noel's parents to eat. Wilma guessed that both Burt and Ericka's clothes had cost more than the bride's wedding dress. Ericka's fancy hat and the partial tulle coming from her under her hat shading her eyes gave for quite a fanciful look.

Wilma was suddenly self-conscious in her homespun dress. Though she'd thought it beautiful at the time she had sewn it, but now it didn't compare with the famous actress's.

Wilma situated herself in the seats across the table from them. She clasped her hands together. "Oh, wasn't the wedding just beautiful." Wilma was so caught up she just rambled for a few moments, and then she realized that she was being stared at and finally slowed down, shutting her mouth.

"I've never been to one quite like this," Ericka said, her tone even.

"Well, I think you totally shocked them both, Burt, when you went up front and gave the bride away. Why, I hadn't even seen you slip in," Doug said.

"Well, after years of being a movie star, you learn how to slip in and slip out unnoticed as possible. Cameras can be brutal hounds," Burt replied dryly.

Conversation went on like that for a bit more, and then Burt and Ericka slipped out, not even saying good-bye to Noel. Wilma couldn't stem the tears any longer. Doug put his arm around his wife and comforted her.

"She didn't even say good-bye to her daughter," Wilma cried out.

"Let's focus on the fact that they came," Doug consoled his wife.

Noel didn't seem like she even noticed their absence, as there was much laughter and play around the food. Then, when it was time to go, instead of the traditional rice bags to throw, Noel had decided on feeding the birds with bread pieces. So each person was given a bag of bread pieces to throw on the bride and groom as they left. Then Noel knew the squirrels and birds would have a feast. So it was through a shower of bread pieces that the couple went out to the parking lot to leave on their honeymoon.

Willy stopped dead in his tracks. He had rented a stretch limo for the occasion to carry his bride away in. The limousine was nowhere in sight. But his beast was parked in its spot and was decorated with strings of cans, starfish, and shells. They'd even tied a toy sand bucket to the back. They had about ten drumsticks hanging from each mirror. And "Just Married" was written on the back window.

Willy ran his fingers through his hair. He was not happy. All the pranks he played on Peter and Sky Blue came flooding in. He looked around to find the two men who had just come to his mind. He spotted Peter. He was rocking back and forth on his heels, his arms crossed with a mischievous smile on his face. He looked around for Sky Blue. When he found him, he too was grinning wildly, and he waved at Willy. Willy rolled his eyes, scared to even open the door.

"We might as well get in. I guess this is still better than leaving in a surrey," he said to his wife.

"I'd go anywhere with you." Noel laughed.

With those words, Willy opened her car door only to have a bucket of sand pour out on her. She screamed and both looked inside the car. It was filled with sand. Willy looked back at Sky Blue, and he just shrugged his shoulders but couldn't quit smiling. He looked at Peter and was rewarded with another grin. Willy slammed the door, rolled his eyes, went to his door, yanked it open, and plopped down in his seat, only to have a bucket of sand pour in his lap. He hit the steering wheel.

"Someone is going to pay for this!"

"I think we are!" Noel giggled.

"You do realize I had a limo waiting to take you away. I'm so sorry to take my bride away in the beast!"

"Well, we might not have a fancy car to leave in, but with a bit of water, we can build ourselves the fanciest sandcastle ever to live in."

Willy smiled at his wife. "I love you."

Then he stared up the car and took off. When he got to the road and put on the brake, his horn went off. Willy pressed the brake again. It went off again. Then he took off and pressed it again and the horn blew again. It was obvious that someone had played yet another prank on them. They'd wired the horn up to the brake sensor pedal, so every time he touched the brake pedal, the horn blew. And it was no ordinary horn either. Someone had gone through the trouble of making a drum roll horn noise. So as they drove down the road, all the well-wishers from the wedding could hear the drum roll over and over again.

Willy turned to Noel. "This is going to get annoying!"

Noel couldn't say a word, for the whole thing was hilarious to her.

Willy went inside the hotel office, leaving a trail of sand behind him in his orange flip-flops, jeans, white t-shirt, and puka shell necklace. Noel had to cover her mouth. He was so adorable, so Willy, she thought.

Willy came back in short order with a key. He had gotten a honeymoon suite up in Monterey Bay for two nights, and then they were going to come back to Moonstone, where they were wed, and stay two nights before heading back to the apartment that Peter and Lilly had vacated to pass to them.

Willy unlocked and opened the door. He set their suitcases down and did what he dreamed of doing, carrying his wife over the threshold for their first night together. Noel, not being familiar with many things, gasped for air when she felt herself being lifted off the ground but held on to his neck, lest she be dropped.

"What are you doing, my crazy husband?" she asked, scared to death.

"I'm carrying my beautiful bride over the threshold and into my heart forever." Willy grinned and then kissed her before setting her down.

He hooked his hands together behind her shoulders. "Today was more than words can express." Willy so loved this woman.

"I agree, and tonight, we can express what there are no words for." She smiled and then whispered, "I'm so glad I saved myself for this moment. And I gladly give the last thing, the only thing of my own, to you."

With that invitation, Willy took his wife into his arms, and as was predicted, sand or no sand, it was a night to remember.

The next morning, when Willy got up to go to the bathroom, he was greeted with a sand castle with a toothpick message sticking out of the top. The message read, "Thanks for making all my dreams come true."

Willy looked around. Noel wasn't in the room. He got worried. He was in the midst of throwing on some clothes when the door opened. "Oh, I was just going to look for you," Willy said with concern.

"I brought my husband a cup of coffee *without* sand from the lobby." Noel flashed him a smile as she set the two cups down on the table and went to her husband.

She put her arms around his waist, and he embraced her. "Good morning to the beat of my heart."

"Any morning is *good* after last night." She smiled up at him, showing her enjoyment of their first night together.

Willy drew her closer and bent and kissed her neck. "I know of a way to make a *good* morning even better."

Some two hours later, they threw their now-cold coffee out and went for mochas in town, leaving a trail of sand behind them.

EPILOGUE

FOURTEEN YEARS LATER

Willy walked in the door of their home after work and was greeted by his four children: ten-year-old Montana (Monti) and eight-year-old Dakota (Dak), the two boys, and Carolina (Lina) and California (Cali), the twin girls age three, came rushing in. "Daddy! Daddy! Daddy's home!"

He hugged them all, and then he did his usual head bopping. He went from oldest to youngest and bopped them all on the head in a rhythm tune while he sang some crazy, "I'm home and lovin' you" kind of greeting with a huge smile. They were all accustomed to it. Noel just stood and watched him, loving him more and more every year they'd been married.

Then he came to her and kissed her like he hadn't seen her in three months. When he came up for air, leaning very close to her ear, he asked, "Hey, are you ready for the song we are to sing Sunday at church?"

Noel put her hands on her hips, her belly protruding out six months with child. "Of course I'm ready."

Willy gave her a mischievous grin, put his hands on Noel's tummy, and said, "Cymbals doesn't agree." He was referring the baby Noel was carrying and continuing their ongoing disagreement over her name. He kept looking at her. "As a matter of fact, I think you need to practice it for me in our bedroom to see if you hit every note just right."

Noel got the message all right; he wanted a private moment with his wife, without tagalongs. She smiled at Willy that smile that still melted him in his shoes and, with a wink, turned to the kids. "Boys, wash up for dinner and get the girls cleaned up and to the table. Keep your hands in your laps until we come and join you in just a minute." She then scooted herself into the bedroom, Willy right on her heels.

She turned and put her arms around his neck. "Just what do you want, Mr. Drummer Boy, the man who makes my heart beat wildly?" She was teasing him, as she knew full well that he didn't want to hear her sing.

Willy knew as much, but he wanted to give full vent to his desires, and desiring intimacy with his wife was very much on his mind, though he'd have to wait until later, when the kids were in bed. So he kissed her passionately until he thought he'd better quit. Then he said, "You're so irresistible, but if I don't stop, dinner will be cold and the kids will be banging on our door." He let up with a smile. "Later, will you join me in the beat of my heart?"

She knew full well what he was asking. She said, "I wouldn't miss it for the world!" Then she went out of the room, leaving a happily married man following her to the dinner table.

"Dad, when are we going on tour again?" Dakota asked.

"Well, son. That depends on your little sister, Cymbals." He paused while cutting his roast and looked over at Noel with raised eyebrows. "Your mother needs this time at home with all of you to prepare for Cymbals to come into the world. So I think it might be a while yet. But maybe three months after your mother delivers, if she is up to it, we will hit the road again. What would you think about that?"

"Oh boy! We would love it!" Dakota said along with his brother and twin sisters clapping and saying, "Wuv it, Daddy! Wuv it!"

"Yeah. I know Sky Blue has been itching to get back on the road. Between Kenzie and me having babies, it has been crazy trying to even book a year in advance. But he's done a great job. Don't you think, Willy?" Noel chimed in.

"Yeah. I mean, it's hard to imagine that we've held together all these years, and now they're like my own family. That's kinda cool. Don't ya think?"

"Certainly not what he thought when I first came along." Noel snorted, remembering the bumpy beginning she'd had with Sky Blue, and shuddered. "You know, though, your mom and dad aren't going to like it. They kinda get attached to the kids, and the baby will be hard to pull from your mom's arms."

Willy was shaking his head. Wilma and Doug adored all their grandchildren, and it was hard when Willy and Noel did their tours with the kids.

"I don't know who is worse, Peter and Lilly, or my parents." Willy did his drum roll on the table.

"You got that right. I mean, Peter and Lilly are like my very flesh," Noel said. "I don't think I'll be the one telling them that we are headed out right after the *not* Cymbals is born." She emphasized that she didn't like his choice of names.

Willy shook his head. "Not to mention that their three kids have hovered over ours like eagles. Though ages are different, they couldn't be better cousins." Willy snickered. "We'll hear it from them for sure." They continued in the light banter until the twins interrupted with a surprise.

"Oh, Daddy, we made you somefing special," Lina said as she hopped down to retrieve it.

"Oh, yes, Daddy, we did." Down went Cali. She clapped her hands, "You gonna wuv it!" she said, both sounding absolutely adorable in their cute baby jibberish.

They came back carrying on a saucer something that Willy was not shocked by but dreaded. Willy leaned down. "What is it, my sweet peas?"

"Oh, it's a supwise," Lina said.

"Tee-da!" Cali flew her hands wide. "We made you a mud pie!"

Lina wiggled her finger and jumped up and down. "And dawady, it haws a worm in it!" She was smiling ear to ear.

"Mommy said you would eat it. Go ahead! It is youwrs!" Cali said as she shoved the mud pie toward her dad's face.

Willy looked over at Noel. She was sucking in her checks to hold her laughter. The boys were laughing, remembering when their mom had done that with them. It had been a hoot.

So, in much laughter, Willy dug out the gummy worms and sucked them down, to everyone's great delight.

signature 2018